CENTRAL PLACES

CENTRAL PLACES

A Novel

DELIA CAI

Ballantine Books
New York

Central Places is a work of fiction. Names, characters, places, and incidents are the products of the author's imagination or are used fictitiously. Any resemblance to actual events, locales, or persons, living or dead, is entirely coincidental.

Published in the United States by Ballantine Books, an imprint of Random House, a division of Penguin Random House LLC, New York.

BALLANTINE is a registered trademark and the colophon is a trademark of Penguin Random House LLC.

LIBRARY OF CONGRESS CATALOGING-IN-PUBLICATION DATA
NAMES: Cai, Delia, author.
TITLE: Central places: a novel / Delia Cai.
DESCRIPTION: First edition. | New York: Ballantine Books, [2023]
IDENTIFIERS: LCCN 2022003012 (print) | LCCN 2022003013 (ebook) |
ISBN 9780593497913 (hardcover; acid-free paper) | ISBN 9780593497920 (ebook)
SUBJECTS: LCGFT: Novels.
CLASSIFICATION: LCC PS3603.A37866 C46 2023 (print) |
LCC PS3603.A37866 (ebook) | DDC 813/.6—dc23/eng/20220302
LC record available at https://lccn.loc.gov/2022003012
LC ebook record available at https://lccn.loc.gov/2022003013

Printed in Canada on acid-free paper

randomhousebooks.com

9 8 7 6 5 4 3 2 1

First Edition

Title-page art by robin_ph © Adobe Stock Photos

Book design by Sara Bereta

For my mother and father, of course

I have always treated English as a weapon
in a power struggle, wielding it against
those who are more powerful than me.
But I falter when using English
as an expression of love.

—Cathy Park Hong, *Minor Feelings*

CENTRAL PLACES

CHAPTER 1

The baby in first class is drooling all over his mother's sweater. It's probably rude to watch this happen without saying anything, but the thought of leaning over and telling a total stranger that her kid is ruining her cashmere while we're hurtling at cruising altitude somewhere above Lake Erie feels like an overreach. Besides, it's not worth disturbing the quiet hum of the plane, not when this baby—I think it's a boy—has been asleep since we left New York, and there's still another hour to go before we hit the Midwest.

So instead, I keep staring, likely thanks to that predictable late twenties biological pull, but also out of envy as I try to think of the last time I felt that untroubled, that indifferent to space and time and turbulence. At least the baby is one of those objectively cute ones: fat cheeks weighing down that soft, milky-pale face, lips scrunched in a rosebud, two ghostly eyebrows suggesting a strain of ancestry that my mother would be able to geo-locate immediately, in the way Chinese women always can, even when afforded only a glimpse through the rearview of whoever might be waiting behind us in the McDonald's drive-through with the same telltale nose bridge. It happened rarely enough in central Illinois that those moments of recognition always resembled a special occasion. From the folds of the baby's blanket toddles one thick leg, tightly furled like a drumstick wrapped with a little gray sock. Next to me in the window seat, Ben yawns awake from his grown man's nap. He follows the direction of my stare and nudges me.

"Hey," Ben says with a grin. "One thing at a time."

I roll my eyes, moving my gaze off the baby and down to Ben's great-grandmother's ring, which I slide up and down my finger again. It's turning into a bad habit. Ben had it resized over Thanksgiving, but I swear it's still loose, and I can't decide if I should tell him or wait until we're back in the city and take it to a jeweler myself. Either would be more useful than endlessly testing the drag of the band against my skin, as if I'm expecting the white gold to shrink down now that it's making itself at home. Even Zadie noticed this new tic the other day, when we were splitting the twenty-dollar hummus plate at brunch and bitching indulgently about how Williamsburg always got so overrun with German tourists for the holidays. "Stop messing with it," she chided, and then picked at her bangs so she could avoid looking directly at the diamond, like she still couldn't believe that the big *E* happened to me first. Here, inside the fluorescent interior of the 737, the ring wiggles over my knuckle with what feels like a promising amount of effort. But wasn't there some scientific explanation about how the cabin pressure makes your fingers swell or something?

Ben's leaning over me now to get a better view of the baby across the aisle. Then, rubbing his jaw thoughtfully, he turns back to me.

"Ours would be like that, right?"

"Like what?" I give him a look. "Asian?"

Ben pretends to be offended. It's part of our ever-running gag, because of course he isn't making this about *that*. "No," he says, smiling impishly. "Quiet."

This makes me laugh. I say that I hope so, and Ben takes another glance.

"And a *little* Asian," he adds, completing the punch line. Because of course, he's a white guy and I'm the Chinese American girlfriend—well, fiancée—so actually, it's always about that.

I indulge Ben with an eye roll and watch him settle back into his nap with a contented grunt, like a whale surfacing long enough to gather oxygen and consult the scenery before returning to the depths. Of course Ben is unbothered enough to joke about babies and drift back off to sleep while I'm still gaming out all the possible scenarios for what happens when we touch down in Illinois, when the protective spell of our life together in New York disappears and he finally meets my parents. He's always been like this, not so much unconcerned by the nuisance of cramped seats and roaring jet engines and the future's greater mysteries as he is drawn to any open flame. Even the apartment Ben had back when we first met, the one right next to the aboveground train, recast adventurously in his eyes: When the J went clattering by, he had the nerve to emit these long, happy sighs about how it proved we were "New Yorkers, baby." After three years together, it shouldn't surprise me how different we are in that way: Ben has always been the seasoned ranger, fully at home in the city and its ever-present potential to turn any day into a personal sitcom episode; a hopeful romantic, buoyed by a belief in a welcoming universe; and the kind of guy who smooths a tense exchange in the Whole Foods line into one of those odd New Yorkian friendships in under twenty minutes. It's probably what makes him such a good photojournalist. Meanwhile, I'm the one who notices the noise and the disorder, the crooked picture frames and the monstrous train barreling by just a few feet away from where we slept—the trail greenhorn who catastrophizes for sport. The other night, I ran this self-assessment by Ted, my boss, when we were working late at the *Current* office, and he said he agreed. "But it's what makes you a brilliant sales rep, Audrey," he added. "You're ready for anything." Ted said this nicely, like my ability to anticipate even the most demanding client's whims without choking on the existential indignities of professionally asking people for money is the most impressive personality trait he can think of.

●

The only times I've ever seen Ben genuinely upset were during occasional incidents like the one earlier this morning, when we were waiting by our gate at LaGuardia. A young white couple asked if we would watch their bags while they hunted down the restroom, which I guess was supposed to be flattering, a coded acknowledgment passing among the four of us as we perched between a family chattering in Farsi and a group of retirees clutching monogrammed luggage. When the couple came back, Ben went off to stretch his legs and locate his daily iced coffee, like it wasn't late December, like the looming enormity of the coming week now speeding toward us wasn't enough to jolt him into consciousness by force. Whether out of reflex or the need to fulfill an ancient feminine custom, I struck up a conversation with the woman, who introduced herself as Erin. She seemed pleasant enough as she unleashed a steady clip of opinions about the morning's traffic, the line at the Terminal B Starbucks, how glad she was to be getting out of the city for the holidays. As she spoke, she kept rustling her unopened magazine, which I realized with a flush of pride was the latest issue of *The Current.* I wanted to ask her what she thought of the big opioid crisis cover story, or at least watch her flip through the inside foldout ad, which I'd spent half of last quarter negotiating for the premium placement and right paper stock. Instead, Erin set the magazine down and began worrying over how the flight would dry out her skin.

"Well, *your* skin is absolutely stunning," she said with a sigh. "I'm jealous."

I could almost hear Erin's neurons whirring as she looked at me, and I waited for the clues she'd been gathering—the shape of my face, the crease above the eyes, the unambiguous black hair—to finish processing. I knew that look well. This was another attempt at classification, not unlike the guessing game my mother used to play in the McDonald's drive-through, or the one I received in greeting when I started kindergarten at Hickory Grove Elementary and the ESL aide materialized unbidden to introduce herself at top volume. By this time, Ben had returned, slightly agitated because he hadn't found coffee that met both his standards for taste and fair-trade certification.

"If you don't mind me asking," Erin finally said as she propped her black ankle boots up on the seat across from the three of us, "where are you from?"

Even though I'd known this was coming, the words bottlenecked at my throat. It had been awhile since anyone in the tristate area asked me this, and I tried to think of the last diversity training they made us undergo at work as I searched for language that felt efficient yet polite. Erin seemed perfectly nice, someone whom I'd bump into while waiting for matcha lattes or ask, as we waited in line for the bathroom at a bar, where she got those booties. It was important to not embarrass her for no reason. But Ben spoke up first.

"Audrey is from the Midwest," he said, leaning over. Ben's face, usually so handsome with that aquiline geometry, darkened. "She grew up in Illinois."

Erin made a *hmm* sound that I wasn't sure if we were meant to hear.

"Hickory Grove?" I offered in my most neutral voice, more so to calm Ben down than to smooth over the creases bunching across Erin's forehead. "It's a small town, outside of Peoria. Pretty much in the middle of nowhere."

Erin frowned, like I'd just ripped into her in rapid-fire Mandarin. *Jesus Christ,* I remember thinking as I waited for her to piece it together already. Ben put his hand over mine and held the woman in the laser beam of his glare.

"If you're wondering what kind of Asian she is," he clarified, "that's really none of your fucking business."

The muscles in Erin's face jumped as her neck colored into a pink smear. I glanced at Ben and tried to catch his eye, to hint that it was okay, he was doing too much; that 10:00 A.M. was a little early for avenging racism. Down, boy.

"Wait," Erin said quickly. "That's not what I meant."

It *was* satisfying to see her look over to her husband, who was actively not listening under the guise of his earbuds and podcast. Erin drilled her eyes at him asking for backup, but he only retreated further inside the depths of the NYU hoodie that, an hour ago, he and Ben had been trading undergraduate memories over. I could sense Ben simmering next to me, but the annoyance I felt stemmed primarily from the knowledge that I was definitely not getting Erin's ankle boot recommendations now. I'd been in New York long enough to know plenty of people like her, who belonged to produce co-ops and book clubs that reread Ta-Nehisi Coates every February, but who, at the first crack in the snow globe, revealed the white-knuckled grip they've had on everything all along. And I knew from the last three years that the fact that I was with Ben, an Ellis Islander's dream in cheekbones and blue irises, only reinforced whatever fuzzy ideas of bonhomie these Erins propped under their worldview. If someone like me was with someone like him, then it was all good and fine, right? The basic fact of my relationship with Ben implied that we'd moved beyond "that stuff," that we really were all the same leaves stemming from one great kohlrabi. It was all subtler, at least, than what I was used to growing up in Hickory Grove, where there usually wasn't a skincare preamble leading up to the questioning.

To Erin's obvious relief, the gate agent interrupted just then to call for group one to board. I almost laughed at the way she vaulted out of the seat and dragged her husband into line in one fluid motion. Honestly, I didn't blame her. The Illinois thing threw everyone for a loop. In fact, that was what Ben said he found most foreign about me when we started dating: my status as a real non-Chicago, Laura Ingalls Wilder–adjacent midwesterner. Once, as proof, I showed him an old picture from a second grade birthday party where Kristen Anderson and I stood in her backyard, bean bags for cornhole in hand and our matching BFF necklaces glinting in the light. Behind us, you could see the neighboring grain elevator, its steel bins lined up like a row of supersized sugar jars. Ben couldn't stop joking about it. "My little country mouse," he loved to tease, until we spent a weekend in that J-train apartment besieged by actual rodents. *New York, baby!* After we gave up on the no-kill traps and finally broke out the glue pads, I told him to never call me a mouse again.

•

Over the intercom now, the pilot announces the start of our descent. I watch Ben snore as I brush tendrils of hair out of his face. He says he needs to get it cut, but I like it shaggier like this. It reminds me of when we first met, back in 2014, and the immediate impression he made at Zadie's Thanksgiving potluck: all those curls and the charisma of a New York lifer. When we met, I'd been in the city for almost two years, but my days at *The Current* kept me too busy to explore much of anything outside of midtown. Ben's intimate familiarity with the city was like touring Neverland under Peter's close supervision. He knew everything about every neighborhood: the best cafés for people watching, the barbershops with the underground speakeasies, the hole-in-the-wall pho joint personally consecrated by Anthony Bourdain. Before Ben Stear, I could count on one hand the number of celebrities I saw walking around in New York—I still wasn't used to living in the center of the world like that. But when I was with him, the city was our personal movie set: On our third date, at the Broadway premiere of his friend's play, I turned to my left and accidentally jostled one of Cynthia Nixon's icy elbows. Meeting Ben's parents had a similarly dazzling effect. Ann and Clement Stear were both Columbia professors, fluent in both Latin and the lingua franca of the Upper Both Sides. They invited us to monthly dinners in their Washington Heights brownstone, where they fed me things like coq au vin, fussed unironically over the neighborhood, and asked lots of questions about how I spent my entire day at *The Current* convincing advertisers to buy a full spread instead of a single page, four-color instead of black and white, in order to finance the type of magazine that in turn paid people like their son for their photographs and journalism. It was easy to like Ben's parents and both of his lawyer sisters, even though I found their family unit intimidating: a comprehensively educated clan of murky Anglo-Saxon origins, the type who would find DNA tests entertaining if they didn't already have a family tree detailed in Great-Grandma Stear's Bible.

The summer after Ben and I met, Ann and Clement invited me to spend August with them upstate, where, like many New Yorkers of a certain lineage and income bracket, they owned a cabin in the Hudson Valley. I was terrified of asking for that much time off at *The Current,* but when I mentioned the A-frame lodge in Beacon to Ted, he waved me off and told me to enjoy myself. "*Everyone* goes away for August," Ted said, glancing at me with what I would later understand as a kind of welcome. Every morning that month, Ben and I would take the family's matching set of clueless retrievers for a hike along the riverfront, and every afternoon, we'd come back to find Ann and Clement arranging an elaborate dinner spread and singing along to the radio, or rubbing aloe on each other's sunburns. Sometimes I tried to picture them screaming at each other in front of the TV, or throwing things out car windows in fury, as an exercise to remind myself how different other people's parents could be. Over the ensuing summers and long weekends, I could feel myself changing into the type of person who picked blueberries, wore L.L.Bean, and entertained her boyfriend's dreams of photojournalistic acclaim while we rolled out pie crust together in his parents' house upstate.

This past summer, our third together, Ben and I spent almost every weekend at the Beacon house. It had been rainy and muggy all season, and as we worked our way through a stack of puzzles and the HBO catalog, we talked about our plans for the coming year. Now that we were halfway through 2017, the reality of the new presidency was finally sinking in, so even though our lease on Bedford Avenue wasn't up until early 2018, there was an urgency about this upcoming move, as if we had to prove to ourselves that whatever happened to the rest of the country, we'd still be fine. More than fine, in fact, after Ann and Clement drove up to join us for the back half of August and, after taking us aside one night, offered to help with a down payment for a real place of our own. A few days later, Ben's sisters came up, too, for Labor Day. Surrounded by his family and the buzzing Hudson River mosquitos, Ben presented me with the family ring at dinner. The moment I said yes, the humidity felt wrung from the night air. Everything, even breathing, suddenly felt easier. "He adores you, and so do we," Ann said later that night when she and I were drying dishes in the kitchen. She smiled, and her approval felt as obvious as a full moon.

•

I put off telling my parents about the engagement until we were well into October. It wasn't hard, since I called only every few months to check in, and these conversations were always curt, half-hour exchanges of information relating to promotions and apartments and how much rain New York was getting lately. It was all surface-level stuff I designed to be unimpeachable, which is how all conversations involving my mother had been since college, when I'd announced the night before graduation that I wasn't going to stay and get my MBA after all, that I was looking at my chance to soak up more of that red-blooded American education my mother always worshipped and turning up my nose, because it "wasn't for me." "How could you?" my mother hissed that night, once she realized the final stage of her daughter-project would never be fully realized. We'd been taking a stroll around the University of Chicago campus in anticipation of the ceremony the next day, and my mother became so furious that she turned and walked away from my dad and me, leaving us to follow her all the way back to the hotel, where she'd dead-bolted the door to the room and left my dad scrambling to book another when it was apparent she wouldn't let either of us in until graduation was over. It took months before she would even speak to me; it had now been years since I'd given her a real piece of news. So when I called about the engagement, my mother grew quiet on the phone. She knew I had a boyfriend but had never actually met Ben, so I didn't know if she found my news surprising, or if she was adding it as evidence to her unifying theory of how disappointing I continued to be. When she finally asked if there was a wedding date set already, I said no and laughed out of surprise that this was the only question she seemed to have about the whole thing. That was when the phone was passed over to my dad. He knew only slightly more about Ben than my mother did; the last time he'd visited me in New York, Ben was conveniently out shooting a refugee camp in Greece. But my dad had seen our shared apartment and understood the meaning of Ben's various shoes interspersed with mine outside our door. Telling my dad about our engagement on the phone, though, meant explaining the Stears' cabin upstate and how I was already planning to spend another Thanksgiving with them there. My dad paused, then asked, if that were the case, would I think about coming home to Hickory Grove for Christmas. "It would be nice to meet Ben," he said.

I told him I would think about it, and later that night, as I relayed the conversation to Ben while we picked over an extra-large rainbow roll—I left the piece with the eel, his favorite, for him—he brightened.

"Of course we should go," Ben said. "I still haven't met your parents. Or, like, any of your childhood friends."

"I'm not really close with anyone back home."

"Well, I need to get to know your mom and dad at least. We just got engaged, remember?"

I knew Ben would want to go, that he found my reluctance confusing, but I got irritated all the same and said that he didn't know what it was like to even think about going back to Hickory Grove after eight years away. I reminded Ben that he'd technically never left his hometown, that he was a guy who'd spent his whole life on this one cluster of islands. Okay, Ben said, but didn't the year he spent backpacking in Thailand count? In response, I stabbed at a piece of salmon and pretended it was an issue of timing: My dad had suggested that we visit for the whole week leading up to Christmas. That was too long for a trip home, right? But Ben shrugged and said his calendar was clear; he was still looking for his next project, and it wasn't like *he* had an office job to answer to in the meantime. That was when I knew I was out of excuses.

Ben has always known that my relationship with my parents, especially my mother, is complicated. When we started dating, it took me more than a year to fill in any real detail beyond the bullet points of my parents' immigrant success story and the resulting Chineseness that still seeped out at the edges of my personality, like when I'd insist on keeping our bedroom window closed at night, no matter the season. "Bad chi," I'd say with a dark expression that wasn't entirely exaggerated, and he was never quite sure how seriously to take me. I liked it that way and wanted to preserve this film of mystery between us for as long as I could, because it meant my life with him in New York was that much more removed from my childhood in Hickory Grove. Of course, Ben tried asking questions: Why didn't I ever go home? Why didn't I talk to my parents more than a few times on the phone every year? Why wasn't I fluent in Mandarin even though I could understand when the nail salon ladies were talking shit about my cuticles? These questions reached a fever pitch right after the election, when self-flagellation over what everyone had gotten wrong about the people from places like Hickory Grove was the thing to do. And I would just try to be funny about it. Once Ben asked me what I wanted to be as a kid, because obviously no one grows up dreaming of slinging ad space for a dying industry, and I'd joked, "Anything that wasn't a farmer or a disappointment." What else was I going to say? How do you explain a former life that's anything less than Rockwellian to a guy whose parents laid out rows of gleaming silverware for Sunday dinners on Riverside Drive? While Ben was being a regular tween roaming New York on his skateboard under Ann and Clement's loose dictates, I was working my way through ACT prep books in the stuffy computer room, or, once I finally got my license, forever gunning it home at eighty miles an hour to beat whatever arbitrary curfew I was under that week that made it impossible to do much of anything in between studying and sleeping and fighting with my mother.

"My parents aren't anything like your parents," I warned Ben that night over sushi in a last-ditch attempt to scare him off the trip. He patiently reminded me that this was a normal next step for us, as necessary as getting the Stear family ring sized properly. Once we took care of this, we could start seriously thinking about apartment hunting and what we wanted to do about the actual wedding. "But we should do this first," he said gently that night. Later, I phoned home and told my dad that it was all settled. Ben and I would spend the week in Hickory Grove for Christmas. Things at *The Current* would be slow enough by the end of the year that Ted wouldn't mind that I was going "off the grid," as he said, like I was heading into the Alaskan bush. Last night, as we were packing and I was agonizing over whether I'd need five-inch leather boots in Illinois, Ben said he was proud of me and that we'd do something fun for New Year's Eve when we got back, like he could already see that I was tensing up for the whole ordeal, like I was a toddler who needed an incentivizing cookie dangled into view.

"You're sure you're up for this?" I asked him again as he shut his suitcase with a satisfied click.

"Of course," he said, never one to turn down an adventure or to consider there could be a place on earth, much less the continental United States, that could ever feel inhospitable.

Objectively, I knew that Ben was charming and likable and a generally aware white guy, so it was silly to worry about introducing him to my parents. But this wasn't a gap year adventure to a far-off locale. This was visiting my tiny midwestern hometown to meet my very impossible-to-impress, very Chinese parents, whom *I* had struggled to get along with my entire life. What if he met them and saw what they were like—and what Hickory Grove was like—and then never saw me the same way again? And what would they think of him, the first guy I'd ever brought home? On his own, my dad would be easy to win over: Ben would deploy his most gleaming smile and accompany him for a round of golf and it would be a done deal, the dowry of approval forked over with little hesitation. But my mother would be a different story. After a lifetime of reminding me of everything I'm not *enough* of—not grateful enough, not obedient enough, not loyal enough to live closer to home or smart enough to do the things she thought America was for—what would she think of Ben? Would she find Ben as inscrutable as everything else I'd chosen for myself, or could he actually be *enough* for her: a successful white mei guo ren from a family of professors and lawyers who was proof that I could get at least one thing right? What Ben knows about my mother are the basics: that she's strict, exacting, judgmental; that she came to America to accompany my father on an engineering scholarship and made it as far as the associate manager level at the downtown department store before giving up on her own all-American career altogether. I always made sure to talk about her in loose platitudes, letting his rewatches of *The Joy Luck Club* and long-form articles about tiger moms color in the lines for me. There was no way to prepare him, anyway; things never went smoothly where my mother was concerned. I remind myself now, as the plane engine rumbles slightly, that no matter what happens, it'll only last a week. We'd get in, check the filial piety box off our to-do list, and get out with plenty of time to spare before the new year. And if we wanted, we'd never have to come back again.

●

The plane begins to circle Chicago. I watch Ben sleep with his head tilted back, cradling his camera bag between his feet. Crammed into the window seat, he resembles an overgrown teenager, his still-gangly arms and legs threatening to unfurl at any moment. I smooth out the collar of his shirt and tighten his seatbelt with a tug so it's no longer draped like a suggestion over his lap. The baby across the aisle stirs and I look back over. This time, I study the mother. She's in her early thirties, beautiful and clearly assured of it, with the same sleek bob a lot of the young international crowd wear around SoHo. She's asleep, too, one hand resting on the back of the baby's head, the other wrapped around her husband's arm, whom I can't see all that well but who I can tell is Asian, likely a Chinese national, too. Even if they weren't sitting in first class, I'd know they were definitely rich. Before I moved to New York, I couldn't always tell the difference between the types—new versus old, Wall Street cash versus Pilgrim money—but I feel pleased recognizing the father's wool slip-ons from a subway ad, which meant, first class notwithstanding, this was a family still upwardly mobile enough to be susceptible to glossy marketing. Good for them, I decide, in order to head off the less generous thought that crosses my mind about how this baby would probably grow up to be any kind of asshole he wanted to be. He'd never have to fight about college majors or business school; he'd never end up doing the mental math on every life decision just to figure out how quickly he could enter the workforce to start paying it all back, while also stockpiling both savings and fealty for the more complicated decades to come with his parents. Because that was the other, realer reason for the visit. Secretly, I'd known the decision was already made the minute my dad hesitated on the phone and explained the additional motive he had for having us home for the holidays. "I have to have a procedure," he admitted. He said something about stress ulcers, which he dismissed right as I noted how weary his voice sounded. I asked if it was expensive, if he needed help paying for it. He ignored that and let a heavy pause import meaning into what he said next, about how it would be nice to have me around. "To help your mom around the house," he lied. What he didn't say was *So I don't have to be alone with her.* I googled *ulcerative colitis* on my phone and frowned. I tried not to think about how it was exactly like my dad to put himself last like this, both in the cadence of our phone conversation and as a line item on the calendar year's health insurance.

"Plus," he added, "it's been a long time since you've been home." *Eight years,* he could have reminded me, but didn't.

The plane shudders briefly and begins its gentle tilt downward. The pilot's voice crackles over the intercom as he promises beautiful weather ahead. I fish around in my purse for my little spray bottle of rosewater, which I spritz shamelessly over my face. Racist or not, Erin was right: The flight *was* dehydrating. Ben loves this stuff, so for good measure, I give him a light spritz on the face as he snores and then wonder if, in the last moments of this flight, before the protective barrier around our life gets peeled back, I should wake him and ask one more time if he's sure we should be doing this. Because what I really should have said when we first discussed the visit over sushi, or maybe years ago at the beginning of our relationship, was that the Audrey Zhou he knew—the confident, polished girlfriend who had the intense job and perfect skin and was always down for whatever adventure he was concocting—she wasn't anything like the Audrey Zhou who grew up in Hickory Grove, the pathetic teenage wallflower whom I thought I'd long since dissembled and left behind in some forgotten storage unit of my mind. And I didn't know which Audrey to expect once we were back in Illinois.

As the plane shudders again, I clutch the armrest and lean over Ben to gaze out the window, where the brown-gray patchwork of fields and subdivisions blur into the gray pane of Lake Michigan. I take a few deep breaths and then look over across the aisle again. This time, the baby is awake, and he's staring back evenly.

CHAPTER 2

Outside the entrance for Terminal B, Ben and I scan the lanes of traffic whizzing by for my dad's SUV. It's just under fifty degrees, barely colder than it was in New York, and the heavy down coat I changed into preemptively in O'Hare is making me sweat. With his camera bag dangling from his left shoulder, Ben hoists my duffel over his right, and I can hear the watery contents shift. Last night, when we were packing, he made fun of me for bringing the entire contents of our bathroom counter, but I was too tired to explain to him that the supply chain for my favorite rice water foam cleanser did not extend into Peoria County, or that if I was facing my mother for a week, I needed to present the most poreless, faultless version of myself. He doesn't say anything about the bag now, and I rub his shoulder blade in thanks. The metaphor of Ben carrying it for me is not lost on either of us.

Now that we're actually off the plane and breathing in the damp Chicago air, the stakes of this entire trip settle like a weight that sinks further into my chest with every passing minute. As we wait for my dad to pick us up, I remind myself to give Ben more credit for simply being here, with a sliver of memorized Mandarin under his belt and a watchful concern that he lets slip when he thinks I'm not looking. Last night, when I reminded Ben that I haven't been back home in Hickory Grove since I left for college, he'd been so shocked. "But you've, like, *seen* your parents, right?" he asked. I shrugged and said they visited occasionally, but it didn't feel important to detail these rare, strained visits, where my mother always managed to find fault with everything from the restaurant noise level to the over-plucked arch of my eyebrows. Anything to telegraph her continued displeasure with my choice to be a sales rep—a barely glorified version of the annoying white women she worked with at the downtown Bergner's for a decade before getting laid off—and a definite waste of the University of Chicago degree she spent my childhood preparing me to secure. "We're just not that close," I'd told him.

"And now your dad's sick?"

No, I said quickly: It was an endoscopy. People got those all the time.

Ben seems like he wants to say something else now as we crane our necks to survey the traffic, but he knows not to press. Instead, he squeezes my hand.

"You know I'm proud of you for doing this," he says again.

"You're the one who wanted to come," I say, as part of another long-running gag where we know who's really doing the favor here.

Ben jokes that I can count this as his Christmas present as a blue Ford Escape, abrupt in its familiarity, pulls up. I see my dad waving at us through the window. He puts on his emergency flashers and hops out, giving me an awkward half hug and releasing me before I can decide whether I should lean into it and make it a real one. As my dad strains to heave one of my bags into the trunk, Ben leaps forward and lifts up the other end easily. I realize I'm holding my breath to see if Ben's going to do it, if he's going to go through and say *ni hao* like I heard him practice while shaving this morning, but he changes course at the last minute and flashes the same smile that's made him the lead image on our dentist's Instagram.

"Here, Mr. Zhou, I've got it," he says instead, pronouncing our last name so it rhymes not with *zoo* but *joe,* the way it's supposed to, although he hasn't quite mastered getting his teeth into the *zh* sound. Still, his effort impresses my dad, and I am slack with relief.

"Call me Feng," my dad says, obviously sizing Ben up for a beat.

"Dad, this is Ben," I say unhelpfully, absorbing how surreal it is to see my fiancé, a six-foot-one white guy wrapped in a brushed wool peacoat, towering slightly over my Chinese father, who looks like he's on his way to the office, all khakis and wrinkled collared shirt. They shake hands briefly. Then my dad slaps the side of the SUV like it's a dependable Thoroughbred. "H Mart?" he proposes.

I get in the passenger seat and give what I hope is a reassuring nod at Ben in the back, where he sits with his camera bag between his knees. As my dad pulls out of the drop-off lane, hazards flashing—I'll have to remind him later—I turn to get a better look at him, curling and uncurling my fingers inside my coat sleeves even as I tell myself that this is the easy part, that my dad has gone his entire life being accommodating, so why should he be any different when it comes to Ben? Now that I'm sitting next to my dad again, I can't decide if he seems older or younger than his fifty-five years. His beard is speckled white now, one silver strand that he missed while shaving quivering on his left cheek. He seems both wider and skinnier; baggier, maybe, than when I saw him last year, when he was in New York for work, and Ben was in Greece, and I was supposed to take a client out to a baseball game. But when my client bailed, I convinced my dad to play hooky for the first time in his life to spend the afternoon in box seats at Yankee Stadium. I remember we said a dozen words to each other the whole game. When it was just the two of us, things felt at least peaceful.

My dad casually asks me to text my mother on his behalf of his safe arrival, so she knows he didn't get into some apocalyptic crash on the interstate, which apparently remains high on the list of things that she obsessively fears, right up there with having a useless, mutinous daughter who moved far away, probably. I do so while avoiding reading too much into the existing text conversation between him and my mother, which is filled with sparse, misspelled texts in English about who noticed they were out of Lactaid and who was going to pick up more of it. Then my dad hands me the dashboard GPS and a jumble of cords. I'm almost positive it's the same Garmin we used when he'd drop me off at marching band events in high school a whole decade ago. "It doesn't stick to the windshield anymore," he grumbles.

I tell him it's okay and pull up my phone, which feels ludicrously sleek next to the GPS in my other hand. "The H Mart on Grand Street, right?"

Ben leans forward, already fully briefed on the pit stop I knew my dad would insist on making, since the drive up to Chicago remained such a rarity for my parents and there were few Asian supermarkets below Cook County.

"It's Whole Foods, but for Asian people," I explained last night of my parents' favorite go-to grocer.

"I *know* what H Mart is," Ben reminded me. "There's one by Astor Place."

Dad pulls the SUV onto the highway, and I look out the window at the gray-green expanse of warehouses and strip malls we drive past and the black tree branches dividing like blood vessels into the chalky sky. It's not quite home—Hickory Grove is still 170 miles away—but the suburban silhouettes are comforting while also being far enough removed that I know I won't see anything, or anyone, too familiar. Ben leans forward from the back seat to ask my dad what he thinks of the Cubs' chances next season, a line I know he prepared based on the intel I'd given him about the mystery of Zhou Feng, whose interests primarily rested on following organized sports and forever attempting to keep the peace. I lean my cheek against the familiar tautness of the seatbelt and close my eyes, listening to Ben and my dad talk. Ben's being his sweetest and most charismatic self, taking care to slow down his speech from his usual manic New Yorker clip. He makes a joke about a pitcher that goes completely over my head, but my dad laughs and asks if Ben would want to hit the golf course with him while we're here sometime, as long as the weather stays this warm.

●

When Ben and I first met three years ago, I'd just gotten promoted at *The Current,* which meant I could finally leave the loft I was splitting in Bushwick with three wannabe writers for a slightly smaller railroad apartment I only had to share with one girl and her Roomba. Most of the time, I was at Zadie's place anyway. Zadie was my first friend in the city: As undergrads, we both interned at the same Chicago PR firm one summer and kept in touch after college, and now that I lived only three subway stops away, she took care to introduce me to her deep network of Brooklyn contacts and, more eagerly on her part, single guy friends. That November, Zadie had scored her first reporting job and moved in with her architect boyfriend. They were throwing a Friendsgiving feast for all of us who were stuck in the city (or, in my case, unwilling to go home) to celebrate their new, successful lives and their shiny, broker-scouted apartment in Clinton Hill. We'd only recently hit our mid-twenties, so for the rest of us, it was our first glimpse inside what we decided was a real adult apartment: one with a dark, skinny stretch of a hallway and no working buzzer, sure, but then the hallway opened up to a cavern of a living room kitted out with built-in shelves, a trash receptacle divided for four types of recycling, an enormous potted monstera, and a real leather sectional.

"Secondhand," Zadie said about the couch with a demure eye roll when I gave the place an appreciative once-over, hoping my compliments made up for the fact that I was an hour late from handling a last-minute work emergency and wearing my usual midtown uniform. Upon scanning Zadie's living room, where everyone was wearing thrifted sweaters and decisively ugly jeans, I felt like a kid playing dress-up in my work blazer and try-hard heeled boots. Everyone else was already chin-deep in the mounds of potatoes and salad and some extreme overachiever's homemade bread, so I stood at the edge of the hallway as Zadie took my coat. In the kitchen, her boyfriend was giving a detailed recap of his turkey roasting technique. I darted toward the bar cart and made myself a drink. It had been a long day, and I was hoping I could manage to eat quickly and slip out without having to talk to too many of Zadie's media friends. When a guy in a Penn sweatshirt—the subject of Zadie's latest Austenian scheme for me, I immediately knew—came over and started telling me about his summer abroad in Beijing, I stifled a groan. He asked me where I was from, and when I said Illinois, he stared at me blankly. "Chicago," he reasoned after a pause, and kept talking. I started scanning the room in search of rescue, which is how I landed on Ben, who was sitting on the rug next to Zadie's giant houseplant, his head poking out between two of the enormous fronds. He was staring right back at me, looking as bored as I did, as he pretended to listen to a girl with a shaved head, whom I vaguely recognized as Zadie's college roommate—Jasmin something? I remember thinking then that Ben seemed out of place within the staid domestic coziness of the evening even though his entire body was positioned in all the right angles to appear deeply interested in the Twitter dramatics everyone on the sectional was discussing. He was even skinnier then, basically a stack of bones under a barely contained dark mop of hair. In his hands, he fiddled with a camera, some old-fashioned model that I could tell still used actual film, but the full weight of his gaze was on me. He held eye contact for a moment, then glanced down at my boots and back up at me, and let a small grin unfurl across his face. I realized then that everyone else had taken their shoes off at the door, and Zadie must have been too polite to say anything. *That* embarrassed me, so I busied myself making a plate of food and then carefully spent most of the rest of the night on the other side of the living room, dodging Beijing's Number One Fan and thinking about how my mother would die if she knew I'd forgotten to leave my shoes at the door of someone's party. When Zadie's boyfriend went to check on the pies, I took his place in the conversational ring around her and quietly asked who the guy with Jasmin was.

"Ben Stear? He and Jas went to high school together." Zadie swiveled her head over to the couch with such immediacy that I winced. "You know, that arty one on the Upper West Side?" So even then I'd known Ben was a New York native. Zadie studied my reaction and tacked on a fact about how Ben only recently moved back to New York after backpacking in Thailand. I'd made a face at this, thinking of the Penn guy openly leering across the room, and Zadie laughed.

"No, Ben's great. He's just always up for whatever. And cute, right?" she said without missing a beat.

At the end of the night, the dozen or so people gathered in the living room clamored to take a group photo. I had gone to make another drink and returned as Ben, camera in hand, was trying to art direct everyone into place. "If you're going to always be carrying that thing around," Jasmin was saying, "you know we're going to put you to work."

It didn't seem fair that he, a newcomer to the group, was automatically the odd one out for the photo, so I told Ben that I could take the picture if he wanted to be in it. Zadie waved from her spot on the couch and told me to stand over next to her, that I should let Ben do his work because he was a "professional." I looked at Ben, only able to make eye contact with the column of his neck. "You're a photographer?" I asked.

"Well, I'm working on it," he said proudly, which felt refreshing. It made me think of the sad little desk in midtown I'd just left, so I said something about how it sounded like a meaningful thing to do. At this, he beamed a little and pretended to check the framing of the group. So far, he said, it was a lot of weddings. I stared at his hands, narrow and elegant around the body of the camera.

"You should get in, though, over by Zadie's right," Ben said. "It'll put you in the center."

I grimaced, not wanting to upstage Zadie. It was her party, after all, and she cared about these kinds of things. Then Ben leaned over to me and said it so quietly and quickly that I barely processed it:

"First rule of photography," he said, throat bobbing. "You put the gorgeous girl in the middle."

I choked on my drink. "Jesus," I said. "I don't even know you."

He jutted his chin out at me in challenge. "But I think you want to."

I forced myself to swallow and said it was nice to meet him, and then I practically bolted over to Zadie to take the picture. If it had been anyone else who said it, I would have found the line cheesy and condescending. But Ben was simply that sure about himself, I could see already as I watched him crack a joke and make the entire room laugh. And he seemed just as sure about me. I was twenty-four, and no one had ever used that word, *gorgeous,* for me before. Ben waved his hand to get everyone to look at him for the shot, and I was too glad for the excuse.

●

I must have dozed off during the drive to H Mart, because I have to peel my cheek off the seatbelt when we park. The grain of the belt has left a patch on my cheek. My dad offers to let me stay in the car to sleep, as if I'm still the little kid he's carting around between errands, back when we'd make a game of how long we could stay out of the house. "No, no," I tell him, "I'm fine." I zip up my coat and get out of the car, and the three of us troop into the grocer together, Ben trailing with his camera slung over one shoulder like a quiver.

Inside, the instant confrontation with ninety thousand square feet of food laid out under a battery of flashing screens and fluorescent bulbs and plastic holly makes me want to stop and massage my temples a little. Ben snaps a few pictures. My dad observes Ben with a bemused expression. "He's very good," my dad remarks to me, as if he can tell just by the way that Ben glides through the produce aisle, even though I am sure that Ben is the first photographer, and journalist, and photojournalist, that my dad has ever met in his entire life. I take the shopping cart from my dad and follow him around as he gradually loses interest in watching Ben and then revs into grocery mode, picking out crates of Asian pears and fat persimmons and twelve whole cartons of the soft tofu on sale for ninety-nine cents each. Ben takes a few pictures of a bin overflowing with bok choy before putting his camera away, which I'm relieved about.

"It's a lot," I apologize as my dad bobs ahead of us in the produce aisles. I think about what else I should preemptively say that I'm sorry for, amid the strangeness of trailing after my dad in this random Chicago suburb H Mart, but Ben squeezes my hand and tells me to stop.

"You're *so* stressed out." He chuckles, and ordinarily this would be all it takes to make me roll my eyes and nod along, but I'm watching my dad closely so we don't lose him in the soy sauce aisle. "Breathe," Ben reminds me. "Everything is going great, okay?"

He takes the cart from me and gestures for me to climb onto the end. I want to humor him, so I do, and he steers the cart past rows of Spam and cellophane noodles, his eyes softening with satisfaction as I try to tell him to slow down but start laughing instead. Maybe this *was* a good idea, bringing my chronically starry-eyed fiancé home. If anyone could handle this trip, it was going to be Ben, Mr. Up for Whatever, and as long as I had him with me, that made me the soon-to-be Mrs. Up for Whatever. And that meant I was truly coming back to this place as a different person than the one who left. How stupid it was to worry about Ben on this trip when being slightly out of place, I realize, has always been his natural element.

•

The morning after her potluck, Zadie, who always knew when a story was afoot, called and demanded to know what I thought of the whole night before casually bringing Ben up.

"Jasmin said he asked a lot of questions about you," she said finally. "Like, if you're single."

I was glad she couldn't see me redden over the phone. "And?"

"I said you're married to *The Current*."

"Wow, thanks."

"It's true. You work like a crazy person. *I* never get to see you."

I said something back about how that wasn't entirely my fault; she was too busy plotting how to get her boyfriend to propose.

"So?" Zadie sniffed. "How about you hurry up and get together with Ben, and then we can be boring Brooklyn gentrifiers together?"

I made a noncommittal sound, allowing myself to think back to Ben calling me gorgeous in the middle of a crowded living room.

"Anyway, he asked for your number, and I gave it to Jasmin." She sighed, clearly unimpressed with the response she was getting from me. "He's very good-looking. And Jas said he interned for Annie Leibovitz once."

"Zadie, I'm not trying to hire the guy."

"I'm just *saying*. He's impressive."

Later that night, after coming home from a run around the park, I got a text message from a number with a 917 area code asking if I was free for a movie on Friday. I opened my calendar on my phone and dragged open a new box, typing in *Date with B?* as if I couldn't believe it could really be that easy. When Friday rolled around, I considered canceling on Ben because there was an outing with the other sales reps on my floor, and I knew that a night spent sucking up to Ted and the rest of management would be infinitely more practical than going to an obscure art house film with some guy, as cute and probably even funny as he was. Work I could always count on; people, less so. But Ben sent me a text at lunch to confirm the movie time and ask what kind of snacks I liked; he even specified where we should meet out in front of the Angelika. The idea that someone was thinking through this category of details for me, after I'd spent the entire week smoothing over a battery of egos at work, felt irresistible. So at seven on the dot, I met him out on the theater's front steps, where he surprised me immediately with a kiss on the cheek.

"You look nice." Ben smiled. "I'm glad you wore those boots again."

I was pleased that he'd noticed. He was wearing a corduroy jacket and jeans and sneakers that matched only in degrees of studied shabbiness, but he was so handsome that it somehow balanced out the way we fit together as he led the way into the theater, holding a tub of popcorn against his chest and taking my elbow to guide me down the aisle. The movie was this indulgent nostalgia trip where the timeline was all jumbled up and the effect was supposed to be purposefully scattering, which I hated, so I spent the whole film watching the light from the scenes change on Ben's face. He was utterly engrossed and didn't speak at all until near the very end, when the credits were rolling and we were sitting quietly in the emptied theater, and then he leaned over and asked if he could kiss me. We made out until they turned the lights on. I couldn't stop blushing, but Ben thought it was the funniest thing in the world, and I remember walking out the door holding hands slicked with popcorn grease, feeling so pleasantly dissociative that I wondered if this was what Zadie meant when she talked about doing ketamine.

It was raining outside the theater, and Ben produced an umbrella instantly, like he'd planned this detail, too. I was still considering how much more impressive that was than any prestigious photography internship when an unshaven man stopped us to ask for a dollar. "Hey, man," Ben said, as casually as if he were greeting a former classmate. For a minute, Ben leaned over to chat—I couldn't hear about what—and then gave the man our umbrella. Before I could say anything, Ben held his jacket heroically over my head and we ran down Houston to find the nearest bar, almost running right into traffic because of the way every atom of our bodies was tilted toward each other.

It was funny how quickly everything happened after that, though it wasn't as if I had a lot of romantic history for comparison. Before Ben, I had Ted and my clients; there wasn't time for anything else. Before New York, college was a string of aimless miscommunications. And before all that, there was high school, and high school revolved around one person, one particular unrequited mess that I made myself stop thinking about a long time ago, since maybe the minute I left Hickory Grove and at last saw my warped memories of all those long drives down Route 91 and locker run-ins for what they were: humiliating and useless and oddly forgettable as soon as I'd breached the county line. With Ben, everything was clear. One night, a few weeks after that movie date, we were cooking dinner at his apartment, and he looked up as he was dicing onions and said, "You know we're good together, right?" Just like that. I was thrilled by this, how he spoke things into being, like God. So I didn't think twice about always picking up the dinner tab or letting him stay with me when his J-train building got condemned at last. We both knew I was making twice as much just on commission as he was, especially when he cut back on the wedding photography and started applying for photojournalism grants in earnest, so we quickly came to an unspoken agreement. Over that first year together, Ben did the cooking and the cleaning, the optimizing of weekend plans, the Black Friday strategizing when it came time to buy a new TV, all while remaining unembarrassed about letting me be the breadwinner. My work friends, who'd all been a little skeptical about the economics of dating a freelance photographer, signed their full letter of support when one of Ben's pictures from the migrant camps in Greece landed on the front page of *The New York Times* and kicked up chatter as a Picture of the Year contender. In short order, Ben had his pick of magazine assignments, which made it possible for us to move to a one-bedroom in Williamsburg, where we've lived ever since.

●

Farther into the bowels of H Mart, my dad holds up a shrink-wrapped packet of pork belly and asks if I still like hong shao rou. I nod and push the cart over to where he's evaluating a few bloody cuts of meat and checking them against a list on his phone. He asks what I think about doing pork tomorrow, brisket Saturday, and maybe a hot pot later in the week, and I tell him we don't have to decide it all now. "I was hoping they'd have lamb," my dad says with a sigh, tucking his phone back into his belt holster. "They don't always have it in stock, but I wanted to do something special since you're home, finally."

Pretending not to notice how his voice bent on the last word, I take the pork belly off his hands and set it in the cart. "You know I'm trying not to eat that much meat anyway," I say.

"Why? Meat is good for you," he replies indignantly, the way I knew he would.

We continue to the seafood section, where the open tanks of king crabs, lobsters, and what looks like an entire school of trout jostling for space are. I instinctively steel myself for Ben to register the smell, but instead he examines the smaller blue crabs crawling on a metal tray nearby and takes a picture. My dad walks over to show Ben the thick brown paper bags stacked nearby and launches into a story about the rare summer when the tiny Asian grocer in Peoria, before it went out of business, had stocked live crabs. This was back when I was maybe seven or eight, and my dad describes how freaked out I was to sit in the car next to the bag of crabs scrabbling against one another all the way home. Ben and my dad share a good laugh over this, and then my dad asks if we should get a few for tonight. I realize he isn't searching for my approval so much as Ben's, so I watch as they crouch around the tray like excited kids, my dad using tongs to coax each reluctant crab into the bag Ben is holding. When one falls to the floor and tries to scuttle away, Ben leans down, picks it up with his hand, and drops it in the bag without hesitation. My dad turns and gives me this obvious look that says, *Okay, I love this guy*. I feel my shoulders lower.

An hour and two overloaded carts later, Ben and I wheel over to the checkout, where a handful of local teenagers stand snapping their gum and arguing over which K-pop act is playing on the speakers. My dad reappears with a few bags of watermelon seeds, his greatest vice, and winks at me as he sets them on the conveyor belt. I glance at the teens. We're still too far out from Hickory Grove to accidentally lock eyes with anyone I might know, so I relax and take my place at the end to bag everything. Ben joins me. Even though he doesn't say anything, I know he's disappointed by all the plastic, and I make a mental note to remind my parents to use those reusable grocery totes I'd sent them a few years ago, at least for the week Ben and I are around.

In the car, my dad and Ben share a bag of watermelon seeds, spitting the shells out into an empty Kleenex box. I turn around and mouth "Thank you" at Ben, and he just gives me that reassuring grin. Then we all settle into the comfort of the SUV for the three-hour drive down the spine of Illinois, where we watch the suburbs and strip malls dematerialize into muddy fields. By now, it's almost five, and the gray December night has already settled in. I sit with my hands in my lap, twisting my ring. From the rearview mirror, I watch Ben observing the smudge of the horizon. He seems thoughtful, and I think back to all the times when he asked me about where I was from and I'd deflected with a quip. I could have made more of an effort. Soon we'll be entering Hickory Grove, and it will be impossible to write off the reality of living under my parents' roof and driving around the same roads and possibly even running into people who wouldn't even recognize me anyway, not after eight years, not after all the pains I've taken to scrape and buff away the remaining edges of the person no one ever totally understood anyway. And even if anyone did recognize me, what better way to go into those encounters than with Ben alongside to help tamp down the old Audrey and offer living proof that the new Audrey, the *real* Audrey, has been doing great.

By the time we take the highway exit for Hickory Grove, it's too dark to recognize much except the vast shadowy shapes of the farms and fields that the town has carved itself out of for decades. I sit up, tense and unnerved to see stars and the familiar profiles coming into view: the dome of the water tower, the endless jagged fencing, the gleaming gas station sign. Ben has dozed off in the back seat, his chin bobbing gently. When I look over at my dad, it feels like it's just the two of us again, driving home from school or possibly one very long grocery store run. When my dad pulls onto Newcastle Court, I can pick out our house immediately by the mismatching porch lights and front-yard maple tree shivering noisily in the wind as if to signal that here, at least, was one thing that figured out how to stay put.

CHAPTER 3

At first, I can't tell if the jabber of Mandarin is real or just part of my dreams, or either way, what it is that my parents would be fighting about: Money, again? Me? How much my mother hates living somewhere that gets so cold in the winter? But then the contours of my room blur into view and I realize the steady stream of consonants is coming not from my parents, but from the China Central Television midday news report on the TV downstairs. I sit up, relieved but also aware I've overslept. We got home after eight last night, while my mother was still at her evening Bible study at the Eastwoods Community Church, and after a quick dinner of steamed crab, I barely had the energy to give Ben a half-hearted tour of the house before escorting him to the apparently renovated basement, where my parents have set up a guest bedroom for Ben. "They're so old-fashioned," I told him, hoping Ben didn't mind sharing the room with a bookshelf of my dad's old textbooks and three DVD towers crammed with every possible movie from the American action canon along with my mother's favorites from the eighties, all covered in a thick film of dust. By then, it was technically eleven in New York and we were both too exhausted from the day to even think of debating the sleeping arrangements, so I climbed upstairs afterward and said good night to my dad, who had retreated into his room at the end of the hallway.

After scrolling through a few emails on my phone, I realize that the sensation of waking up in my childhood bed isn't nearly as disorienting as I thought it would feel, as if my body and my subconscious actually know *too* well exactly where we are: everything as familiar as any given morning in high school, when I'd bolt up from my alarm and cycle through the usual anxieties over which class might have a pop quiz and which songs I could burn onto the CD mix to trade with Kyle Weber that would finally make him see me as more than a friend. It's unnerving, this realization that if I don't push too hard, I could easily forget the last eight years of my life in New York and peer into the mirror hanging on the back of my door to find the same teenager, plagued with whiteheads and unrequited longing, late for class. I reach for my ring on the nightstand and slide it on, turning it over and over on my finger like a rosary as I take a better view of my old bedroom. Thankfully, there are plenty of visible cues that give away the passage of time: the appliance boxes in the corner, as if my parents gave up on putting certain things away and resigned them to the purgatory of my room. My old flute case sits under a cake of dust on the dresser. There are the school portraits, hung up in ascending order, my hands folded primly as my Picture Day outfits get successively nicer, peaking with the velour tracksuit I wore freshman year, right before my mother got laid off and we lost her employee discount. There's a framed photo from the days of my figure skating classes from fourth grade, and a handful from family vacations—my face noticeably tense as I stand next to a sign for the St. Louis arch. Proof of life. Hanging from an uncurled ribbon of Scotch tape are a few Polaroids I put up in high school, and I take care to not look too closely at them.

I pull on a pair of stiff jeans and a sweater from my carry-on, then remember to knock twice before entering the upstairs bathroom that my dad and I share. It's funny to see the contents of my makeup bag spilling out on the counter, next to my dad's wet toothbrush and extra-large jar of Tums. We moved into this house when I was four, after my dad finished his PhD and got a job with the manufacturing corporation in downtown Peoria, also after my parents officially stopped pretending they would ever sleep in the same room again.

Whatever negotiation occurred that gave my mother rule of the downstairs bedroom and relegated my dad and me to the top floor, like occupants in a tenant house, is evidently still in effect two decades later. I take a steadying breath and carefully wash my face, making sure to dab on an extra bit of serum and concealer and to slap my cheeks lightly to make them seem more glowy, healthy, happy to be here. I almost feel good about the resulting effect until I knock over my liquid foundation and watch its contents drip down the drain. *Fuck,* I hiss at myself. *Get it together.*

Downstairs, Ben sits at the kitchen table with my dad, who is eating a bowl of congee with kimchi and pork floss and keeping one eye on CCTV on the living room TV. If the smell from the open kimchi jar bothers Ben, he doesn't let on. He's also eating a bowl of plain congee that he's apparently tried to season with salt and pepper, judging by the shakers standing next to him. When Ben sees me, he winks from across the table and then lets his attention slide back over to the TV, where the newscaster talking in rapid-fire Mandarin clearly has him spellbound. Part of me is relieved Ben knows to maintain a chaste distance in front of my parents, but I can't help but wish he'd at least come over and walk me through this next part as I register my mother standing at the kitchen island, dabbing a Clorox wipe at the smudges on the suitcase I left downstairs last night.

"Mom, you don't have to do that," I say in greeting while avoiding having to look at her directly. "It's just going to get banged up again when we fly back."

The smell of the kimchi makes my stomach curl, and I move to the nearest kitchen cabinet in search of the matcha latte ingredients that I know we don't have. I pretend to consult the contents of the cabinet—canisters of loose-leaf oolong, a jar of Tylenol Extra Strength, Ziploc bags, and three tubes of aluminum foil—as I let the corners of my mother sink into my periphery: the mannish short hair, jet black from her zealous box dye efforts; the pilling elbow of her sweater; the familiar floral print of her loose cotton pants.

"You should take better care of your things," she intones.

"So," I say, "I guess you've met Ben?"

My mother shrugs like I've asked her about the weather and gives me a frown. "You slept in late."

I glance at her without meeting her gaze. The tattooed eyebrows she must have gotten done on her last trip to China give her the effect of an angry bird, and for a moment, I feel powerful for making this observation and not saying it out loud, knowing she's scanning my face in return for something to comment on. She just can't help herself. From the corner of my eye, I sense Ben watching our interaction and wish I could tell him that *this* is why I've shielded my life from my mother for so long. My dad uses this moment to announce that they got bagels, which I now see wrapped in Kroger packaging on the counter. I reach for them, pretending to busy myself with untwisting the plastic sleeve as I await my mother's verdict.

"Your color's off," she says finally. "Are you sick?" Then she eyes my bare feet on the hardwood floor and makes a pained sound that I'm not wearing one of the guest slippers she keeps on the rack by the front door.

"I'm fine." I hold my jaw carefully as I say it, working to keep my voice neutral. It was a dumb move to leave my foundation open on the sink like that. The bagels are stuck together, and when I pry one out, I pretend not to notice it's already stale and focus on tying off the sleeve with a meticulous knot.

"Are you even going to look at me?" my mother asks now, satisfied with her opening salvo. "I haven't seen you in years, and I don't even get a hug?"

I can feel my face get hot. I move to the fridge and check for cream cheese that I also know we don't have.

"Probably shouldn't get too close," I say. "Especially if I'm sick." I keep my voice light, and this rhetorical pirouette annoys her. I can only wonder what Ben thinks of this entire conversation, of the way my mother and I are circling each other in the kitchen like boxers assessing each other's weaknesses, knowing this is only round one.

The last time my mother and I were together, it was right after

Ben and I met, when she and my dad came up to New York to visit because they had Easter off. We were having dinner at one of those high-end hot pot places on the Lower East Side that I thought would impress them. But my mother was still able to find fault with the menu and the noise, asking me irritably as we ate about when I was going to *really* settle down, as if my New York life was just a vacation, as if the chaos of the restaurant was yet another sign that I should have followed the twenty-year plan she'd set out for me. At the end of the night, when the waiter brought the check, I set my card down with a decisive clatter. My dad protested immediately. What we were supposed to do was go back and forth on it, but I was exhausted from working a sixty-hour week and said something briskly like, "We all know I make more than both of you," a comment as irrefutable as the checks I had started sending home every few months to help with the mortgage. Of course, part of me felt smug about it, after all the grief my mother had given me in the years since college about robbing myself of a real shot at success. That's when the table went quiet. My dad gave me a look. Later, as I walked my parents out the door and hailed a cab to get them back to their midtown hotel, my mother said quietly, angrily, "You didn't have to shame us like that." It was another critique born out of desperation, I later realized, after a night when she had exhausted her usual topics of displeasure: my life, my appearance, the crime rate in Brooklyn. The fattest paycheck in the world wouldn't have made a dent in my mother's internal calculus of doing *enough* if I wasn't respectful enough or grateful enough first.

Now I'm the one standing in her kitchen grinding my molars, aware that she currently holds the power to embarrass me in return. This acknowledgment seems to pass between us like an understanding toward our mutually assured destruction. *If you scare Ben away,* I silently telegraph to her now, *I'll* really *never forgive you.*

"You know, I'm not that hungry," I say, abandoning my efforts to make this bagel breakfast happen and tipping it into the trash bin under the sink, where it lands with a thud. "Ben and I should get going, actually. We have errands to run."

On cue, Ben sails over to the sink, empty bowl in hand, hair slicked back from his shower. He compliments the congee and flashes a wide grin at my mother. The comforting frost of Ben's cologne shakes me out of my defensive posture, and I can't resist touching his arm to make sure it's really him. My mother's gaze flicks over to him. It's not clear if she seems impressed that Ben is here, saving me from the rest of her critiques, and also *here,* towering with his princely, agreeable confidence in her home. Seeing Ben next to my mother is at least proof that I haven't simply dreamed up the past eight years, and I watch the tip of her mouth turn upward slightly at him as he thanks her for breakfast. Not even my mother is immune from Ben's charms, I start to think, until she glances back at me and mutters in unmistakable Mandarin, "So skinny." I pretend not to hear and tell Ben we're going for a drive. Over my shoulder, I make sure to ask my mother in the sweetest, most winning Sales Rep of the Month voice if I can pick up anything for her from the store.

●

In the garage, my still-shiny Acura sits waiting, and I know Ben is trying to puzzle out its existence next to my dad's car and my mother's battered Accord.

"You know how people have love languages?" I try to joke. "It's like that, but gifts were my dad's guilt language."

Ben does not ask what it is my dad had to be guilty about, and I'm relieved. I take another deep breath in the driver's seat. Ben buckles in and then kisses me gently on the side of my head. I try not to think about how, if we were in New York right now, we'd be reading the paper in bed or deciding where to meet Zadie and her boyfriend for our usual languorous brunch. Ben glances at me to see if I want to talk more, but I shake my head, so he adjusts the strap of his camera around his shoulder and asks where we're headed.

"You know you don't have to bring that," I say, pointing to his camera. "We're just going out for a drive. Nothing photogenic."

"I'm sure we'll find something." He smiles when he says this, moving his hand automatically to the tendons of my shoulder, assessing how tense I am. "Your mom's really coming out of the gate hot," he ventures.

"That was nothing," I say, pulling the car out of the garage and letting the remains of my first in-person conversation with my mother in almost three years fade in favor of the muscle memory as I tilt the rearview mirror in place and position my hands at ten and two. "Just wait."

As we pull onto Route 91, I keep busy pointing out everything I recognize to Ben: the bright blue water tower, the Casey's general store where Kristen and I got pizza after school, the WELCOME TO HICKORY GROVE sign updated with the latest population figure—1,300, which I guess must include all the new subdivisions along 91 now. The remaining stretches are composed of stripped cornfields and soybean fields cast gray and clammy in the late December light, the way skin does after you wear a Band-Aid too long. We're driving in the vague southward direction toward Peoria, where we could be downtown in thirty minutes if we wanted a view of the depressing riverfront and the nondescript building where my dad has worked for more than two decades. I watch Ben look out the window, and I try to describe how the late summer fields of corn blurred together like the pile from a plush carpet when you drove by, how September was the best time of the year to be in Hickory Grove if you had a choice about it. When we pass a neighboring farm, he sits up and watches the black shape of the cattle herd from the window, asks if we can circle around so he can take a picture. Afterward, we shoot down 91 toward Peoria for a while, and I wince only once when we pass a billboard with a blown-out picture of a baby on it staring down at us like some pro-life Doctor T. J. Eckleburg. Thankfully, Ben's too busy fussing with his camera to see it. Here on the outskirts of Hickory Grove, the speed limit on the highway is sixty-five, but cars behind us speed past, clearly annoyed with my leisurely seventy. I guess I'm out of practice. I tell Ben that I can't believe Kristen Anderson and I used to drive around town going ninety when no one was around.

"Kristen—she's your best friend?" He's heard me mention her name before.

"She *was,*" I clarify, because of course now I count Zadie as my closest friend. But Kristen was the one I grew up with, the one who let me borrow her Harry Potter books and showed me how to shave my legs and kept my awful crush on Kyle Weber completely secret all while maintaining her starter position on the softball team.

"We met in first grade. She's the one from that picture I showed you," I say, squinting at the road. Ben pats my leg and then squeezes it gently, like a melon he's testing.

"Does she still live around here?"

"No." Then I backtrack. "Well, her parents do."

"So she might be back for the holidays?"

I sigh and remind him that I haven't been in touch with anyone from Hickory Grove in years. And yet, as we drive, I know instantly where the turnoff is for Kristen's house, just like I know the shortcut that leads to the best neighborhood for selling Girl Scout cookies, or the gravel road you'd want to get to the one bar in town—what was it called again, Finnegan's? something ostentatiously Irish—or which route Kyle used to drive me home from youth group in his ridiculous Mustang, or which exit got you to the Presbyterian church that ran the vacation Bible school. We drive by the Hickory Grove Baptist and Lutheran churches, too, and Ben asks which one my mother goes to. To show him, I get off 91 and take Allen Road over to the newer part of Hickory Grove, the part that's mushroomed up around the new subdivisions, and I wait to see Ben's face as all four stories of Eastwoods Community Church loom into view, glassy as a condo development, its lawn miraculously green for late December. "Oh my god," he mutters unironically as we loop into the Eastwoods parking lot, which is easily four or five acres itself. At the entrance is a new mural, a scene of Jesus sitting on a hill surrounded by children with carefully varied skin tones. The clouds above Jesus's head spell out JOHN 3:16. Ben asks what that's supposed to mean.

I look at Ben. "You're serious?"

"Is it from the Bible?"

Now I'm fighting back a laugh. "It's kind of the big one."

"The Bible's got greatest hits?" He's teasing, but I realize he doesn't actually know the verse. So I recite it for him. It surprises both of us, and I quickly steer out of the parking lot and back onto Allen. We'll see the church up close for its Christmas show, I tell Ben. My mother volunteers with the planning committee, so we'll definitely have to go.

By now, I remember that I haven't eaten yet, so I drive until I see the familiar green-and-tan sign of a woman clutching a baguette come into view. I wonder for a moment if Ben has ever actually been inside a Panera. "It's no Zabar's," I quip apologetically, and he laughs, eternally a good sport. Inside, I half expect to see Kristen with her olive-green cap and apron secretly reading *The Half-Blood Prince* under the counter. The last time I checked her Instagram years ago, I saw she'd gotten married and moved to Cedar Rapids. Like Ben said, there was no reason to suspect she *wouldn't* be home for the holidays, but there are five days to go before Christmas, and occupational therapists in Iowa don't get that much PTO, right? And even if she was back in town, why would she be operating the bagel slicer at her old high school job? Still, the paranoia, and maybe a little guilt that makes me want to check whether she's here, leave me crabby, or at least aware that I'm starving. The girl at the counter—probably a college kid home for break—stares conspicuously at Ben's camera, and I can feel him vibrate from the undisguised admiration. He smiles and pretends to be casual as he explains that he's a photojournalist, which of course impresses her. Then Ben adds that we're from New York, which opens up the conversational floodgates for them both. It's funny, the way Ben's professionalized chattiness resembles midwestern nicety. While she takes his order and tries not to blush too much, I check a few emails on my phone and answer a text from Zadie asking how things are going. I send her back an emoji that could be grinning or baring its teeth, depending on the situation. After Ben snaps photos of the cashier standing at the pastry counter, I order a cinnamon crunch bagel and something called a green tea chiller, which seems to be the closest thing I'll get to matcha in Illinois. We eat quietly in one of the booths, where I sit facing north so that I can keep an eye on the entrance. Ben has ordered a salad, which sort of feels like a waste of being at Panera, but then I remember how he gallantly insisted that I not tell my parents that he's usually vegetarian. Judging by my dad's equation of meat with hospitality, Ben's going to need all the arugula he can get.

Ben's also checking his phone and tells me he's expecting a call from Simon, his agent, about potential locations for his next shoot. I nod along and am relieved when he spends half an hour catching up on email so I can look at my phone, too, though with all my clients out for the holidays, my inbox is annoyingly empty of distractions. By now, it's midafternoon. When Ben asks where I want to go next, I say that I need to stop by Walmart for a few things, but that there's one more place we should visit first. He watches me when we're back in the car, waiting for the light to change. I drum my fingers on the steering wheel and reach for the radio, which somehow remains preset at the same station I'd programmed years ago: a loosely indie rock station that's still playing the Killers even now. I start singing along, and he watches in amazement. "You never do this in New York," Ben says.

"I never *drive* in New York."

Ben watches me so openly that I can feel the heat rise in my face. It reminds me of when I caught him staring at Zadie's party. All these years, and I'm still unused to the intensity of his attention, like I'm a puzzle he's working out, or an undiscovered species granting him an audience. Half of his job hinges on his ability to make everyone feel this way, I remind myself, and I tell him to stop so half-heartedly that Ben just smirks and shakes his head.

•

Half an hour later, I spot the turnoff for Legion Hall Road. They've paved the road over again, and the street sign has been replaced, but soon we're sitting in the student lot of the high school, which has a new wing and also an entire second story now. I make a mental note to ask Zadie's boyfriend, the architect, how they could simply build an entire new level on top of an existing foundation. Was that structurally sound? From behind the auditorium, we can see the neat edges of the track and the football field. Ben grins as he scans the Hickory Grove High School sign at the building entrance. I can tell he's fixated on the mascot painted below the school's name: a cartoon Dalmatian wearing a firefighter hat and brandishing a hose, in honor of the Hickory Grove Chiefs. I don't tell him it used to be the other kind of chief, one that wore a feather headdress at pep rallies until Ashley Davis started a petition to change it. There are a dozen or so cars in the parking lot, which confuses me because I know school's supposed to be out for the year. But then I see a girl drive up and get out of her truck with a bat bag over her shoulder, and it resurfaces a faint memory of Kristen complaining about the winter clinic that the softball team was forced to endure over Christmas breaks.

Ben allows for a minute of poetic silence before he asks me how I feel about being back here, and I grasp in the corner of my seat for the lever that lets me lower myself all the way back so the school and the girl scurrying inside are now in my peripheral view.

"You know I didn't like it here," I say with a dramatic sigh, and Ben laughs. We're both aware this is an understatement, based on the bits about growing up that I've fed him over the years.

"Well, no one loved high school," Ben says, probably reasonably, though I want to tell him that enduring the teenage gauntlet here in this former all-white farming village turned slightly less white suburb, where there were maybe four other people who looked like you in the entire school—not counting Grace Nader, who was Lebanese but also extremely pretty by central Illinoian standards, all that shining hair and tiny frame, so everyone assumed she was simply very tan—while you carried the weight of two Chinese immigrants' expectations for you to validate their entire life choices and tried not to think too hard about which classmates used to call you "Snake Eyes" back in preschool—it wasn't exactly John Hughes shit. Instead,

I point to the hulking body of the auditorium and tell Ben brightly that's where we all watched the Obama inauguration senior year. I mention this to change the subject, but doing so just reminds me of how different Ben's version of that day is. He'd been a sophomore at NYU and got bussed down to DC the night before with a group of students to witness history and then get blackout drunk on the National Mall. He even got laid on that trip. Meanwhile, I'd spent the next morning in this musty auditorium, watching the fabric of the projector screen flap ominously as we waited to see if we'd witness the assassination attempt that all the kids with the really Republican dads loved warning us about. I imagine telling Ben about that, how secretly satisfying the horror on his face would be.

"Was that your favorite part?" Ben is asking me, and I realize I've zoned out.

"What?"

"Watching the inauguration. Was that your favorite part of high school?"

"No. I don't know."

"Come on," he says. "It couldn't have been all bad."

He has a point. After all, school was not only where I got out from under my mother's thumb for eight hours a day, but it was also something that came easily. The instructions for earning my teachers' approval were neatly printed out on the syllabi, and the general expectations for our football-obsessed high school loosely revolved around getting everyone to an accredited state college anyway. It was all infinitely clearer to navigate than the ever-moving goalposts at home, where my mother was fixated not only on academic success, but also on how tenuous any real hold on that success was and how carefully you had to move through the world to prevent accidents or stupidity from undoing all your hard work. The problem was that my mother couldn't understand, even as I got the good grades and the coveted first chair in band, how I still managed to find creative new ways to fuck things up: by oversleeping and missing a test, by giving myself pneumonia in March when I sat outside in a swimsuit in forty-degree weather so I could get a tan that would match Nicole Bentley's after she got back from Cancún, and once, while speeding home in order to make curfew, by hitting a deer and thereby denting the precious Acura. Why didn't I see the deer? Why didn't I swerve the other way? These were the endless pieces of evidence that I was inherently careless and warranted tight supervision. No wonder school was a relief, a place where I had friends and structure and a last name that was unpronounceable but alphabetically useful for one thing: making sure I had the locker next to Kyle Weber every year. I loved getting up in the morning because it meant seeing Kyle, always with his skateboard and a blue Gatorade in hand. Like every other athletic-enough guy, he was on the football team, but once he spotted a copy of *Alternative Press* that I'd bought at Hot Topic in my locker, we found out we shared the same obsession for that particular mid-2000s cross section of indie and pop punk. Every day, during those stolen minutes at our lockers between each class, we'd discuss new bands we'd found on Myspace or briefly review the CDs we'd burned for each other the night before. I found myself waking up and counting down the minutes before I'd see Kyle, and he'd cheerfully high-five me once every morning, chanting, "Weber and Zhou, back of the alphabet crew," before English, then again in the afternoon before he rushed off to practice. I didn't even care that Kyle said my last name wrong; everyone in Hickory Grove pronounced it as *zoo* anyway, and it wasn't until I got to New York that I remembered it wasn't actually supposed to sound that way. His family went to the same church as Kristen's, and throughout freshman year, those stolen locker moments and the brief youth group sightings were the only times I got to be around Kyle up close, because, at school, he was legitimately popular. When we first learned about planetary gravity in physics, I remember thinking, *Oh, like Kyle.* He drew everything and everyone toward him, because he not only was funny and always shared his weed and had those dimples, but also maintained a degree of street cred for having a supernice mom, who ran the concession stand during Friday home games and turned out to be, in what felt like a total novelty to everyone at Hickory Grove, Mexican. "But, like, you can't even tell," as

Nicole Bentley—who was dance-team popular and whose family also went to Kristen's church—would say during sleepovers at Kristen's. I should have asked her why having one mom like Fran Weber was cool but having two parents like mine wasn't. Thank god for Kristen, the kind of best friend who'd change the subject, or invite me to youth group with all of them, or share her fries at lunch, or let me cry for an hour on the phone when we found out Nicole and Kyle had gone Facebook official. Even after all these years, I can picture the two of them slow-dancing at senior prom, Nicole in her spangled mermaid dress and Kyle in a bow tie, their matching purity rings glinting.

"Audrey?" Ben prods again, and I realize I've been making a face. He asks me what I'm thinking about.

"Prom," I half lie. "Prom was, um, not bad."

"Really?"

"I was on prom court, if you can believe it."

Ben makes a sound to signify being impressed, though I wonder if it's appalling to be almost twenty-eight years old and sound proud of this. He asks if I had a date.

"Of course," I say, as if I hadn't spent a good half of senior year giving myself stress hives about finding one. "Alex Bentley."

Ben squints into the middle distance. "I thought you had a thing for a different guy. Kevin something?"

Kyle, I want to say, though I'm touched that Ben half remembers a name from old conversations we'd had about our romantic histories, back when New York Audrey could be self-deprecating about having a crush on her locker-mate from a safe geographic remove.

"Alex was a kicker on the football team," I say instead. Which was true, except Alex was also Nicole's brother and a year behind us in school. When it was clear I wasn't going to score a real prom date, Nicole set me up with Alex for the benefit of our shared friend group and the limo her parents rented for all of us. And I'd agreed, of course, because it meant that I could be around Kyle the whole night. I start telling Ben about how carefully I had to pitch the Hickory Grove prom to my mother as a traditional ritual that all good, well-rounded college-bound Americans participated in, and how she eventually agreed to amend her ban on boys and dating for the one night. "Don't kiss him," she warned. I had never kissed anyone at that point, and definitely did not plan to try it with Nicole's little brother—he was cute but still a junior—but I couldn't believe my mother felt her authority over me extended into even this part of my teenage life. "Kissing gives you diseases," she said, like she was warning me away from doing illegal drugs.

"Can you believe that?" I roll my eyes, like this is just another inside joke Ben and I share about how impossible it was to grow up in a small town with parents who had plenty to be terrified about—drunk drivers, the casual gun ownership, the regular meth busts across the river in East Peoria, the general ebb and flow of oxy getting palmed between upperclassmen in the Hickory Grove High School bathrooms—but of course, my mother picked *kissing* as the greatest danger.

Ben's nodding, but he's also frowning in slight concern. "So what happened?" he asks.

I take a deep breath and move my gaze to the ceiling of the car. I shouldn't have tried to bullshit Ben on this fake happy memory, not when prom night in actuality had been lackluster and humiliating. There was the matter of my mother trying to dictate my life down to this final, personal degree about Alex. There was the residual indignity of knowing the teachers had rigged the prom court vote to get me and Ashley Davis, who was Black, on it—"to get a little color up there," as I overheard Mrs. Reid say to another teacher one day when I was making copies in the faculty lounge during lunch, followed by "She doesn't even look that Asian." Like Nicole, Mrs. Reid deemed the ability to pass, somewhat, as a compliment, which felt worse. The dress I bought at the mall downtown was supposed to be silver, but it washed out into white in the pictures, so that I looked like a terrified child bride in all of them. And I'd had a headache that morning that hadn't gone away—this was back when my mother's distrust of Western medicine extended to Tylenol, which I guess was her interpretation of the pill problem a lot of kids at school had—and of course, there was also the dread of being around Kyle and Nicole all night and forced to witness the way they draped over each other. Alex and I shared one slow dance made cumbersome by the blue-and-orange cast he wore on his arm, and I found it so mortifying that I complained about the headache and spent the rest of the night glowering at a table with Kristen. As she and I watched our seventeen- and eighteen-year-old peers attempt club moves in the ballroom of the Peoria Holiday Inn, we agreed the whole affair paled in comparison to the Harry Potter convention up in Chicago that we'd driven up to the weekend before.

Later, as Alex was driving me home, he offered to stop by CVS to buy me Tylenol, which was cute. In the empty parking lot afterward, he kissed me, and I remember thinking that the kiss itself really wasn't anything like what my mother had warned me of, nor was it like what Kristen and I read about in *Cosmo:* just wet, neutral contact that could have been helped out with a smear of Carmex. No sparks, but there wasn't anything to be afraid of, either. It helped that Alex was younger, as if our age difference lowered the stakes. I remember thinking he wasn't as cute as Kyle was, and not nearly as funny—this part I leave out as I relay the rest of the prom story to Ben—but Alex had been so clearly nervous about the whole situation that I felt magnanimous telling him to keep going. I knew what to expect of sex by then—thank you, Kristen's dial-up at home, where we spent afternoons reading dirty Harry Potter fan fiction—but I hadn't put a lot of thought into what it really entailed beyond its basic illicit allure. But I was so intoxicated by the power I felt when Alex admitted that he'd never done this before. I told him that I hadn't, either, but wasn't prom night as good an excuse as any? We agreed that we might as well get it over with. I remember Alex had a little beaded Jesus fish ornament hanging off his rearview mirror, because that's what I focused on the whole time. In the end, sex also didn't feel the way the Draco Malfoy fics or Kristen's youth pastor said it would. I spent the entire drive home brushing ancient Doritos crumbs left all over Alex's back seat off my dress, waiting for whatever guilt was supposed to arrive and feeling only slight annoyance as Alex toyed nervously with the radio. Afterward, he walked me to my porch and tried to kiss me good night. I asked him not to tell anyone what happened, and he nodded, like we both agreed that keeping it a secret made it glamorous and not at all like we were both relieved the evening was done. Part of me wanted to wake my mother up and tell her what happened, to throw the baldness of my rebellion in her face—*Look, Ma, I took Tylenol! Look, Ma, I lost my virginity in the back seat of a Wrangler!*—and see what would happen.

But I didn't. I was graduating in a matter of weeks, and nothing mattered except how quickly I could leave high school and Hickory Grove. Kristen and I had spent our whole lives promising each other we'd get as far away from our sleepy hometown as we could, but when she got a full ride to play Division II softball in Iowa and I got into the University of Chicago, we both felt like we had failed.

"At least you're moving to a city," she said, and sighed.

"At least you're leaving the state," I reminded her, disappointed, too, that she was leaving right after graduation for summer training.

She was genuinely excited about Iowa, though, and as we walked around Dick's Sporting Goods on those last days of senior year picking out sports bras we imagined we'd casually wear around the boys in our respective dorms, she told me she was officially over high school, and it was important we both put as much distance as we could between it and our shiny imminent futures as adults. At the time, I'd been angling for a way to tell Kristen about prom night. I'd waited so that I could make it seem like it was some casual thing I almost forgot about, but one look at Kristen's determined face—all our babyish memories already fast receding in her mind's eye—and I knew no one actually needed to know about the ten minutes in the back of Alex Bentley's car.

As I wrap the story up to Ben with a wry, disaffected joke about how Alex and I never spoke again, I immediately feel stupid. What was the point of telling Ben all this crap about prom? Did I think it would prove to him how stifling it was to grow up here? Was it to give him a window into my teenage angst and whatever issues I've been working out ever since? Or, if I'm honest with myself, was it not about Ben at all, and only because I wanted to replay that night so I could soak up one final, lingering shred of satisfaction that came with doing something actually rebellious, before summer came and the humiliation of my unrequited crush on Kyle became complete? I finally make myself meet Ben's gaze, to see how horrified this story makes him, but he's staring at me so tenderly that I pretend I have to adjust my seat. "Audrey," he begins to say, and then we're thankfully interrupted by the sound of his phone going off. I can tell by the ringtone that it's Simon, his agent.

"Sorry," Ben says with a grimace, and paws at his pocket. "I have to get back to him on this one thing."

I wave my hand to say that it's fine. It's getting late in the afternoon anyway, so I start driving toward Walmart while Ben asks Simon how it's going in New York. By now, I've gotten the hang of my old car again, so I can steer with one hand and reach for Ben's with the other, squeezing it with relief as Hickory Grove High School becomes a dot in the rearview.

●

As he and Simon talk, I look over at Ben and think more satisfied thoughts about how he's proof that, despite everything that happened to me growing up in this town, I'd at least made it out and created this whole new interesting life for myself, with a handsome, witty soon-to-be-husband who took photographs of people and lived with me in a nice apartment with a balcony view of Manhattan. By any standard that wasn't my mother's, I'd done exceptionally well for myself. If only everyone here knew. It was almost too bad that I deleted my Facebook after college; maybe there was worth in keeping those photos and connections intact as living evidence that Hickory High Audrey and New York Audrey have become two entirely different people.

The Walmart's packed. I wrap my parka tightly around me as

Ben and I get out of the car. The sun is setting, and I begin running through a list of final odds and ends that I want to pick up here: some foundation so my mother won't comment on my color again, hand moisturizer, booze definitely. It's gotten colder now, and I'm so focused on getting between those sliding doors of the supermarket as quickly as possible that I don't hear my name being called, not until Ben gently touches my arm.

"I think that guy knows you?"

That's when I stop and recognize a voice that is so clear and cheerful that I think I must be only imagining it. Then I turn around and come face-to-face with Kyle Weber.

"Audrey Zhou." He's grinning. "I knew it was you."

CHAPTER 4

Standing in the Walmart parking lot, I stare at Kyle and swallow to keep at bay the same vertigo from this morning that made me afraid to blink and discover that the last eight years have only been a wild dream, and I'm actually still a teenager, car keys in hand.

"Kyle?" I turn his name over in my mouth like I've forgotten how to pronounce it.

"I thought I recognized that car." Kyle stretches his arms out, and I go in for the automatic clasp that I've honed from greeting everyone from clients to Ben's friends, but upon entering Kyle's physical orbit, I feel too aware of the thick cotton of his hoodie, the wary angles of my elbows, the architecture of his rib cage, and it takes me a millisecond too long to remember to step back. Unreal, to *smell* him and feel my brain stammer in recognition. It's not quite the high school Kyle odor of Axe and deodorant and weed, but whatever warm base note that was there all along has remained unchanged. Now Kyle is holding me out in front of him, as if to get a better view. "You should have told me you were back," he says.

His face is serious, and I worry immediately that he's angry, even though I tell myself he has no good reason to be, not after everything that happened the last time we saw each other. But then Kyle breaks out in that wide smile that lifts even the tips of his ears up. "Christ, it's good to see you," he says.

"It's been awhile," I say peaceably, and take another step back.

"Your hair's shorter now. Looks rad."

I grimace to try to keep the blush from spreading. "What are you doing here?"

He laughs like I've just told him an amazing joke. "I live here?" Then he pauses. "Well, I mean, I'm staying with my mom for Christmas. But I'm over in Morton now. I teach at the high school."

"You're a *teacher*?" The things I would know if I hadn't deleted Facebook. From the corner of my eye, I'm aware Ben is ping-ponging his head back and forth between this conversation.

"World history," Kyle says, his back straightening with pride.

"Shit," I say, despite myself. "That's what your mom used to teach, right?"

"I can't believe you remember that." Kyle seems amused, like he can tell that I'm spinning out just under the surface of my manners. He asks if I'm still in New York, and I nod and explain that I'm back for Christmas. Ben coughs lightly then. I jerk around and grab his arm, like I haven't just remembered that he's standing there.

"Ben," I say, nearly thrusting my fiancé toward my old crush like a weapon. "This is my . . ." There's a slim moment of space as I consider the right modifier to use and then decide I don't need one. "This is Kyle."

While Kyle pumps Ben's hand up and down, enthusiastic as a missionary, I take the moment to study my old crush. He looks almost exactly the same, with that quick, compact frame he made as much use of as a running back as he did on his beloved skateboard; those wide, heavy-lidded eyes; the thick, attentive eyebrows that always seemed cocked in invitation. And of course, there's that broad mouth punctuated with a set of dimples, giving him the appearance of someone treating adulthood as a prank he can always take back, only now he's grown into the soft baritone of his voice and traded his checkerboard Vans for a pair of teacherly white sneakers. There are the beginnings of a beard, too, which would be new. Or maybe he simply forgot to shave.

"Ben's meeting the parents." I hold my hand up, Stear diamond glitzing on cue, by way of explanation. Is it my imagination, or does Kyle's left eyebrow arch as he gazes at it?

"Oh, wow," he says. "Congrats."

"Thanks," I say for the second time. Ben rubs his hands together from the evening chill, and I realize how bizarre it is that the three of us are standing in the parking lot: my fiancé, my high school crush, and me. I glance at Kyle to see if he's thinking the same thing, but he's smiling like this is a completely ordinary encounter to be having.

"Well," Ben says, "it's nice to finally meet one of Audrey's high school friends."

I can feel the weight of Ben's attention on me, and I'm suddenly terrified that if he looks hard enough, he will bore straight into the mainline of all the teenage memories that are unspooling in my brain now that the inner vault's been cracked by the last person I wanted to see at Walmart.

"Aud and I go *way* back," Kyle says. "Locker buddies since what, sixth grade?" He gives me a wink and I want to stop him from saying what I know he's about to say next: "Weber and Zhou, back of the alphabet crew!"

Ben makes an amused *hmm* sound through his nose; Kyle's mispronunciation of my last name embarrasses me in this moment even though it never did before. There's a pause. Awkwardly, I start to ask Kyle how his mom is, but my phone buzzes with a text from my dad reminding me to pick up Lactaid. It's just what I need to shake myself back into how the normal progression of this day was supposed to unfold.

"Well, we should probably go." I jerk my thumb in the direction of the Walmart and make an excuse about how Ben and I have to get back for dinner. Kyle nods.

"If you guys aren't too busy later, I was about to go get some beers at Sullivan's," he says. "You should come."

Sullivan's! *That* was the name of the local bar I'd been trying to think of earlier, when we were driving around. Before today, it had been years since I'd even thought about that little watering hole on Alta Lane, but now I can picture it immediately. "God, that place is still around?" I say weakly.

Kyle grins and says it's clear that a reunion is in order. I turn to Ben to ask if he wants to go, but Ben pinballs a glance off Kyle and back to me. "It's been a long day," he intones. I ask Kyle if we could do it tomorrow.

"Tomorrow's great." He shrugs. "School's out until after New Year's, so I'm around whenever, really."

Ben slowly takes a step back, toward the Walmart entrance. Kyle takes the hint. "I'll text you," he says, turning to me. "Same number, right?"

I tell myself it's an innocent question, that he isn't insinuating anything about why he never heard back from me after all this time, and I say yes.

"Great. Listen, I know you're a fancy New Yorker now and all," Kyle says, backpedaling away as if he isn't ready to turn around yet. "But this?" For a second I think he is motioning at the space between me and him, then I realize he is motioning at me and the ground. "It feels right. Audrey Zhou, home at last," he finishes, and waves goodbye.

●

For the next hour, as Ben and I troop around the cavernous Walmart, I throw anything that looks useful into our cart in an effort to distract myself: a quart of contact solution that I know I don't need, two bottles of foundation from the makeup aisle in case I feel like trying the extra shade, and an eight-pack of toothbrushes even though I know we both packed ours. Ben watches me in amusement and stops only to add paper towels, which he must have noticed my parents were low on. In the liquor aisle, I pile bottle after bottle of cabernet in the cart, along with a case of Sapporo for my dad. Of course Kyle is here—and not just *here* at the Walmart Supercenter, primary supplier of Hickory Grove's produce, home goods, and basic firearms, but *here in town* already for the holidays, because that was the kind of person Kyle always was. I knew that. Did I really think I could have gone a whole week here without running into him?

Ben pushes the cart along beside me wordlessly, but I know he's confused. *Who's this mystery guy, popping out of the woodwork like a Hallmark movie plot twist?* I can almost hear him asking, though I know he won't. It isn't like I never told Ben anything about my romantic past, and I'd joked about Kyle plenty of times, part of some self-deprecating bit about how I had nothing to show for crushing on another girl's boyfriend other than a bunch of useless CDs sitting somewhere in the glove compartment of my Acura. A Taylor Swift song as old as time, but now that I'm thinking about it, I can't remember how much detail I've really given Ben. And why would I have gotten into the specifics? It wasn't like I ever expected him to meet Kyle.

"So," I say finally on the drive home, keeping my tone light, like I'm setting up for a punch line. "Remember I said I had a guy friend I had a thing for in high school?"

"Sure."

"Well"—I pretend to study the speedometer—"that was him."

"*That* guy?"

I look at Ben, who's smirking. "What's so funny?"

"He's not really what I pictured."

"What do you mean?"

"You know. I thought you said he played football." Ben pretends to flex in an exaggerated sweep of his arms.

"Well, it was high school, not the NFL." I roll my eyes. "Plus, everyone played. Kind of like how everyone went to church, or knew, like, all the same country songs. It was just in the air."

"You midwesterners contain multitudes." He's kidding, and while I'm glad he doesn't seem freaked out by the whole run-in with a former crush, I can't quite get it together to laugh along.

When we get home and start hauling the Walmart bags out of the car, Ben asks, "So, you really never fessed up to him? Only because he dated your friend?"

I swallow and know that my face is turning red.

"It's kind of cute," Ben says nicely, though I can tell he's a little tickled by the small-town melodrama of it all.

"Honestly, it was nothing. Just high school stuff."

I know I'm supposed to say that, with the benefit of hindsight and geographic distance and my life as New Audrey. But I also know that Ben, as a normal self-respecting person, wouldn't understand the truth. He'd find it downright masochistic that, once Nicole and Kyle started dating in earnest sophomore year, I didn't have the sense to back off and tend to my heartbreak in private. Of course it made me hate Nicole to the point where I was constantly fantasizing about something awful happening to her—a wardrobe mishap at homecoming, rejection from all her top colleges, maybe even a mysterious reversal to the Bentley farmland fortune. Anything that would even up the unfair odds life doled out to us. But at the same time, I also *welcomed* Kyle and Nicole's relationship, because by virtue of Nicole's friendship with Kristen, the four of us started hanging out together, first at youth group, then at school, too. Then it was trips to the mall and the movies, and I was so fucking excited to go from Kyle's locker-mate who liked the same bands as him to Kyle's actual *friend* who hung out with him in public all the time, rooting Kristen on at her softball games and getting celebratory Steak 'n Shake after his. So what if Nicole was there, too, forever twining her arm around Kyle's? It was enough to get ferried around Hickory Grove in that white Mustang with the orange racing stripe, to have his number to text when it was time to plan Nicole's birthday, to watch our conversations veer away from Nicole and toward the subjects of school and college and our parents—his demanding dad, my impossible mom—in those stolen moments alone in his car when he dropped me off last after youth group, to sit and eat lunch in the cafeteria with some of his friends from the team.

Later that year, when Kristen started dating Cody Reynolds, the quarterback, I had another chance to bow out. I could have accepted that being the perpetual fifth wheel was beneath me. But I didn't, because how else would I end up in situations like Nicole's sweet sixteenth, sitting on the edge of her in-ground pool and feeling Kyle's hand on the back of my neck, rubbing in leftover sunscreen with friendly diligence. "You missed a spot," he'd said casually, leaving me unable to look anyone in the eye for hours.

Among the five of us, I still believed Kyle and I felt a specific affinity for each other, partly because of our locker-mate situation and love for the Killers, and partly because, thanks to either the Mexican part of his identity or his general awareness of what it was like to not totally fit in, he seemed to get how I felt whenever Nicole would quote *Seinfeld* and I'd have to admit that I'd never seen the show, or when I always had to go home early because of my mother's strict curfew. It wasn't like Kyle and I were in exactly the same boat—the name *Kyle Weber* got him by in school in a way *Audrey Zhou* never would—but there was an understanding. Before him, I didn't know anyone else who even tried to get it. I mean, there were kids like Grace Nader and Jake Patel, who were cool, so they didn't count; Vivian Leung, who led the debate team and laughed at me when I told her I didn't actually speak any Mandarin, so I avoided her at all costs; and Ashley Davis, who got moved out of honors English sophomore year after her semester-long campaign to decolonize the reading list. Maybe if I'd been braver and less intimidated by Ashley's fearlessness, I could have befriended her and the small group of Black girlfriends she ate lunch with every day. But I wasn't, so I didn't. And I depended on my tenuous bond with Kyle instead: When Nicole said she was jealous of how the two of us never needed a tan, or when Cody Reynolds would make a terrible Cinco de Mayo wisecrack, all it took was for me and Kyle to glance at each other from across his basement foosball table to know we were thinking the same thing. After prom, I waited to see if Kyle would act differently toward me, darkly hoping that Alex had let our secret slip and that would startle Kyle into a kind of jealousy. But nothing happened, and I felt so pathetic about the whole thing that I kept my mouth shut extra tight for the rest of senior year, waiting for Nicole and Kyle to finish making out every morning so I could get to my locker. I would be the patient and selfless good friend even if it crushed me, I decided. It had to count for something in the long run.

"It must be crazy to run into him now," Ben says in the garage, right before we go inside. "I mean, what are the chances?"

I arrange my face carefully to affect a convincing amount of wonder at running into Kyle within the first day of being back in Hickory Grove. "Small world," I say with a shrug, letting Ben content himself with this catchall rationale.

●

Dinner with Ben's family was always an event straight out of a lifestyle spread, inaugurated first by the inevitable baroque still life his mom loved assembling out of elegant blades of cheese and crostini—"for grazing," she'd encourage, which always had the effect of making me feel like a small deer—followed by bright, zippy salads and astute wine pairings and, without fail, some type of entrée that required three separate garnishes. Crammed into his parents' dining room, we would spend the night embroiled in debates about everything from the mayor's obsessive gym habits to the latest HBO prestige flick. I liked sitting back and watching Ben argue with his sisters—I'd never met a family that actually *enjoyed* shouting at each other like this before ferociously hugging goodbye at the train station—and the dinners always left me feeling full and clever and civically engaged.

But dinner tonight with my parents, I know, will be something else entirely, and as we unpack our haul from the plastic Walmart bags—of course I forgot to grab the reusable ones when we left this morning, and Ben honestly seems more sullen about that than running into my high school crush—I mutter a few last-minute reminders to Ben that are really meant to prepare *me* for what to expect from the inevitable awkward affair in which my parents will be intimidated by his quick English and white people table manners. I warn Ben that it's going to be a literally quiet dinner, because even if there wasn't the language barrier, my parents are just simply not the type to have heated opinions about Damon Lindelof's cinematic genius. He tells me to relax. "Besides," Ben says, "I bet your parents' cooking is amazing."

There is, at least, a lot of it: tightly packed bowls of rice—purple for my dad, white for the rest of us—and then four or five platters of food that my dad must have spent the afternoon cooking: the braised pork belly we bought at H Mart; delicately stir-fried chives and eggs, a favorite childhood dish; steamed bass; stir-fried eggplant; and, inexplicably, a couple of steaks that my dad grilled and slathered with A.1. sauce. He must have picked the most white person thing he could put on the table to make Ben feel at home. An edge of guilt about Ben's vegetarianism, and also the fact that we spent the entire afternoon avoiding the house, presses steadily at the back of my head. We're eating in the dining room, which is how I can tell my parents are trying to make an occasion of it. Growing up, we always did dinner around the kitchen table, where my mother could have a view of the TV in the living room and everything was easier to wipe down. The dining room was more of a life-sized diorama for showing off the extendable mahogany table when, say, my mother was hosting the Eastwoods Bible study; otherwise, it sat empty and encased in plastic lining to protect from wayward scratches. Tonight, the plastic's come off. My parents are on one side, Ben and me on the other, with the two remaining chairs pushed out, as if we're waiting for another couple to join us. We're even eating off the nice dishes, which feel so unfamiliar that I'm running my finger over the scalloped edges of my plate and wondering vaguely if my dad's fortieth birthday was the last time we used these.

Ben announces that everything smells "absolutely" delicious. My mother smiles tightly at him, which seems promising. If she can stop critiquing me for a second to decide if she likes Ben or not, then this will all be a *lot* easier. My dad, at least, is a clear fan. Ben settles easily into dinner and starts asking him questions about what it was like growing up outside of Shanghai and coming to St. Paul in the eighties for his doctorate. The effect is clearly flattering; it's likely been ages since someone has paid this kind of attention to my dad. Ben is leaning forward with his elbow on the table in what I suppose is his go-to interviewing stance. I can't help thinking how good he looks and how he seems already more comfortable with my parents than I could have ever pictured. I want to throw my arms around him and thank him, somehow, but then I realize that as I'm watching Ben, my mother has been watching me. "Did you both meet in school?" Ben is asking, and my dad nods and describes how they'd both been students at the Wuhan Institute of Technology, bonding over their obsession with *Roman Holiday* and a shared ambition to get out of the country as China juddered into modernization.

"She only married me because I was coming to America," my dad says, half teasing my mother, who gives him a look that passes between them too quickly for Ben to notice. My dad pretends not to see it and explains to Ben that it was a big deal to come to America for school back then; they weren't just sending any average Joe out to represent the Middle Kingdom. Ben makes all the right sympathetic sounds as my dad begins describing those St. Paul years, when he was working on his PhD at the University of Minnesota and helping my mother, who came with him dreaming of her own adventures in American ascent, get acclimated.

"It must have been hard," Ben prods.

"It *was,*" my dad says, tilting his head toward me. "Especially when this one came around by accident!"

My mother's mouth presses into a thin line, probably thinking about how that "accident" derailed her plans of studying economics—she'd always been obsessed with how unseen forces shaped individual choice, as if once she mastered the basic rules, she could beat the system herself—and thereby her entire life. "Of course I thought about an abortion," she told me once, when I was maybe ten. She didn't want to start a family as a twenty-four-year-old on WIC. She wanted to be like my dad and get an American degree and become one of those well-liked, well-rounded American women she saw on TV who worked in an office and went on vacations; her decision to marry my dad had been a practical strategy for realizing those ambitions. She never imagined that, instead, she'd be stuck at home raising a daughter who wouldn't even grow up to have the sense to be appreciative about it. When my mother's water broke while she was reading book titles to practice her English in the public library, she'd called a cab for the first and possibly only time in her life to get to the university hospital. My dad had been at a conference that weekend and rushed home to find my mother cradling a nubbin of hair and blanket in her arms, her precious *Roman Holiday* VHS playing stubbornly on the little hospital TV. She was the one to name me Audrey, of course. My dad agreed because he liked the way that *A* and *Z* bookended my initials, as if it meant his daughter would contain the whole universe of possibility that came in between.

"Feng," my mother admonishes now, and then says in Mandarin, "you shouldn't be saying these things."

Ben glances at the three of us, uncomprehending. Before I can answer, my dad, emboldened by the attention, launches into a story about the time I fell out of my high chair as a baby when my mother was home alone with me and trying to take a shower. I was fine, just scared. But my mother was so panicked that she called 911 and tried to explain what was going on to the perplexed operator, who couldn't quite make out her accented English anyway, before she realized they probably charged you to call for a doctor in the beautiful country, so she hung up and simply sat with me on the couch, her hair still half sudsy with shampoo, until my dad came home. My dad tells this story with a grin, as if it is the funniest thing in the world. "That's how we started! With almost nothing," he says, punctuating his story with a soft belch.

"It was like that for my great-great-grandparents, too," Ben says earnestly.

I stare down at my plate so he can't see my face, and so I can't tell if my dad is flattered or confused at being lumped together with German bookkeepers who sailed through Ellis Island a hundred years ago. Ben doesn't seem to notice and is now trying a second bite of everything, even the pork belly and steak, as I pick at everything myself. It's all so much heavier and saltier than the meals we cook at home, but Ben makes a show of digging in. My mother watches him eat. She cuts her eyes to my dad.

"Why are you telling him all these things about us?" my mother says in Mandarin, but it's clear from her tone that she's saying something disapproving, and Ben stiffens. A flash of exasperation moves over my dad's face.

"You're being crazy," he mutters back to her, in Mandarin, too. "I'm helping Ben get to know the family."

"You're embarrassing yourself," she hisses back, and I know what she really means is that he is embarrassing her.

"Guys," I cut in, in English, and give them a look. My face is burning again, and I can barely meet Ben's gaze as I apologize to him, though no one's sure what about, exactly. But it's enough to suck any marginal semblance of normalcy out of the room, and the four of us fall silent as we eat. I resist the urge to recoil as my dad delicately pulls a fish bone from his mouth, setting it neatly on a napkin. My mother, apparently finished with participating in conversation, fields WeChat messages from her enormous phone, the keyboard sounds audible and grating. I wonder dully in between bites of eggplant if she's doing it on purpose, like some kind of black-ops CIA program designed to wear down the opposition. It's a classic move, the way she simply shuts down the conversation whenever she wants to, like the way she dead-bolted the hotel room before graduation or when she'd give me the silent treatment for weeks after a big fight. When I was even younger, she'd lock herself in her room to cry for hours, leaving me bewildered in the hallway, trying to slip drawings under her door that I made in apology for breaking a drinking glass at dinner or losing a jacket during recess. Sometimes that worked and she would come out and accept my apology doodles. When I got older, she preferred them in writing. An apology wasn't enough; there had to be a degree of self-assessment, too, an explanation of behavior and a promise toward improvement. Pro-and-con lists were her favorite tool in this; so many times she made me write down a list of my personal strengths and weaknesses. Weaknesses: I was reckless, impulsive, clumsy. Strengths: I was

smart but, most of all, lucky. Once, she let me write down *good at eating grapefruit* because that was a point of pride for her, that I could stomach the bitter pink fruit when most people found it too sour. Whenever she was in a good mood, we would sit together after dinner and I'd watch her peel a whole grapefruit, pulling the skins apart to leave the plump sections naked and fully intact. And then I would eat the whole thing.

I want to say something about how rude it is that my mother is on her phone during our first dinner as a family, but I'd feel like a hypocrite because I'm itching to check my phone, too, which I left in my purse upstairs. As annoyed as I am with my parents right now, I'm also still thinking about the run-in with Kyle and wondering, like a fidgety preteen, if he's really going to text me about going to Sullivan's. In a last-ditch attempt to make conversation, I tell my parents about the fact that Ben and I are planning to move to a new apartment next year. Ben perks up and supplies the fact that Ann and Clement are helping with the down payment, which I immediately wish he hadn't brought up. I watch my dad's face carefully, unsure if the idea of someone's parents buying his only child a place to live is as much a hit to his pride as me unthinkingly picking up the dinner check in New York. But he seems excited and asks Ben what neighborhoods we're looking at, as if he knows any places in New York other than Williamsburg, where we live, and Yankee Stadium. My mother's face is the one that changes with this news. I watch her and wonder if whatever line item she's adding is going under her column of "pros."

●

After dinner, Ben offers to do the dishes, which pleases both parents. My dad puts up a half-hearted fight as a courtesy, then wanders into the living room to catch the Bears highlights, and my mother goes to her room and gets on the phone with a church friend. I almost breathe a sigh of relief to be left alone in the kitchen with Ben to rinse plates.

"So," I say. "Big day one, right?"

"I think I've been in literal conflict zones that were less tense."

"I told you it would be like this."

Ben chuckles and then sets the dishes down, drying his hands briefly on his jeans so he can put his arms around me. "It's not so bad," he says more seriously.

"I can't believe I'm putting you through this."

"Come on," he says. "It's your family. They're part of the package."

I peek at my dad, who is engrossed in the news in the living room, and use this as an opportunity to give Ben a long kiss. It catches him off guard, but he automatically moves his hand up to rub the back of my neck. I pull away and tilt my head toward the basement in invitation.

"I should finish the dishes," Ben says. Still, he allows himself to be tugged away from the sink, and we sneak downstairs to the guest room. I assume this is breaking an unsaid rule with my parents, but it feels urgent to not role-play someone's disappointing daughter, or someone's old high school friend, or some sad ghost wandering around Hickory Grove for a few minutes, at least.

Ben is taking forever to unbutton his shirt. "Leave it," I say, and climb over him. For a few minutes, we try to make it work, but I can tell Ben is preoccupied by the thought of all those unwashed dishes and I stop. I ask if everything is okay even as we both reach for our pants.

Ben plants a kiss on the top of my head and gives me an apologetic smile. "Sorry, I'm just, you know. Exhausted."

"Okay."

"Plus"—he glances toward the ceiling—"your parents are right there."

I sigh, knowing he has a point. It's sweet that he's trying to be respectful, even when I wish he could table the impulse just this once. Back in the kitchen, Ben insists he's got the dishes covered, so I go upstairs to take a long shower and then lie on my bed with my hair in the towel and Walmart's best excuse for a face mask smeared on and sinking into my pores. I take off my ring and set it on the bedside table. Who am I kidding, it *was* unwise that I was trying to sneak in a quickie with my parents barely ten feet above us. I know Ben was right, and I know why I wanted to do it anyway, because it would have kept me from doing exactly this: spinning out in my childhood bedroom as I think about that run-in with Kyle and what it means.

●

After high school ended, I was finally rewarded for my masochistic patience: Kristen moved into her athlete dorm in Iowa to begin training, and Nicole went off to tour Europe with her grandparents, leaving Kyle and me alone in Hickory Grove for the summer.

"You need to tell him what's up," Kristen chided when we said goodbye on her driveway, punching me lightly on the shoulder to emphasize her point. "It's literally now or never, Aud."

Whatever envy I had about Kristen getting to leave Hickory Grove first to begin her new life as a college athlete soon dissolved under the realization that I had Kyle's attention all to myself for three months. It was only a matter of time, I decided, until he and Nicole broke up like every other high school couple. I just had to stick it out. Every morning, I made it a point to check Facebook to see if their relationship status changed, as if I were keeping tabs on some great geopolitical event. It never did.

That summer fell on one of those years when the manufacturing corporation downtown renegotiated its contract with the labor union, which meant everyone who worked the office jobs, including both my dad and Kyle's dad, had to practice stepping in at the plants if things didn't go well and the workers went on strike. I didn't learn until years later that this made my dad—as well as everyone else's who worked at the office—what people like Ben's friends called a *scab.* My dad was assigned to the second shift, so I didn't see him for most of that summer as he underwent nightly training and then slept all day. It left me antsy and unwilling to hang around the house, especially at night with my mother, who grudgingly allowed, now that I had gotten into the University of Chicago, that there was nothing left for me to study for. I half expected Kyle to completely forget about me once Nicole and Kristen were gone, but he must have been in the same limbo, stuck counting down the days until he headed off to Illinois State, where his older brother and his father had both graduated from. Once he started inviting me over to his house to hang out, probably out of habit, I couldn't find any reason not to go. It didn't feel like any form of betrayal to Nicole when I was so sure their breakup was all but ensured.

That was the summer when Kyle's parents also got divorced—something that I watched my parents for signs of, too, because I was fascinated by the idea that after your children grew up, you could admit things went wrong and kind of start all over. By June, Kyle's dad moved out and left their enormous house on Radnor Road to his mother. I wasn't entirely sure what she did in it all the time. That was another way I rationalized always being over at the Weber house; his mother was always cooking for three, Kyle would explain to me sheepishly when he asked me to stay for dinner. I liked Mrs. Weber and found her school reputation as the cool mom well deserved. She asked me to call her Fran and kept the kitchen stocked with seltzer and homemade puppy chow and hummus—things that didn't exist in my house. Most important, she didn't care what Kyle and I did, so we spent those days either watching MTV in the basement, where Kyle showed me how to smoke weed and shotgun a Coors, or driving aimlessly around in his Mustang. A few times, we snuck into Sullivan's whenever one of Kyle's brother's friends was bartending. If I thought about it, I could still picture the way he'd put his hand on the headrest of my seat as he backed out of Sullivan's curved driveway, when we had to leave before it got dark and real adults started filing in.

It was easily the most thrilling summer of my life. If either of us found it odd to hang out without Kristen or Nicole, we never mentioned it. I definitely wasn't going to say anything, not when it meant that I could spend whole afternoons lying on the carpet in

Kyle's basement and listening, at top volume, to *Sam's Town,* or the new All Time Low record, or sometimes even Nicole's favorite Carrie Underwood album, which, in the sanctity of the Weber basement, we could both admit was pretty catchy. Then he would play me the CDs he burned for Nicole, these little mixes that he mailed off dutifully at the beginning of the summer, and occasionally, she would want to Skype him from Europe. I'd go outside and listen to the sprinklers spatter across the driveway to give them privacy. But those occasions got rarer as July slid into August. When Fran got sick of us hanging around the house, we would hang out at my house, or drive down to Detweiller Park, where we'd pass one of his clumsily rolled joints in peace, our fingers brushing so often as we handed it back and forth that it felt natural.

A few weeks before the end of the summer, Kristen came home for the weekend. I thought I'd be happy to see her, but as I drove us around Hickory Grove and listened to Kristen gush about her roommates and the campus Quidditch team and her brand-new boyfriend from the baseball team—things she hadn't bothered to tell me about over the phone all summer—I found myself annoyed with how immersed she already was in her new life, and I realized ungenerously that her presence, even for a weekend, cut into the limited time I had left to spend alone with Kyle. When Kristen stopped to ask about Kyle and whether I'd finally made my move, I said coolly that everything was "chill" and then changed the subject. Compared to Kristen's grown-up adventures, my summer mooning over a high school crush felt juvenile even then. I was relieved when she went back to Iowa.

The truth, of course, was that I fell even harder for Kyle that summer. And I knew if I got to have him only for a few months, then I wanted it to be perfect. So even when we were hanging out in his basement, stoned out of our minds to the point where the carpet seemed to shimmer between us, the stereo cooing straight into our ears, I was resolved to not break the spell. I wouldn't ruin this, I promised myself. Which meant not saying or doing anything that felt drastic, right up until the night before I left for Chicago.

When I get up to wash the mask off my face, I consider how I should tell Ben about all this. The memory of all those humid days and nights hanging out with Kyle feels at odds with the narrative of Hickory Grove that I've given him over the years. "It couldn't have been all bad," Ben said when we were peering out at my high school. And it wasn't. There had been good parts, like the nights when Kyle would try to teach me how to skateboard, his hands gently gripping my wrists as I wobbled on his driveway, before we gave up and spent hours speeding up and down Route 91, talking about how Illinois State University wasn't even that far of a trip from Chicago, and why Mayday Parade wasn't as good now that Jason Lancaster had left the band, and whether we thought God actually cared if we got high sometimes. And then Kyle would tell me quietly that he didn't talk about this kind of stuff to anyone else, and could we always be friends? How I'd wanted nothing more, and maybe that was the problem all along.

CHAPTER 5

The next morning, before the sun's up, I drive down to the Gold's Gym across the street from Eastwoods and spend an hour on one of the treadmills upstairs, as if running will somehow put space between myself and the events of last night. Christmas is in four days, so they're playing carols nonstop both at Gold's front desk and on the radio as I drive home. When I get back, everyone's still asleep, and I'm relieved—and a little cheered from the carols, I have to admit—to not have to start off my second day at home in a defensive crouch again.

After showering, I can hear the familiar sounds of my mother making tea downstairs along with the CCTV broadcaster's staccato of Mandarin, so I take special care in the bathroom, tweezing my eyebrows and applying the foundation I picked up from Walmart last night, even though both types I grabbed are several shades too light. Still. The aim is to appear as wholesome, well rested, and undisappointing as possible. This is what I've always been good at, putting on a face.

As I swipe on mascara, the sensation of leaning over this bathroom sink and peering at the mirror speckled with calcified toothpaste surfaces the memory of a morning from junior year, when I spent an hour trying to get the winged edges of my eyeliner just right, using the cheap electric-blue pencil Kristen and I had bought one weekend at Hot Topic. I made it all the way to the garage before my mother yanked me back in the house and scrubbed it off herself with a dry paper towel. She said I looked like Julia Roberts in *Pretty Woman*—"*So low-quality,*" she'd thundered. Only after it was gone was I allowed to get in my car and drive to school. What she didn't know was that I reapplied the blue over my poor, raw eyelids in the car, and it was all worth it when Kyle commented on it right before first period. "Looks rad," he'd said then, too. Amazing, how I could picture exactly what he wore that day: a gray beanie, torn dark-wash jeans, a white long-sleeved shirt underneath—in what my eighteen-year-old self had believed was the height of irony—a D.A.R.E. T-shirt.

My phone buzzes on the sink counter, and I want to groan at the way my pulse flutters a little. It's Pavlovian, I tell myself, this response to Kyle's name flashing across my screen right as I'm doing my makeup in my old bathroom. Kristen would die if she knew what was going on, and for a second, I fantasize about picking up the phone and texting her. What if she *is* back in Hickory Grove, too, like Ben said? Christ. He must think it's totally pathetic that I haven't kept in touch with anyone I grew up with, even if he's too nice to ever say it aloud. I quickly tap through the notification to read Kyle's text, which suggests that we meet at Sullivan's at nine tonight. *Also my mom says hi,* he adds.

In the kitchen, my mother is eating a bowl of congee and pecking at her iPad. I gingerly pour myself oolong tea from the kettle and sit down next to her.

"You look better," she comments, surprising me. I open my mouth to say thanks when she glances at me over her bowl. "Something's wrong with your eyebrows, though. So thin."

I will myself to not say anything, and she changes the subject.

"Don't forget," she says. "Eastwoods is having their Christmas show tomorrow night. Your father probably won't come, since his endoscopy is in the morning. But I got us all tickets, just in case."

I nod peaceably.

"You could check the church out in the meantime," she says. "They have openings for next summer."

"What for?"

She sets her tea down and stares at me as if she has spent her whole life waiting for me to guess the correct answer already. "Where else would you have the wedding?" she asks.

"Jesus Christ, Mom." I feel the shadow of a headache coming on.

"What?"

"I'm not sure why you would think Ben and I want to get married *here,* in Hickory Grove."

"New York is so expensive. You tell me that all the time."

"Yeah, but even if we do have a wedding, we'd have it at home," I say, and then wince, knowing I have committed a grave error.

"*This* is your home."

"All of our friends are in New York. Ben's family, too. We can't ask them to all come out to the middle of nowhere. Besides," I add. "We haven't even started planning the wedding. You're being way too intense about this."

She furrows her brow and then gets up abruptly.

"Mom—"

"I'm just trying to be helpful," she snaps.

"Jesus, I'm sorry, okay? Why are you *mad*?"

My mother gives me that look again, like she can't believe I still don't know. "I have to go to the church to help with rehearsals," she says tightly. "Dinner's at seven."

For the next hour, I sit alone in the kitchen, trying to scrub my brain of that interaction by flicking through emails and apartment listing updates and greeting my dad before he heads into the office. I wish I had an office I could retreat to, or that there would be some spectacular client emergency that would require me to get on a plane and hustle back to New York. As much as I complained about work to Ben and Zadie, some sick part of me loved when those client crises came up and made everyone act like the future of global peace was at stake instead of an issue as inconsequential as page count or invoice dates, things we all knew didn't solve any real problems in the world but that made us all feel capable and important anyway. Selling ads for a magazine like *The Current* was never something Ben and my friends understood—much less my parents—but I had to admit that I liked the constant theater of the transaction. At least in sales, everyone always had a clear agenda. Without work to focus on, I can feel the gears in my head coming unhinged. How was it possible that Ben and I had been in Hickory Grove for only two days? And what was the point of coming all this way if my dad was still going in to work and my mother was pulling all these long volunteer days at the church? I guess I should be thrilled that the only thing my mother can think of nagging me about is the location of the future wedding. Does it mean she likes Ben, and that she's actually happy about the whole thing? I turn my ring over in my hand in agitation; today it definitely feels too loose. I'm still staring stonily at it when Ben comes upstairs, sleepy but freshly shaved.

"Forgot I packed this," he says, holding out a small tin he'd wrapped in a Ziploc bag. It's my matcha powder, from our supply at home.

I clutch the tin to my chest, jumping up to refill the kettle. He chuckles and plants a quick kiss on me. Whatever awkwardness might be left over from our failed quickie last night melts away as I relax again at the sight of him—and, sure, the thought of getting my caffeine fix properly. Classic Ben, thinking one step ahead of my snobbiest cravings. We sip the matcha, and then I wait for him to slurp down a bowl of congee that my mother left on the stove before grabbing my keys and telling him I have a surprise for him, too, in a way. In the car, Ben asks me if I've been keeping up with the news and then reads aloud a few headlines about the latest patch of wildfires outside of Los Angeles.

"So late in the year?" I ask.

"I know," Ben says. "There's a chance they'll get pretty bad."

I reach over to rub his knee reassuringly, but when I look over, Ben is lost in thought. Neither of us wants to say it out loud, but we both know that if Ben's right, it's going to be a newsworthy—and photo-worthy—story, maybe on par with the shots he did in Greece. As Ben types on his phone, I can already imagine which contacts he's putting feelers out to, which editors will get back to him first, how things on fire always make for the most dramatic visuals.

I take the long way down toward Peoria so we can swing through Grandview Drive, which was supposed to be the surprise. I wanted Ben to see how all the skeletal oaks and hickories framed the Illinois River perfectly, but Ben is still on his phone, texting with Simon. I thought he'd want to take some pictures of the view, but then I realize he's left his camera at home. Probably a good thing, I decide. He deserves a break.

It takes a good half hour to get all the way across town, past the RV park and the strip malls and my dad's golf course of preference, which, like the Eastwoods lawn, is curiously green for December. It's surprising that it hasn't snowed here yet. When Ben finally puts his phone down, he asks what I think about running into Kyle yesterday and if we really are going to a bar with him tonight.

"Is it dumb?" I ask. "We don't have to."

"But you want to, right?"

I mumble something about how I haven't seen Kyle in a while, and it was the polite thing to do.

"So you guys were, like, what, pretty close?"

"No," I say quickly. "It was a small high school."

Ben watches me drive. "Are there more?"

"More what?"

"Secret high school friends who are going to pop out of nowhere." He smirks. "I just want to be on my A game, you know."

"No," I say, and laugh. "There's not going to be anyone else. I told you. I haven't talked to anyone from high school in years. Honestly, I didn't have a lot of friends to begin with."

"What about that one girl? Kristy something."

"Kristen?" I make that laugh again. "No, come on, I promise. No more Walmart encounters."

The parking lot at the Owens Center is nearly full, which makes my plan to take Ben ice-skating feel a little uncreative, as if all the parents of school-age kids in Hickory Grove and I had the same idea for keeping our respective dependents from going stir-crazy at home. Ben yawns and starts buttoning up his coat when I park in the farthest corner of the lot.

"Wait," I say, suddenly determined to make the morning feel slightly less family-friendly. I unclip my seatbelt and give Ben a look as I start unzipping my jeans.

"Hold on," he says. "What are you doing?"

I motion to the back seat. "Let's finish what we started last night."

Ben glances around. "Here? Really?" he asks, and then he grins. "I guess parking lots are kind of your thing."

I zip my pants back up with a scowl. When I slam the car door on my way out, Ben shakes his head at me, like a parent who refuses to be provoked. He says he's sorry, that he's just feeling tired and also backed up from last night's dinner, all that meat and white rice. It irks me that he insists on being the adult here, immune to whatever's in the Hickory Grove air that's making me feel like a teenager again. And I wish he hadn't brought up the whole prom night thing, even though objectively I know it's a good joke.

"What is *with* you?" he asks, chuckling and pulling me in for a kiss now that we are standing up. "There's plenty of time for that when we get back home." I already know he means New York, which reminds me of the way my mother looked at me this morning when I'd made the same reference.

"Sorry," I say. "I'm wound up. My mom and I got into it a little this morning."

"Did something happen?"

"It's fine."

"Audrey"—Ben pats my hand—"you know we can talk about this stuff. We *should* talk about it."

"She's just never happy with me." I shrug. "And she probably never will be."

"You're mad."

"It's *fine,*" I repeat, locking the car and walking toward the rec center. Ben jogs a little to catch up.

Inside, there's a buzz of activity as parents carrying coats and rental skates chase kids past the concession stand, toward the gleaming white of the ice rink visible from our end of the lobby. At the rental counter, Ben leans over and asks the high schooler on duty for a demonstration on how to lace the skates up, and while she blushes and shows him, I yank mine on as tightly as I can before buying myself a Diet Coke from the vending machine and taking a quick scan of everyone here for the free skate session today. A morning figure skating class has recently ended, and I watch as a group of girls on the cusp of middle school age stalk by me on their blades while in deep discussion about the spring recital. I try to remember if they're at the age where you still worship your mother or the one where you start to hate her.

My phone buzzes in my pocket, but I resist the urge to check it, knowing there's no reason for it to be Kyle since we've already confirmed plans for tonight. While last night's run-in with him might have been inevitable, at least the low-lying dread I've been carrying over the possibility of seeing Kyle ever again is gone. Tonight at Sullivan's, we'll have a perfectly civil catch-up beer where neither of us addresses the reason we've gone eight years without speaking, and that will be it. There's no reason I'd need to make it anything else. When Ben wraps up his skate-counter charm offensive and waddles over to me, I unbutton my coat and leave it on the bench—"It's *fine,*" I say a third time that morning when Ben looks around worriedly, as if the Hickory Grove preteens will make off with our outerwear—and we make our way out onto the ice.

●

I thought it would be fun to take Ben skating so he could play tourist, even if we are just in Hickory Grove. Back in New York, he was always the one with the home field advantage in planning little surprise activities like this. Whenever the weekend came around, I never knew for sure whether we'd end up at a restaurant opening, or pop-up gallery, or neighborhood block party, but I trusted Ben's intuition for where and when interesting things were always happening and his knack—on the rare slow weekend—for inventing adventure on our own when needed. Once, early in our relationship, we were kicking around Chinatown before a lunch reservation, and he suggested that we get massages. I was skeptical. Sometimes I took clients out for pampering, but we always went to these expensive spas uptown, not some tiny joint crammed between a dim sum shop and the Bowery Street HSBC Bank branch.

"Those forty-an-hour places?" I said, wrinkling my nose slightly. "Aren't they kind of shady?"

Ben rolled his eyes and told me not to be so racist. Then, without consulting his phone, he led me inside an herb shop and up a flight of stairs in the back that opened up to the massage parlor. Ben was, of course, greeted as a regular. We were led up another set of stairs to a small room curtained off to the side. I stripped down to my underwear, but Ben rolled his eyes at me, so I took that off, too, and laid my face down on a massage table that, as far as I could tell, was lined with one giant paper towel. I watched Ben poke a hole at the end of his table where the face went and did the same. When I lay down, the torn edges of the paper towel flapped by my mouth. Out of habit, I covered my ass with one of the provided sheets, though Ben snickered at this. "Relax," he instructed.

Through our paper towel face holes, we watched two sets of men's feet come in. I hadn't considered the possibility of having a random guy working me over, but I felt both too panicked and too naked to say anything by then. In my ear, my masseuse introduced himself as Frank, which I knew was absolutely a lie told for the benefit of white customers, but I was happy to play along even as Frank plunged an elbow into my back. I had to grip the table to keep from jerking away. Forget deep tissue—this was an exorcism. Still, I said nothing. As Frank dug into my shoulders, then my calves, and then, yes, even my bare ass, it hurt so much that I fantasized all hour on how exactly I'd berate Ben for not preparing me for any of this. But I could hear Ben making satisfied noises on the other side of our little room as he asked for more pressure, then less pressure. I knew intellectually that I could ask the same of Frank, that if this poor man knew how much agony I was in, he'd easily let up. Wasn't that my job, to speak the right combination of words and get what I wanted from clients? It should have been second nature. But Frank likely already thought of me as a dumb ABC who couldn't even greet him back in Mandarin, and I bet he was wondering what I was doing here with a white guy like Ben in the first place. The thought of that horrified me, so I let myself be kneaded like a glob of human dough while I stewed over how pleasant Ben's voice became as he got sleepier during the massage. What was that like, to just confidently ask things of the world without wondering if someone would be annoyed by the burden of your needs? As Frank pried my hamstrings apart, I lay there resisting the urge to scream into my stupid little paper towel face hole.

After our hour was up, Ben and I stood in the windowless foyer as he paid for our sessions in cash. "A hundred even, with tip!" he said wondrously to me, though I was barely listening. "What a steal."

I remember standing there dazed, sure I was going to wake up fully bruised in the morning and of how Ben and I would joke about it as evidence of another adventure accomplished. On our way out, I tipped Frank again separately.

●

Out on the ice, Ben suggests that we hold hands. We wiggle our way around the perimeter once, then a little faster as my feet recall the old slicing and gliding motions from those fourth grade lessons. Ben yelps as I pick up speed. It hits me that he's *nervous*. For Ben, the one who runs half-marathons on a whim and convinces me to do the Polar Bear plunge every year and brings me to excruciating Chinese bodywork sessions, feeling distrustful of his body must be totally foreign. I want to wince when I see the uncomfortable angle of his ankles in the rental skates, so I slow down and watch Ben edge along the rink. He's trying so hard. The group of preteens from earlier swoop by us, heedlessly veering too close. I watch Ben hover in the air for a second before he falls, crashing onto his elbows and knees. It happens so quickly and feels so shocking in that moment to see him splayed on the ice, unwieldy as a cartoon crane, that I barely swallow a laugh. I work on composing my face and skate over to him to help him up.

"I think I sprained something," he says tightly. We hobble over to the edge of the rink, where Ben takes his skates off and feels around his right ankle. His face is flushed pink, so I know he's more embarrassed than actually hurt. It's almost cute. I ask if he's okay, and he shakes his head, looking crestfallen.

It's obvious that we're done for the day, so we walk slowly back to the car. I watch Ben putting weight delicately on his ankle and twisting his face in response. He asks hopefully if there's a CityMD around; I do a quick search on my phone and offer the downtown urgent care as an option. "Is it close?" he asks, and I have to tell him it would be a forty-minute drive. Ben sighs and says he probably just needs to go home and rest.

"I'm so sorry," I say, feeling like I should take responsibility for throwing Ben out on the rink like that. "I thought it would be fun."

"Well, it's no Rockefeller Center," he mumbles, and I guess I'm relieved he's able to kid around about it.

The nearest CVS is only ten minutes away, so I drive us over to pick up an ice pack and medical tape in apology. When we're pulling out of the parking lot, I realize with a jolt that this is where Alex Bentley and I had sex after prom. But Ben is leaning back in his seat with his eyes closed, and it doesn't seem like the best time to pick up that bit again. At a stoplight, I scroll through Instagram quickly to see if I can find Nicole's brother. Maybe he's back in town, too? But a million different Alex Bentleys appear under the search bar, so I give up.

●

At home, Ben says he's exhausted. The experience of his body, so used to trekking around foreign terrain and running races, betraying him even just this once unnerves him, I know, so I leave him alone in the basement to lick his wounds while I decide to try tidying things up in my room.

In the closet, I sort through a pile of books and folders still stuffed with homework, the pencil marks faded into a thin silver. There's the copy of *Prisoner of Azkaban* that Kristen must have loaned me ages ago. Out of instinct, I flick through the paperback, its spine cracked so completely that it lies flat on the carpet. The fulsomeness of Kristen's handwriting in the margins makes me close it quickly. Then I close my hands around the slim hardcover of my senior yearbook. I can't resist the urge to page through it, and halfway in, I find what I must have been searching for: a picture from the graduation spread that a yearbook staffer snapped of Kyle and me standing in line for our diplomas. The sight of Kyle as I've always remembered him, with a Blink-182 shirt peeking out from under his half-zipped graduation gown and—god!—that ill-fated buzz cut, makes me pause. In the picture, Kyle and I are in mid-conversation, while everyone else stares ahead. It looks like he's telling me an outrageous story: I have my hand in front of my mouth in mock horror.

While I'm taking a photo of the page with my phone so I can show Kyle at the bar, there's a bizarre ringing that erupts from somewhere downstairs, and it takes me a moment to realize it's coming from the landline. After I locate the home phone downstairs in the kitchen, I find that it's a medical receptionist on the other end, calling from the hospital in Peoria where my dad is supposed to have his endoscopy tomorrow. She's apologetic. There's been a change in the outpatient schedule, and they're short-staffed from the holidays. Would my dad mind terribly if his procedure, since it's elective, got moved back a few days? With a sinking heart, I ask her how soon they can get my dad back in, and she says that they have only a few slots left for December. Would the twenty-ninth work? She's polite and tells me they have more openings in the new year, but I try to negotiate anyway.

"What about the twenty-fifth?" I ask, the day before Ben and I are supposed to go back to New York. She's quiet for a minute.

"That's Christmas," she says finally, like she feels sorry to be the one to break it to me.

I try not to sigh too audibly into the phone before I tell her to put us down for the twenty-ninth, that I'll check with my dad when he gets back. Back in my room, I look up how much it would cost to change our flight back to New York on my work laptop. Luckily, I'm still logged in to Ben's American Airlines account, so I can tell he has plenty of points to make it doable, but I make a note to ask him properly later since he paid for our flight here. Technically, he'd used the points he earned from all the traveling for his shoots, which, sure, stemmed from a career that I funded in the first year of our relationship, but if nothing else, my mother raised me with an iron-clad aversion to accepting things from others: help, validation, airline miles. "*Only trust family,*" she'd thundered once, though in the context of her own dead parents and a life marooned in the middle of America with a disobedient daughter and an indifferent husband, I remember thinking it wasn't like she had a lot of options.

To distract myself from the thought of having to stay in town for a few extra days, I go downstairs and stretch out on the living room sofa, where flakes of pleather shed like pieces of eggshell, and allow myself to click through all the apartment listing updates I'd seen in my email this morning. Ben and I usually liked to go through these together, but I figure I'll save any good ones to show him later.

For the rest of the afternoon, I scroll through listings for classic sixes on the Upper East Side, gut-renovated brownstones in Park Slope, and a handful of gleaming new condos only a few blocks away from our current block in Williamsburg. The latter I bookmark since they're actually within our budget—thanks to Ann and Clement Stear's help—even though I know Ben has his heart set on having more space. Somewhere with room for his photography equipment and his bike and maybe even a nursery, he'd teased. He wants to move south, near Bed-Stuy or Crown Heights, where the space per dollar ratio evened out better. "Broaden your horizons," he teased me when I said I liked where we were, so close to the East River. We'd probably have to get a place that needed a lot of work, he added, but it would be fun, because it would be ours forever. It was easy to let Ben talk me into his vision whenever we debated neighborhoods, because it seemed like he was thinking seven steps ahead. And that was what I had fallen in love with, this ability to smooth away the edges and take care of everything for me, to hold the possibilities of life up like a complicated garment that he would always help me get zipped into, and all I had to do was hold my arms out.

CHAPTER 6

For dinner that night, Dad makes fish stew and a stir-fry that leaves the entire house smelling like oyster sauce. He shows Ben how to operate the family rice cooker, which makes Ben feel useful now that his ice rink embarrassment has been forgotten after an afternoon nap. Then my dad asks if Ben wants to hit the driving range tomorrow, to make full use of his PTO day now that his procedure has been pushed back. As I set the table, I observe their growing friendship. It makes me happy to think my dad likes Ben so much already. It also makes me wonder how often the prospect of a golfing partner comes up.

If my mother is still pissed about this morning's conversation about the nonexistent wedding, she hides it well and spends most of dinner asking Ben more questions about his work. I bet he thinks she's trying to get to know him better, when she's actually trying to figure out just how successful Ben really is—and preventing my dad from steering the conversation again. I feel like I should cut in, but I have to admit that I'm curious how Ben will hold up under interrogation. He's being sweet and a little extra bubbly from the wine we picked up at Walmart last night as he patiently shows my mother pictures on his phone from this year's trip to Puerto Rico, where his photographs of hurricane wreckage won him a grant from Getty Images. It reminds me of how excited he was about the California wildfires this morning, and how if this were any other week, he'd be itching to see the action up close. While I'm gauging my mother's reaction to Ben's pictures, I wish there was a way I could telegraph to her all the adventure and fame Ben is probably giving up by being here in Hickory Grove, patiently explaining his work in clear, slow English. My dad asks if it's dangerous, all this traveling in search of conflict and disaster, and Ben smiles beatifically.

"I get very, very lucky," he says, and then looks over at me and squeezes my hand. "It's all thanks to Audrey," he adds. "She's supported me every step of the way. I couldn't do this without her, especially when I was starting out."

My mother shoots me a meaningful glance after she hands Ben's phone back. I make a point to not make eye contact. Does she get Ben's insinuation that I covered rent for a year before his career took off, and if so, would she think it was a measure of my own success or a failure on my part to find a man who didn't have start-up costs? And is she even impressed by the reality of Ben's work as a photojournalist, or simply dismayed by his pictures of barefoot children and muddy Red Cross tents? I've lost my ability to be able to read her mood as well as I used to, but I know I'll receive the official judgment on Ben soon enough. After dinner, I offer to do the dishes while Ben and my dad catch the end of a game on TV; I can hear my mother's slippers shuffling across the tile as she carries over the last plates from the dinner table.

"Well?" I ask when she sets the dishes on the counter. It seems as good a time as any to get it over with. "What do you think?"

"About what?"

"Ben," I say. "Do you like him or what?"

At this, my mother snorts, and that only irritates me more. "When have you ever cared about what I think?" she says. She doesn't mention the MBA thing or the moving to New York thing, but she doesn't have to.

I'm suddenly clenching a sudsy drinking glass in my hand. Jesus. She really can't ever have a normal conversation, can she? Now that she's gained the upper hand again, my mother seems satisfied with herself. She crosses her arms as she eyes my dad and Ben in the living room, who are both egging on some numbered figure on the TV screen, and she shrugs.

"You've clearly made up your mind," she says finally. "So I know it doesn't matter. But I just didn't think you'd end up with a man like *that*."

"What, because he's white?"

She makes a *tsk* sound with her tongue in annoyance. "That's not what I meant."

"So what is it?"

My mother shrugs again. "I don't like him for you," she says, clearly enjoying the rage that's building up in my jaw.

I turn back to the dishes, forcing myself to concentrate on the fraying sponge in my hand as I scrub at the same glass I've been cleaning during this whole infuriating conversation. She fucking loves this, withholding just enough so that it'll drive me insane. As a kid, I'd run myself ragged trying to figure out whatever it was my mother wanted out of me on any given day, like a show dog leaping through the day's designated arrangement of hoops. At least now I see it clearly enough that I can refuse to play her games. I'm not going to guess. I bet she just can't stand the fact that I've made my own life without her, with someone as great as Ben, and that it's better than anything she could have done for herself.

"Well, you obviously don't think Ben is good enough," I say from the sink, secretly pleased with how calm I'm keeping my voice. "But you don't even think *I'm* good enough. So you're right. I guess I don't care."

Behind me, I hear her slam the rest of the dishes on the counter and leave the kitchen, and I can't help but feel triumphant.

Up in my room, I dig through both suitcases to find the wrap dress I packed for the big Eastwoods Christmas show. It was an old standby I wore regularly both to work and drinks with Zadie, but now that I have it on and can see how much of my chest it leaves bare, I realize that passing this dress off as a church outfit in Hickory Grove was a little ridiculous. Who was I kidding? Still, I take extra care to let my mascara dry between each coat and add a dab of lipstick, which helps me feel a little more like New York Audrey getting ready for a night out versus whoever it is that I feel like now, leaning over the upstairs sink in my parents' house in Illinois.

"Ready?" Ben pretends to knock as he pokes his head inside the bathroom.

I work to keep my face straight as I take in what he's apparently wearing to Sullivan's: the carefully cuffed corduroy trousers, the thick cashmere sweater with the wooden toggle buttons, suede Chelsea boots in hand. He's clearly making an effort, and even though I know *I'm* going to be overdressed for a small-town dive bar on a Wednesday, seeing Ben attempt to spruce up for the occasion feels kind of hilarious. I notice the camera hanging off his shoulder and resist the urge to roll my eyes—we're back on field trip mode, I guess. But then I think back to his fall on the ice this morning and about the patient way he flipped through his photos for my parents at dinner, and I decide it's probably the brattiest thing in the world to feel annoyed that Ben is trying *too* hard. If I'm not careful, I'm going to turn into my fucking mother.

Ben gives me a cheerful kiss. "Weren't you saving that dress for the church thing?"

Smoothing the sweater against his chest, I bite back the urge to unbutton it so that the childish toggles aren't so obvious. "It's Hickory Grove," I say with a wave of my hand. "No one's going to know if I wear something, like, five times in a row."

He reaches back to give me a squeeze, but I bat his hand away. "I have to talk to you," I say, feeling guilty now for putting this off all afternoon. "There's been a change of plans."

"Yeah?"

"My dad's procedure got pushed back a few days."

"Oh." Ben looks relieved, but then his mouth curves slightly. "So we're staying longer, right?"

"*You* don't have to," I say quickly. "But I should. I talked to Ted earlier, and he said it was okay. It's like, four extra days."

"You're okay with that?"

"I don't think I have a choice." I wait a beat to see if Ben will say that *of course* he'll stay and volunteer up his points, especially considering this trip was his idea in the first place.

"Let me check some things," Ben says finally. "I'm sure that's fine."

"I feel bad."

"Don't. We'll figure this out." Ben shakes his head. "It's not your fault."

This annoys me more than the sweater; I want to tell Ben that of course I know that. After bidding goodbye to my dad, who's working on another packet of watermelon seeds over the kitchen counter, and warning him that we'll be coming home late out of some holdover teenage compulsion, Ben and I arrive at Sullivan's later than I hoped. I don't have any reason to believe Kyle's improved upon his high school grasp of punctuality, but it stresses me out, especially after spending the drive updating Ben on the condos I bookmarked from the apartment listings earlier that afternoon only to hear him sigh. I half expected him to tell me to "broaden my horizons" again, so I'd dropped the subject, but I can't help sulking now as we circle the Sullivan's parking lot because sure, he can't promise to stay in Hickory Grove with me for a few extra days, but I'm the one who has to commit to moving neighborhoods next year. As we take a third turn around the lot, I realize I'm clutching the steering wheel so hard my knuckles are turning white.

"There's a spot," Ben points out mildly.

"Too small." I clench my hands more tightly around the wheel and eye the enormous Dodge monstrosity that I'd have to negotiate my way around.

"I think you can make it work."

I don't know if it's his tone, or the fact that we're late, or the resignation over this trip's extended timeline, but I snap and tell Ben that if he's so sure, he should get out and try it himself. The end of my sentence ends with a terrible silence, and we both pause to absorb it before I take a breath and apologize.

"Do you want me to do it?" Ben asks patiently.

"No. It's fine." Another deep breath. "I'm just kind of freaking out."

"Yeah, I can tell." Ben pats my leg and offers to stay sober tonight so he can drive us back. "Seems like you could use a night off," he says with such kindness that I lean my forehead against the steering wheel and let off a long, apologetic sigh. Classic Ben, seeing to the details, the still-open parking spots, and yet humoring me when I want to do things the hard way. Why was I so stressed out about extending our trip? This was *Ben.* Of course we'd figure it out.

I end up pulling out of the lot and parking on the side of the road, the Acura tilting ten degrees into the ditch. It's almost ten, but I'm chastened enough by my outburst in the car that it's easy to muscle myself into a better mood. From the parking lot, we can hear the live music inside—someone's doing her best Faith Hill impression—and Ben finds my hand as he follows me in. It's nice, I realize now, to be the one showing him around. There's that funny little half step right before the door, and I hop over it in time and turn to warn Ben, feeling proud that I remembered.

●

This was the kind of assurance he probably carried with him all the time in New York, especially back when we first met, when I still confused the Chrysler Building with the Empire State. But I remind myself that it wasn't just Ben's geographic edge that thrilled me, but his innate membership into the whole other world inlaid with the city grid: the cool, academic parents; the cabin upstate; the intimidating friends; the long evenings lingering over dinner in upscale restaurants. One night, early in our relationship, we'd gone out with Simon and a few of Ben's friends to a spot in the West Village famous for roast chicken so heedfully sourced I was surprised we didn't get an ecology lesson from the server. We were sitting on the patio, slack with relief that the August humidity had finally broken and happy to be celebrating Ben signing with Simon's agency. I remember feeling nervous: This was the first major life event that I was celebrating with Ben's friends, who were all artists or professional creatives, especially when I suspected they still couldn't quite understand what the deal was with Ben's new girlfriend, who kept her cardigan on because she was thawing from a day in the *Current* office's industrial conditioning.

One of Ben's friends, Jasmin—the one who'd originally brought him to Zadie's potluck—was recounting the story of a recent camping trip to Maine with friends from her Bushwick socialists collective. We were all listening intently over plates scraped conscientiously clean of the chicken, which had unfortunately been worth the hype; I'd even taken a picture and posted the meal on Instagram as part of a post congratulating Ben's success. Jasmin was telling the story in that theatrical way I'd found that New Yorkers automatically employed under the assumption that each of them was the hero in their personal coming-of-age film, and I found it comforting to watch Jasmin play director and screenwriter and starlet all at once. What a relief, after another long day embroiled in conversations with clients where each comment was coded in a million different ways to various degrees of effect on the final budget number that may or may not guarantee the future of *The Current* and journalism for a few more months. I was content to sit back and sip the chardonnay Simon ordered for the table, which helped with my nerves especially as Ben's friends got progressively drunker. Ben had his hand on my knee and looked thrilled by Jasmin's camping escapades.

"We should go this fall," he said to me. "There's a great spot in the Poconos my parents used to take us to when we were kids. I'd love to show you."

The other friends at the table nodded eagerly. I remember noting with satisfaction how we had presented as a rather photogenically mixed group: Ben's agent, Simon, and the girl on my right were Black; Jasmin was Asian, too, possibly Filipino. If I had worried that Ben was the kind of guy who acted like some citizen of the world but who only actually hung out with his white NYU friends, this night put me at ease—so much, in fact, that I snorted and rolled my eyes and said louder than I intended, "I don't think my parents came to America so that I could sleep on the ground *on purpose*."

It was supposed to be funny! I thought I was riffing on another bit Ben and I already had between us at that point, about how I was so obviously the high-maintenance one in the relationship, the one who wanted the shiny one-bedroom on Bedford, who'd rather go to the store and buy bread like a normal capitalist instead of spending a Saturday afternoon coaxing along homemade sourdough. At any rate, my comment forced the conversation to pause. I glanced around and smiled, feeling suddenly stupid. Simon gave me a charitable grin and said that he agreed with me, though as the dinner's official host, I knew he was being nice.

"Oh, your parents are immigrants, too?" Jasmin asked. I nodded. In a rush of recognition, she told me about her mom, who still worked at a nail salon in Flushing, and how she'd put Jasmin and her brother through school by herself while they all shared a one-bedroom apartment with an auntie. It was her mom, Jasmin sighed, who inspired her path into community organizing, which I thought was an interesting way to describe the tweeting frenzies Ben told me Jas rolled out during her daytime graphic design job. Then Jasmin asked what *my* parents did. The way she pounded the table in her enthusiasm about her mom made me realize I should probably lie.

"Well," I said instead, "my dad's an engineer."

I could see the way Jasmin's face flickered, like I had tricked her. She leaned back, rubbing her freshly buzzed head.

"And my mom used to manage inventory at a department store," I added, wondering if anyone at the table even knew what a Bergner's was. "It's like a Macy's, except—"

Jasmin cut me off. "Well, that's pretty different," she said flatly.

I swallowed thickly. The tension at the table seemed to congeal with every passing second.

"Well, they started off kind of poor here, right?" Ben said defensively, though I wish he hadn't said anything at all.

Jasmin looked at me, but I was too mortified to meet her gaze. The others at the table seemed to be sending each other a silent radio warning: *The Asians are fighting!* Ben's agent sat back and poured himself another glass of wine. I eventually said something about how my dad came here as a grad student. This made Jasmin snicker and sit back, running a hand over her buzzed hair almost protectively.

"So they were *broke,*" she said. "Not poor."

"Hey," Simon said serenely. "We're all here, right? We're living the dream, right?"

"Plus," Ben added. "Audrey grew up in, like, the middle of nowhere. In this crazy conservative town." He said this as if, on the scale of whether my middle-class parents deserved the same amount of sympathy as Jasmin's single nail-tech mom, this evened out the math. While everyone at the table made apologetic sounds, I wanted to point out that, technically, Peoria *County* had gone blue since 1992, in no small part because of the private university located downtown, and it was the surrounding counties that earned the red, gun-wielding, God-fearing reputation. Part of me wondered if Jasmin would change her calculus on my parents if she knew how much my mother hated working at Bergner's, and that she always blamed my existence for having to do so. Surely that would earn me a few points in Jasmin's scale of worthwhile hardship.

Later that night, after we said goodbye to his friends, Ben and I walked up to Union Square to catch the L train. Usually when we walked, I let Ben stay half a step ahead, his purposeful strides carrying the both of us to the next interesting event or landmark. But that night, I forced myself to walk faster than him, my hands tightly pretzeled across my chest. Panting slightly to keep up, Ben asked what was wrong. I said it was *nothing,* the word coming out with sharper edges than either of us expected. I thought about how obscene it was that we'd even try to debate whose parents had it harder when we'd all just polished off plates of seventy-dollar chicken. Compared to the pains Ben's friends undertook to examine their cortado-fueled lives, my mother's lifelong visions of unfettered capitalist ambition seemed so straightforward. At least she was never apologetic about wanting and having things. Ben watched me walk on with a neutral, almost journalistic remove. This was the first time he had seen me angry, and we were both almost curious to see what was going to happen.

"Is this about what Jasmin said?" he said finally, when we were descending the two flights of stairs for the L train. He rubbed one of my shoulders cautiously, like he was testing the temperament of a stray cat, and I stood there deciding if I wanted to let him keep doing it or not. "She made things kind of awkward, right?"

I said something about how it was his night, his dinner, and I didn't want to ruin it.

"Jas gets like that," he said, and sighed. "She never turns the lecture off."

I shrugged, but allowed Ben to work his way to my other shoulder. Maybe he didn't totally get it, but at least he always came close.

●

Inside Sullivan's, it's now impossible to ignore how overdressed Ben and I are. I decide to keep my coat on, embarrassed for real about wearing a designer dress when the other women in the bar are wearing jeans and sweatshirts. Ben's sweater seems even more ludicrous; I don't comment on it and hope Ben won't, either.

"Your friend is over there." He taps my shoulder and inclines his head toward where Kyle is leaning against the bar.

Unlike us, Kyle looks perfectly in place, the hood of his black sweatshirt half pulled over his head as he nods to the thrum of the cover band, a can of Miller Lite in hand as he reaches the other around to fuss with the back of his hair—a nervous habit I recognize with crushing immediacy. I want to take a second to survey the bar and see how much it's changed, if at all, from the summer when the two of us snuck in here to drink, but I'm so self-conscious of sticking out like a sore, brushed wool–wrapped thumb that I make a beeline for Kyle in an attempt to appear purposeful.

"You made it." Kyle extracts me from the crowd and gives me a quick, firm hug. He greets Ben and makes two more Miller Lites materialize with a wave to the bartender. I fish for my wallet in protest. "Just drink the beer, Aud," Kyle says.

Ben gingerly sips at his designated beer for the evening, which is so many degrees removed from the locally brewed IPAs he loves so much back home that it probably barely registers as alcohol. I watch him scan the bar and try to interpret it through his eyes: the spotty Christmas lights, the signs announcing Thursday penny-pitchers in Papyrus font, the pedestrian pitch of the cover band, the general droopy damp feel of the place. I can't tell what he thinks, though I do note that Kyle and I are the only two people in the bar who aren't white.

"So," Ben says finally, "this is where you drank in high school?"

I shake my head.

"Audrey was too focused to party," Kyle says, his dimples unfurling. "That's how everyone knew she was going places."

The fact that he doesn't mention our secret summer drinking sessions here is a relief. Kyle tips his head back to finish his beer, seeming to consider Ben, who has turned to the bar to order a Tito's and soda, apparently abandoning the beer. I bite back a frown. Ben must have forgotten offering to drive us home.

"You look great, by the way," Kyle says in my ear, interrupting this thought as he touches the toe of his sneakers to my boots. "I like these."

"I think I look like an asshole," I admit.

"Well, so what?"

We both briefly eye each other, and I drop my gaze to unbutton my coat. Because it's warm in the bar, I tell myself. But also because I want to watch Kyle's eyes rake over the decidedly new Audrey in front of him, the one who wears necklines like this and looms slightly over him in these impossible shoes. But Kyle just squeezes my arm and then politely turns his attention to Ben to ask where he's from. The toggles of Ben's sweater quiver from the enthusiasm of his response.

"I guess Hickory Grove doesn't really compare to New York," Kyle says graciously.

Ben gives the bar a once-over, either for generous effect or to stall. "It's nice," he says. "Everyone's really friendly."

I resist the urge to roll my eyes; midwestern niceties aside, *everyone everywhere* is friendly to Ben.

"Well," Kyle says, giving me a wink, "it's not exactly the City of Lights."

I can tell that Ben is trying to catch my eye while he's struggling not to laugh, because even if Kyle hadn't confused the nickname for Paris with New York's, he would have hated the cliché all the same. Kyle asks where in the city we live, and Ben tells him, out of habit, that we're off the Bedford stop in Williamsburg. Watching Kyle blink politely from the total lack of geographic context this response gives him is excruciating. I ignore both of them and pretend to watch the band for a moment.

Through the bar entrance, a gust of cold air ushers in a trio of girls—probably college kids, back for the holiday break and tickled by the nostalgia of drinking in their hometown bar again—who bump up against Ben at the bar and start flirting immediately, aware that cheekbones like those are a novelty in this zip code. "You're, like, a photographer?" I hear one of them ask and turn to see her touch the body of his camera, and I already know the whole spiel that Ben is going to give them, like the girl at Panera and the girl at the skating rink, and how they're going to ask him to take their picture, and how he'll oblige, of course, to be nice. I turn away, aware that my nostrils are flaring in an ugly way my mother used to hate, and use the opportunity to study Kyle from the corner of my eye.

The door opens again, and now all these guys our age stream in, swaggering like a pack of original alphas returning to their hunting ground. When they wave at Kyle, I realize with a jerk that they're our old classmates. I place a few of them and can't help but gape a little, both at the novelty of hearing their names for the first time in almost a decade as Kyle calls out at them and at the way these guys look now, softer at the edges, as if their bodies have just started to lose the plot on that twenties metabolism. Bryan Johnson's jawline has smoothed into his dad's, I realize. Danny Howard is as enormous as ever and likely still everyone's contact for dirt cheap weed. There's Cameron Evans, the homecoming king wattage of his smile as bright as ever, though his comb-over is a different story. There are Joe and Luke Richter, whose dad had been the youth pastor over at Eastwoods; they'd been the shining example at Hickory Grove High that you had to believe in Jesus in order to be cool, at least until the brothers went to college and channeled their zeal into an especially paranoid slant of Libertarianism, per the very last time I had checked on Facebook.

I pretend to sip at my empty beer can while glancing around. Luke actually recognizes me immediately, and he leans down to give me a bearish hug. At least he gives my dress a deserving gawk. I scan the group again and realize I'm searching for Alex Bentley, my old prom date, even though he'd been a year behind us and probably doesn't have a reason to be around these guys. Next to Ben, it's suddenly hard to imagine a time when Bryan and Danny and Cameron and everyone commanded the school, now that they're so clearly aging into their barely squarer-jawed versions of their dads, likely with the same gripes about the news and the weather and the Bears. I glance between Ben and Kyle and wonder what the two of them would think of each other if we were all back in high school right now, if Kyle's casual star power by virtue of being cute and on the football team would have impressed Ben's assured worldliness and debate club convictions, though who knows what Ben would have been like if he'd been a Hickory Grover, too.

I offer to buy the group a round of shots, which amazingly costs twenty dollars total, then Kyle does the same. By the time I'm downing one of the beers that Cameron Evans has started handing out, I realize I'm drunker than I've been in a long time. I almost feel bad that Ben has been sticking to ginger ale after that second drink, now that I know he hasn't forgotten about driving home after all. When Ben goes off to find the bathroom, I make a mental note to be nicer to him tonight, especially after snapping in the car. Then the band strikes up a particularly twangy number about the usual—fried chicken, cold beer, pickup trucks—and Kyle asks if I want to go outside to vape.

"I always loved this song," I tell Kyle as we make our way toward the door. It's gotten crowded inside Sullivan's, and some people are bobbing along to the live band's chorus in a way I'd find cringey by proxy if I wasn't six drinks deep. "None of my friends in New York even listen to stuff like this. Can you believe that?"

Kyle takes my hand to spin me in a circle. It's corny and I want to hate it, but instead I clutch my Miller Lite and laugh as we tumble out into the night. And I realize how much I've missed him. When I cut off contact with Kyle after that summer, after we went our separate paths to Chicago and ISU, I'd done it out of self-preservation. I knew I never wanted to feel like that again, about anyone. Now, I realize in my drunkenness, the essential shape of whatever those emotions had been is starting to resurface under my chest. Stammering a little, I say something to Kyle about how alien it feels to see all those guys again, Cameron and Bryan and Joe and Luke, and how funny it is that we're all back here together again. Kyle produces a vape pen from his hoodie pocket and hands it to me first. I haven't smoked weed in years and take a greedy draw.

"Well, Ben seems great," Kyle says, watching me.

"He really is."

I pass the vape over to him, refusing to let my mind linger over the fact that Kyle is putting his mouth right where mine has just been.

"I can't believe I'm marrying him," I add. Then I make a face as a cough threatens to push against my throat. "Honestly, I can't believe I'm getting married at all."

"It's pretty crazy," he concedes.

"You know, my mom and I have already gotten in a fight about the wedding. I don't even know if Ben and I will have one, honestly."

Kyle asks if things have gotten better with my mother, and I shake my head. "Sucks," he says with such an emphatic earnestness that I have to grin.

"It's whatever." I take another draw when he passes the vape back and wonder aloud about what everyone else is doing inside. "You know, I can't believe you're in touch with all those guys."

"It's not so hard. Everyone's mostly around. Aren't you and Kristen still tight?"

"No."

"Wow. Really?"

"We had a dumb fight in college." I shrug. "And then I couldn't get off work to go to her wedding. So she's probably mad about that, too."

Kyle gives me a curious look, but he's too polite to press further. The music inside ends, and I shiver even though it's not even that cold. Kyle turns his head away to exhale. Somewhere, an engine sputters. I scan the parking lot and ask if Kyle held on to that Mustang, half hoping it'll materialize in the dark. He laughs and says no, that he'd gotten rid of it.

"Shit," I say. "I can't believe I'll never see that car again."

We stand in silence, as if holding our own memorial for his Mustang. When Kyle speaks again, his voice is thoughtful. "You know, I still can't believe you're here, Aud. I thought I was never going to see *you* again."

I didn't expect him to say it right out loud like that, so I take a swig of my beer to give myself a beat, but then I realize that I've already finished it. "What do you mean?" I ask.

"Come on." Kyle smiles to let me know he isn't upset. "It's been years. It's kind of weird, right?"

I watch the cartilage of Kyle's throat bob up and down, the glint of the parking lot streetlamp against the rims of his eyes. Refamiliarizing myself with the contours of his face and comparing them with the way I thought I remembered his face all this time feels as good as putting on those skates this morning and taking those wide, arcing loops around the rink. I just wish Kyle didn't have to complicate such a good moment like this.

"Sure," I say. "I guess it's weird."

"But everything's okay? With us?" he asks. "You're not mad?"

"Why would I be mad?"

Kyle looks like he's going to say something but then decides against it. Instead, the door opens and the group of girls who were hitting on Ben earlier squeeze by, knocking me off-balance and into Kyle's shoulder. He steadies me, his hand on the lower half of my spine, reminding me instantly of the time we'd gotten partnered up in youth group to do trust falls, how sheepish I'd been about Kristen and Nicole watching Kyle catch me. If only Kristen could see us now, I think wildly as Kyle asks if I'm okay and I pretend to dust myself off.

"Here." He tugs my elbow over to the right so I'm not as close to the door, in case it opens again. Then, after a pause, he says, "I just missed you, Audrey. That's all."

"I missed you, too."

"You did?"

The music inside has started up again, and I pretend to be distracted by it.

"Look, I should have kept in touch better, okay?" I say. "But everything's cool, I promise."

I suggest that we go back inside, where Ben greets our return with a couple of beers and a glass of water in his hand. He hands Kyle the beer and the water to me. I gulp it down through the plastic straw—a peace offering from the bottom of his annoying environmentalist heart, I know, for talking to those girls for so long—and enjoy the brief freeze the ice exacts on my brain. Kyle seems like he still wants to say more to me, but the band strikes up the first bars of "Wagon Wheel," and everyone starts singing. I give in and join, too, a little surprised I haven't forgotten any of the words. Kyle gives me a sly grin and glances at Ben, who's scrolling intently on his phone. I move next to Ben to give him an encouraging squeeze on the arm, and then I notice he's actually googling the lyrics. Kyle watches me figure this out. He doesn't even have to say anything—he just gives me this wink, and it's like a joke passes between us unspoken. I have to cover my mouth to keep from bursting into laughter and fail because I'm drunker and higher than I realize. Ben asks what's so funny, and I shake my head. As the entire crowd finishes up the chorus, I turn to the bar, heady and gleeful, and ask for another drink.

CHAPTER 7

Dinner the next night is reheated leftovers rushed through so we can get to Eastwoods early and score a good parking spot. In the back of my dad's SUV, I can feel my brain thudding through my skull even after I spent the whole day in bed, pretending I had to work when I was really trying to sleep off the worst hangover I'd had in years. Ben, of course, was fine. He came up to my room to check on me in the morning before heading out to the golf course. I barely managed to down the glass of water he brought me before asking him to go easy on my dad. "Right, like how you went easy on those beers last night?" He smirked, practically swimming in endorphins from an early jog around the neighborhood and general self-righteousness over not being the one who threw up in the ditch outside Sullivan's at two in the morning.

In the car, I reach into my purse and count out three more Advils and swallow them dry. My mother glances back at me and says something in Mandarin about how all that ibuprofen will tear my stomach up just like my dad's, and then *I'd* be the one getting an endoscopy one day. Sensing no response from me, she decides to switch gears and announces nicely how great it is that we're all going to the show together, as if she hasn't spent the last two days making it clear how nonnegotiable tonight was, as if the three of us haven't all been actively conspiring to spend as little time with her as possible in the lead-up to the Eastwoods Christmas show. Ben pats me supportively on the knee.

I lean back and eye my mother, who's sitting in the front passenger seat, knowing that what she's really annoyed about is the conversation we relitigated at dinner about the wedding and how she still thought it should be at Eastwoods. Now that I know she's ambivalent at best about Ben, I don't understand why she's so obsessed. Maybe it should be touching that she has such strong wedding venue opinions, but the whole thing makes me think about how none of the major events in my life has ever met her expectations: My birth? An accident. Prom? A major bacterial risk. College graduation? She literally locked herself in a hotel room during the ceremony. At this rate, I should do everyone a favor and get it over with at city hall to save all of us the disappointment.

At dinner, I'd tried explaining to my mother about how small weddings were in vogue now. I really thought there was a chance she would understand. It isn't like I expected my parents to kick in any money, and we definitely weren't going to ask Ben's parents, now that they were basically writing us a check for our apartment next year. The apartment felt more important anyway, and as far as I knew, my parents' own wedding hadn't been fancy or expensive, either. They'd simply gone to the local government office in Wuhan to sign the papers, and then spent the rest of the morning shopping for a suitcase for my dad to bring to St. Paul. Marriage hadn't even been their primary errand of the day.

"You know, you don't even have to come," I said to my mother finally at dinner. "It can be like graduation. Just show up for the pictures and leave."

This made Ben stare straight down at his plate, which he'd been picking at artfully to make it seem like he was eating more of the brisket than he really was, and I saw my dad tense up, too. I waited to see how my mother would respond to this challenge, if she'd take the bait and get angry and let Ben see how quickly these fights could unfurl. But she was ultimately more fixated on the show, so she said nothing except that we needed to leave in twenty minutes.

We finished dinner in silence before changing into our respective church clothes: I put on the wrap dress from last night even though I knew it reeked slightly of weed, and Ben trotted out a different button-down. My dad, who originally thought he'd gotten a free pass to get out of the show because of his endoscopy, gamely put a work shirt on. My mother chose a cardigan with ruffles on it, which felt too girlish for a woman nearing sixty, as anti-feminist as it probably was for me to think that. Before we left, Ben took a photo of the three of us standing together in the living room. My dad offered to take one of the two of us, but I knew the idea of someone else using Ben's camera made him uncomfortable, so I said we didn't need one.

We take Alta Lane past Sullivan's to get across town to Eastwoods. I can't tell if it's the headache lifting, but as I watch the bar and the subdivisions we pass flash by in a twinkly blur of Christmas lights, I feel relatively buoyant. Of course I shouldn't have overdone it last night, but it *had* been fun being inside Sullivan's again and generally enjoying a night out without any clients or Ben's friends to worry about impressing. Whatever nervousness I'd had about seeing Kyle dissolved by the time we shared our second vape break. That was when I showed Kyle the yearbook photos on my phone from earlier that afternoon, before Ben came outside to find me.

This morning I texted Kyle to see if he and his mom were going to the Eastwoods thing tonight, and I felt disappointed when he said they had tickets for the Christmas Day performance. I didn't know how to say that I wanted to see him again, soon. As if summoned by this wish, there's a telltale buzz from inside my purse. I pull my bag up on my lap so I can check my phone without taking it out. It's Kyle, saying how rad last night was. I ignore the pleasant twist in my stomach and text back a description of the day's hangover. In return, Kyle says he's having a few people over for a bonfire tomorrow night. Do Ben and I want to come? I respond immediately.

When we arrive, I realize that not only has Eastwoods added the new wing that Ben and I saw from our drive two days ago, but there's also an espresso café, a juice bar, and enough parking to rival the downtown mall. As we stream in with the earliest of the evangelical Hickory Grove flock to the auditorium, we pass a sign that cheerfully announces the church gym's renovation, and Ben gives me a bemused look. We locate our seats over in what an usher in a bright red shirt proclaiming HAVE A VERY EASTWOODS CHRISTMAS specifies is the "orchestra," which at first feels like a dramatic stretch but then I realize is appropriate terminology; the main auditorium inside the church has also been upgraded so that there's a new balcony level. Evidently, all the volunteering my mother has done with the planning committee has earned us VIP spots, and we find ourselves only ten rows back from the stage. My mother files in first, then I follow with Ben and my dad behind into the plush seats. Onstage, a man with a goatee strums a guitar and sings an old Chris Tomlin song as animated lyrics flash on two eighty-foot projector screens.

I've always told Ben that I'd grown up somewhat religious, that it was as natural as knowing the difference between combines and cultipackers if you grew up here. Even if I went along to Kristen's youth group only for the off chance that I'd end up next to Kyle at the end of the night when we joined hands in prayer, the sum total of all the worship services and mission trips and weekend car wash fundraisers had done its work infusing me with a basic nondenominational Christian education. To Ben, the fact that I not only had read the entire Bible but, when pressed, could also quote from it had been endlessly fascinating; once or twice it served as a decent party trick in front of his friends. Now, though, as we sit in the enormous auditorium eyeing the giant gold cross suspended from the ceiling, I take a babyish pleasure in noting how Ben is the odd one out here as he studies the program with a tourist's interest.

My mother has brought her own Bible along and flips through it like she's cramming for a midterm. She'd started attending Eastwoods the year I entered high school, after Bergner's laid her off and both of her parents passed away from heart attacks within the fall semester. I barely remembered the short phone calls that each came at four in the morning announcing the events; my mother stayed in China for a month each time, which I remembered clearly only because I had selfishly enjoyed getting to stay up late at Kristen's house to watch the Lord of the Rings series in her absence. It was probably a shame how religion happened to the two of us via such separate processes when it could have been something to bond over, even if I got into Jesus only to fit in, whereas for my mother, it was less a matter of believing one specific dude actually came back from the dead two thousand years ago than about having tried-and-true rules to follow for guaranteed results in an otherwise turbulent universe.

As the lights begin to dim, the abrupt keen of an electric guitar cuts through the air, and the curtain lifts on the church worship band, helmed entirely by men dressed like they all worked in the same downtown office as my dad in their gingham shirts, ripping into the intro to "Joy to the World." The crowd roars. It's too bizarre not to laugh, even when my mother gives me a look. From there, we're treated to a full hour of the best of the Eastwoods Worship Collective's repertoire: There's a country version of "Do You Hear What I Hear?," a contemporary remix of "O Come, All Ye Faithful," and, from what I can tell is my mom's favorite, a full choir for "Mary, Did You Know?," paired with someone's teenage daughter doing a self-serious interpretive dance onstage. Even Ben is stunned by the production value of the random light show that erupts during "Silent Night." In between each performance, one of the associate pastors serves as a sort of holy emcee, introducing the next act as enthusiastically as a wedding DJ.

To avoid getting overwhelmed by the strobe lights, I sneak a glance at my mother's face. I can tell that she wishes the choir would get more airtime, probably because she had performed in her school's Lunar New Year variety shows as a student. In another life, with another set of language skills, maybe she could have been one of the sopranos up there. In this moment, feeling soft all over from the singing and the strumming and my waning hangover, I decide to try to remember that it has never been easy for my mother. She had come to the United States with my dad and this whole idea of how things would go before she got pregnant with me and everything changed. And we hadn't always been at each other's throats. Before we moved to Hickory Grove and she got that department store job, there had been those early years in St. Paul, when I was too young to be turned into a project. This was when my mother stayed home with me all day, watching TV Land and helping me dress and re-dress the two Barbies we bought from some garage sale. This was when she used to call me her "xin gan"—her heart and liver—and I remember thinking how grisly that phrase was, after I grew up, once the fights began over curfew and grades and why I couldn't seem to get things right when I had every privilege stacked in my favor. Why couldn't my mother be normal and call me things like "honey" and "sweetie" like everyone else's parents did, I began wondering, instead of equating me with the bloody vital organs inside her body? Was that why we really fought so much, because I wanted her to be somebody else the way she probably wanted me to be smarter and better behaved and sometimes nonexistent? Or did we grow apart just because we stopped sharing a language for expressing ourselves to each other, once I lost my childhood Mandarin? There couldn't have been only one reason. Sometimes we fought simply because I was angry about things like having the whole history class in eighth grade eye me when we talked about Japanese internment. And I'm sure we sometimes fought for reasons that *she* never told me: how lonely it was raising a family in central Illinois where no neighbors knew Mandarin, how boring it was to work at a department store all day making sure everything was neatly folded for bored white people to riffle through, how to pass the stretches of time my dad spent away examining manufacturing equipment in other midwestern towns, or how she got to see her parents only once every few years via those humid summer trips until those 4:00 A.M. phone calls arrived.

Tonight, as the spectacle of the Eastwoods Christmas show

unfolds, I watch my dazzled mother lift her phone every few minutes to take pictures that I know she'll study for weeks. It's embarrassing, like I'm watching a kid believe in Santa, and I want to tell her what I figured out a long time ago, that doing drugs or even drinking six Miller Lites in a row could actually give you the same sensation of experiencing God's approval far more consistently than singing along to words from an ancient book.

•

During the intermission, my mother stays resolutely in her seat, like she's terrified to miss even a nanosecond. The rest of us venture out for a reprieve. In the women's bathroom, I touch up my lipstick and try to fluff my bare eyelashes a little—my mother was so anxious to get to the church that I didn't have time to put on any real makeup. When I go to pee, underneath the stall I can hear two women washing their hands and discussing someone's daughter, who's apparently pregnant again. One asks if it's the boyfriend's, and the other, whose voice sounds almost familiar, assures her that it's "definitely" not God's. They both snicker. It's pretty funny for bitchy church gossip three days before Christmas, and my mouth is still in a half smile from it when I'm washing my hands in the sink and look up right as Kristen walks into the bathroom.

"Oh, fuck," I blurt out.

It's her. Even though it's been years, I recognize Kristen instantly—that same strawberry-blond hair, the athletic build, the asymmetrical spray of freckles across her nose. For a minute, I'm so happy to see her that I want to tell her about that immaculate conception joke, but then I watch Kristen's eyes narrow as she stands there in the doorway. I know we're both thinking about the last time we ever heard from each other, when I'd gotten the invite to her wedding and I couldn't take time off from *The Current*'s sales retreat to go. I had been surprised that I'd been invited at all, considering the last time when we'd actually seen each other in the flesh was freshman year at college, when she drove up to Chicago to surprise me for my birthday, and it ended with both of us screaming at each other in my dorm hall parking lot. Incredibly, I notice that Kristen is pregnant. I wipe my hands quickly on my dress.

"It's *me,*" I tell her when she doesn't say anything. I'm unable to stop staring at Kristen's belly. She's wearing a dress made of this drapey jersey material that makes her body look like a magic trick waiting to be unveiled. It feels impossible to not acknowledge, but now Kristen is stepping around me to get to a stall.

"*Hey,*" I say, flinging my arm up without thinking against the nearest open stall so I can block her way. For a wild moment, I think she must be confused. "Kris? It's Audrey."

Kristen squints at me, and for a minute, I wonder if maybe *I'm* the one who's confused. Wouldn't it have been funny, to be on the other side mistaking one white girl for another? But of course it's Kristen. From this close, I can see the vague puckered dimple on her right earlobe, where we'd tried to pierce it with her mother's sewing needle one night after youth group.

"D-don't you recognize me?" I stammer. Kristen seems to be staring straight at my forehead, her pale eyebrows arched in irritation.

"Of course I do," she says finally, glancing at the other women in the Eastwoods bathroom, as if trying to tell me she doesn't want to cause a scene. I swallow and wait for Kristen to say something else. Instead, she just asks, "So can I pee or what?"

Her bluntness almost makes me laugh. There really was no one else like her. "I didn't know you were in town," I say slowly. Part of me is still waiting for Kristen to register that it's me. The other part knows that I deserve whatever mind game she's playing—if completely warranted hostility could be counted as a mind game—because Kristen has every reason to brush me off. Maybe Kyle could excuse years of radio silence over a catch-up vape outside Sullivan's, but Kristen was always going to be a different story.

This realization makes me almost thankful I've got my arm against the stall for support, especially now that the other women in the bathroom have begun to stare at this decidedly un-midwestern confrontation. If it bothers Kristen, she doesn't let on. Instead, she studies me carefully now, and the coldness radiating from her voice makes everything begin to fully sink in.

"Of course I'm in town," she says impatiently. "My family still lives here. So does yours, last time I checked." She notices that I can't stop staring at her belly, and she crosses her arms protectively over herself.

"Well, this is weird," I joke weakly. Now that the shock has worn off, a twinge of annoyance has crept in. Why can't Kristen play along, the way you're supposed to in these kinds of conversations, and just be normal and act like everything is fine so we can say we'll do lunch and then never speak again?

Kristen exhales, and her eyebrows go flying. "Can we not do this right now?"

"Do what?"

I can feel blood drain from my face as Kristen gives me a look like she knows I'm playing dumb and wants me to know that, actually, *this* is worse than blowing her off after high school. Over the intercom, they announce the five-minute warning for everyone to get back to their seats. Nearly everyone darts out the door like the Holy Spirit is personally calling them. I stay put, intent on acting like everything is fine and normal in this megachurch restroom, even if the effort might kill me.

"Kris," I say again, aware of how pleading my voice sounds. "What are you talking about?"

"This." Kristen waves at the space between us the same way Kyle had gestured toward the space between me and the Walmart parking lot when we ran into each other. Then she blows a strand of hair out of her face in boredom, which feels so crushingly familiar that I drop my arm and suddenly want to cry. "I can't do this right now, Audrey."

Kristen steps around me and slams the bathroom stall door shut behind her. The two remaining women in the bathroom finish pretending to rinse their hands in the sink. Even the way they flick water from their hands feels loaded with judgment. I make myself check my makeup in the mirror as if my nonexistent mascara might be rubbing off before exiting the bathroom at a slight run and sliding back into my seat as the strobe lights return.

•

The second half of the show opens with the night's headliner: the senior pastor's message. I dully wonder if it's blasphemous to pop another Advil as he talks about hope and generosity and, coincidentally, how helpful Jesus personally would find it if everyone could chip in for the next stage of the church's long-term vision, i.e., the rec center renovation. I check the program and groan inwardly. There's still another hour to go.

Ben notices me clenching and unclenching my hands and gives me a quizzical glance. "Everything okay?" he mouths, and I nod stiffly. Even if we weren't in a packed auditorium listening to the pastor recite Proverbs 11, I'm not sure I could find the words to explain the run-in with Kristen in the bathroom. Vaguely, I can already picture my mother saying I shouldn't have downed all that Advil in the car.

So Kristen is home. And she's definitely mad at me. I shut my eyes and try to push the image of her glaring at me in the restroom to the furthest corner of my mind, as if I can simply drag and drop the memory into the same unmarked file where I've been keeping all this other crap that somehow keeps coming up now that I'm in Hickory Grove. It's obvious now that this whole trip was a mistake, which makes the fact of my dad's endoscopy getting pushed back and having to stay here four extra days suddenly unbearable, especially if I'm going to have to actively avoid places where I might run into Kristen again.

After the sermon finally ends, the Eastwoods youth choir files onstage and begins humming. I count at least four teens who don't seem obviously white, which seems promising. *Good luck,* I mentally beam in their direction, turning my ring meditatively and letting myself be carried by their voices. *Hope you guys get the fuck out of here.* The lights dim further, and a single spotlight demarcates a soloist who's stepping forward and smiling girlishly in the light as she sings. People are crying, I realize, and then I rush to rub away the swelling sensation behind my own eyeballs. Ben notices and pats my hand. I want to explain to him that it isn't the music or, like, the Holy Spirit; I'm crying because I just saw my old best friend, and she didn't want anything to do with me, and I probably deserved that. Ben leans into my right ear and asks if I want to go, and I shake my head.

Then, suddenly, we're in the final number, the one where you can tell they pulled out all the stops. The strobe light returns, as do the adult choir and the worship band and the interpretive dancer. A wall of sound descends on our uplifted faces. From the rafters, five snare drummers are lowered down, like pop stars at Madison Square Garden, and their legs bizarrely air-march in unison like puppets. Somewhere up on the balcony, a confetti cannon launches red and green confetti through the air. The audience stands up to applaud as the offering plates are hustled out efficiently by volunteers. Ben lifts his camera up and snaps away. I give the thought of Kristen one last shove into the back of my mind and decide to keep it there. My mother claps and claps and claps. Her eyes are shining. The way she remains sitting as straight-backed as a schoolgirl makes me wonder if this is something she looked forward to not just all winter, but all year.

In the lobby, Ben and I wait next to a painting of blond Jesus as my mother dashes off to use the restroom at last. I'm clutching my coat and feeling dazed, if not by the awesome gravity of a specific child's birth from thousands of years ago, then at least by the enormous stimulus overload that has been confetti-blasted into our faces. Ben looks exhausted, and I don't blame him—experiencing the entirety of Eastwoods on top of a day of golfing and dealing with my hungover self has stretched even his nerves. But he still nods along as my dad shows Ben the iPhone pictures he took of the show. They're probably blurry and unfocused and terribly mediocre to his photojournalist eyes, but Ben compliments my dad anyway out of that instinct that always drives him to welcome the world and all its graininess into his line of sight, so unlike whatever demented mutation inside me that prefers years-long absences and graceless restroom encounters. That's what I've always loved most about Ben, and I know now it's also why I need him. I let my gaze drift, searching through the crowd for signs of Kristen, if only to confirm that I hadn't hallucinated her appearance. Instead, I recognize Ashley Davis standing with her parents and grandmother, the four of them looking lost in the crowd of white people. Then my eyes land on a woman in a thick gray coat who's speaking to one of the choir members; her face seems to materialize in pieces from high school memory. It's Mrs. Reid, my old biology teacher, the one whom I'd overheard saying that I didn't look "that Asian" in the teachers' lounge the week before prom. It was her in the bathroom, gossiping about someone's daughter and dropping that immaculate conception line. I stare at Mrs. Reid as she moves through the crowd with that familiar birdlike uncertainty and wait for the recognition to give in to the blinding rage I'd felt after that day in the teachers' lounge. But I'm either sedated by all the talk of mercy and joy in the air or simply too hungover to summon the energy. I watch Mrs. Reid bid the choir member goodbye and walk out the door with her balding husband, past a girl with her parents who resembles Nicole from the back. Out of habit, I search for Alex again, but he's nowhere to be found. Maybe he wasn't home yet for Christmas.

During the drive home, my mother gazes ahead while my dad speeds down the highway, like he can't put enough miles between us and the dangling snare drummers. Ben and I sit in the back again like two high schoolers being chaperoned. "Such a beautiful church," my mother says, and sighs. And then: "I don't understand why you won't get married there."

"Mom," I mutter. "Can we not do this right now?"

My dad glances over at my mother nervously, but she seems too calm to pick a real fight.

"Are his parents stingy?" my mother wonders aloud almost dreamily in Mandarin, though I'm annoyed she switches languages on purpose to leave Ben out. "If they're buying you an apartment, surely they can fly out for a wedding."

"*Mom,*" I say, gritting my teeth.

"After all this boy's mooching," she adds. "He should let you have this."

So there it was. She didn't like that I'd been the one supporting Ben for so long, like she couldn't believe a relationship where a voluntary give-and-take was possible, not after the lifetime she spent buffeted by the rising or falling tides of my dad's job. I want to tell my mother that isn't how actual normal relationships work—that there isn't this invisible ledger we had to square up with each other—but I don't know the words for it in Mandarin and I don't want to say it out loud in English for Ben to hear.

"I just don't understand why you want to make things more difficult than they have to be," my mother finally says out loud, and I appreciate the fact that she does it in English.

"It *is* a beautiful church," Ben says, assuming that we're still discussing the wedding venue potential of Eastwoods. "But it's too much, you know? Too big."

"They seat up to three thousand," my dad chimes in. "I read about it in the program."

"I think we want to keep things simple." Ben looks over at me in the dark car. "Not to be dramatic, but I could marry Audrey at, like, Whole Foods, and I'd be happy."

It's cheesy, but I allow it and he squeezes my knee protectively. My mother says nothing. It's possible she has no idea what Whole Foods is. As we pass a streetlight, I can see in the glow that her brow is slightly furrowed, as if she finds Ben's idea of contentment in the face of all this wide-open venue space and general opportunity entirely foreign. It reminds me of the time we took our first vacation as a family, back when I was maybe six or seven and my dad decided we were going to drive down to St. Louis and see the arch. Basic midwestern weekend trip fare, but for my parents then, it was like going to Disney World: My dad long obsessed over the arch as an international feat of engineering, while my mother was excited to take pictures of a monument that her friends back in China would recognize. It was Fourth of July weekend, so hot that we all got sunburns standing in line while my parents argued over who'd left the water bottles in the car. I was tired and hungry and was under some kind of impression that there would be food once we got to the top—I think my dad had joked that they would be selling hot dogs—so I broke down in tears when we got off the tiny elevator onto the observation deck and there was nothing. While the other kids and families busily posed for pictures with the view, I refused to stand still for my mother, who'd even invested in a Polaroid camera for the occasion. Picture after picture of me came out terrible, leaving my parents not only in the awkward position of having to tend to my tantrum in front of all these other white families, but also horribly aware they were wasting all this expensive film and the precious time they'd paid for in order to see what it was like to stand at the top of the world for twenty minutes. I screamed and screamed as they begged me to stand for just one decent picture that they could send home or pin up on the fridge. Finally, after detailed promises of ice cream, my mother got a shot she deemed worthy. When we filed back into the elevator, I remember hiccuping in my tantrum's aftershock and watching my mother hold the final Polaroid between her two fingers in the harsher fluorescent light and looking disappointed. "What a waste," she'd grumbled quietly to herself, though of course I overheard. She really hadn't asked for much.

These were the types of stories I never told Ben about my family, because at first, I thought they were too depressing, and then, once I got to know the Stears, because I knew he'd never understand. And then, once we got engaged, they felt irrelevant. However clumsily my parents put the weight of their expectations on each other—and me—it wasn't going to matter, because Ben would be the part of my family that mattered most. My mother's comment about whether the Stears were rich or stingy missed the entire point: It wasn't just that Ben's family had the silverware and the cabin upstate; it was the absence of debt to each other in their lives that had enchanted me from the start.

CHAPTER 8

At the Peoria mall the next afternoon, Ben and I are splitting a pretzel at the food court. He wipes his hand on a napkin between each bite like he can't stand having cinnamon sugar on his fingers a second longer than necessary. "You know I have to go," he's saying. "It's a huge opportunity."

Without asking Ben if he wants it, I jab the last piece into the tub of cream cheese sitting between us on the rickety food court table. Then, still chewing, I get up to throw away his greasy napkins and the cream cheese in the nearest bin. It's the closest I can come to admitting that I'm furious. We'd both gotten up late and were eating breakfast by ourselves in the kitchen this morning—I was mulling over last night's encounter with Kristen and wondering if she'd show up to Kyle's bonfire tonight—when Ben cleared his throat, and I realized I hadn't been listening. I should have known he had bad news from the way he kept fidgeting as he pulled up photos he'd seen online from the fires in LA. They were getting worse, Ben said. It was turning into the biggest story of the year. So instead of staying with me to see my dad through his delayed endoscopy, Ben was leaving Hickory Grove tomorrow—December 24—to fly out to California and cover the fires. I held my face carefully as Ben reeled off the statistics: Close to a thousand structures had already burned, and they were even getting the celebrities in Calabasas to evacuate. Wasn't that *exciting*? "Well, you know what I mean," he'd amended.

His contact at a local fire department had told him to get over there as soon as possible because this wasn't just any old wildfire story. It was the apocalypse. California burning on *Christmas*? That was huge. He'd already booked a red-eye out of O'Hare for 11:00 P.M. tomorrow night.

"You really can't sit this one out?" I asked tightly at breakfast, using my thumb to crush a stray grain of rice that someone forgot to wipe up from dinner against the grain of the kitchen table.

"Audrey. It's Pulitzer material." Ben ignores my sarcasm and smiles half-dreamily, like he can already hear the *Times* front page editor calling on the phone. "Everyone's going to see these pictures. Maybe I'll get a bigger contract. We could move into a *really* nice place next year."

"So you're just going to leave me here?" I said, and he gave me a look.

"You could come with me," Ben said.

"To LA?" I shook my head. "What about my dad?"

Ben didn't have anything to say about that, and we made the forty-minute drive downtown to the mall in silence. "Is it because it's Christmas Eve?" Ben finally asked, squeezing my shoulder. "After the church thing last night, you know, I get that it's important to you." He watched my face for a response and then sighed when I gave him none. "I'll make it up to you when I get back," he said. "This fire will burn out soon. It's way past time for the rainy season, which is why I have to get over there, like, yesterday."

I want to remind Ben that this entire trip had been his idea, and now I'm the one who has to stay in Hickory Grove longer than we ever planned while Ben jets off to LA. What happened to sticking this out together? And what was I going to do with my parents without Ben as our guest buffer? It makes me almost wish Ben would push harder for me to come with him even though we both know that would be stupid. What was I going to do out there, carry his camera bag all day?

As we start making a loop around the upper level of the mall, I sense his guilt in the deferential half step that he's walking behind me. It isn't a fair situation for either of us, I guess. And it definitely isn't fair to be angry about some ill-timed wildfires ruining my Christmas plans. What could I say? *Hey, would it be cool if you please give up this amazing professional opportunity so that I, a grown woman, don't have to be alone with my parents for the holidays?* Haven't I been the one who's always encouraging Ben to be more ambitious and take his work seriously? Did I *really* want him to pass up this assignment? Besides, it's not like what Ben thinks, that I'm just childishly mad because it's *Christmas.* Since I've been in New York, I only ever used the holiday as a reminder to send my parents a check or buy them whatever functional and unglamorous necessity they needed in the moment, like a new water heater.

It isn't like my family had any real traditions of our own. When I was growing up, any occasion to remind my parents of how tight money was, or how flimsy their grasp on whatever picture of suburban success they measured themselves against, only ever proved to be more trouble than it was worth. The Christmas I learned about in school and on ABC Family felt like a foreign custom I could only observe from afar, though one year, in third grade, Kristen's family did bring me along to visit the mall Santa. By then, I was pretty bearish on Christmas already, but the off chance that the bearded man sitting outside the JCPenney was legit and capable of miracles made me consider how, exactly, I should word my wish for my parents to stop screaming at each other for a few weeks. I figured if this Santa guy was all about peace on earth, then it wouldn't be such a big deal to ask for a little of that for our home on Newcastle. So, in total seriousness, I asked Santa if he'd work his Christmas spirit magic on my parents, no gift wrap required. The man tugged nervously at his velour suit and mumbled something about trying his best, and I remember getting off his lap and reflecting on how Santa seemed way more decisive in the movies. What a rip-off!

This year, my mother will have her Bible study and the Christmas service at Eastwoods, and my dad and I might get it together enough to put *It's a Wonderful Life* on TV, and that would be it. Who cares if Ben's sitting with us on the couch or not? Except, of course, I guess

I did think things would be a little different. Isn't that why Ben and I were here, why I let my dad dramatize a routine procedure into an event I *absolutely* had to come home for, why I let Ben convince me that this was the dutiful thing you do when you're grown-up and living the life you've always wanted and can spare an extra week or two to pay off whatever outstanding balance you have with your past, so that you can finally move on? Isn't it why Ben and I are at the mall in the first place, because I wanted to buy my parents real presents in, like, actual wrapping paper for once, like a normal person?

Ben is doing that thing where he's watching me closely, waiting to see when I might round the corner on my mood. "You're annoyed," he concludes as we pass a patchy Santa ringing for the Salvation Army near the escalator.

"No, I'm not," I say. "You just *decided* you were going to LA. You didn't even talk to me about it."

"I told you about it the other day. In the car, when we were going to the ice rink."

"No, you didn't."

"I did."

I exhale through my nose.

"I thought you knew what I meant when I brought the wildfires up."

I think back to two days ago, when we were driving to the Owens Center and he'd been on his phone, engrossed in the news. And I know he's right. Of *course* Ben was referring to the fires in the context of his work. What did I think he was doing, making casual chitchat about Los Angeles to pass the time? This was the reality of his job, and it wasn't his fault. And in light of how patient and great Ben has been here this whole time—defending me to my mother in the car last night, taking my dad out golfing, letting me drive around Hickory Grove moodily, being polite to Kyle, surprising me with my matcha—I know I shouldn't begrudge him this. I make myself stop grinding my teeth and take Ben's hand in a sign of reluctant peacemaking.

•

As we loop around the former JCPenney entrance, I decide to push this whole thing about Ben going to LA into the back of my brain, where the encounter with Kristen at Eastwoods has already become diffuse, and let myself absorb the generic carols piped in overhead and the chatter of everyone shopping around us. Now that Ben will be leaving soon, I'm thinking of all the things I still want to tell him and won't have time for, like the way I can imagine my teen self milling around this mall on a typical weekend, eating pretzels and ducking into stores that sold the kind of clothing they promised us kids in California wore all the time in between surf sessions and hosting cookouts on the beach. I want to tell Ben about the time I dared Kristen to get her cartilage piercing at the Piercing Pagoda on the first floor, about how she actually went through with it and was such a good sport that, even when it got infected, she didn't blame me. Or the time when we ran into Kyle and Nicole after school at the food court when they were clearly fighting, so Kristen assigned me the job of keeping Kyle occupied while she and Nicole went to the bathroom to hash things out. There were a million stories like that attached to our ritual of driving into Peoria and going to the mall; this was one of the few places our parents let us roam unsupervised and also possibly the only indoor activity that reliably took up an entire Saturday afternoon. I know Ben probably thinks malls are soulless and boring—he decided to leave his camera in the car—but if we were in better moods, I'd want to try to describe these memories to him, or at least tell Ben about how I saw Kristen last night. Instead, wordlessly, we do a lap around the top floor and then take the escalator down to the lower level.

"Do you want another pretzel?" I suggest uselessly to Ben as we pass the downstairs Auntie Anne's outpost, and he shakes his head, saying he needs to "cool it" on the carbs. He pats his stomach, which I suppose does look rounder than when he's operating on his usual diet of fast-casual salads and Soylent back home.

"I think it's all the rice," Ben says. "We haven't exactly been eating organic."

"Well, I'm sure you'll be able to find a good acai bowl in LA," I say as a joke, to show that things between us are okay, that I don't care that much anymore about him ditching me to parachute in for a wildfire.

Ben makes a face. "You know I'm going there for work, right? This fire isn't funny. People are dying."

"*Okay,* sorry," I say through my teeth.

We stop inside Bath & Body Works, which seems like a promising place to scout out a gift for my mother. Ben takes a whiff of the Christmas Blessings candle on display and recoils. I pick up one emblazoned with a generic image of a sandy beach and wish I could make a wisecrack to Ben about how the tropical scent had just the right base note of imperialism underneath. But he's grumpy now, and I know I should feel bad that my parents' meat-centric meals are probably making him feel sick. The shop is crowded, and I watch as Ben holds himself unhappily around the dozen or so other women in the store, who are sneaking glances at him in the same way girls everywhere in Hickory Grove have looked at him. In an effort to get us out of the store as quickly as possible, I grab one of the premade gift baskets at the counter, even though it's obviously going to be a pain to figure out how to wrap properly. It's the lazy option to go with some employee's taste in candles and lotions, all of which will bewilder my mother as much as the coil pots I used to bring home from first-grade art class, but I've already lost the morning's motivation for shopping.

Balancing the gift basket on my hip, I wave to Ben and gesture over to the long line. "Wait outside," I mouth, and he shrugs and parks himself on the bench outside, next to a few other men waiting for their wives and daughters to finish sussing out the difference between gingerbread and Vanilla Bean Noel body butter. He's still prickly about the acai bowl joke and just as bored with this dull, pedestrian mall errand as he has been by Hickory Grove over the past four days, I suspect. Could I blame him? Last year for Christmas, we got flown to Bali so he could shoot a tourism board campaign—not exactly Pulitzer-level stuff, but we did get to surf and swim at this five-star resort for a week in exchange. The year before, it was a trip to Mexico City, where Ben insisted we try to only speak Spanish; our first Christmas had been a spur-of-the-moment escape to Stockholm. No wonder being in a mall in central Illinois makes him want to charge headfirst into a wildfire. My phone buzzes inside my coat pocket, and I shift the weight of the gift basket to my other hip to pick up. It's Zadie.

"Hey," I say with a rush of relief. I apologize and tell her I've been meaning to call.

"Whatever," she chirps. "How's Christmas in the boonies?" I can hear an ambulance siren in the background on her end.

"It's, um, fine."

"How are the parents? What do they think of Ben?"

"Well, my dad has found the golf partner of his dreams."

"Sounds promising." Zadie laughs. She fills me in on her week in New York, how her boyfriend's parents are crashing at their apartment, how ugly the tree at 30 Rock is this year. By comparison, she says, a week in Illinois sounds practically idyllic.

"It would be if I didn't keep running into people from high school," I say.

"What's *that* like?"

"My old best friend won't talk to me."

"Wow. Okay, what a bitch," Zadie concludes. "What else?"

The idea of trying to explain the situation with Kristen in a packed mall seems ludicrous. I'd fill her in when I got back. "There's this guy friend," I add. "He's not so bad. We've been catching up."

"*Really.* Say more."

"It's not like that."

"Either way, I'm not judging," Zadie says unconvincingly. As our conversation moves to matters of our New York apartments—how she swears they need a bigger place, especially when potential in-laws visit; how I'm still looking at neighborhoods with Ben—Zadie says she has to send me a listing she'd seen on her block in Clinton Hill. "Within walking distance," she intones. "Just imagine."

"Send it over," I say. "I don't know what Ben might think. He's very in love with Bed-Stuy."

"Yeah, but he's more in love with you, right?"

I sigh and say it'll all come down to what Ben's parents think, probably, since they're paying for it anyway. Zadie whistles. "Can't argue with the American dream," she says.

If we had longer to talk, I could give Zadie the full backstory on those neighborhood negotiations, how Ben and I spent a weekend over the summer touring places to get a sense of what we wanted, before I knew Ben was going to propose and that his parents would offer to help us buy a place. I was too busy at work to check rental listings, so the places we toured were mostly spots in Bed-Stuy that Ben was interested in. At our third open house, on Hancock, we toured a brownstone with a patio and a wall of built-ins that Ben eyed as he spoke to the owners, slyly sprinkling in facts he'd googled about the neighborhood's history. They were renting out the top floor for now, but Ben eventually got it out that they were considering putting the whole place up for sale, which only excited Ben more. We ended up staying too long chatting with the owners that we missed the open house at the one place I'd suggested, an apartment in a newer building I'd liked for its proximity to the train—it wasn't going to be easy to get from Bed-Stuy to midtown—and besides, it came with a brand-new laundry unit, too. It was dark and rainy by the time we left the place on Hancock. I was trudging a few steps in front of Ben, who noticed and asked if I was annoyed that we ran out of time. The line of negotiation I'd prepared to convince Ben to give the condo a chance felt like a nonstarter, given how much he loved the Hancock place. This was the flip side of Ben's enthusiasm for handling the details; he took everything upon himself so naturally that I think he forgot I sometimes wanted in on the big moves, too.

"Those places always just look like their pictures," Ben said about the condo in what I guess he thought was a reassuring voice. "Totally soulless. We probably didn't miss anything."

The wet leaves on the sidewalk gleamed in the streetlight as we walked to the train. To fill the silence, he said cheerfully that this felt like the neighborhood for us.

"You could get a bike," he said, when I pointed out how moving to a new neighborhood would complicate my commute.

I tried to picture myself bicycling to the office in my heels and a suit skirt and let the thought go before I got too angry. So instead I said that it was nice there were so many churches nearby as we passed one with a whitewash facade and two brass seraphim peering out from the concrete alcoves. Ben gazed at it mildly, as if he never would have noticed otherwise.

"It *is* a very Black neighborhood," he mused. I couldn't decide what he wanted me to say in response to that.

A few blocks from the subway, we wound up taking a wrong turn and found ourselves on a dimly lit street. It was dark enough by then that we almost didn't see the man walking toward us, leaning heavily on his right foot, until he stopped to ask Ben and me for change. Even though it was barely past six, it felt much later at night. I remember darting my eyes over to Ben, thinking back to our first date when Ben had given his umbrella to a guy off the street. Now, he wavered for a second.

"Sorry, man," Ben said finally. The man mumbled something and walked by, and Ben took my hand and guided me quickly down the sidewalk. I said nothing.

Later, we let the tension of the day erupt into a small fight over this hypothetical move to Bed-Stuy. Ben asked me if it was because the man on the sidewalk scared me. I said I didn't care about that, that I was mad because he never asked my opinion on the places we'd seen that day. "You never ask me how I feel," I shouted at him. Ben looked truly shocked at this.

"I ask you all the time," he said. "*You* never tell me how you feel."

Later that week, when we went up to Beacon for the rest of August, things still felt strained, but by the time Ben proposed, we'd both completely forgotten about the fight. It was his dad, Clement, who brought up the subject of apartment hunting shortly before Great-Grandma Stear's ring was settled on my finger. I remember clutching my salad fork at dinner as Ben gave his father the basics of what we were hunting for once our lease was up in the new year. Then Clement asked why we were bothering with renting. "It's a buyer's market," he boomed over the table. What was the point of being a parent, he asked, if he couldn't help out his offspring in moments like these? Ben immediately showed him the listing for that brownstone on Hancock we'd seen. I wanted to say that we couldn't possibly accept their help, because things couldn't actually be that easy. If the fact of simply having Ann and Clement as parents could whisk away an entire brownstone-sized problem, what did that mean? Ben just smiled back at me, and under the Stears' tablecloth, he reached for my hand.

•

After I bid goodbye to Zadie on the phone and pay for the gift basket, I find Ben perched on one of the massage chairs outside where the Wet Seal used to be. Uselessly, I tuck the gift receipt in my pocket with the full knowledge that even if my mom hates this gift, we'd rather have it sit moldering in the closet for years before we took it back or threw it away.

"All done?" he asks.

I tell him there's a sporting goods outlet downstairs, and that it's my best bet for tracking down a Cubs sweatshirt for my dad. Ben exhales and rubs his temples, and I ask if he wants to take a break.

"Whatever you want," he says, the brightness in his voice clearly forced.

"We could get lunch? Do you feel like Panera again?"

"I'd rather not." He runs his hand through his hair with a sigh. "Christ, this really is the boonies, isn't it?"

I know he's not being serious, but it's less funny to hear him say it now than when Zadie, who has at least passing familiarity with her grandparents' farm in Pennsylvania, said it. Then Ben's phone buzzes, and he walks away from me to answer it, likely to coordinate logistics for LA. I twist the shopping bag in my fingers and stare up at the mall ceiling for a minute, exhaling. At least Kyle's bonfire is tonight. It's probably just what Ben and I need: an excuse to be around other people and get out of each other's faces after the past four days. This is what Hickory Grove did to people, I knew: shrinking the world down and blowing the stakes up so that we wasted our energy arguing over minor details when, in the end, Ben and I both actually want the same exact thing.

CHAPTER 9

The night feels practically balmy for being three weeks into December. It's only forty degrees, the sky is clear, and I even notice a few holdout leaves trembling on the oaks at the end of the Weber lawn as I help Kyle drag lawn chairs from the garage to the backyard, wondering if he's also thinking about the inaugural bonfire he held for the youth group after he and his dad built the pit all in one weekend, as he'd loved reminding us. I keep stopping to roll up the sleeves of the jacket I borrowed from my dad for tonight. It was probably overkill to have hassled Ben about his coat choice after I insisted on bringing my giant winter parka to Hickory Grove. For all I can tell, it might not even snow while we're here.

Ben and I are still peeved with each other from earlier at the mall, and I'm surprised he came tonight, especially after complaining about his stomach again after dinner. I watch Ben standing on the other side of the yard, checking his phone and drinking a beer with a few of the guys—Danny Howard, Cameron Evans, Joe and Luke Richter—he met at Sullivan's the other night. In total, there are about two dozen people here, including the guys from the team, a handful of townie friends whom Kyle must have collected over the past years, and a few random faces I vaguely recognize from high school, who definitely weren't going to remember me. How is it that Kyle has kept in touch with so many of our classmates? Even Jake

Patel is here, and while he and I at least nod politely to each other in recognition, we keep our distance as if we're still circling each other in the school cafeteria, like visitors from alternate universes who can't be seen at the same time.

Miraculously, Ben seems to be getting along with the guys from the team, or at least he's acting like it to make a point to me. We're both good at putting on a face like that. It's why we work so well with strangers in our jobs: He likes to study and document them in beautiful photos; I like figuring out what would get someone to part with a few more dollars in the marketing budget. In the car ride over, I listened to Ben reel off more statistics about the fires in California, as if he needed to justify his trip to me, and then I asked if he wanted me to drive him up to O'Hare. I wasn't sure if I offered because I wanted to prove that I wasn't mad or because I wanted to show him I was being the bigger person here. But Ben shrugged and said he'd get a rental, that his red-eye out to LAX came out of his points and included a voucher for Hertz. "A total steal," he remarked.

"Lucky you," I said almost meanly, but Ben stared at my face long enough that I felt chastened to be the one wearing a full face of makeup to a bonfire.

Kyle's house, like the homes of most kids we'd known with dads in high-up manager jobs downtown, looks like a mansion compared with my parents' place on Newcastle. We're out in an older part of Hickory Grove that hasn't quite gotten partitioned off into subdivisions yet, so the Webers' enormous backyard bumps up against the woods, making it the ideal setup for a sprawling party, not that Kyle's dad let him throw any back when we were in school. Maybe this is Kyle's way of making up for lost time. I wonder how many times Nicole has been to this house. Across the yard, Kyle is dragging a dead branch toward the fire, enthusiastic as a puppy, and he calls on the guys Ben's with to help. Danny, Cameron, the Richter boys, and a few others eagerly join in to drag over branches from the edge of the woods and break them down. I watch Ben standing uneasily at the edge of the group, holding a branch that I can tell even from here is too green to snap properly in half, though he tries. He has his camera slung around his shoulder and is wearing that dumb sweater with the wooden toggle buttons again.

Even though my beer is only half finished, I duck inside the house to find Kyle's mother, Fran, so I can give her the bouquet of carnations we'd picked up with a twenty-four-pack at Walmart on the way here. She's standing at the kitchen island inside making a cocktail and doesn't seem remotely surprised to see me. "These are for you," I say in greeting, brandishing the flowers.

Fran comes over to give me a half hug as she holds the shaker in one hand. I feel myself automatically relax in her presence. She's just as I remembered, all soft arms and polished glasses and that wide, dimpled grin that's been copied and pasted over to Kyle. Standing in her kitchen, I'm reminded of the nights when she joined in on the movie marathons that he and I arranged during that summer, and how Kyle and I would drive to the movie theater across town to get an enormous tub of fresh popcorn—Fran's favorite thing in the whole world—for the occasion.

"It's good to see you," I say, so genuinely that it shocks me a little.

"How about a real drink?" Fran asks me, raising her eyebrows at my PBR.

I pull up a stool next to her and find a knife to slice up a lime for her. The island drawer catches slightly on its tracks, like it always did when I helped put away silverware after all those dinners at the Weber house. Fran asks me warm, teacherly questions about how I'm doing, how my parents are doing. My phone buzzes, and I see that it's a text from Ben. *WHERE ARE YOU,* he asks, like I haven't been inside for only a few minutes. I turn back to Fran and wonder vaguely what she does with herself in this huge house on all the days Kyle isn't home.

"So how's New York?" she's asking. "Kyle tells me you've been so busy that you haven't been able to come home much."

"Yeah," I say lamely, somehow unable to summon my New Audrey enthusiasm in front of Fran. "My job gets pretty crazy."

"Not working too hard, I hope."

I shrug as she pours the vodka.

"Well, we always knew you'd make it big." She glances out the glass door; Kyle is out of range to shoot any disapproving looks toward. "You had *focus*."

Her eyes crinkle at the corners like Kyle's do when he laughs. And I have the same thought that I always used to have being around Fran: *This is nice. This is what normal moms are like.* Moms who made cocktails and asked questions without holding up some unseen yardstick to your answers. I tell her that I heard Kyle's also a teacher now, just like she was, over at Morton. She must be proud.

Fran allows herself a satisfied smile. "You know, between you and me, I was worried."

"About Kyle?"

"Well, you know. He was a little lost for a while with Illinois State and everything." She gives me a knowing look. "Change isn't really his thing."

I try to act like I know what she's talking about. Sure, Kyle had never been a great student. But he'd wanted to go to ISU, like his dad and older brother, for as long as I'd known him. I couldn't imagine why his mother would be saying that he'd had a hard time.

"Well," I say, "he seems to be doing great now."

Fran nods and gives my arm a squeeze. "Don't let me keep you from the party," she says. "I know you're not here to see me."

"Come on. I like talking to you, Fran." It's the most genuine thing I've said all night. "I've missed you."

"Me!" She chuckles and pours the contents of her shaker in a large tumbler and hands it to me. "You missed Kyle."

She squeezes my shoulder as she leaves. Warmed by her heavy pour, I clutch my glass and wander back outside, observing the successfully roaring fire and the generally much boozier state of the party. Ben and a few of the other guys are crouched down next to the fire, feeding it logs with the careful attention of a team of surgeons. I can't bring myself to sidle up alongside Ben to take his temperature and figure out if he secretly wants to leave, which he probably does, so instead I circle the picnic table where a few people have laid out more beers, assorted bags of Lays chips, and, I see with a sense of recognition, a casserole from Fran. Is it pathetic or kind of nice, to know that Kyle asked his mom to whip up some chicken divan for his grown-up party in her house? There's a woman standing in front of the casserole dish, and it isn't until she turns around that I realize why she seems so familiar.

"Nicole?"

She's smaller than I remember, her hair cut short and no longer bottle blond. But it's Nicole Bentley all the same: the girl whose parents still own half the land in the township; who set me up with her younger brother, Alex, for prom; who jostled with me for Kristen's friendship throughout school; who got to be Kyle's high school girlfriend and would now always be the one everyone else came after. Nicole looks blankly at me for a moment until her features knit together in recognition. We hug awkwardly, automatically. I haven't seen her since she went off to Europe that summer.

"Wow. Hi," she says.

"How are you? How's, uh, your family?" I ask, basically regurgitating the questions Fran had just asked me.

She blinks and tucks a strand of hair behind her ear. "Still here, I guess. Yours?"

"Yeah, same." It's strange, meeting like this without Kristen as our nexus, the only place we really overlapped besides, well, Kyle. Nicole had been popular in the way that tall girls who drove real sports cars and had handsome brothers were. "Do you, um, also live around here?" I ask, trying to modulate my voice so that it doesn't sound like I'd be judging either way.

"I'm in Eureka now. Forty minutes east."

"That's cool," I say. So even Nicole stuck around.

"I like to be close to home."

"Close is good," I echo faintly.

"You're, like, in New York, right?"

I nod. We both stare at each other and then the fire for a moment, uneasy, and then Nicole is the first to ask, "So, do you talk to Kristen anymore?"

The memory of Kristen's face in the Eastwoods bathroom rises to the surface. I finish my drink and then, to stall for time, I ask if she does. Nicole shrugs and lifts her plate with the casserole on it.

"We have dinner every now and then," she says. So *they're* still on speaking terms, at least. I guess she won the long game for Kristen's friendship. "She's already back for Christmas, actually. I think she was supposed to come tonight," Nicole goes on. "But she's, like, *so* pregnant. You should see her."

I blink and pretend to be surprised by this news, like I hadn't been almost personally bodychecked by Kristen and her unborn child when I blocked her way to the Eastwoods bathroom stall. "Maybe I will," I say. God, I sound so disingenuous. "It's been a while."

Nicole makes a *hmm* sound.

"I guess we fell out of touch?" I say like it's a question, like Nicole continues to be the one who knows all the right things to say and the right clothes to wear. It isn't like I plan on seeing Nicole again ever, but it doesn't seem like the time or the place even now, as we shiver slightly away from the bonfire, to explain what happened: that Kristen and I tried to stay close after high school. We really had. But that first summer apart *did* change us: I was too jealous of Kristen's jump-started life in Iowa and treated even her phone calls as an encroachment on the fast-waning time I had alone with Kyle. She tried to remedy our growing distance once the fall semester started with regular texts and Skype sessions, even the occasional postcard from the random towns around the Midwest she traveled to for tournaments. But we both got busy. Finally, over Presidents' Day weekend that February, Kristen drove up to Chicago to surprise me for my birthday; she'd bought tickets to a regional Harry Potter convention and showed up with her costume already on. All I remember is how horrified I was to see her standing at the entrance of my dorm in a wig and fake robes, ready to whisk me off to the convention center. I'd walked up to the building with my sorority sisters, and we were all drunk from a day party. When I saw Kristen, I started laughing, and the girls I was with joined in, too. I'll never forget the way Kristen's face fell as she ripped her wig off, or how she refused to look at me as she stuffed everything in the trunk of her car while I half-heartedly pleaded with her to stay. Then Kristen screamed at me, in front of all my college friends, which made me so angry that I shut down and coldly told her to grow up and get over herself. Up until our run-in at Eastwoods last night, that had been the last time we'd seen each other.

"I guess I'm surprised," Nicole says politely. "You guys were so close."

She allows for a pause that indicates she knows more than she's letting on, and I realize there's no way Kristen hasn't already told Nicole everything, especially if they're still getting dinner all the time. Somehow, it's infuriating that Nicole isn't even being remotely bitchy about rubbing this in. But maybe that's why Nicole was always the one who got the popular friends and the teachers' attention and Kyle: She was ultimately a lot nicer than she had any right to be.

"Well." I clatter the ice cubes in my glass for effect. "I'm going to go get another drink. You want anything?"

Nicole gives me a tight smile, like she feels bad for me. "No, thank you."

I should be more embarrassed about what happened with Kristen, I remind myself as I trudge across the yard toward the cooler. Isn't your high school best friend supposed to be the one who ends up as your maid of honor, the one you call when you need a serious heart-to-heart or even just when you're on Facebook and see that the former prom king is selling fake vitamin supplements now? Ben frequently went on camping trips with his entire gang of LaGuardia High classmates. And of course, Kyle is clearly, like, best friends with everyone here even almost a decade later, even if he lives in the next county over. Moody now, I grab another PBR and commandeer one of the empty lawn chairs around the bonfire. Several partygoers have started making s'mores, including Kyle, who waves and comes over with a skewer and two slightly smoking marshmallows in hand. He's sweating from the fire, or maybe the effort of breaking down those branches earlier, and I can feel the humid musk of his body temperature as he sits down.

"I saw you and Nicole talking. Didn't know you guys were still tight." He offers me one of the marshmallows.

"We're not," I say casually. "But you guys are, what? Friends?"

"Yeah, I mean, Eureka's pretty close."

"It's not awkward?"

"Why, because we dated, like, a million years ago?" He pushes his hands into the deep pockets of his jacket. "I don't know. It's nice that we chill together sometimes. Especially after everything that happened with her brother."

"What are you talking about?"

"You don't know? About Alex?"

"No." I scan the backyard, like I expect Alex Bentley to materialize. "Is he here?"

Kyle is silent for a moment, and I look over at where the guys are playing flip cup on the Ping-Pong table he hauled up from the basement. Ben is studiously shotgunning a beer.

"Alex died, like, three or four years ago."

"What?"

"Yeah."

I smile stupidly, like I'm waiting to be let in on the punch line. "Alex from *prom*?" As if there's another Alex Bentley in Hickory Grove he could be talking about.

"Yeah."

"What happened?"

Kyle's brow is furrowed. "Fuck," he says. "I'm sorry. I thought you knew."

I look over to where Nicole is eating her plate of casserole a few yards away with her customary entourage of girlfriends, whom I don't all recognize but probably should. What exactly did I ask Nicole about her family, when we were talking earlier? Had she thought I was being polite and not bringing the obvious up? And when she asked if I'd talked to Kristen, was that what she really meant: Did I know what happened to Alex? Because if anyone was going to tell me, it would have been Kristen.

"They said it was an overdose," Kyle says gently now. "I think Nicole was the one who found him."

I have to stand up now, tilting my head upward away from the smoke, as if that's the reason my eyes are stinging now. Wiping the last shreds of marshmallow goo against my jeans, I mutter an excuse about having to use the bathroom and trip a little on my way back to the house. At the last minute, I veer off around the hedges, glancing behind me first to see if Kyle is watching me blatantly lie about where I'm going. It's too dark to tell, so I keep walking past the porch and the driveway until I'm out on the sidewalk, pacing by the line of cars everyone parked along the Webers' street. The way I trip on the sidewalk again makes it obvious that I can't drive, so I tell myself that I'm just going to sit in my car for a minute. In the back of my throat, I can taste something sour.

The third car down from Kyle's house makes me jerk to a stop. There's a dent in the fender and a thick crust of dried salt along the base, but it's Alex Bentley's Wrangler all the same, down to the FIGHTING ILLINI license plate holder. For a minute I think I'm hallucinating, until I realize Nicole must have driven it here—the Bentleys must have kept the car. Maybe it was Nicole's now. My chest tightens as I glance around the dark street before stepping closer to the car, touching my forehead to the cold window on the driver's side. I can barely make out the beaded fish ornament hanging from the rearview mirror before I stagger back. There's that fuzzy taste at the back of my throat—maybe that last beer—and I lean over the grass and wait to see if I'm actually going to vomit. When we were at Sullivan's the other night and I threw up in the ditch after all those shots Cameron Evans bought, it had almost felt fun, like I was making up for a teenage experience I'd never had. But this feels like something much worse than beer is about to come up, except I don't even get the relief of letting it all out; it leans there in the back of my throat like it's making a point. The thought of Ben finding me out here makes me straighten up and swallow whatever it is and shudder. How could I be this surprised? I read the articles, watched the talking heads, understood that this was an epidemic involving actual people but, of course, not anyone I knew in fucking Williamsburg. On the plane here, I had read *The Current*'s latest exposé with the same removed concern I reserved for the war in Syria and wondered whether this meant a few pharma clients were going to be mad. But *Alex Bentley*? Nicole's little brother whom I made promise not to tell anyone about those fifteen minutes in the CVS parking lot? Whose sister I used to dream up endlessly awful scenarios about having something bad happen to her? It's this thought that makes me lean over the grass again. I wait a few more minutes to make sure I'm not going to vomit, and then I uselessly wipe my mouth with the back of my hand and realize that I'm standing out here alone on the Webers' street, peering into a car that isn't mine. The next house down is at least a hundred yards away, and the lights are off, but I walk quickly back toward the Weber house like I'm about to be caught.

Now that I'm not squinting straight into Alex's old car, I decide that I've overreacted. It's been *years;* Kyle said so himself. And it isn't even like I knew Alex well. I probably haven't thought about him for more than a few minutes, max, since that awkward night after prom. Hadn't I deleted his friend request after graduation without a second thought? I take a deep breath as I reenter the backyard, concentrating on looking like I'd just needed to take a totally normal stroll around the house. I remind myself that I don't even know Nicole anymore, Kristen and I haven't spoken in forever, and I've only barely reconnected with Kyle. Of course I wouldn't have kept track of Alex, and no one expected me to anyway.

Kyle has remained in the same spot by the fire, and I lower myself next to him sheepishly. "You good?" he asks, and offers me a sip of his beer. I know I shouldn't since my mouth still tastes gross, but I accept anyway. If Kyle can tell I didn't exactly bail mid-conversation to use the bathroom, he's nice enough to not say anything about it. Why would Kyle suspect anything less than a normal reaction to a tragic—but old—piece of news? These things were always so straightforward for him: staying loyal to a girlfriend all summer, grieving her dead brother, accepting the half-assed friendship of someone who catapults back into town after eight years, all without question.

"I should have told you about Alex sooner," Kyle says after a beat. "They had the funeral over at Eastwoods. The whole town came."

"It's not your fault," I say.

He tilts his head like he isn't sure he agrees. I try to think of something nice to say about Alex, but all I can remember is the blue-and-orange cast—Hickory High School colors—that he wore to prom and the Doritos crumbs scattered across the back seat of the Wrangler. I barely knew the guy, I remind myself, trying not to wonder if anyone ever vacuumed those crumbs up. I blurt it out before even thinking: "I lost my virginity to Alex, you know."

As soon as I say it, I'm mortified. I can tell by the look on Kyle's face that he'd never known; Alex must have kept our secret after all. Now I'm trotting out this claim on his memory like it makes up for the fact that I had no idea he's been dead for years. Kyle waits to see if I'll say anything else, and I consider all the things I'd rather do—jump through the fire, hide in the woods, endure another trip to the mall with Ben—than face Kyle's judgmental gaze.

"Jesus," he says, and then somehow, incredibly, he starts giggling.

"It's not funny!" I say quickly. "That was a shitty thing to say. I just meant, you know, I liked him. As a person. He was a good guy."

"He *was* a good one," Kyle agrees, and wipes his eyes, which leaves his bottom eyelashes stuck together in little triangles.

Across the yard, I barely hear Ben's camera clicking away as I try to think of what I can say to Kyle. What he must have thought of me before this, when he assumed that I knew about Nicole's brother and *still* didn't come home for the funeral and *still* didn't say anything to him—or anyone else—over the past years. And even when he thought I knew and did nothing, he still wanted to be around me and invite me to a party at his house, like I hadn't totally betrayed Nicole or Kristen or even Kyle himself during all this time. This was a person who's never asked anything of me at all, not even the decency to show up for the past that I'm so busy trying to leave behind.

Across the yard, the flip cup team that Ben is on wins their game, and I see him celebrate with a chest bump from Luke Richter, whose girth knocks him off-balance. Ben spills beer from his plastic cup as he looks around, proud and victorious, until his gaze lands on me sitting next to Kyle, and he shakes his head, like he isn't surprised. Kyle and I watch Ben set his beer down and walk over to us.

"What's with him?" Kyle asks.

I sigh. "I don't think he likes it here."

We watch as someone—maybe Cameron—staggers off to the edge of the woods to pee.

"What's not to like?" Kyle says in a deadpan voice, and we start laughing so hard I have to hold on to the side of my lawn chair.

My eyes are watering now, especially from the smoke, so I stand up to wave it away from my face. Ben has now made his way over, and I'm surprised to see that he's buttoned his coat all the way up. "I think I have a headache," he says, swaying on the spot. "I think we should go."

"You were literally *just* playing flip cup," I say, rolling my eyes. "I thought you were having fun."

"Well, *you* sure are." Ben's eyes dart over toward Kyle and then back to me.

"Yeah, we're talking about Nicole's dead brother. It's a real fucking party."

Kyle gives me a glance, and I realize he's never heard me talk like that before. Ben, however, stares at me blearily. He's absolutely wasted, I realize. "Who's Nicole?" he asks.

I throw my hands up. "Forget it. If you want to go home, call a cab. I'm staying." I want to say something about how ridiculous it is that *he's* being pissy, now that I've decided to not make the LA thing a big deal.

Ben wrinkles his nose and gets his phone out, visibly struggling with entering his passcode. "Do you guys even *have* Uber here?" he sneers drunkenly. "Or should I hitch a ride on someone's tractor?"

I hear Kyle choke on his beer as I yank Ben's elbow over to the side, where no one can hear us. He leans unsteadily on a lawn chair.

"Are you serious right now?" I ask through gritted teeth.

"Come on, Aud. It was a *joke*. I'm sorry." He holds his phone up and sways. "See, it's coming. In, like, forty-five minutes." He snickers to himself.

I turn to Kyle and apologize for having to go. Kyle asks if I'm sure, but then the lawn chair Ben is leaning on collapses, and he falls over on the grass, cursing. I give Kyle a look and ask if it's okay to leave my car here for the night.

When the black Honda finally pulls up, a tired woman with a Cubs baseball hat in the front seat, I corral Ben into the back. Sobered a little from our wait sitting out on Kyle's front porch, Ben hiccups slightly to himself. As soon as I get in the back seat, he thrusts his head in my lap, his angular body bent oddly on the seat.

"I get it now," he mumbles sleepily.

"What?" I'm annoyed, but I push his hair out of his face all the same.

But Ben just closes his eyes. I'm relieved when he stops talking.

CHAPTER 10

Now that it's finally Christmas Eve, even the ride my dad gives me back to Kyle's house so I can pick up my car the next morning feels like a cheery errand. On the way, we stop at the Starbucks drive-through and order peppermint hot chocolates to toast his last day in the office for the year. We should go out for dinner, my dad suggests. I'm dubious about what restaurants in town might be open tonight, but he's optimistic and says he'll look into it.

Once we get to Kyle's house, I make a point not to linger before I unlock the car and drive toward Gold's Gym to get a few miles in, as moderately hungover as I am from last night's bonfire. On my way home, I note the burly Santa stationed in front of the Walmart entrance and the twinkling nativity scene between the Best Buy and Menards. Even the gas stations are decked out in red and green lights, and the tiny Lutheran church by the high school rings out hymns that the wind carries across the fields and empty subdivision lots so that I can hear them later with ethereal clarity in my room while drying off from a shower.

Ben is leaving for LA tonight. "At least I'm staying for dinner," he prods, as if that somehow undoes the fact that he's hightailing it out of Hickory Grove without me. It's pointless to stay sulky about it—even getting mad at him at the mall yesterday, I realize now, was a waste of time. I should be happy that he came on this trip at all, that we could still share part of Christmas Eve together, because who knows how long he'll be in LA? In an attempt to make peace, I spend the rest of the morning with Ben downstairs in the guestroom, tending to his more severe hangover and checking apartment listings as if we're back home, having a lazy Sunday. I'm glad neither of us sees the point of relitigating the LA trip, that we're both trying to act normally, which entails, on my end, not wondering about my dead old prom date, and definitely not wondering about what everyone in Hickory Grove must have said about me when I didn't show up to Alex Bentley's funeral. Which was a selfish view of it anyway, I remind myself as Ben gingerly rubs his forehead. No one would have thought about me at all.

By the time we got home from the bonfire, it was midnight, and Ben was still drunk. Once I got him downstairs and into bed, he turned sad and needy. He pleaded with me to stay in the guestroom with him, and then he asked me over and over about where I'd gone off to during the bonfire. As I tucked him in, I noticed the bedspread and the pillow are so brand new that they smelled like the plastic packaging. I told Ben I'd been in the house talking with Kyle's mom—there was no easy way to account for the time I spent peering into Alex Bentley's old Wrangler—but Ben kept forgetting and asking me again. "You kept disappearing," he said pointedly, and I bit my lip to keep from telling him that he was being ridiculous. While I waited for him to fall asleep, I paged through back issues of the magazines he'd brought from New York, as if he'd secretly known how boring this trip would be.

Looking at apartments now puts both of us in a better mood. As we sip matcha and mull over the listings, I think about what it was like back when Ben first moved in with me and how easy our life together felt. The ensuing years' worth of apartments and trips and weekends upstate had all involved similarly smooth adjustments, so why did being in Hickory Grove bring out this tension that turned Ben reckless and paranoid and me wild with annoyance at 3:00 A.M. to find that, out of all the emergency reading material Ben packed, he hadn't thought to bring along even a single issue of *The Current*. It's clear this place is driving us both crazy, but I remind myself now that I need to have some perspective. Being here in Hickory Grove wasn't our real life. New York, and whatever new apartment we found together: *That* was real life. I point out one of the Clinton Hill listings I bookmarked, knowing Ben would like it, and mention that it faces a community garden, and isn't that nice? Ben nods. He's still subdued from his headache and, I know, the vague knowledge that he behaved badly last night. I'm glad he doesn't seem to remember the finer details. We scroll through a few more listings, then stop at photographs of a sunny three-bedroom with an address that, as I confirm on my phone, would put us on the edge of Clinton Hill and Bed-Stuy, fifteen minutes from Zadie. It's like a compromise we willed into existence. I scroll down for the price. "This is nice," I say peaceably.

Ben peers at the laptop screen. "It's, like, a condo, though."

"Would that be so bad?" I wish he'd focus instead on all the space, how we could both have an office.

He sighs. "I just love that prewar look, you know."

I remind him of the mice at his old apartment by the J train. Prewar problems, I joke, but from the frown on his face, I know it's already a hard no, and he's working up how to say it.

"I guess I just don't see myself as the type of person who lives in a place like this," he says finally, tapping a fingernail at the photo of the glassy building. "It's so new and soulless. I'd feel like a carpetbagger, you know?"

I tell him he can't be serious, and he asks what I mean by that. Shouldn't we be conscientious about these things, he wants to know, when all those shiny condo buildings did was displace local residents?

"I mean, if we're buying a place in Bed-Stuy, we're gentrifying anyway," I say slowly. "I don't think it matters what *kind* of building it is."

He makes a face. "Of course it does. If we're moving into someplace historic, it's like we're helping to preserve it."

"Right," I snort. "I'm sure that's what the neighbors will call it."

"Come on," Ben says. "Let's not fight."

I open my mouth to say that I didn't realize we were, but he shuts the laptop and starts stroking my hair. It feels so nice that I move my hand to the back of his neck, rubbing it the way I know he likes and debating whether we can sneak in a quickie at last, now that Ben seems in good spirits and less constipated and my parents are out of the house. Maybe that's what we need to defuse all the tension from yesterday, between the strained mall trip and the bonfire: a little normal couple time without having to talk or explain a decade's worth of history.

"It *would* be nice to have all that space," Ben says, closing his eyes and leaning into the neck rub like a satisfied cat.

I move in closer and use both hands now, feeling the tendons of his neck and shoulders finally start to loosen. "If it's space you want," I say without thinking, "we can always move out here."

Ben's eyes widen; I feel the muscles in his neck snap back to attention. He looks so horrified in that moment that I have to turn away. So I get up like I have to get a glass of water and pretend to laugh off my own dumb joke as I'm climbing the stairs. When I flick the light on in the upstairs bathroom, my face feels warped from the effort.

●

In honor of Christmas Eve—and Ben's last night in Hickory Grove—my dad announces with a distressing amount of flourish that we're going out for dinner after all. I consider mentioning the new downtown trattoria I found on Yelp while I was at the gym this morning, but I'd checked the menu online and hated the idea of my parents having to puzzle over how to pronounce *cacio e pepe* to some tired server. The local Applebee's has been out of the question ever since the time my dad tried to order fajitas and totally butchered the pronunciation. It would have been easy to overlook the server's derision had she not taken it a step further and cloyingly assured my dad that no, the *fajeetas* were not *velly spicy*. This was in middle school, and all I could think about was how angry I was that my dad hadn't stuck to his usual grilled chicken, because then we wouldn't even be in a situation where he was getting mocked by a waiter for what, not knowing a *third* language? But thankfully, my dad has already made up his mind on tonight's spot. To give Ben enough time to drive up to O'Hare and make his flight, we decide to arrive at the Hickory Grove Olive Garden at five.

The promise of a change in scenery perks me up. Going out to a restaurant feels like what regular families are supposed to do after an afternoon of high-quality bonding, instead of what we'd all really done, tucked away in our respective office cubicles/Eastwoods Bible studies/parts of the house watching the various TVs and, on my part, scrolling through old *Journal Star* articles about Alex Bentley's death on my phone. I notice that my mother even dresses up for the dinner; she is wearing the same cardigan she wore to the church Christmas show, and my dad has shaved for the event. I decide to put the Sullivan's/church wrap dress back on and add a thick cable knit sweater over it to head off any comments from my mother on the neckline.

I know I should cringe the moment we set foot inside Olive Garden. If the plastic grapevines tacked up overhead aren't cheesy enough, the knockoff Jules Chéret prints framed by the doorway make me avert my eyes while we wait at the host stand and I shift in my boots, wondering if anyone else in here knows or cares that those posters are actually French. Ben notices them immediately, and I can tell it bothers him more than the prospect of limp calamari and breadsticks. It's funny how he doesn't even try to disguise his disdain, I realize, and this dampens whatever genial feeling I had about him from this morning and our apartment hunting, which was probably a waste of time anyway. In the back of my mind, I already know Ben has his heart set on the place we saw on Hancock, and I'll be lucky if he even humors me with a few more open houses to tour once we get back to New York.

We're seated immediately in a booth in the back. My parents settle in happily while I do a quick scan of the restaurant, even though I know in the back of my head that Kristen's family always drives out to see her grandma in Bloomington for Christmas Eve, making the possibility of another run-in unlikely. When the server comes by and offers us the wine list, my dad pretends to study it instead of waving it away as he usually would. "Maybe one glass of cabernet," he says. I offer, probably too eagerly, to go in on a bottle with him.

My mom grimaces. "Should you really be drinking? Who's going to drive?"

I glance at Ben, wondering if he'll offer, but he's preoccupied with flipping through the laminated pages of the menu.

"Just one glass, then," my dad says softly. "A small one."

I narrow my eyes at Ben and flip to the back of my menu, where all the cocktails are, and order the Italian margarita. The server tilts her head toward Ben, and he asks for an iced tea. My mother orders one, too, then gets up to seek out the restroom. After badgering my dad about washing his hands, too, she gives me a look when I don't immediately follow them both. I pretend not to see. Ben shifts unhappily in the vinyl booth while they're gone, alternating between staring dolefully around the restaurant and then back at the menu.

"I think I'm gonna get the shrimp scampi," I announce for no real reason other than to keep the conversation from rolling to a dead stop.

Ben rolls his eyes. "Aud, we're literally in the middle of nowhere," he says. "Do you really want to order *seafood*?"

I slap the menu down on the table. "You know, it wouldn't kill you to be less of a snob for this one night," I say.

It comes out nastier than I intended, and I know I should walk it back, but I'm too overcome with the need to eat overcooked pasta for an uninterrupted hour without wondering what Ben thinks, what Ben wants, what Ben feels. He falls silent, and I read the menu over again with a pretend studiousness, like I need to also consider the chicken cacciatore. Thankfully, my parents return from the restroom at the same time, though if I was hoping that they'd help carry the conversation, I'm deeply mistaken. My mother gets out her phone and begins checking her WeChat messages. She's been quiet since our minor snit during the drive home from Eastwoods. My dad looks over at her and pulls out his phone, too. It's supposed to snow tonight, he announces. That's good, I say encouragingly. We haven't gotten any so far.

"Just in time for Christmas," my dad agrees.

My mother sighs. "I wish you weren't drinking if the roads are going to be bad tonight." She says it in Mandarin; I look at Ben, who doesn't seem to care.

"It won't start until late," my dad says in English, patting her hand on the table. My mother moves her hand away. Ben's still sourly inspecting the menu. I ask if he's going to be able to handle the drive to Chicago if the weather's going to be bad.

He frowns and checks the weather on his phone, too, as if expecting a conflicting report. "It'll be fine," he says. "Besides, you know I've driven through way worse, right?" I'm almost surprised he doesn't whip out more photos of Puerto Rico.

After the waiter takes our order, the four of us sit in further silence. I glance at the tables around us full of other families, each concerning themselves with gossip or work drama or the needs of a whimpering baby in a high chair. The one at the table to our left has been fussy and inconsolable since we sat down, so unlike the slumbering baby from our flight from New York. Both sets of grandparents at the table are fixated on how to soothe him, which I decide must be the whole point of kids—something to fill the silence.

When our food arrives, we all breathe a sigh of relief as the server rains down a flurry of Parmesan onto our plates and then disappears. I twirl my fork into the mound of scampi and stick it in my mouth. The result is unequivocally disappointing—the pasta *is* overcooked, and even though I try not to count, I note the three lone nubs of shrimp. Who's the snob now? I watch my parents dig into their chicken Alfredo. There was a point when I would think it sweet that they ordered the same thing, and only later would it occur to me that perhaps it was the one meal they memorized how to order, the safe bet producing the least amount of confusion from a college sophomore who couldn't wait until her shift was over. Ben's picking at his Greek salad, and I feel myself sigh with my whole body. My mother takes a small bite of chicken, then squints at a table behind us.

"Isn't that one of your friends, Audrey?" she asks.

My dad looks over, too. "It's the guy who was running back when you were in school." He thinks for a sec. "Kevin something?"

I snap my head up, and sure enough, Kyle is sitting at a booth with Fran. They've just finished eating. How did I not see them when we came in? I catch his mother's eye and wave, and then Kyle whirls around, his face broadening like a sunbeam. Has it really been only twenty-four hours since we last saw each other at the bonfire? Ben stares straight down at his salad, and I hear him mumble it so quietly that I almost miss it. "This fucking place," he says.

My mother presses her lips into a thin line and asks if we should go say hello; even she knows that's the proper Hickory Grove etiquette. Though my parents apparently don't remember Kyle by name, they've met him enough times to feel that suburban compulsion to go make small talk. But Kyle and his mother are already coming over to us. Fran is wearing a knit sweater that has tiny jingle bells sewn on it—the sort of Christmas sweater my New York friends and I would wear ironically—and Kyle has on a pressed collared shirt underneath the usual hoodie, which is kind of endearing to see. "Mr. and Mrs. Zhou, how's it going?" Kyle says in greeting. "This is my mom."

My parents stand up from the booth and reach across the table to shake Mrs. Weber's hand. Fran nicely says that she thinks they've met before, at graduation. "I still think about how great Audrey's speech was," she says, shrewdly going in for my mother's ego. "We were so thrilled to have her as our valedictorian."

Predictably, my mother grins, reminded of probably the one day in her life she was proud of me. "That was a good day," she allows.

Ben looks up at last. "I didn't know you were valedictorian," he says to me.

"Of course she was," my mother says immediately. "Four-point-three GPA. The highest at their school, ever."

I decide to ignore Ben here and instead ask my mother how she remembered that. She shakes her head like I've personally offended her. Meanwhile, my dad uses this opportunity to ask Kyle if he's still playing football. Kyle says no, then gestures to introduce the only two who haven't met: Fran and my fiancé, but he doesn't elaborate beyond just "Mom, this is Ben," and I wonder if that means Fran somehow already knows the whole deal. Fran asks Ben how he likes Hickory Grove, and to his credit, Ben maintains a straight face and says it's been "lovely" to stay with the Zhous for the holidays. It's obvious to everyone how he pronounces *Zhous* so it rhymes with *joes* and not *zoos,* which is how Kyle says it. The six of us regard one another for a beat. I can feel the hostility emanating from Ben, and I tell myself it's because he's tired and crabby and probably hungry, considering his subpar Greek salad.

"Looks like we're not the only ones catching an early dinner," Fran says, and asks if we're going to tonight's show at Eastwoods as well. My mother perks up at this and explains that we'd all gone the first night. I give Kyle a quick glance, and we both try not to roll our eyes as our mothers discuss Eastwoods Christmas shows from the past years, like two band groupies comparing notes. No wonder he and Fran are dressed up.

"Oh, you guys got the Alfredo? Great choice," Kyle says amid our mothers' cross-talk, grinning at my dad. "I always get that." My dad nods eagerly, as if there's no gourmand whose taste matters to him more than Kyle, even though I'd notice he'd mostly been pushing his Alfredo around on his plate.

Talk quickly turns to the mild threat of snow tonight, then how unseasonably warm the winter has been so far. My dad retells a joke about buying out the rock salt at Menards in preparation for a recent blizzard that didn't bear out; I watch Kyle's mom laugh wholeheartedly. Then my mother asks Kyle what he is doing now, and he tells her about the world history classes he is teaching at Morton High School. I can tell she isn't sure whether to be impressed, either from a lifetime of admiring the American education system or wishing her own offspring lived closer to home. Ben stares stonily at his salad, probably thinking about how it is wilting, and thereby losing all remaining appeal, as we speak.

"It sounds like you're doing well," my mother says finally to Kyle, in that coded motherly way that means she is actually complimenting Fran.

"So is Audrey, of course," Fran says, completing the volley on cue. "She's made us all very proud here in Hickory Grove."

"I wish she lived closer to home, like Kyle does."

I ditch the shitty cocktail straw and sip directly from my Italian margarita until the ice hits my teeth.

"Well," Fran says diplomatically, "in any case, I'm glad these two have always stayed in touch. They practically came up together, didn't they? Look at them now."

Kyle is trying to catch my eye, but my face feels too hot to hold his gaze for long.

"It's good to stay close with old friends," my dad offers, reasonably.

Ben clears his throat. "Well," he says curtly now, "enjoy the show tonight." For a second, I assume he's just being New York polite—it was the kind of definitive conversational closer I'd give to a coworker I ran into on the weekend, or the rare overly chatty stranger on the subway. But then Ben's mouth tilts upward in a smirk. Fran rearranges her face to cover her surprise.

"We should be heading over anyway," Kyle says after pretending to check his phone for the time. As they leave, Kyle shoots me an arched eyebrow, and I can feel my face burning. My dad blinks in confusion. Meanwhile, my mother has her arms crossed, and she holds my gaze without expression, like even she understands what happened.

●

It's only a little after six when we get home, and after my parents retreat into their usual corners of the house, I go into the kitchen to pour myself a glass of wine. Ben has brought his suitcase up by the front door. He has a little over four hours left to drive up to Chicago and catch his flight, but instead he's leaning against the counter, gathering up the full force of the anger he's had simmering since we left Olive Garden.

"What did she mean," he hisses, "that you guys have 'always stayed in touch'?"

I spend a minute trying to wedge the cork back into the bottle so I can save the wine, but then I give up. I ask Ben what he's talking about.

"Kyle's mom. She said you guys *always* stayed in touch. I thought you told me that you and Kyle haven't talked for years."

"We *haven't.*" I swallow, rubbing my temple. "Fran doesn't know what she's talking about."

"So what happened?"

"Nothing."

Ben crosses his arms.

"*Nothing,*" I repeat. "I swear to god, Ben."

When his expression doesn't change, I switch tactics and soften my voice.

"Kyle and I lost touch because I was an asshole and never came home after college," I say. It doesn't escape me how sensual the idiom *losing touch* feels in that context, making it all seem bigger than simply choosing not to pick up the phone over and over. "That's all there is."

Ben rakes a hand through his hair. "So what," he says, agitated. "You guys still *talked*?"

I frown. "No. I cut things off."

Vividly now, I remember the last text exchange we had. Kyle had asked me if I'd heard that Cameron Evans was getting married while I was pregaming at someone's apartment in Wicker Park, early freshman year. I said no, and he linked me to the engagement announcement in the *Peoria Journal Star*. I'd meant to respond when one of my sorority sisters saw the text over my shoulder. "Who's that?" she asked. I put my phone away immediately and said it was no one important. After that, I never responded. It was that easy. But I don't say any of this to Ben. I just tell him he's overreacting.

"You're not getting my point, Audrey," he says, glaring at me. "Even if that's true, why would you do that? Cut Kyle off completely?"

"What do you mean?"

"I mean"—Ben exhales—"did something happen?"

"No."

"Are you lying to me?"

I blink. He's never accused me of lying before, and I have to take a second to absorb his face.

"No." Now I'm mad, too. "You're reading too much into this. The thing Kyle's mom said at dinner is just like, her being a mom and assuming everyone stays friends forever after high school. Which was not the deal with me and Kyle."

"So what is the deal?"

"Oh my *god,* Ben." I'm gripping the counter so hard that I can see the tendons quivering over my knuckles. On top of everything else—Ben's surprise departure, all the ways he was an asshole at dinner, the exhaustion I have felt from the weight of juggling everyone's needs the entire week, his included—it feels almost laughable that Ben is what, *jealous*? Like I'm going to leave him for a guy I barely know anymore? Like I haven't spent this entire week watching him flirt his way up and down Hickory Grove, brandishing his stupid camera like a fishing lure with the Panera counter girl and all the girls at Sullivan's?

"Come on, Audrey," Ben sneers now. "You and this guy. Something's up. We've been here for, like, four days and I'm watching you guys gaze into each other's eyes by the fire. I don't know if you recall, but we're *engaged.* We're about to buy a home together. What are you doing?"

I'm shaking so much that I can barely set the glass down. I want to say that it isn't us buying the apartment—it's Ann and Clement doing it and letting us live there.

"You're being crazy," I snap. "I can't hang out with a friend while we're here?"

"Why won't you just admit it?" Ben is pacing in the kitchen. "You guys have history. *Something* happened."

The way Ben makes it sound like Kyle and I actually dated is so ludicrous that I start laughing. I tell him he has no idea what he's talking about, that he's making a huge deal out of this imagined past.

"This isn't funny." Ben watches me down the glass of wine and pour another one for myself. "Do you have any idea how this makes me feel? Up until, like, a week ago, I didn't even know this guy existed. You could have at least *warned* me, Audrey." He takes a glance around the kitchen. "This is so messed up. I thought this week was going to be tough, but I didn't think it would be like this. You didn't prepare me for anything. I feel . . ." and here he stops, considering what he's going to say, and then hardens his face in triumphant resolve. "Tricked."

"You're the one who wanted to come here," I hiss. "This was your idea. This whole trip was for *you*."

We both eye the kitchen clock. Ben has to leave soon or he'll risk missing his flight, and we both know he'd never let that happen. For a minute, Ben holds his face in his hands, tortured by his existential fear of having to be the bad guy who has to leave mid-argument. I could apologize. I could tell him it's okay, that everyone gets a little jealous, and he should go and we'll figure it out later, but I find myself wishing he would hurry up and leave so I can have space to think. Right now, I can barely stand to look at him, leaning against the sink in a sweater I'd bought him for his birthday, insisting that he hand-wash so it wouldn't pill so obviously the way it is now. I think back to when Ben couldn't even snap that branch in half for the bonfire, and it makes me hate him a little. It's just the rage and maybe the lackluster scampi summoning these thoughts, I know, which is why I want this whole argument to be over.

"You know, this is kind of insane. Like you could just tell me that everything is fine and I have nothing to worry about, but you're being so . . ." Ben pauses. "Evasive. And angry. Why didn't you tell me about this guy before?"

"I've been *trying,* Ben. It's like all this stuff with my parents. You know it's not easy for me."

"It should be. You should be able to talk about how you feel. It shouldn't be these bullshit mind games all the time."

I'm silent for a moment.

"See, you're doing it again," he says, and I suddenly feel like I'm going to scream. "You shouldn't need to think this over. You should be able to just tell me."

"It doesn't even fucking matter," I say. "You won't get it."

"Audrey, come on." His desire to fight is spent, I can tell, and he tries to hold my hand. I know if I could step back for a moment, I'd see how I'm fighting with him exactly the same way that my mother fought with me and with my dad: by shutting myself down and then feeling for all the soft parts of his psyche and sharpening my knives. I know it hurts Ben that I'm not immediately capitulating, that I'm refusing to play along and make up, but even the fact that he expects a tidy resolution—one that fits with his travel schedule—makes me more furious. I can feel a tightness settling inside my chest and stretching out as I yank my hand out of Ben's grip. His face falls and then turns stony.

"This is so messed up," Ben says now. He's talking fast so I can't see how hurt he is. "You talk about being home like something seriously traumatic happened to you, or like you were really poor, or whatever."

Broke, not poor, I want to remind him. I can almost hear Jasmin's voice in my ear.

"But as far as I can tell, you're just another girl who thinks everything is your parents' fault, or because some guy you liked a million years ago rejected you." Ben knows he's being mean now, too, because he won't look me in the eye anymore. "How have you not gotten over all of this already? Grow up, Audrey. *Everyone* grows up feeling different."

The house is dead silent. I wonder if my parents can hear us.

"That," I say, "is a really white thing for you to say."

"What does that have to do with anything?"

I shake my head. I don't trust myself to speak.

Ben's expression darkens. "Is this how it's always going to be, Audrey? Come on, I never bring your race up. *Ever.* Is this how it's going to be?"

We stare at each other for a moment, and then he tries to walk over to me. I shudder, and we both draw back and glance at the kitchen clock. Somehow I can't actually believe it when he leans over and picks up his suitcase.

"You're really leaving?" I ask.

"I'm not missing that flight."

I can see the way his hand is clenching the handle of his bag. "I can't believe you," I say.

"What do you want me to do, Audrey?" Ben hisses. "I'm not losing out on this trip because of you. I'm not going to wait around to see if you'll ever be ready to talk about things like a real person, or if you just want to keep taking your mommy issues out on me here. Get a grip. I can't deal with you when you're like this."

He turns on his heel and heads for the front door. I can feel the door slamming from the kitchen. The whole house shudders, then falls quiet.

CHAPTER 11

I storm up to my room. The blood pounding in my head—helped along by the wine, which I'm now swigging directly from the bottle, and that imposter margarita from dinner—makes it impossible to think. I want to call Zadie, but she's always covering the breaking news desk over Christmas, and besides, haven't we reached that life stage where we're supposed to stop running to each other with every little glitch in our relationships, now that our primary loyalty and responsibilities as confidants belong to our *real* better halves? Why that happened, I wasn't sure I wanted to know. And whether Ben yelling at me to grow up and me yelling back and pulling the race card qualified as a fixable relationship setback anyway, I also don't want to consider. So I sit on my bed and finish the cabernet instead, until my phone buzzes and I clutch at it, hoping it's either Zadie, telepathically sensing my panic, or Ben, calling from the road. Maybe he knows what he said was over the line, and he wants to apologize already. But then I look down at the screen and see that it's Kyle.

"Hey," he says over the phone. "We just got back from Eastwoods. I thought I'd call and see how you are. That thing at dinner was kind of weird, right?"

"Yeah. Christ." I try to sit up. "I'm really sorry about that."

"I don't think you have anything to apologize for."

"We both know that's not true."

He's quiet for a moment. "Is everything okay?"

I lie back on my bed and try to think of a good way to answer as the ceiling starts to spin. The shock of my fight with Ben hasn't fully sunk in yet, so even if I wanted to relive it in detail to Kyle—and he'd listen, of course, because hadn't I done the same for him all the times back whenever he and Nicole were on the outs? but also, wasn't having a blowup with my fiancé different from talking someone through sophomoric squabbles? *was it?*—I can't even think of where I'd begin. I keep waiting for Kyle to disconnect or to ask if I'm still on the line, but a whole minute passes and then another one, and then I feel unreasonable and apologize again.

"It's cool," Kyle says, like he has all the time in the world. "Do you, um, want to talk about it?"

"I think I need to get out of this house."

He asks if I want to go to Sullivan's, and I hiccup into the phone. Kyle takes this as a yes and says he'll pick me up. In the bathroom, I wash off my makeup, which is all dried and smeared from this day that felt like it would never end, and consider changing out of the dress from dinner. But the challenge of coming up with something else wearable from the dregs of my suitcase seems stupidly hard, and it isn't like I'll be gone for more than an hour.

When I see the headlights arcing down the cul-de-sac from my window, I pad downstairs and slip out the front door, pulling on a pair of my mother's tennis shoes on the front porch as Kyle's car idles quietly in the driveway. It occurs to me I should probably tell someone where I'm going; I'm not sure if this technically qualifies as sneaking out if I'm not a teenager breaking curfew. But my parents are in for the night, and Ben is on his way to O'Hare. Like I told Kyle: I just need to get out of the house. Maybe going to a bar with him right now isn't as sensible as going back upstairs and putting myself to bed, but it isn't a crime, either, and I'm definitely not a kid anymore.

It doesn't seem right that it's Kyle's new, practical Camry idling at the curb instead of his old Mustang, and when I climb in, I peek into the back seat a little surprised it isn't still covered with football pads and discarded hoodies and loose curls of weed. Kyle hands me his vape by way of greeting, and we spend the drive to Sullivan's flicking between the Top 40 station and the same indie rock standby my car still has as the preset, then when both of those go into commercial break, I find the local country station and leave it on when Kyle starts humming. As I take a deep draw from his vape, I fidget again with my ring and turn it 180 degrees, so the knob of the diamond faces inward. The fewer things to remind me of Ben right now, the better.

I assume Sullivan's is going to be dead on Christmas Eve, but instead we find about a dozen people at the bar sucking down draft beers and smoking not-so-secretly indoors. It's mostly older guys, middle-aged men in camo jackets and baseball caps. A cluster of them at the bar drink noisily and watch the small overhead TV, but the college types crowding around some arcade games in the back add a sense of normalcy, like this could be any regular night in town. The bartender nods to us as we come in. "Keep an eye on the snow," he says. "We're supposed to get a few inches tonight."

I shoot a glance at Kyle. "Should we go?"

He shrugs and holds up his fingers for two beers. "We'll be quick. I'll get you home before it gets bad."

I find a table in the corner, next to the arcade game with the plastic rifle controllers, and when Kyle comes back with a couple of Bud Lights and an ice water, I drink mine down eagerly. "That one's yours, too." Kyle slides the other beer to me.

"I'm sorry Ben was a dick at dinner," I say finally. "He's not usually like that."

"He seemed annoyed." Kyle props his head up with his elbow.

"And I'm sorry Fran had to see that," I add.

"I wouldn't worry. She doesn't get too upset about random stuff like that."

"Yeah. 'Cause she's, like, a normal mom."

"Well, I don't know about that."

"You know what I mean," I say, leaning on my elbows, eager to talk about anything that isn't my own family or my pissy fiancé. "Fran's so fucking cool. And you guys are so close."

"Well, we kind of have to be."

"Because of the stuff with your dad?"

It's Kyle's turn to shrug, and then he asks if my parents are glad to have me home. I say something dismissive about barely even seeing my mother since we've been here, and how my dad's endoscopy got rescheduled to the twenty-ninth, at six in the morning, like it isn't inconvenient enough already to have to stay those extra days in Hickory Grove. I wait for Kyle to say it's nice that my parents are still together, at least. Instead he simply says that it's good that I'm home to take care of them.

"I don't really know if I'm actually helping by being here," I say with a sigh. "We came all this way so they could meet Ben, and now I don't know what the point is since he left. For work," I add quickly.

Now that we're really alone—without all those others at the bonfire and without Ben hovering nearby—I feel more self-conscious about having Kyle's attention focused on me. It makes me glad that I'm drinking, because at least that could explain why my face feels so hot.

"It's not his fault," I continue about Ben, wondering if he's made his flight yet. "He's just doing his job."

"Does this happen a lot?"

I frown. "No. Maybe, like, a few times a year." I take a sip of beer. "It's my fault anyway. This trip got to be longer than either of us expected. It was a lot to ask."

Kyle nods, and I don't know if it's because he knows the unsaid part, that it's a lot for anyone to meet *my* parents, specifically. We both seem to consider the ring on my finger for a minute. He asks if I like Ben's parents, and I tell him about Ann and Clement and their townhouse and the cabin upstate.

"So they're loaded."

"Yeah." I laugh. "It's so wild. They're even helping me and Ben buy a place." I think back to the *other* argument Ben and I had, this morning, over the apartments, and how I can already picture moving into the prewar on Hancock because, well, that's the place Ben liked the most and that's what ultimately mattered if his parents are involved. I explain this to Kyle, hoping it provides some kind of context, but Kyle just raises his eyebrows.

"I thought you liked your current neighborhood," he says. "Williamstown?"

"Williams*burg*," I correct automatically, and then rub my forehead self-consciously. "Shit. Sorry." *Who's the asshole now?*

Kyle pulls my hand away from my face, laughing. I'm waiting for him to pass judgment on the whole apartment situation—what a classic first-world problem—but instead he exhales through his teeth and says peaceably that relationships are complicated. We drink silently for a few minutes, me and my Bud Light and Kyle and his cup of ice water. To steer the conversation away from Ben, I ask Kyle if he's ever brought anybody he was dating back here to Hickory Grove. "A few times," Kyle says. I immediately envision a bunch of faceless girls in ISU garb flanking his college self.

"How has that gone? Did you introduce them to Fran?"

He crumples up the paper straw wrapper and flicks it across the table, then says something about how picky his mother is.

"Well," I say, not a little smugly, "they can't all be Nicole Bentleys."

Kyle makes a face. "Oh, my mom did not like Nicole."

"Really."

He nods sheepishly. I think about Nicole threading her arm around Kyle's in the school hallway, the way she slid herself into Kyle's car when we carpooled to youth group, how her perfume filling up the entire back seat made even my mouth water. I swallow and ask if he's dating anyone right now. He shakes his head immediately like he's relieved. "I, like, *just* got my life together, Aud," he says solemnly. "I'm not trying to drag anyone else in any time soon."

Now Kyle looks embarrassed, and I realize that even though we've fallen back into our high school friendship easily over the past week, I don't actually know that much about his life from the past eight years. I try to ask him more questions about it—how he liked ISU, how he wound up teaching world history—but he seems, I don't know, hesitant? I want to push, especially because I feel guilty about him spending Christmas Eve in a shitty bar with me, but Kyle doesn't let me: Instead, he asks endlessly polite questions about New York, like which train I take to work and what I usually do on weekends. I feel moronic even imagining how I'd explain my usual routines of overtipping on Chinatown massages or staring at my phone while in line for a matcha latte, pretending to think about the chain of sheer human effort it took strangers on the other side of the planet to harvest and grind and ship the green powder all the way to whatever overpriced Brooklyn café I was at trying to stave off a hangover for nine dollars. I can't explain this shit to Kyle any more than I can explain how quickly my fight with Ben in the kitchen tonight had gone off the rails. Once I get home and think it all over, I know I'll realize how unreasonable I must have been to have provoked Ben into losing his cool for maybe the first time ever in our three years together. But for now, I want to pick at my anger the way I'm fussing with the paper label on the beer bottle. So I default to what seems to have worked so well with Kyle over the past week: reminiscing.

"Do you remember when we first met?" I ask, feeling relaxed now that the two beers are working into my system in tandem with the wine and marg from earlier tonight. "What was it, *twelve* years ago? Freshman year?"

"Of course." Kyle smiles now. "Weber and Zhou, back of the alphabet crew."

There had been a concert downtown the night before, one of those rare stopovers B-string acts sometimes made en route from Chicago to St. Louis. Because school started the next day, I wasn't allowed to go, and I hadn't expected to see almost everyone else show up for class in matching Green Day concert tees. I ask Kyle if he remembers this.

"Shit," he says. "That really was so long ago."

"You had one of the shirts," I accuse.

"No, definitely not."

"Of course you did. You loved Green Day."

Kyle shakes his head again. "I don't know what's going on with your memory, but I *definitely* didn't go to that show."

I ask if he's sure. I can detect the faintest cloying note in my voice. I know I'm on the verge of flirting with him outright.

"Yeah, 'cause, um, my dad grounded me that whole summer and made me start going to youth group." Kyle props his other elbow up on the table and sinks the weight of his chin onto his palms. "Besides, we met way before that. In sixth grade, after I moved here."

"You remember that?"

"I think it was my first day as the new kid, 'cause I remember being so nervous. You and Kristen were in front of me in the lunch line, talking, like, a million miles an hour."

"*That* I believe."

"You were so mad about some teacher who was being a dick to you. Because they got you mixed up with Vivian Leung in class."

I feel sheepish, not in the least because of the mention of Kristen. I mumble something about how I thought everyone was being a dick to me back then.

"I mean, they probably were. The whole school was white as fuck," he says. "And I remember seeing you and feeling, like, okay. You know. It wasn't going to be me versus everyone else."

"There *were* others," I remind him. "It wasn't just the two of us. Vivian and Jake and Ashley went to middle school with us."

"Still. It felt that way, didn't it?"

We are quiet for a moment. The satisfaction of knowing that Kyle has preserved this memory for so long lingers.

"You should have told me," I say. "We could have been friends sooner. I wouldn't have had that dumb crush on you first."

The words remain suspended in the air as we seem to consider each other carefully now. I can see from the window that tiny white flakes are starting to fall outside; we're already staying out too late. Kyle takes a sip of water, and when he looks back up, he's smiling so boyishly it feels unbearable.

"A crush, huh?" he says.

I stuff my hands in the pockets of my coat. He can't actually be surprised, can he? How could that be possible when I spent my entire adolescence so visibly fixated on him, this kid with the braces and the hair gelled up in spikes and the musty ISU hoodie he kept all the time in his locker that he gave me to tie around my waist when I got my period after gym class; who grew up into the boy with a skateboard attached to his hand and the perpetual funk of weed and Nicole's perfume floating around his shoulders. And now here he is, a fully grown man who moves with a teacher's deprecating slouch and needs a shave.

I clear my throat and announce that I'm getting the next round. As I hop off the stool, Kyle grips my arm. I assume he's going to say something in response to my sudden awkward admission, but instead he cuts his eyes over to the group of men who've been drinking at the bar since we came in; they're all probably locals or guys who drove in from any of the more rural towns in the county. I tell Kyle it's fine and then I grin, thinking of all the stories I could tell him about the weirdos I deal with in New York on a daily basis. At the bar, I offer the guys a quick nod in typical Hickory Grove greeting and wait for the bartender to return from his smoke break. As I wait, I can feel one of the men, the short one wearing a dirty baseball cap, rake his eyes slowly over me.

"So," he says. "What are you?"

I'm still buzzing from quasi-flirting with Kyle, so I mishear it and shrug and give him a quick smile. "I'm good," I say, feeling generous for indulging a random barfly, on Christmas Eve no less. "How are you?"

This guy with the cap looks at his friends and then back to me, and then I realize that wasn't what he asked. "No," he says, sighing like I'm too stupid to understand. "I said, *what* are you?"

I'm aware that I'm holding my breath as I try to classify what's happening. Is this like the incident with Erin at the airport, where I should just be nice? It doesn't feel like it, based on the way this guy is staring at my throat. Now I can't believe I took my sweater off in

Kyle's car, that I'm wearing this horrible wrap dress with the neckline from dinner. Maybe this is like when I was at Zadie's potluck and that guy was telling me about his year abroad in Beijing a little too eagerly. Nothing I haven't dealt with before, I remind myself as I try to level my gaze with this guy's. Except, in my gut, I know this isn't either of those kinds of encounters; the only thing I can remember that ever made me feel this frozen to the spot was when that Applebee's waiter giggled and told my dad the food wasn't "*velly* spicy," or when Mitchell Hoffman chased me around the playground screaming "snake eyes" over and over. That's what this feels like, as if I'm seven years old again searching for a place to hide amid the monkey bars. And I know I have to say something—fuck, *anything*—because the longer I wait, the worse this could get.

"Japanese? Are you a fucking Jap?" the man with the cap prompts me, a leer curling his mouth upward. "Do you even speak English?" He starts laughing, looking over at his friends as I feel my face burn.

In the back of my throat, I can taste the scampi from dinner. Then there's the weight of Kyle's hand on my back, the sound of his voice asking what's going on. The stiff way he's standing reminds me of all those Friday home games I spent in the band section scanning the field in between plays and finding Kyle tensed in that preparatory crouch, so unlike the usual shuffling mosey that he carried himself with between classes.

"It's fine," I finally say. I can feel how hot my face is, but now that Kyle's here, my vision is able to widen out to the entire bar again.

Without looking at me, Kyle fixes a glare onto the men and asks again what's going on. There's a single, terrible moment as the man stares at his two companions and then back at Kyle, a sneer on his face. I realize he's completely drunk. "Check it out," he snorts to his friends, tilting his head toward us like he's just seen something entertaining at the zoo. "Beaner to the rescue." Then he turns away, distracted by something on the TV.

Kyle already has both hands on my shoulders as he steers me away from the bar. I struggle to meet his eye, hoping he didn't hear what the guy said, though judging by the way Kyle's face has changed, I know he has. Once we're outside in the parking lot, I shrug his hands off me and we stand in self-conscious silence. It's snowing now, but neither of us makes a move toward his car.

"You okay?" Kyle says.

I nod, forcing myself to pick out a single snowflake to track as it flutters to the ground.

"That stuff probably doesn't happen in New York, right?"

"Not like that."

"I'm so sorry, Aud."

I ask if he's okay. Kyle digs his hands into the pockets of his jacket. The snow is starting to gather in the crinkle of his hood. "Nothing I haven't heard before."

Wordlessly, Kyle hands me his vape again, and we both take a long draw. Then he stares at me for a moment before pulling me into a hug. The immediacy of his body, warm and bony as he wraps his arms around my shoulders, makes me pretend like I have to clear my throat. I feel my way to the keys in his jacket pocket. "Let's get out of here," I suggest.

●

The snow's starting to leave a light dusting on the cars in the lot. Kyle tells me to wait inside the Camry while he pops open the trunk and produces a small brush to wipe off what's already crystallizing on the windshield. His hoodie is drenched through by the time he gets inside the car. The country station we left on the radio blares as we get out on the road; I flinch and punch it off. Both of us say something about how fast it's coming down now, and I notice Kyle's forehead creasing as he pulls onto Alta Lane, which is already slick. He picks the most familiar route he knows, which is the winding country road that leads back toward the high school, the same route he's driven a million times giving me rides home from youth group. I peek at my phone to see if Ben's texted me yet. There's no reason he'd know about what just happened at the bar, but my blank screen revives a plume of anger over the fact that he wasn't here, as irrational as it is to believe Ben's presence in Hickory Grove would have shielded me from a random racist, and that he couldn't even be bothered to let me know he made his flight. The car inches along as the wind outside picks up speed. Neither Kyle nor I will admit that we are spooked by the sudden snowstorm, not when the adrenaline rush from the encounter at the bar has barely begun to wear off.

"That stuff makes me so mad sometimes," Kyle says quietly. "I don't know how you stand it," he adds. "Because I know I only deal with it half the time. Most people can't tell."

"Yeah, well . . ." I sigh. "Half the time is still a lot, right?"

"Is this why you never came back?"

I sigh again and lean my head against the car window. Now that we've left Sullivan's, I'm shaking, which Kyle mistakes for chills. He reaches over to turn up the heat.

"It was a lot of things," I say finally.

"Well"—Kyle glances at me and smiles humorlessly—"I figured you had a good reason for leaving and forgetting all about me."

The thought of ever forgetting Kyle, especially as I'm feeling the world spin around me in his car, makes me snort. It's only a millisecond of hurt that flashes over Kyle's face, but it seems to sober me up immediately. I tell him I'm sorry. "You know I could never forget about you," I say, and wish I could add, *Trust me, I tried.*

The weight of that minimal confession hangs in the air in the car between us. Kyle drives on. Whether he's lost in thought or simply focusing on the road, I can't tell. Outside, the wind picks up and we can feel each gust shoving against the car. Without the radio, it's so quiet inside the Camry that I find myself returning to the mash of all the Hickory Grove memories I've been trying so hard to keep stuffed in the back of my head. Now that Kyle and I are shivering alone in his car like this, everything's spilling back out, and it's impossible to look over at him and not think back to that summer we had together, how there never was a place where I'd felt safer than sitting next to him in the passenger seat, whether we were in the middle of a snowstorm, or whiling away the hours of that last August night before I left for Chicago for good. That evening, we'd driven Kyle's Mustang around Hickory Grove and parts of Peoria in loops; Kyle had insisted that I see my hometown in its entirety before I left, as a sort of goodbye tour. It was one of those warm, muggy nights where we drove with the windows down, our favorite song by The Format turned up so loud it felt like we could hardly see, and as we clattered across the Murray Baker Bridge toward Detweiller Park, I remember being terrified we'd drive off the bridge into the river, and then thinking for a millisecond, as the wind blew my hair into my mouth and all over the passenger seat and Kyle whooped from how fast we were going, *Would it be so bad?* To die right then with a crash and a bang, like life couldn't possibly offer anything better than driving around with the first boy you loved. How I could have said right then how I felt about him; how I could feel the words pressing against my teeth, and still I held them there, unwilling to break whatever spell or curse suspended us in that moment, because I had to remind myself that this was enough. It was possible I only ever got to have this.

Another gust of wind forces Kyle's entire Camry to shudder, and neither of us admits aloud that we can feel the car veer a few inches toward the edge of the road. It's enough to shake me out of this useless remembrance, and I'm almost grateful to have the storm to keep my mind busy playing out all the scenarios where this night ends with Kyle and me crashing into a snowy ditch, instead of sinking deeper into the memory of *that* summer night, which hadn't ended with us barreling off the bridge after all, though maybe I would have chosen that over the pathetically plain heartbreak that came later. But there was no reason to go there now; it was for the good of our concentration—and what this renewed friendship between Kyle and me has become—to stop the tape there.

With the curtains of snow swirling furiously around us, it's impossible to tell where we are, so I get my phone out again to check and notice my battery is only at 5 percent. Fuck. I should have thought to charge my phone at Sullivan's, because according to the tiny blue dot on my screen, we are still only a few miles out from the bar. What was barely a fifteen-minute drive on a clear night has taken us more than half an hour, and we weren't even halfway back to my house. Kyle's knuckles gleam white in the watery glow from his dashboard, and he manages to say something about how the storm really snuck up on us before he stops short for a barely visible intersection, and we both feel the brakes buckle underneath our feet.

"Shit," Kyle mutters.

"This is bad, isn't it?"

He says he's seen worse, which reminds me of how Ben had also said that at dinner when I asked if he was okay driving to the airport. I check my phone again to see if he's texted me. The battery shifts to 2 percent, and I stuff the phone back into my pocket miserably.

"Should we go *back*?" I ask.

Kyle shakes his head. "Let's get you home."

The car lurches again as we pull out of the intersection. At this rate, we'll be stuck crawling along the highway for at least an hour until we get to Newcastle, assuming we don't hit the ice or slide off the road. Meanwhile, I realize Kyle's house is only another mile out. I tell him that we should go there, and he looks at me like I'm crazy.

"It's going to be too much for you to drive all the way to my parents' place and then back," I say. "We should wait it out, and your house is closer."

Kyle is dubious. But it's late, he says. And what about my parents?

"What about them? It's just going to be a few hours." I'm nodding, mostly to convince myself that this is the practical move when you're inching along a dark road in the middle of a surprise blizzard. "Besides, what about Fran? She's home alone. What if the power goes out?"

Kyle is quiet for a minute as he thinks it over. "But," he says, "it's Christmas Eve. Don't you want to be home?"

This makes me laugh. "Give me a break," I say, and Kyle says nothing. "Look," I add, hoping he doesn't notice the quaver in my voice as another gust of wind rattles the car. Even if I trusted Kyle's driving with my life, I couldn't deny that it was feeling a little bit like we were in a rowboat out in open sea. "We need to get off the road."

"Are you sure?"

"You know I'm right. It can't snow like this forever."

I check my phone again. It's at 1 percent now, and it's almost midnight. It *is* sound logic, I tell myself, because it isn't safe to be driving in this. Even if Kyle and I made it to my house, there was no way I'd let him try to go it alone back to his place, and the thought of posting Kyle up—where, on the living room couch? in the guest room where Ben slept?—makes my head ache. Kyle glances quickly at me and then nods. We crawl along for another half hour, then take the turnoff toward Kyle's subdivision. Right before my phone dies, I check the weather. The snow is supposed to let up around three, I tell Kyle. He promises to drive me home as soon as it clears up, and I shrug.

"Honestly, whatever," I say. "It's not like I have anywhere to be."

"Who's 'whatever' about Christmas?"

"A fucking adult?" This makes us both laugh, and it suddenly feels okay in the car again, now that we have a plan and a shared understanding that yeah, it's pretty messed up that I'm using a blizzard as my latest excuse to avoid my house. Kyle smirks and consults the road.

"I think we could be okay," he says. "But if you're too scared, then yeah. Let's just go back to my house."

"I'm not *scared*," I say, even as we feel his car scrabbling on the pavement. Kyle tries to brake again, and his Camry slides halfway into the other lane before he's able to steer us back.

We drive in silence the rest of the way, and it isn't until we reach the entrance to his subdivision and Kyle takes a hand off the steering wheel to give me a gentle pat on the knee that I notice I've sunk my fingernails into his arm. He asks if I'm okay and watches me extricate my grip.

"Is this weird?" he asks as we inch around the parked cars on the street.

"No. Why would it be?"

Kyle's relaxed now that we're close to his house. "You know what's funny?" he asks. "The the other night at the bonfire, Joe and Cameron and some of the guys were asking me if we ever were, um, together. I think the exact words they used were 'So did you and Zhou ever screw?'"

"Seriously?" I can't help but laugh at the rhyme. I know now that Joe and Cameron were only ever going to be harmless suburban dads-to-be, but it's hard to accept the idea of their popular football captain selves even remembering me, much less picking up on what I thought had always been a secret crush on Kyle.

Kyle looks at me quickly. "Sorry. That's probably gross. I was trying to think of something to distract us."

I said I wasn't offended. "But you know, Alex and I did hook up," I add, uselessly.

Kyle snorts. "Yeah, you mentioned that."

"I can't believe Alex never told you."

Kyle makes a *hmm* sound at the back of his throat. "That was your first?"

"Yeah."

"Mine was Nicole. But I mean, everyone knew about that."

"Yeah."

He shrugs. "Whatever. I just thought it was funny how Joe and Cameron said it. Like they were being so . . ."

"What?" I say. "Assholey?"

"No. It was like they were jealous." Kyle smiles to himself. "I think Joe always had a thing for you, you know."

"That's definitely not true."

"Why not?"

I frown. "I used to sit in front of him in biology. He never said a word to me."

"Well, you were sort of terrifying in school. Didn't you know that?"

I stare ahead as we take the final turn down Kyle's street. "No. I thought people just didn't like me," I say.

"Jesus, Audrey. Even I was scared of you for a long time," he says. "You were so *serious* all the time. No one wanted to mess with you."

We pull into his driveway. He reaches under his seat to activate the sensor for the garage door, and we wait for the door to roll up. When it doesn't, Kyle curses under his breath and parks the car in the driveway instead. "Here," he says, holding out a hand and pulling me up the slushy driveway incline, where the snow is starting to harden into ice. Inside, the Weber house is silent, pungent with the pine needles of the tree Kyle must have hauled home from the supermarket, and we brush the melting snow off ourselves. I have him turn around so I can dust the back of his hoodie, and then we stop and look at each other, nerves still racing, and it seems like Kyle's going to say something. Instead, he turns to pick up my coat and shakes it out more fully, rehanging it so that it will dry properly on the rack. A yawn overcomes me before I can stop it, which Kyle takes as a signal.

"So, um, the guest room is kind of filled with my mom's scrapbooking crap," he says as I follow him to his room upstairs. The posters of the German cars and the DIY punk bands are gone, but there's the same bookshelf crammed with CD cases, the same twin bed, which I only ever saw covered in laundry. Now the bed has been made, at least, and Kyle walks over to his dresser, pulling out a shirt and sweatpants from the middle drawer.

"Bathroom's on the right." He jerks his head toward the hallway. I roll my eyes and say that I know. We're whispering so we don't wake up Fran, I decide. Not because of how bizarre this feels, to be silently debating who gets the bed in the middle of the night on Christmas Eve.

"If you need me, I'm gonna crash in the basement."

"No, come on. I can take the couch."

"Don't make this a thing, Aud."

I make a face in surrender, even though I'm not sure he can see it in the dark, and ask if I can charge my phone. Kyle rummages around the bottom drawer and sets the cord with the shirt and sweats in my hands. Then he puts both hands on my shoulders, like he did at the bar, only this time his face is so close I can feel the warmth radiating from it. *Like the sun,* I manage to think.

"Good night, okay?" Kyle says in my ear, and then leaves.

I can feel the blood rush to my face as I sit down on his bed, considering the turn of events of the last twenty-four hours and wishing I could get on the phone and call someone about it. Not Zadie, not my New York friends—they'd never get it, not when they've all lived in comfortable geographic proximity to their pasts and, as a result, remained unfamiliar with how the act of migration cleaved your time space continuum into a strict before and after. But who else was there? Not Kristen, who hated me. Not anyone else from Hickory Grove whom I cut out of my life, as easy as hitting delete, so many years ago. I try to think of what to text Ben, if I *should* text Ben. But if he can't send me a simple message assuring me that he made his flight, I certainly don't need to keep him updated on my every movement in Hickory Grove. I slam the phone and the cord on Kyle's nightstand.

The shirt Kyle gave me is an old Fall Out Boy tee from a concert I remember he drove all the way to St. Louis for junior year. I pull on the sweatpants, which bag at my ankles only a little, up over my Spanx. Then I feel ridiculous and take them off along with the rubbery underwear, pulling the pants over my bare ass this time, the cotton snagging on my ring. Then I crawl into bed. The sheets have been washed recently. I can smell the detergent along with Kyle, piney and bodied with the slight stink of weed, that same summer pond warmth that has apparently remained even after all this time.

Outside, the wind shrieks. I wonder if Kyle's car will be buried under the snow tomorrow, if by some sleight of the universe's hand, time itself will glitch and I'll be stuck in the Weber home indefinitely, left to drink cocktails with Fran all day in the kitchen in an endless continuation of that last summer before I left. Downstairs, the grandfather clock chimes softly. It's midnight. I get up out of bed and walk downstairs, through the living room, and peel open the door to the basement. The light is on. I keep going until I see Kyle standing at the foot of the couch, rubbing his eye with one hand and holding a set of sheets with the other. He stares at me sleepily, like he can't tell if he's still awake. If I close my eyes, I could pretend this is still senior year.

I go over to him and touch the edge of his chin with my hand, letting the edge of his face scrape against my palm. Right before I kiss him, we both inhale out of mutual surprise, or maybe to ready ourselves, the way divers do before they plunge into an unexplored trench. He drops the sheets and folds himself around me. My hand scrabbles against his shoulder to find a secure place to hold on to, partly to steady myself, partly to confirm that he is actually there, and to make sure I'm here, too. When I work my way to the hem of his shirt, I feel like I've been waiting my whole life to tug it upward. There is a softness to Kyle's body I haven't anticipated, the nudging give of his belly, the hollow under his jaw where I bury my head against the downy lawn of his chest. I feel his shoulder blades shift under my hands, and then it's like I'm clawing at him to let me in.

Neither of us bothers to turn the basement light off before I pull off my clothes and get down on the couch. I couldn't have said something if I tried. We tentatively put our bodies in the correct places, like teenagers who aren't sure if we're getting it right. From the reflection in the TV screen, I watch Kyle's bare ass jutting in rhythm and feel myself detaching and hating that I still instinctively know how unflattering the angle of my body is, half hanging off the same leather sectional we'd spent that whole summer lying around on. For a second, I wonder if Ben's missed his flight because of the snow. He'd be so mad, and it would serve him right. Then Kyle stops and asks if everything is okay, and I know we will both die of embarrassment right there if I don't tell him to keep going. "Sorry," I say, and I hope Kyle knows I'm referring to the past eight years in addition to this present moment. I dig my hands into his hair and remind myself who this is and where we are, though I already know I'm going to have to blot out the funny angle of Kyle's elbow, the annoying buzz of the ceiling light, the undignified way we're both an inch away from falling off the couch entirely whenever I end up thinking about this again. Closing my eyes helps.

CHAPTER 12

It's almost noon by the time Kyle and I leave for home. I'm flooring his Camry like we're fleeing the scene of a crime, grateful that Kyle doesn't question my insistence on driving, like he understands how humiliating I'd find it to be taken home like a delinquent even though I'm not sure if I'm actually frantic to get back or if I just want to put as much space as possible between myself and Kyle's bedroom. It's the former, I decide. It's Christmas morning, after all, and my parents have definitely noticed by now that I'm not in the house. I try to remind myself that I'm twenty-seven years old and don't owe them an explanation, but I can't bring myself to slow down. What if Ben never made his flight after all and drove back to Hickory Grove, and he's waiting at home for me? What would my parents say, to find him on their doorstep in the middle of the night, all three of them unable to explain where I was? How long would it have taken for Ben to do the math and arrive at the conclusion that's been obvious to him all along?

I'm staring straight ahead, thankful the plows have already gone through the roads once. Kyle says nothing from the passenger seat, and I briefly wonder if he's gearing himself up to say something along the lines of *So that was a mistake.* I'm not sure I want to know what he's thinking as I consider how far back I'd go if a time portal conveniently opened up on Route 91 for me to drive through. Would I rewind things back to last night? Eight years ago? To sixth grade, when I must have glanced back at him in the lunch line and seen the skateboard and energy drink and his dimples smiling over at me and thought, *Okay, him*? But Kyle simply sits with his hands folded between his knees. He was the one who tried to be responsible and set an alarm on the nightstand clock radio when we'd gone up to his room to sleep, but the snowstorm knocked the power out and scrambled everything. I woke up to Kyle shaking me, his morning breath sour and unavoidable as he handed me a glass of sink water. I'd fallen asleep with my hand curled into a fist, my ring still turned in so that it left a diamond-sized welt on the inside of my palm. We couldn't even tell how late it was until I finally found my phone and the cord—which I'd never actually plugged in last night—and saw the ten missed calls from my mother before the screen went blank. To save time, I voted against taking a shower and pulled my dress back on from the night before. Neither of us could look at each other as we dashed down the stairs, Kyle pausing to kiss his mother good morning before we sprinted out and brushed the snow from the car, where Kyle used the brush while I frantically wiped at it with my hands, as if that would help save time. Fran had been making waffles; if she was surprised to see me, she didn't let on.

All the homes along Newcastle are covered in soft icing from the snowstorm. My parents haven't even shoveled the driveway yet, so I park at the curb. I half expect to see them standing outside, like soldiers waiting to intercept a prisoner exchange. But there's no one waiting outside, only the snowman inflatable next door bobbing in greeting.

"Do you want me to come in with you?" Kyle asks as we both get out.

"No," I say tightly. "You should just go."

Kyle asks if I'm sure. I say yes, so impatient to get inside that when Kyle leans toward me for a hug, I flinch. He backs away, then edges over to the driver's side of the car, cupping my elbow gently for a second as he steps around me in the snow. Then he gets in the car and drives off. I watch the Camry disappear into the fold of the subdivision, then walk into the house. They have Lite Rock 107 playing carols in the living room, and I'm almost prepared to walk into some strange alternate universe where Ben, having magically changed his mind about LA and driven back to Hickory Grove through the snowstorm, is opening presents with my parents in the dining room. It's how I'd secretly pictured this trip would end up, fantasy case scenario, but instead, it's only my parents sitting at the kitchen table, quietly eating lunch: my dad with his trusty jar of kimchi stinking up the entire room, my mother tapping at her phone. I'm not as disappointed as I thought I'd be, but I'm also suddenly aware that I should have taken that shower. My mother looks up from her phone and rakes her eyes up and down the dress I'm still wearing from last night. She asks where I've been, and her voice is even and steady, like she's compacted her anger into each syllable of the question, even though I can see that she's shaking.

"I went for a drive last night," I say lamely. Even if I woke up earlier, it's doubtful I could come up with any kind of believable lie.

"In the storm?"

"Yeah. So I got snowed in."

"Snowed in *where*?" my mother asks, her voice raised.

"At a friend's."

My dad frowns. "But your car is still in the garage."

"I got picked up," I say. "Really, I'm okay. I'm sorry if I made you worry."

My mom snorts. "Of course we were worried. I was going to call the *police*." She waits for me to react. "On *Christmas*," she emphasizes, when she isn't satisfied with the level of remorse on my face.

I keep saying that I'm sorry. My dad nods, eager to get this all over with, and points to the stove, saying there's warm congee left.

"Who was it?" my mother asks.

I act like I don't hear her and say I'm going to take a shower.

"Audrey." My mother's voice is hard. "Who were you with?"

"It was just Kyle," I say finally. "Okay? Everything's fine. I'm going to take a shower."

In my room, I peel that awful dress off like it's toxic waste. Thank god I at least thought to put my Spanx back on, as clammy as the spandex felt this morning; it seems to have mitigated the overall whore factor of my look at least a little bit. My mother has followed me and watches me undress from the doorway, keeping her distance like I'm contagious. The exhaustion of the night before is starting to sink in, but I dig through my purse to find my phone—I never did charge it, after going to find Kyle in the basement—and plug it in, hoping Ben hasn't mysteriously detected whatever tremor this morning might have set off all the way in California. I'm disappointed when my screen shows I haven't got any new messages.

"What did you do this time?" my mother asks from the doorway, narrowing her eyes. Now that Ben's gone, she's fully switched to Mandarin. I wrap a threadbare towel around me, hoping to step around her to get to the bathroom. My mother stands resolutely in the middle of the doorframe. She clarifies her question. "What were you doing with Kyle last night?"

"We were just hanging out," I say, aware of how flippant my English sounds in response. "It's not a big deal, Mom. I had to get out of the house."

"For the whole night?"

"I told you. We got snowed in."

She glances at my dress, crumpled on the carpet. Then she turns back to me, staring at what I know from a quick scan in Kyle's bathroom mirror this morning is the incriminating patch of dark pink on my neck.

"Something happened," she says.

I blink hard and rub my eyes. Christ. In the entirety of our relationship, my mother and I have barely discussed sex outside of one terrifying moment in college when she found my birth control pills stowed in my medicine cabinet during a visit. To explain to her the intricacies of my relationship with Kyle—not to mention Ben—feels impossible. I look around my childhood room, at the pile of laundry and old folders I still haven't thrown away and the Harry Potter paperback I'd borrowed from Kristen ages ago, as if there's a secret code for how to defuse my mom's anger, a secret Old Audrey left for me to deflect the nuclear reaction about to unfold.

"Tell me right now," she demands, her voice rising another octave.

I tell her I don't want to talk about it, but of course, this makes her angrier.

"I was upset last night after fighting with Ben," I say finally, looking down into the patterns of the quilt on my bed. "Kyle and I met up to talk."

"To *talk*?"

"Come on. You know how long I've known him. You know how it is," I say, wondering how obvious this flattery tactic is, where I imply she understands me better than she actually does. That one used to work when I was a kid, when we were close.

"You know that boy is"—and here she switches back to English—"*low quality*. He dropped out of college!"

I blink and ask my mother what she's talking about. Kyle went to ISU, I say. I remember vividly the day he got his acceptance letter and showed it to everyone in study hall. She shakes her head, switching back to Mandarin to explain with the fullest extent of her derision.

"No, he dropped out halfway through. And then he went to community college."

"How do you know that?"

Exasperated, she gestures with her hands. "Everyone knows!"

"Even if that's true," I manage weakly, "what does that have to do with anything? I thought you liked Kyle." Somehow this manages to upset me even more. Have I misremembered everything about this place?

"Not as a partner for you."

"Okay, well, no one said I'm trying to turn him into my *partner*. I'm still with Ky—" I correct myself. "I mean, Ben."

My mother looks at me, shaking her head at my mix-up, and makes a *tsk* sound with her tongue against the back of her teeth. "Low quality," she repeats.

"Mom." I am starting to lose my patience. "You can't say that. Kyle is my friend."

"You haven't even talked to him in years," she says derisively. "Some friend."

"I'm not discussing this with you." I try to sidestep her, and she grabs my arm hard.

"You know," she says tightly, and I know she's winding herself up for a blowout. It's like watching a storm gather. "I thought maybe there was a chance you've changed. But you're exactly the same ungrateful brat."

I stare at the carpet. As much as I hated fighting with Ben, even if it turns out that was *it* and we never come back from this fight, I'd choose it a million times over doing this with my mother. As she begins shouting in her hard, barking Mandarin, I'm reminded exactly why I've spent the past years avoiding Hickory Grove—and her.

"Look at you," she sneers. "You're twenty-seven years old. You have everything. *Everything,* including a free apartment from a rich man's parents. You don't even have to worry about taking care of your own family, who gave you all of this in the first place. And you don't even care. You have so much you think you can throw something like this away for one night with this boy who probably barely remembers you."

Standing straight-backed in my room, as I clutch my towel around me, my mother steadily raises the volume on her evisceration about how this confirms what she's known my whole life, that this is classic, selfish irresponsible Audrey, just another example that proves what a careless disappointment I have always been. So reckless, so impulsive, so disrespectful of everything she and my dad—but mostly her—sacrificed so that I could stomp around like a toddler who's grown tired of all her toys. My mother uses a Mandarin word to describe me, *huai,* that could mean "bad," or "evil," or "broken," depending on the exact context. After that, I stop parsing the sounds coming out of her mouth for meaning, and maybe because of that, I start to detect the razor edge of envy in her voice as she berates me for imploding my whole future once again. "You think you're ready to marry someone?" She's seething, flecks of saliva hitting me in the face. "You have one single fight and then you run the other way, like a coward. You have no idea what it takes."

I wonder what would happen if I pushed her out of the way and left, if I walked downstairs and out of the house. I could make it down the driveway in my towel and even wade through the snow for a few miles until I got, well, where? Where would I even go? Back to Kyle's house? I can't even think about facing him, not after the way he clumsily handed me my underwear this morning with the tips of his fingers. I shouldn't have had those beers at Sullivan's, but I can still remember lying awake in his twin bed and wondering, *Was that it? That was all?* How was it possible? I think about how Kyle handed me a glass of water when we woke up and how I'd sipped it and even the water tasted wrong, like the fuzzy inside of a freezer. No, I couldn't go back to Kyle's even in this escape fantasy. I'd have to walk all the way to the outskirts of Hickory Grove, then, and find a way to get myself to New York so I could never come back again. Staying away had been the right idea all along.

"You always do this," my mother is screaming, winding herself up for her closing arguments. "I can't believe I put everything I had into you, and you still turned out like this, ruining everything."

"You don't even *like* Ben," I hiss. "Why are you so fucking worked up about my relationship anyway? It isn't any of your business."

She looks at me like I've slapped her, or possibly because she has to take a second to parse through the rapid-fire English I've flung at her.

"Of course it is. Your life is my life," she says. "How could you even say that to me, your own mother—"

"Stop. Just stop," I say. The molars in the back of my mouth ache from how furiously I've been grinding them. "I'm so fucking sick of this. You're always blaming me for your own shit. But no one asked you to have me. No one made you come over here and give up your whole entire life."

My mother glares at me. "What did you say?"

I move my gaze briefly to hers, then back to where I can hold it more steadily, studying the tendons in her neck and the chenille sweater she has on, which strikes me as a hilariously cheerful shade of yellow. This was something I used to do all the time: stare at her skin and bones and fingernails, wondering how on earth I came from those same cells. And I realize that she isn't only furious because this is her worst nightmare coming true, but that I'm ruining another hand-gifted chance at the kind of fantasy she used to dream about. My mother had spent my entire childhood exhausting herself in an attempt to discipline everything careless and weak out of me, to keep me on the straight and narrow so that she and my father could springboard me into the greatest heights possible. And here I was, on the precipice of marriage and adulthood and a wholly foreign life, despite having never learned. No wonder she wasn't wasting her time deciding whether she liked Ben; she was waiting to see if I'd screw things up all by myself.

"It's not my fault," I say finally, "that you made the mistake of coming here, and maybe even being with Dad, and ending up in some farm town in the middle of nowhere. I'm sorry that's how your life in America worked out, okay? I'm sorry you ended up as a nobody living in a nothing place."

My mother has one hand balled into a fist, like she's going to hit me, which is how I know words are failing her. The thought is so absurd that I almost will it to happen. I want to feel her tiny, bony hand connect with my face. Neither of us is looking at the other. I'm staring at the wallpaper that my mother stuck up when we first moved to this house; somehow even in this moment, I can imagine her bursting with pride when she hung it herself in what felt like the most American act, to wallpaper your daughter's room with twirling elephants. Then I think about the time in preschool when we first moved to this house, when I got in a fight with the girls living down the street because they made fun of the way I couldn't say the *th* sound in *thank you,* because my parents always pronounced it their way: *sank you.* I'd told my mother about this when I came home, thrilling slightly at the delusion I had where she would transform into the kind of sitcom mom who would march me back down to the neighbors' house and tell those girls off for me. Instead, my actual mother had given me an exasperated look and asked what it was that I'd done to make the neighbors not like me.

"Why can't you ever be on my side when I mess up?" I ask now, just like I'd asked back then. I'm horrified to realize that my face is wet, that I can barely rein in the quiver in my voice.

My mother smooths the folds of her sweater and walks over to the door. *Tell me it isn't all my fault,* I suddenly want to beg. *Tell me I haven't actually burned it all down.*

"You always do this," she hisses, before slamming the door shut behind her.

Just like that, I'm not twenty-seven-year-old Audrey anymore. I'm maybe six or seven, trying to ignore those same neighbor girls at the bus stop while they tug their eyelids back and scream made-up consonants at me. I'm staring at the flat yellow grain of Mrs. Gorsuch's desk as she explains to my mother that it looks like I could use another year in kindergarten, to learn how to better socialize, she says nicely, or at least so I can learn to not bite other kids like Mitchell Hoffman, who laughed at me when we were doing self-portraits in art class and I tried to use the same apricot crayon he did for skin color, telling me I should use a darker shade, some crayon named *tumbleweed*. I'm aware of my mother staring at the back of my neck, unable to imagine that it's the entire American education system to blame and not this disappointing daughter who wasn't even supposed to be born in the first place. I'm at the kindergarten graduation ceremony a year later, wearing the plastic cap and gown like everyone else but looming a full head taller than the nearest boy. My stomach is hurting from eating lunch too fast, from being nervous about seeing my parents in the middle of the day. And when they line us up on the makeshift stage to receive our diplomas, I'm shitting myself. It isn't obvious what's happened until it's my turn to go up and shake Mrs. Gorsuch's hand, and everyone and their parents see the stain on the white gown. I'm being yanked off the stage so quickly that I never even get my fake diploma or the Pizza Hut gift certificate rolled up inside. In the parking lot, my mother shakes me so furiously I can feel my teeth rattling. Wasn't she constantly telling me that she'd given up everything to be in America, which meant she gave up everything so *I* could be *here*? So why was it so hard to behave, to do things right? "What is wrong with you?" she couldn't stop saying. "How could you do this to me?" I'm at the top of the St. Louis arch, cracking under pressure as my mother screams at me to smile.

CHAPTER 13

For the next two days, I stay as far away from my mother as possible. It's easy enough since I can hear her move through the house slamming pots, pans, doors. She snaps at my dad for not rewrapping the TV remote control in Saran wrap now that Ben is gone, now that we don't have to hide the way our family works anymore. When we cross paths in the kitchen for breakfast, I hover tensely at the sink to gauge how angry she is. If she at least acknowledged my presence in the room, there would be hope that this would pass within days. But she moves around me like I'm a piece of furniture, which tells me we're still at the full silent treatment stage, which sometimes went on for weeks back when I was in high school.

At least Christmas is over. The past week's worth of laundry has accumulated in a mound in my closet, and even though I know it's only a matter of lugging it all down to the basement instead of my usual four-block trek to the laundromat, I put it off again today in favor of heading to Gold's in the most passable shirt and sweatpants I've rummaged from the pile.

At the gym, I up the treadmill speed until the repetitive whir lulls me into a trance state, which allows me to alternate between each mini TV screen within eyeshot like a lab rat considering a Food Network segment on making pigs in a blanket, the Weather Channel's snowfall forecast, and the drowning porters in the back half of the *Titanic* with the same unblinking consideration. The only break in this attempt at self-hypnosis, about an hour in, comes in the form of Joe and Luke Richter's entrance into the weight room, which I view from my perch overlooking the lower level of the gym. I keep my dad's Cubs cap on, as if the thin disguise will help keep me unseen. Watching them reminds me of the way Kyle described Joe's old crush on me, and that just reminds me of Kyle. I make myself watch the runners looping around the indoor track instead and mull over what difference it made, cardio-wise, whether you ran in place or in small, arbitrary circles. It makes me miss my real gym back in New York with the scented towels and liters of Aesop body balm and the odd run-in with towering models in the locker room, but I decide that I like the anonymity afforded by everyone's basketball shorts and unironic T-shirts at Gold's, the way Lite Rock 107 is still indiscriminately pumping Mariah Carey into the air. Here, no one's congratulating me on moving to New York. Here, no one knows that my mother and my high school best friend and my high school crush—and soon, probably, my fiancé—all hate me.

After showering and then realizing I've forgotten to bring my blow-dryer, I grit my teeth through the freezing walk to the car, where I hunch in the seat and hold up my wet hair to the air vents, waiting for the heat to reach full capacity. Then I spend the day exactly like I did yesterday: driving around Hickory Grove. It begins aimlessly at first, then slowly morphs into a kind of pilgrimage back to the Owens Center, the high school, the water tower where someone has spray-painted LOCK HER UP!, except the spacing is bad and it reads more like LOOK HER UP!, the mall downtown again. Without Ben in the car, I don't even have to act like I'm summoning any particular memories as I drive and let the scenery wash over like sleet on the windshield.

At a stoplight, I kick off my shoes and peel off the socks so I can press my bare foot against the gas pedal. When I get hungry, I loop around in circles until I recognize something with a drive-through where I can order a flat gray burger and a bag of curly fries that I eat slowly in the parking lot, just like yesterday. At first, I let the engine idle as I eat so that I can keep the radio and the heat on, but then I think about what Ben's most environmentalist friends would say and turn the car off completely, until my fingers feel as cold and damp as the fries and I turn the car on again.

If it weren't for the fact that I promised to stay for my dad's procedure in two days, I tell myself, I'd be on the next flight to New York. But it isn't as if anything good actually awaits me there, either: just an empty apartment where I'd simmer in this same exact dread where I don't know what to do with any of the emails Ben has been sending me since he's been in LA, first explaining how he'll likely have spotty cell service throughout the days, then emphasizing how sorry he was about our fight and how he feels bad about the way we left things. I used to like being in the city during this subdued twilight in between Christmas and New Year's, how you could almost go all day without seeing more than a handful of people until sunset, when everyone emerged from their apartments to pick up takeout and walk the dogs. I can't think of anyone to be logically mad at for missing out on those rare days of quiet in New York this year, so I decide to blame Ben, the wildfires, and the gastroenterologist who moved my dad's endoscopy all at once.

I drive into Peoria's downtown proper, where I peer impassively at the cluster of apartment complexes, the brick office buildings, the enormous St. Mary's Cathedral we were warned away from as kids because that's where homeless people liked to shoot up, supposedly. There is just enough vertical variation to give Peoria a semblance of a skyline between the Twin Towers condominiums, which loom as if conscientious of that foreboding name, and the peak of the old Commerce Bank counterbalancing the ugly slab of the Chase tower. I can't remember which building used to be the one where my dad worked, before the manufacturing corporation moved all its bigger offices to Chicago last spring and he started commuting to the remaining campus across the river. I get off the highway and take the exit for St. Francis Medical Center, like I'm practicing for when my mother and I will drive my dad over the day after tomorrow. After circling the hospital, I venture closer to the riverfront, which is a mostly unremarkable stretch of concrete and fencing interrupted by a few effortfully picturesque spots paid for by the city's chamber of commerce, including the little plaza where everyone takes their prom pictures out in front of the Mark Twain Hotel. I vaguely wonder if I should go home and pack my bags and check myself in, maybe for a whole year. Then I notice the NO VACANCY sign in the window. I look at the plaza again and remember how confused Alex Bentley was at prom when I explained that my parents weren't going to meet us at the riverfront for pictures, like all the other parents. They didn't know that was expected of them, and I hadn't asked. It was easier to rely on Fran and her DSLR.

My phone buzzes; it's another text from Kyle asking how I'm doing. He's sent several of these since we last saw each other on Christmas morning, and I also haven't answered a single one. What could I say? The fact that I'd gotten mad at my fiancé and then gotten drunk and slept with my high school crush would be enough of a cliché without acknowledging what it felt like to get what I thought I'd wanted all this time. If I had sex with Kyle and nothing even felt different afterward, then it meant whatever part of me that still secretly believed he and I were special, that this central underpinning of my entire teenage life was the only good thing about growing up here—it had always been wrong. The fantasy I'd nursed about Kyle after all this time was identical to the one I had throughout high school: empty and delusional and useless, a total waste of time that I'd fallen for yet again. My mother was right—I never learned. This is what I always did. The only real outcome of sleeping with my high school crush was the shame in realizing she and Ben had seen it all coming.

I know I should respond to Ben, at least. But how was I supposed to admit to cheating on my fiancé over Gmail? What would even go in the subject line? And what part of California was he in where he can't just call? It's wiser, I remind myself, to wait until we can get on the phone. Because if I respond to anything now, I'll have to say something about Kyle, and then I'd have to wait until whenever Ben wandered back into decent Wi-Fi again to reply. What was the rush? There was no point in saying anything now when he's busy saving, or at least documenting, the world. I try to push the half-hearted explanations I've drafted in my head—along with remaining memories of the fight I had with my mother on Christmas—out of my mind as I make a loop around the hospital campus.

I thought, at least, that I'd miss Ben more. We felt like such a team at the beginning of this trip: two New Yorkers determined to make the most out of their voluntary immersive experience in Middle America for the week. Only a few days ago, I was convinced Ben was my lifeline, my irrefutable evidence that no matter how awkward dinners with my parents were or how many subpar bagels we stomached, I had a tether back to my New York life. My real life. But now I find myself struggling to remember the five days we actually spent in Hickory Grove together. I drive past cemeteries and country clubs and snowed-under apple orchards, and I can't even remember if I pointed them out to Ben at all.

As I continue driving, I wait for the guilt around the actual betrayal to come, for the part of my decision-making frontal cortex that was suppressed by the Bud Lights and the snowstorm and the suburban basement ambience to light back up, to remember that I cheated on Ben: my fiancé, the guy who rescued me from the tedium of Zadie's potluck party years ago and who's been rescuing me from the slow lane I would have remained stuck in ever since. Intellectually, I remind myself how terrible it is to have done this to a guy who brought me into his world, who planned everything perfectly and only ever asked me to go along. Ben made my life beautiful and exciting, the lens of his attention bringing into focus a life I'd always dreamed of, set against a seamless rhythm of art and music and restaurants and adventure and most of all, the easy surety of always having a place to be. There *was* something wrong with me, to look so baldly at all that and dissolve it in one night.

I keep thinking about the way Ben's face twisted when we fought and I said the thing about him being white. Ben was angry and jealous and heartbroken, I tell myself. Not *racist.* I was being dramatic because we'd never fought like that before. There were the normal arguments, over how much money he spent on new camera equipment, how little effort I made with his friends, or, okay, once how unbothered I was when I took a potential client out to lunch and he'd propositioned me right there at the sushi counter, which I told Ben about as a joke. It wasn't like that kind of thing was totally unheard of, but it sent Ben on this whole spiral on the state of gender dynamics and what it meant that we as a society had to deal with creepy dudes, though by "society" I suppose he meant people who made six figures and lived in Williamsburg and cared about matcha. In hindsight, I knew he'd been angry for regular reasons, the way a normal guy would be when his girlfriend even jokingly entertains the idea of sleeping with someone else, but Ben had otherwise always been rather good about the jealousy thing. You can't be too possessive if you live life like it's all a big backpacking trip, I guess. Besides, it isn't as if Ben, a good-looking dude in New York, didn't get his share of attention. I try to picture him together with one of the yoga-bodied moms who gaze at him too long in the Trader Joe's line, or with one of the other photojournalists he sometimes went on shoots with, the type who chain-smoked cigarettes like it was still cool and wore combat boots unironically. I try to evaluate how these hypothetical affairs would make me feel and prepare for the jealousy to flare up in my chest. But even this mental exercise feels exhausting. It's only been two days, I tell myself. I'm allowed to think things over until I decide how, exactly, to explain to Ben that this attraction to Kyle has always existed on a plane separate from the real world he and I lived in, that what happened on Christmas Eve hewed closer to pure reflex than an actual decision. It was the smart thing to do, to get clear on that first, I decide, before whatever happens next.

It's getting late. I know I should go home for dinner, and that my dad's feelings will be hurt again if I show up late, slinking into my room without a word, like I did last night. Even if he didn't overhear the specifics of the fight with my mother on Christmas, he can sense the tensile stress pervading the house. Last night, after I got home, he'd been watching the highlights of an old football game. I thought for a minute that he was going to ask if I was okay, but instead he just told me there was chicken and tofu in the fridge if I was hungry. Later, when I looked, I saw rows of glass containers full of untouched food. He must be cooking out of anxiety around his procedure. It was the part in the long-running script of our family interactions where I should have said yes, helped myself to the leftovers, maybe even sat down and deigned to watch one of the movies in the American Action Classics DVD set he apparently got me for Christmas. "Dad, you know you can stream everything now," I said flatly when he presented the box to me yesterday morning. He said he knew that, but wasn't there something to be said for owning a copy forever?

I'm still thinking about my dad's commitment to the Bruce Willises and Tom Cruises of the world as I drive back down Knoxville Avenue in the faint direction of home. At a stoplight, I lean my head against the window and see a billboard for the Golden Corral around the corner, a comically bright eyesore advertising the restaurant's buffet and fondue fountain, the curtains of chocolate shining luminously in the gray December dusk. We used to eat dinner there every few weeks in high school, whenever my parents felt either especially exhausted or especially good-natured. My dad loved that chocolate fountain; we would tear through our plates of mediocre mashed potatoes and meatloaf so we could get to the dessert bar and spend an hour dipping little marshmallows and pretzels and chunks of pineapple on a toothpick into the fountain's depths. I stare at the billboard and then switch my turn signal from left to right, even as the car behind me honks in irritation.

Inside, Golden Corral is only a little dingier than I remembered it, and they've also added a small roasting spit by the side dishes, so that three chickens rotate hilariously in sync.

"Just one?" The hostess raises an eyebrow.

I shrug and dig my hands into the pockets of my grungy gym sweatshirt as I slink into the dining room after her. I can imagine her internal debate on whether to put me in a booth, where I'd be visually out of the way, or at one of the four-tops, which are less in demand. In the end, she gives me a corner booth and smiles with what I know is bewilderment by my loner status, the gym attire, and the early mealtime; perhaps against her better judgment, she was thinking about how the respective oddity of all three factors was compounded by the Asianness of it all.

"Can I get you anything to drink?"

"Tito's on the rocks?" I ask hopefully.

She suppresses a laugh. "Anything *else* I can get you?"

"Have you dined with us before?"

Yeah, I want to tell her, *I used to come with my parents back when they gave a shit about pretending we were a regular American family.* Instead, I nod, and she flutters away. I unzip my sweatshirt, let it pool on the booth so that no one takes my seat, then stumble over to the buffet tables in my stained gym T-shirt, picking up a plate still warm from the dishwasher. The hostess comes by later with a Sprite that I didn't ask for and sets it down. She looks mildly at the three plates I got myself: fried chicken drumsticks and baked beans and mashed potatoes and a cut of skirt steak and fried shrimp and plain spaghetti noodles, and a baked potato and a slice of berry cobbler and, inexplicably, a lone slice of pizza. The cheese is already congealing in a thick mass. I know I'll eat it all anyway. "Good girl," she says, and squeezes my shoulder affectionately. I'm about to bite into a drumstick of fried chicken, but I have to set it down because my mouth is watering so fast that it hurts.

●

After waking up at one in the afternoon from a dreamless, unsatisfying sleep that leaves me nauseated, like I shouldn't have gotten up at all, I glance out my window at the front yard, where the snow seems like it's starting to melt. After finding my phone and plugging it in, I ignore Ben's latest email and then realize Kyle has left several voicemails for me. As I debate whether I want to listen, a text from him pops up: *I'm outside.* For a second, I consider ignoring it and going back to sleep, but then he sends a second one. *You know I can see you through the window, right?*

Grudgingly, I put on sweats and shuffle into a pair of slippers that my mother has left by the doorway. Kyle's Camry is waiting outside, but when he doesn't make any moves to get out, I march over to his window. He grins at me as he rolls it down, like it's totally normal for him to have cornered me at my parents' house. I ask him what he's doing here. In response, Kyle opens the passenger-side door. "Get in," he says. "Let's go for a drive."

I look back at the house; my mother is at Eastwoods and my dad is out getting groceries. The only excuse I have is the fact that I don't quite want to face Kyle yet.

"Come on," he says. His voice is gentle, like he's trying to convince a feral animal to come closer. The late December chill is cutting directly through the cotton of my sweatpants.

"Can I change first?" I say, sliding in. "I'm not really dressed to go anywhere."

Kyle says I look fine. "I kind of like the slippers," he adds.

We drive wordlessly along Route 91 and turn down Knoxville, taking it past the usual strip malls and the Walmart Supercenter. After that, we take an exit off the highway that sends us winding down the road off Detweiller. I allow myself to watch Kyle's hands on the steering wheel and then move my gaze up to his arms and then his neck and then, at last, the corner of his face, though I stop when he glances over at me. Casually, Kyle asks if my dad's procedure is still happening tomorrow, and I say yes and that I'm glad it'll all be over soon. We both know I mean this whole trip.

"So, the other night," Kyle starts, and I lean my head back, rubbing my forehead. "I get you probably don't want to get into it, judging by the way you've been avoiding me."

I can feel my face turn red, and I mumble something about being busy, even though we both know he's right. "We really don't have to do this," I say feebly.

Kyle is quiet. "I didn't know you felt that way about me," he finally says.

"That was a long time ago." I stare carefully straight ahead. "What happened with us after the bar was just a bad idea. I was in a weird place because of Ben and everything."

"Yeah. You were pretty upset."

"Well, I'm sorry. It wasn't really fair to you." I shift in my seat.

"I didn't think of it like that," he says slowly, turning up the heat in the car again. "You seemed so sad, even when I saw you at Olive Garden. I wanted to, like, be there for you."

"Jesus Christ, Kyle."

"What?"

"I didn't need your pity."

"That's not what I meant." He frowns. I watch the park come into view, digging my fingernails into my palms. Had he picked this spot on purpose? "I just mean that I wanted it, too," Kyle says, softly again. "I've thought about it before."

The snowfall from Christmas has softened now to a thick cake, and from our spot in the small gravel lot we watch kids bundled up in snow pants and crunching polyester coats as they glide down the infamous Detweiller hill with a shriek. When it's clear that I'm not going to respond, Kyle tries to change the subject, working to keep a smile on his face.

"Remember when we used to come here in the summer? And smoke all that weed?"

I can tell he isn't sure what else to say. It frustrates me, but it isn't like I know what I want from him in this moment, either. I can't even decide if I'm still angry, and if I am, why I'd be angry with Kyle specifically. I shouldn't have gotten into the car. Not today, not Christmas Eve, possibly not even a decade ago when he first offered me a lift home from youth group. I cross my legs ungracefully in the seat as we both watch the kids sledding. I wait for Kyle to explain why we came here to this park of all places, and I wonder if he's thinking of the same night I am, those last hours we were together before I left for college in August, the final crescendo of that summer when we drove down here, with that old album from the Format turned up and the windows down, Kyle going so fast that we practically flew over the train tracks at every crossing, the fleeting thought as we traversed the Murray Baker Bridge that I might die right there because things between us would never be like this again, everything would change once I drove up to Chicago and put Hickory Grove in the rearview. I remember we'd spent the better part of our drive discussing whether we should learn how to smoke cigarettes properly. Maybe I was the one to ask him if he knew how, if it was like smoking the sloppily rolled joints he always offered me, and he was probably thrilled by the idea of trying it together.

It had been one of those final velvety nights in August, the part of the summer when we were no longer impressed by lightning bugs or the way the humidity cupped our faces like an old friend. We drove across the bridge and back and then came down to Detweiller, the most notorious spot in Hickory Grove for smoking, sledding, and making out—and the perfect place, we agreed, to break open the pack of Newports we'd bought at a gas station along the way. I remember my ears were ringing from the music in the car, and I was so sure that something would happen: Why else would Kyle bring me to this dark, secluded place on my last night in town? We found an old picnic table and sat on it with our feet on the bench, and as we passed a cigarette between us, I thought about what I would say as soon as he leaned over and finally did it, how I'd pretend *that* was my first real kiss, not the messy one Alex Bentley gave me in the car after prom.

But Kyle just talked and smoked without making any motion to sit closer to me on that dilapidated wooden table, and in the end, I leaned over and laid my head on his shoulder, right at the crook of his sweaty neck, and waited, tense as a bowstring, for the magical moment to hurry up and unfold. Instead, Kyle just continued telling me some stupid story, neither shaking me off nor leaning into me, and so I sat there and felt more monstrous and unwanted than I had my entire life, all too aware of the horrible weight of my own head. After a few agonizing minutes—maybe it hadn't even been that long—I gingerly lifted my head up and acted like nothing happened, the heat rising from my face like something radioactive. The next day, after I'd driven up to Chicago and moved into the dorm and said goodbye to my parents, my new roommate handed me a handle of Burnett's and said we should celebrate our new independence by blacking out, I took it as a sign.

"Actually, you did know, didn't you?" I say now to Kyle as I scan uselessly for a picnic table I know no longer exists.

"Know what?"

I wait to see if I feel anything as I look at his round brown eyes one by one, like I'm examining him with a clinical detachment. I half expect him to say, *I thought you didn't want to talk about it.* Instead, I wonder if Kyle really might just be the dumb stoner everyone else always thought he was.

"You knew how I felt about you," I say. I realize I'm livid. "Back then. I know I never said anything, but it was so obvious."

Kyle frowns. When he doesn't say anything, I know I'm right.

"Jesus Christ, Kyle." My face is getting hot, ashamed that I'm still angling for this basic affirmation, some kind of evidence that I haven't been totally alone my entire life here, from a guy a whole decade too late. Kyle nervously jostles the keys in his coat pocket.

"I'm sorry," he says after an excruciating minute. "I was an idiot."

I can feel the muscles around my jaw jump from how hard I'm clenching my teeth. Kyle leans toward me, and I flinch. Suddenly I can't imagine how we could have ever been undressed in front of each other.

"We were kids," he says, quietly now. "I'm not saying that's an excuse. But, like, I didn't know what I was doing." Now I can't look at him. "What do you want me to say, Aud?" Kyle asks softly. "You show up here after all this time, and I feel like I have to explain the person I was, like, a million years ago. I don't know how to do that." We watch the sledders plummet down the hill, screaming at the top of their lungs. "I'm not someone who always had a plan," he says. "I'm not like you."

"I'm just saying," I say. "All that time? You could have told me to back off. And I would have."

"Audrey," he says. His voice has a hardness to it. "Give me a break.

I was probably thinking about school, or whatever fight I was having with Nicole. Or my parents' divorce. I had a lot going on that summer, too, you know."

"What would have happened if I'd told you?"

Kyle blinks. "Honestly? I don't know."

I stare at the handle on the inside of the car, my ears burning.

"I liked being friends with you, and I didn't think about it that much more," he says now, in a kinder tone. "You can't be mad about that." Kyle puts a hand on my shoulder, squeezing it now, which only annoys me. "Is that why you slept with me? Because you wanted to prove something to me?"

I shrug. It feels cruel, but also like I'm owed this at least.

"Okay," he says slowly.

Kyle watches me, and I lean forward, resting my head on the dashboard.

"Well, that sucks," he says when it's clear I'm not going to say anything else. "Because that did mean a lot to me. I thought we wanted it for the same reasons, you know? I guess I wasn't totally honest with you about things back in high school. But I'm trying now."

I tell him I want to go home. He sighs and reluctantly starts the car.

"Besides," Kyle says finally, "does it really matter?"

"Does what matter?"

"If we had talked about it. Or, like, dated in high school."

I look away so he doesn't see how hurt I am. "What do you mean?" I say. "Everything could have been different. Maybe I wouldn't have moved away for college."

Kyle laughs, rubbing his chin thoughtfully. "Audrey, you were never going to be that person."

"You don't know that."

"I know *you*."

What I wonder in this moment, as I ball my hands up inside the sleeves of my jacket in irritation, is whether this was ever true. It certainly isn't now, not after we've spent most of this past week exclusively going over things that happened to us almost a decade ago, which I know is my fault because I've been either too selfish or too scared to ask about Kyle's actual life, the one where he dropped out of school and moved back home and somehow still moved on with his life better than I did.

"No, you don't," I say. "We actually barely know each other now. Like, you didn't even tell me what happened with college."

"What?" Even as he says it, he flushes red. So it was true. "Did my mom tell you about ISU?" he asks.

"No. *My* mother told me."

He stares at the dashboard, scowling slightly, and finally says it happened sophomore year.

"How did that happen?" I decide he owes me this explanation at least, if he can't explain everything else. "You should have told me."

"It doesn't matter. It's not like you were around."

I hike my arms up farther into my coat. Now we're both mad.

"I have to meet my parents for dinner now," I say. "Can you just take me back?"

CHAPTER 14

When I get home, my dad is chopping onions in the kitchen. He's wearing the Cubs hoodie I got him for Christmas, though when I try to recall the exact moment I must have handed it toward him after coming home that morning and the ensuing fallout with my mother, my memory is blank.

"You're just in time." He hands me an oil-stained apron, and I tie it on alongside a reluctant mental reminder that I should be spending time with the one person on earth who doesn't think I'm a total disappointment. I ask what he's making.

"It's a surprise."

"Shouldn't you be taking it easy? Your procedure's tomorrow."

I survey the kitchen island, where produce is spilling out of a dozen Walmart bags: brussels sprouts, onions, garlic, celery, olive oil—the cheap kind that comes in a plastic bottle instead of glass, which I feel guilty for noticing—next to a whole pink chicken, barely defrosted, by the sink. My dad has his iPad propped up against the toaster; it's an internet recipe for "easy-peasy" roast chicken. Briefly, I think about how Ben's mother, Ann, knows exactly how to roast a chicken right, with anchovy butter and rosemary potatoes and homemade croutons she toasts in the leftover drippings. An old Stear family recipe, she told me when I asked. Definitely not the type that comes up with a cursory Google search. I watch my dad pat the chicken with a paper towel and note the tense angles that I'm holding my body in, and I remind myself to take a few breaths in an attempt to uncoil the tension left over from the afternoon with Kyle. After our conversation at the sledding hill, I was too angry with him and with myself to say anything beyond muttering a goodbye when I got out of the car. Even now, I know that Kyle is probably right, that I'm borderline batshit for blaming him for being a regular eighteen-year-old guy who didn't know what he wanted back in high school. As if I know any better eight years later, after likely torching my relationship with Ben and spending all my time wandering senselessly around my hometown.

My dad interrupts this self-pitying by putting me on brussels sprouts duty. As I wash my hands in the kitchen sink, I take my ring off. It's been sliding around so loosely that I know at least I've been correct about one thing from the past couple of weeks, which is that I should have had it resized. I put the ring in the pocket of my sweatpants for safekeeping. The sprouts, as I rinse them in the colander, don't look so great. I pull off most of the wilted leaves and then soak them in a bowl of ice water, to try to revive them as much as I can—another trick that Ann taught me. My dad busies himself with seasoning the chicken. I recognize the spice shakers he set out on the table as the same plastic McCormick vials of paprika and garlic salt from my years living at home. I know instantly that these are the same shakers; no one's bothered to throw them out even though they're fossilized by now from disuse. It now becomes very clear that my dad has no idea what he's doing. I want to ask what's gotten into him. Why roast chicken, and why tonight? We did a duck every now and then for things like Lunar New Year, but never chicken. Still, it seems cruel to question my dad as he hums along to the radio. Maybe he thinks roast chicken is something that regular white people like Ben had, and he'd planned this as one of this week's dinners, even though now it'll be for only the two of us. My mother is nowhere in sight.

I wait to see if my dad will ask where I've been, or where Ben is, or even just whatever the fuck happened on Christmas. I can't tell if my mother has bothered to fill him in on what she gleaned from her fight with me. As my dad adjusts the brightness on his iPad, I consider how, if we were in a movie, this would be the scene where my dad and I finally have a heart-to-heart—our first in what, decades? a lifetime?—and we come to a kind of understanding where he tells me everything is going to be okay and that Ben will of course forgive me and nothing bad will ever happen again. But he doesn't ask, and I can't bring myself to be the little kid who petitions for the hug. I used to be angrier about this, back when I thought it couldn't simply be the fact that my parents grew up somewhere completely different and therefore had no idea how to handle emotions through the avenues standardized by Disney and ABC Family. I thought my parents just didn't care. Once, I tried to articulate this difference between our families to Ben, and I may as well have been speaking another language. "What do you mean your parents don't care about your life?" he'd asked, and I wanted to say that that wasn't exactly right, that they always made sure I was clothed and fed and set on the interstate expressway to upper middle-class success. But when it came to asking how I felt about current events, or which teachers I liked, or what the deal is, these past few days, with my very obvious, partially Golden Corral–fueled breakdown, neither of my parents had the vocabulary to begin to ask. Especially not my dad. Even though my mother and I were constantly at each other's throats, the antagonism made us familiar with each other. Anything we couldn't say directly to each other eventually came out mid-argument. Meanwhile, the lack of conflict left my relationship with my dad mostly blank, demarcated more by what it wasn't than anything else. I guess we both decided that was good enough. We were two separate circles in a Venn diagram: He liked golf, the geometry of a cantilever bridge, and, I suspected, Fox News. What would we have ever talked about? The subject of my mother, and the way we both orbited her whims, was verboten; I knew he knew how impossible she made things, but when I'd complain, he'd ask me to go easy on her, like *she* was the one who needed a break. And I guess that made me suspicious, even though he tried to be there for me in all these little ways that didn't involve words but a lot of driving and random gifts. Even the times I asked questions about his childhood or *his* parents, my dad either acted self-conscious or said he didn't remember back that far. The few photographs saved from China were small black-and-white school portraits, plus one with his parents on what I assumed was their farm, where my dad is looking stoically into the camera, his face square and upturned like it is now.

We're moving around each other easily in the kitchen and making comments about the chicken and the sprouts and the general state of the house. My dad points out things that need to be fixed and says brightly that maybe new kitchen tiles would add to the market value of the house, because eventually he and my mother might want a change of scenery after more than twenty years here. Moving's such a pain, I warn him, thinking about the whole ordeal Ben and I will have to put ourselves through when our lease is up in a few months, assuming he still wants to be around me—much less live with me—by then. I really should respond to one of his emails.

Shyly, my dad wonders aloud how much a down payment is in New York anyway. He's asking because he wants to know how much money Ben's parents are giving us, and I can't bear to tell him, not when I know it's several times his salary as a senior civil engineer in Middle America. I fantasize about telling him the truth about how much I don't want to move, how I don't even want to talk to Ben, even though the alternative is downright sophomoric, because eventually, the true extent of the damage between us will be revealed, and either it's all over or Ben will begin outlining his master plan for fixing everything immediately, bloodless as a packing checklist, and I don't even fucking know if that would somehow be worse. I want to tell my dad about how I thought seeing Kyle today would resolve things, but how, instead, it made all the wondering and agonizing even worse, the indignity of holding on to those feelings for this long unbearable. What did I really think would happen—that Kyle and I would ride off into the sunset together? I didn't want that. I liked my life the way it was, before Ben and I came here and everything fell apart. I imagine finally coming clean to my dad about how I've resented the way my mother rules so much of my life and how

I hated the way she must have limited his, too, and that I'm sometimes angry with him for letting her do it. If we *were* in a movie, or at least belonged to a family like the Stears, this would be the part where the lighting gets all glowy and my father gives me sage, fatherly wisdom, and we would sit down to dinner as a happy family, or at least two-thirds of one.

Instead, we're uselessly cooking a roast chicken together. When was the last time we even did something like this? I remember being a kid and sitting in that old student apartment in St. Paul making dumplings by hand with my parents, balling the raw pork up just right and sealing the skin closed with quick little pinches. I'd always been so sad that mine didn't look nearly as nice as my mother's, which were all perfectly shaped like gold ingots. I worried mine wouldn't taste as good, but then somehow, when everything came out pan-fried and golden, all the dumplings appeared identical. I caught on only years later that my dad had simply made sure the ugly ones were all on his plate. Then there were those few years when I shunned *all* the food my parents made because it wasn't what I had at Kristen's house. At first, my mother tried to adapt. She attempted those quizzical mainstays like meatloaf and lasagna before giving up because I *still* complained that nothing tasted right. I started tagging along when my dad went grocery shopping every Sunday so I could personally pick out nine boxes of TV dinners in the frozen aisle: one for every weeknight and two for lunch and dinner on the weekend; it was a miracle I'm not the one with the ulcers in the family after all those Marie Callender's chicken pot pies and Kid Cuisine chicken nuggets and endless boxes of frozen chicken Alfredo. It wasn't until I was in fourth or fifth grade that my mother stopped cooking almost entirely, at first because she was busy with her job at the department store, and then all at once, as if she had turned in an unspoken two-week notice. In between my TV dinners, my dad made me plenty of Cup Noodles and congee and an ever-evolving form of egg drop soup that I craved because sometimes we got it at the cheap Chinese buffets in town, except that at home, it was never as good, and nothing my dad added—chicken broth, a little pork fat, tapioca flour—seemed to make a difference. A long time later, when Zadie was dating this chef who worked at the new Asian fusion restaurant on the Lower East Side, I learned that the trick was cornstarch, and I remember wondering why we never just looked it up on the internet. Maybe that hadn't been how life worked then. Still, my dad never stopped trying. He bought all-American-seeming cookbooks at neighborhood yard sales and set them out for me to page through, pleading with me to at least dog-ear the recipes that seemed promising.

But it wasn't that I wanted the scalloped potatoes instead of tofu, or that I wanted to eat food that wasn't cooked in pots and pans forever coated with remnants of oyster sauce and chili oil. By adolescence, I simply wanted nothing from these parents who spoke English with such heavy accents, who barely understood why I needed to buy expensive maxi pads every month instead of learning to roll up balls of toilet paper like the imaginary frugal, practical daughter they'd wished for instead. It had been easier, when I was little, to participate in the bowling alley trips or the Saturday matinees or the drives down to Glen Oak Park. But once I wised up to the unique embarrassment of my parents the way preteens always did, the only way my dad and I really spent time together was all these in-between moments, when I thought nothing was happening, like when he drove me to skating lessons at the Owens Center or when we went to the old Cub Foods for groceries, before it went out of business, and then chose the nearby Target to mill around and browse the DVD selection. When we were really bored, or if one of us had gotten in trouble with my mother and we needed to kill an extra hour, we went to the Menards, where my dad liked to walk the aisles looking at the thousands of doorknobs, the endless variations of window shades. If I kept quiet and pushed the Menards shopping cart around, my dad would end the day by buying me a gift. In grade school, it was the *Grease* soundtrack: I'd watched the movie at Kristen's house during a sleepover and became immediately obsessed with Sandy's epic romance with Danny Zuko, and especially the transformation she underwent to become worthy of his love. The cover insert of the CD was an image of Olivia Newton-John and John Travolta cuddled up together in a way that was PG-13 in its suggestiveness, but my dad knew that it was sexy enough to offend my mother. After two hours examining tiles at Menards, we went to Circuit City and he bought the CD for me under the condition that I throw the cover insert away, so that if my mother ever found it, she wouldn't be mad. By then, my mother already envied our little errand days together enough, to the point where I knew to pause at the front door when we came home so I could rearrange my face and make it seem like we didn't have too much fun getting groceries.

We'd gone on one of those errand runs on my sixteenth birthday. I'd been especially sulky after being allowed to have a small pizza party the night before with friends from band and honors English. My parents took us to a pizzeria near the mall, where they split a single cheese pizza in the restaurant and my friends and I took over the party room they rented in the back, guzzling Dr Pepper and ordering four extra-large pepperoni pies all by ourselves, which felt like some awesome power. I was morose in the car the next day because the party was over, and I hated the way I felt back in my normal boring life, where I had to study for biology and wait for something interesting to happen to me again. My dad took me out for ice cream to cheer me up. In the car outside the Cold Stone Creamery, he handed me a sleek white box. "Happy birthday," he said. It was a white iPod Video, dense and pearlescent as I peeled the plastic protective film back. I was astonished. A few high schoolers on the school bus had one of these, but I didn't even own a regular iPod yet; my Panasonic CD player had shamed me no end. To this day, I have no idea how my dad knew how much I'd coveted the one Cameron Evans showed us on the bus—Cameron even let me listen to an Eminem music video he'd downloaded, but the volume was so loud on his earbuds that I gave the iPod back immediately. I hadn't even dreamed that it was a gift I could ask for, so it felt ludicrously illicit to palm the beveled edges of the iPod Video in my hand.

"I don't think I'm supposed to have this," I said quietly, already noticing a fingerprint on the screen and wiping it away with the edge of my knockoff Abercrombie & Fitch tee.

"I wanted you to have something nice," my dad said. Then he shifted in the seat of his car. "Keep it safe, okay?"

In my excitement, I took this to mean that I had to take good care of the iPod, so I missed his warning, or maybe just didn't understand. In any case, I kept it in my backpack and imagined about how I'd pull it out on the bus with the right amount of indifference. Every night after homework, I spent hours on the family computer, downloading songs from Napster like Kristen showed me and making playlists to show off at school. Two weeks later, the iPod felt so natural in my hand that I forgot to be careful with it—I forgot that I'd ever existed without it—and I was in the car with my mother, driving back from a band concert. She was in a good mood; I'd had a solo during the show that was small but flawlessly executed. As a reward, she allowed me to listen to the indie station on the radio, as long as I kept the volume low, and when a particular song—I think it was from the Killers—came on, mournful and keening about how badly they wanted to get out of some small town, too, my mother asked me if I knew the name of the song. I'd downloaded it to my iPod the week before, so I got it out of my backpack and said, "Wait, I can look it up." I felt the air in the car vanish as she glanced over at me and frowned and asked whose iPod it was. Still not able to sense the danger I was in, I said it was mine, and she asked where I'd gotten it. "Dad got it for me for my birthday," I said unthinkingly, and turned back to scrolling the little white wheel to find the right song. She asked me to hand the iPod to her.

When we got home, my mother ripped into my dad with all the usual accusations as soon as we set foot in the living room: He'd gone behind her back, he was spoiling me, I was going to grow up a stupid little American brat. It took a lot of tearful explanation on my part to even clue my dad in about what specifically she was so mad about, and I'll never forget the way his face changed. It wasn't his fault; he'd been working late for the past few nights and was exhausted, and there had been no way to know that this particular storm was coming. He looked at me and just said, "You weren't supposed to tell." I knew then that this whole thing was on me. I should have been smarter and better able to protect my parents from all this fighting. The silent treatment that followed from my mother lasted for a month, culminating with a dinnertime announcement—read aloud from a sheet of loose-leaf notebook paper—delineating all the ways both my dad and I would make this up to her to recoup the $300 extravagance. The life of an immigrant family felt that fragile to her, I suppose, but it would be decades before I even began to understand the kind of long-compounding fear that drove my mom to hurl a two-week-old iPod out the window as we sped down the freeway.

●

While we wait for the chicken to cook, my dad goes outside to shovel the driveway. I try to do as much damage control on the meal as I can, unearthing a small, hard lump of butter in the fridge that I slide uselessly on the chicken's skin and dusting it with an ancient tin of black pepper as best as I can. The sprouts are doing no better; I can already tell they will be mushy and tasteless, and I don't even bother trying with them. When my dad comes back in, he busies himself with setting the kitchen table. He goes into the guest bathroom and brings out a long-forgotten candle we stuck in there once, because that seemed like a thing that families we saw on TV and in commercials did. I don't think it's ever been lit. He strikes a match and holds it to the wick, and I can smell the artificial lavender in the air, so that now in addition to being overcooked and underseasoned, dinner is going to smell slightly of soap, too.

"That's nice," I lie, opening the fridge and nearly going slack with relief when I see there are still a couple of Sapporos left. I crack the caps off, and set them down at our places at the kitchen table. My dad puts a dingy oven mitt on each hand to drag the chicken out of the oven and begins carving it with an inherent confidence, as if slicing poultry is something baked into any dad's DNA, no matter where he came from. Even from the kitchen table, I can tell that the chicken is going to be tough and dry—we barely let it defrost, much less marinate—but whether my dad notices this or not, he keeps it to himself and seems delighted that we have cooked a small bird in our kitchen together. "Do you want to take a picture?" my dad asks, brandishing his knife.

I have to laugh and get my phone out to snap a photo of him with the chicken, as if it's Thanksgiving and not just the two of us sitting at the kitchen table. I set out the sprouts. He carves a few more pieces of the chicken and then gives up and sets the whole pan on the table, serving me a bowl of white rice steaming from the rice cooker and him a bowl of leftover purple rice, warmed up from the microwave. He looks approvingly at me as I tug one of the chicken thighs off the bird, and then tugs the other one off and puts it in my bowl of rice, too. I tell him I couldn't possibly eat two *and* any of the other food, but he insists.

"So are you nervous?" I finally ask. "About tomorrow."

"They said it's probably ulcers. And the doctor is very good. I will be fine."

"I know. But . . ." I serve myself the brussels sprouts, cringing at the charred, sulfuric smell that's getting mixed up with the lavender candle. "They're putting a camera in your stomach? That's a big deal."

My dad shrugs and tilts his glasses up his nose. "I'm not worried. But I'm glad you'll be here for it."

"Me, too," I say, delicately putting a forkful of the dry chicken in my mouth and hoping that if I just hold it there, it will dissolve so I don't have to chew it too much. He asks what I think of it. "You've never made roast chicken before," I say instead. "What's up?"

My dad smiles to himself and gets out his phone, and for a minute I wonder if he didn't hear me.

"Dad? Why the, uh . . ." I say the Mandarin words for *white people food*. "Did you see it on the Cooking Channel or what?"

He says something about how he hasn't felt that hungry lately and that he's noticed I haven't been eating much, either. "So I thought I'd mix it up," he says, and then he holds out his phone to me. I stare for a minute before I recognize the photo he had pulled up. It's a photo *I* took, or rather, a screenshot from an Instagram I posted from two years ago. I peer closer and see that it's a shot of the dinner Ben and I had that night at the fancy restaurant in the West Village, where we'd gone with his agent and his friends, and then Jasmin accused my parents of not being poor enough to count as real immigrants. We'd ordered the famed roast chicken that everyone had been raving about, dressed with wild garlic mustard and watercress salsa verde. It's about the furthest cry from this dry remnant of a chicken with jar pesto dumped on top as Times Square is from the Hickory Grove Walmart Supercenter, but I feel the burning in my nose shift to my forehead and the corners of my eyes.

"Dad, you look at what I post?" I ask.

"Of course. But I don't leave any comments," he says quickly. "I know your friends would see them."

"I didn't even know you, like, followed me," I say quietly, staring at the piece of chicken and rice on my plate.

"I don't have an account. But I check yours sometimes. I like to know what you're doing."

"Dad."

He puts his phone away and then digs into the chicken, chewing it with a question mark on his face. "It's not as nice as the New York chicken, is it?" he asks.

I stand up and carve myself another slice of the chicken. "Honestly?" I say. "This is pretty good."

We finish our dinner listening to the Eagles on the radio. After I wash the dishes and set the roasting pan to soak in the sink, I pack the leftover chicken and sprouts in an enormous Tupperware and stick it in the very back of the fridge, where it will be forgotten until it starts to smell, so my dad doesn't feel guilty about eventually throwing it away. I think about how glad I am that Ben didn't have to eat this meal, or that I didn't have to watch him pretend to like it.

CHAPTER 15

The pork buns my mother hands me in the waiting room have clotted into one mass in the plastic container, and I consider refusing them altogether. It was still dark when we got up to drive my dad to the hospital, and none of us bothered to eat breakfast—my dad because of medical protocol, and my mother and I not so much out of solidarity as from our shared neurosis about being late. Once my dad was admitted—he looked almost happy to be surrounded by the crisp, clean order of the hospital; this was a man who trusted American science with his life—my mother produced containers of buns she must have packed last night. I accept mine but am skeptical about how long they've been sitting at room temperature. My mother doesn't seem to care, and she wordlessly gnaws on one while answering WeChat messages, unaware that the pinging notifications are grating on the nerves of everyone else in the waiting room. When she gets up to use the restroom, I reach over and turn the sound off on her phone.

"I'm going to try to find a microwave," I say when she comes back, holding up my container of buns. Maybe I can nuke any potential salmonella out of them. Besides, without Ben or my dad around, I'm uneasy about spending even a couple of hours alone with her, especially after our fight on Christmas. She shrugs at me without looking up from her phone, which feels like a neutral and therefore overall good sign. Whatever she thinks of our fight, or how I've been avoiding her for the past four days, at least she's not giving me the total silent treatment anymore. She even used her regular voice to ask me to fill out the intake paperwork when we first arrived. It's possible she's decided to forgive me, or to pretend the screaming never happened. Sometimes my mother did that—just magically decided to get over things—and we could go years before one of us re-excavated the original issue. After the time I hit a deer with my new Acura, it took her weeks to even acknowledge that I was in the same room as her until I came home from school to find her making baozi in the kitchen. She waved me over and handed me a rolling pin, already floured, and that was it, until my birthday rolled around and I was told there wouldn't be a party: a punishment that was only 365 days delayed. We were learning about the New Testament in youth group that year, and I remember being annoyed that even God seemed to get over things faster than my mother. As hard as I tried to guess the inner workings of her disappointment, I usually just had to wait until she decided things were fine again.

I pick a hallway and start walking in search of a microwave. It's pointless to resent my mother for the fight when I have only a few more days left in Hickory Grove. Soon, I'd return to New York and my mother would recede to the voice on the phone who didn't understand my life and didn't want to. Christ. What would it be like to have the kind of mother in whom I could confide about how mortifying it was to confront Kyle yesterday, or how indifferent I feel hearing Ben leave all these voicemails on my phone, his voice sounding harried but excited. It's surreal to know he's somehow having *fun* in LA, trekking around with the firefighter unit he got embedded with and somehow looking handsome in the picture he posted on Twitter last night with his face all smudged with soot. The photos he took of the damage in Calabasas were everywhere yesterday; I even saw one flash by when my dad was watching the news. But, much like the wishfulness I'd felt cooking with my dad last night, I know this fantasy would require a rewiring of our entire family. If I want to tell my mother how I felt about Kyle and Ben, I'd have to tell her so many other things first, and I'd have to know things about her, too. Like what it must have been like to leave *her* hometown—and her entire home country—behind and forfeit a lifetime's worth of unrequited crushes and complicated friendships and sense of belonging. What did that choice feel like, and would she have done it like this, if she could do it all over again? But what language would this imaginary conversation even happen in? Because it isn't as if I have the grammar for this strain of rootless shame in Mandarin, and she definitely wouldn't understand it in English. And besides, if we had that kind of relationship, we probably wouldn't be here in this hospital in the first place, waiting for the doctors to explain how stress burned all these holes through my dad's stomach lining. It was like what I told Kyle at Detweiller Park yesterday: Everything could have been different.

Still on the hunt for a microwave, I veer down another linoleum-tiled hallway and accidentally lock eyes with a passing doctor, who's wearing a surgical mask and removing her gloves. I find myself a little surprised that she looks Asian, vaguely Chinese, even. She's wearing a white coat and stops and nods, a kind of code for the two of us acknowledging each other in this midsized hospital in a midsized city in a midsized state. *Blink once if you're what I think you are,* I want to say, wondering if this was how my mother felt whenever she'd see another Asian person in Hickory Grove, too. Instead I explain that I'm searching for a microwave and hold up my Tupperware by way of explanation. She glances at the buns and points down the hallway, jerking her fingers to the right.

Once I find the break room, I watch the container of buns spin inside the spattered microwave and check my reflection in the screen of my phone, where I'm monitoring the massive breakout I woke up to this morning, as if even my skin wants to revert to its teenage days, too. At the edge of my hairline, there's a streak of my mother's Pond's left over from where I'd slathered it on in my hurry to get downstairs this morning, and I wipe it away. I study the break room bulletin board full of roommate notices typed in Comic Sans, a handwritten offer to teach guitar lessons, a NARCAN brochure, a fundraising flyer for the Alex Bentley Memorial Fund, which I force myself to read until the words begin to swim and lose meaning. I move my gaze over to the emergency charts pinned to the walls: There's one demonstrating the mechanics of CPR and another that gives instructions on how to prepare for a tornado drill. This last one kicks up a memory of being herded into the school bathrooms on the first Tuesday of every month so we could practice kneeling on the dirty tile floors and covering our heads, like that would have made any difference once chunks of cement started raining down. After we moved into the house on Newcastle, my parents hadn't understood why the siren was going off during our first storm that spring. I'd clutched the tornado safety printout the firefighters at school gave us and screamed for them to come into the basement with me—it was still unfurnished, all beams and cement—and I'd thought only to bring a blanket for myself. I recall watching my parents crouch on the bare concrete floor and hold hands tightly; it was maybe the only time in memory that I could remember them physically comforting each other. That was the hallmark of my childhood here, I realize, my parents' fear. There was so much to be scared of: tornados and kissing diseases and carcinogens and loud music and pain pills and not going to the right college and gun owners and the huddle of teens at the mall food court who were some of the only Black people my parents had really seen in their life outside of the TV screen. My parents lived their lives here so afraid of everything. Why on earth did I ever want to come back and be reminded of all that?

•

As I bite into one of the buns, testing the filling with my tongue to see if it's warmed up enough, my phone buzzes. It's Ben. After consulting the clock on the wall, I decide to pick up.

"Hey." His voice sounds tinny and marred by the static.

I should be happy to hear from him. It probably means something that he remembered the day of my dad's procedure, that even after everything that's happened, even after I haven't responded to a single one of his emails, he keeps trying. I manage a polite hi.

"How's your dad?"

"He's in there right now," I say. "We're just waiting around. Thanks for asking."

"I've been thinking about you. I want to make sure things are okay." I'm not sure if he means my dad or the entire status of our relationship. "*Are* things okay?" he presses.

I swallow. "My dad says it's ulcers."

"I mean with us."

I pretend to study the CPR charts and wonder when someone will come and kick me out for taking up space from people who actually have important things to do, like saving lives and not avoiding their mothers. I reach to fidget with my ring, and then I remember that I left it in my sweatpants last night while cooking with my dad. Ben repeats himself on the phone, as if he thinks I can't hear him.

"Yeah," I finally say. "We're fine."

"It doesn't sound like it."

I can picture the look on his face, the one he makes when he thinks we're getting ripped off at the flea market. I guess this is the moment to tell him about Kyle, but here? In this random hospital break room? I glance toward the door, trying to gauge if this is an appropriate time to drop a bomb like that over the phone. Ben is working hard to sound patient, and I realize he probably thinks I'm still mad at him about LA.

"I've been trying to give you space," he says. "But you know I had to be here. I mean, I got A1 in the *Times* yesterday."

"I'm happy for you."

"Come on. Be happy for *us*." He pauses. "We're a team."

Funny, I want to say. *I used to think so, too.* But then I remember how Kyle shook me awake Christmas morning and bite the inside of my cheek instead. I know I should find Ben's tone encouraging. It's clear he hasn't written things off even after I said all those things to him in my parents' kitchen, but I remind myself it's because he doesn't know everything yet.

"Look. Do you want to talk about things right now? I've got a few minutes. We're loading up the truck for the day."

I take another bite of the bun, hoping the sound of my chewing gives me plausible cover. I know I'm punishing him with my silence, which is pretty rich after being the one on the other end of it with my mother these past few days, but what does Ben want? To hash out a fight over a shitty connection while I'm standing in the middle of a hospital?

Ben sighs again. "Audrey, help me out here," he says, slightly annoyed now. "Is it just this? Or is there something else going on? You know I can never really tell with you."

This, I know, is the part where I confess to sleeping with another guy and then not telling him right away, and also probably apologize for subjecting Ben to Hickory Grove in the first place, but I can't make my mouth form the words. It shouldn't even count, I think suddenly. The Audrey who followed Kyle into the basement wasn't the real Audrey who's talking to her fiancé on the phone now. It would never happen again, and apparently, based on how terribly our afternoon at Detweiller Park went, I wouldn't be surprised if Kyle and I never spoke again. I hate how even as this thought crosses my mind, I want to throw the rest of my bun into the trash. Why the idea of a definitive end with Kyle nauseates me more than the inevitable blowup with Ben, whom I've built an actual entire life with, I don't want to know.

"I wish we could talk everything over, face-to-face," Ben says, as if prodding me to stick to some preordained script.

"Well," I say, "we can't. And that's not really my fault."

Now I can picture his annoyed face perfectly.

"I didn't say it was," he mumbles. "Come on, I'm trying here. I know I fucked up."

"I have to go," I lie. "My mom wants me to get lunch for her."

He emits a sigh so long I think about hanging up midway through. "Okay," Ben says. "Give her my love."

I'm still thinking about what a ridiculous thing that is to say, all things about my mother considered, as I find my way back to the waiting room and extend the other bun, warm and puffy, to my mom. She looks up at me in faint surprise and takes it. I check my phone, trying to ignore how fast my heart feels in my chest. I can't tell if it's from guilt for not telling Ben about Kyle, or if it's because talking to Ben again reminds me of our fight, and now I'm just angry.

"How much longer is it supposed to be?" I ask.

She shrugs, and I marvel irritably at how calm she seems in comparison. I would have thought that a hospital waiting room would encourage her neuroses to be on full display, her long-awaited nightmare of something going wrong finally come true.

"Ben says hi," I lie, to gauge her mood.

"You're talking to each other?"

"Yeah."

"So things are fixed?"

I fit the lid back over the empty plastic container. "I don't know."

"Well," she says, "maybe for the best. You're not ready for marriage anyway."

I give her a look. "Okay. So now you *don't* want me to stay with Ben. It would be great if you could make up your mind."

"*Aiya,*" she says sharply, the word as natural as an exhale, as if I'm getting on her nerves now. I glance around the waiting room, trying to see if anyone can overhear our conversation, conducted half in English and half in Mandarin, as if it matters. "If you want to be married, be married," she says. "I'm done caring, honestly. Do whatever it is you think you want."

I'm fully irritated now, but I can't keep standing in front of her, so I sit one chair away as if it physically pains me to be next to my mother. The clock on the waiting room wall has barely moved. I stare resolutely straight ahead as my mom plays *Candy Crush,* as if she hasn't just devastated me in a few choice words, as usual. I wonder where the Asian doctor I passed in the hallway is and if she hates it here, too. Then I think about what I'm eventually going to have to say to Ben, if it's possible that even when he finds out about Kyle, once we're back in New York and have the time and energy and ability to hash things out without the general suffocating effect of Hickory Grove, things could still work out. My mother seemed set in her assessment, but maybe I was being melodramatic—and too harsh with Ben on the phone. All he ever wanted was for me to tell him the full story. I hadn't been very good at it.

"You know, if it were up to me, I wouldn't have introduced you to Ben. We wouldn't have come here," I say finally to my mother in a low voice, staring straight ahead. If she hears me, she gives no indication. I try again: "You never liked him, did you?"

"I expected better."

I swallow. At least it's out there now, her blatant disapproval.

"Well, I guess you'll get your wish," I manage to mumble. "We might break up and then I'll be miserable forever like you." At this, she says nothing.

Just then, a graying doctor enters the waiting room and makes a beeline for me and my mother without hesitation. It helps being the only Asian family in the room.

"Mrs. Zhou?"

I cringe slightly at the way he pronounces it, *Mrs. Zoo,* like she's a nursery rhyme character. It's okay when Kyle and his mother say it, but I realize I hate how it sounds in anyone else's mouth. My mother nods and stands up effortfully straight.

"I have news about your husband."

I hear the words as if they're coming through a thick fog. Later, I realize I can't remember exactly what he said, and that it's only my mother's habit of relitigating conversations over and over that will help me feel rooted to this moment. I watch as the doctor explains to my mother the reason for the delay, that they had to take my father to get an abdominal CT. And the reason he needed a CT was because, during the endoscopy, amid the ulcers punctuating the lining of his stomach, they'd found a mass, immovable and obvious. It's early stage, it's localized, it's treatable, he assures us repeatedly.

My father probably will not die, at least not for years. My mother's face has gone white, but she says nothing.

"There are a lot of options now," the doctor says, glancing at me skeptically when my mother doesn't seem to react at first. He says more things about making an appointment to go over a treatment plan, and I watch my mother's hands shake as she taps on her phone, the app she has that converts pinyin to the full Mandarin symbols freezing at all the wrong times as the doctor speaks, which annoys him.

"She's taking notes," I hear myself saying through the fog.

The doctor turns to me. "Do *you* understand what I'm saying?" I hold my jaw carefully when I say yes. He checks the watch on his wrist and then sighs. "Well, we caught it early," he reminds us. "You people got lucky."

We're allowed to see my father in the outpatient room, where he is sitting on the edge of his bed and putting his socks on. He looks normal, possibly even more upbeat than usual. I find myself holding on to the edge of the doorframe. How is it possible? Ben's grandmother died of breast cancer the year before, but she was ninety. My father is only midway through his fifties. My mother surveys him with her hands on her hips. I wonder if this news has moved her. Instead, she makes a remark about how clean the room is.

"Hospitals have to be," my dad says admiringly, and I imagine that to both of them, rooms like this remain something of a marvel, everything fitted out for a specific function, scrubbed assiduously clean the way white people facilities always are.

I move over and sit beside my dad on the bed, asking weakly how he's feeling. He shrugs, and in that moment I think about how funny it is that he and my mother both resort to the same tic when they have no words. Maybe it's simpler than trying to root out the specific English phrase for it, or because they don't see the point of putting words to a feeling when we all understand already.

"I always told you to eat less red meat," my mother says, acknowledging the elephant in the room. I glare at my mother, shocked that she would just bring it up like that, but my dad only nods mindlessly, as if he's a schoolkid who knows what he's done.

"Jesus Christ, Mom," I say. "Really?"

She glances at me. "It's true. I have been telling him for years. See what happens when you don't listen to me?"

I ball up my fists. "Are you really blaming Dad for getting cancer?"

My mother wheels around and looks at me. "Do you know why we're here *now*? This idiot kept putting his endoscopy off because he kept trying to get you to come home. He wanted you to be here."

"So it's my fault?" I meet her eyes for the first time all day. Even though I know she's scared, I want to take her by the shoulders and shake her. "What the fuck, Mom?"

"Audrey." My dad raises his hand. For a second I can see the exhaustion flash in his face, and I move to touch his shoulder, a show of solidarity. But he shrugs it off and finishes putting on his shoes and gets up.

I stare at my mother. "You're unbelievable. Who says that?"

"You're so sensitive," she snaps. "Of course I can say these things. I'm his wife. *I'm* the one who's going to take care of him."

"Why does it always have to be someone's fault, Mom? People get cancer all the time. People *die* all the time," I add, then pause for a millisecond as I squeeze the back of my teeth together and let that word wash over me, like if I say it out loud like this, then by the logic of the universe, it won't happen. "It doesn't always have to be for a reason. Sometimes things just happen, okay?"

My mother's hands shake again as she looks away, and then my dad says quietly but with gruff finality, "That's enough."

In the car ride home, my parents are silent. My dad sits in the passenger seat next to me as I drive the family SUV. None of us speak, and I feel whatever was left of my nerves fraying as I speed down the highway back to Hickory Grove. I keep glancing at my phone, and I realize I'm waiting for Kyle to intuit that something's gone wrong again, for him to scoop me up in his Camry and ferry me to a place where I don't have to think about all this. What a pathetic thought. I need to get a grip. So instead, I think about what this means, how even I know the rules for what a good Chinese daughter does next. How else will my parents manage the paperwork alone, much less the endless mediation between themselves and the hospital and the insurance people and the doctors who talk too fast for them to write everything down already? If my dad wanted me home for moral support during a basic endoscopy, what will he need now that he actually has cancer? When I woke up this morning, I reminded myself that I had only a few days left in Hickory Grove. I was so close to being free of this place. And now this. I know my mother is right: There is a part of this that's my fault. If I had come home earlier, maybe we would have caught the cancer even sooner.

"Aiya, Audrey," my mother snaps from the back seat. "You're going way too fast."

I look down and realize I'm almost up to ninety an hour. When we get to the house, my mom goes inside first and says she's going to make tea. My dad lingers, and I hold the door open for him while waiting for the garage door to roll shut.

"You don't have to worry," he says, putting his hand heavily on my shoulder like I'm the one who needs to be comforted. "I'm going to be fine."

This, I know, is one of those moments when, if I end up without a father in the next few years, I'll regret not having said anything, not even a *You know I love you* at least. He nods at me, like he knows I'm studying the coffee brown of his irises, the sunspots on his face, the patchy eyebrows that were passed down to me before I spent years plucking them away. I think about saying, *I know,* or *You're going to be okay, Dad.* Instead, I back away and go inside, every bone inside me crumbling with shame.

CHAPTER 16

The road to Sullivan's has been completely cleared of snow. As I skirt around potholes on Alta Lane, I reach for the radio but then stop. I can't tell if it's because I like the quiet of the car, or if I'm punishing myself, like there's something profane about the idea of tuning in to the Top 40 on such an awful day. It's the former, I decide. I should enjoy the silence while I can, before I go back to New York, where even the sidewalk chatter through the bedroom window always woke me or implanted strange, talkative dreams. That's *if* I ever get back to New York, which—now that my stay in Hickory Grove has been extended a second time—feels like a real question mark.

After my parents and I got home from the hospital this morning, I moved my flight back again and then emailed Ted about using the rest of my PTO, though I still wasn't sure what I would do with the extra days here. It isn't like my dad is suddenly visibly more cancer-ridden than before we got his diagnosis, but it felt like the right thing to stay in Hickory Grove through the first few days of January. Plus, the sooner I get back to New York, the sooner I'll have to face Ben now that the LA fires are finally under control. I don't think I'm ready for the follow-up to our lukewarm hospital phone conversation just yet. I'd replayed it over in my head all afternoon when I was doing laundry, barely remembering to check the pocket of my sweatpants for Ben's ring and plunking it back on my finger.

The parking lot for Sullivan's is nearly empty. I'd thought about calling Kyle when the idea first came to me, once I found myself veering in the direction of the bar on my drive after a particularly wordless dinner with my parents. But considering how awkwardly he and I had left things when he dropped me off yesterday, I doubt Kyle would have even picked up the phone.

Inside, I take a quick scan to make sure there aren't any obvious racists at the bar and that Kyle isn't magically waiting for me at a corner table. There are a few college kids in the back talking loudly about their various acronymed extracurriculars and a pregnant woman sitting at the bar with her coat draped on the stool next to her. She needs a trim for those split ends, I think as I situate myself a few seats down from her and order a Blue Moon. Then I turn around and my eyes widen. It's Kristen.

"You've got to be kidding me."

I don't realize I've said this out loud until Kristen looks over and makes eye contact, and for a minute, I think we're both going to burst out laughing at how inevitable this was. For a second, I'm almost happy to see her—the shock of seeing her is blunted by how badly I want to tell her about my dad and ask her what I should do, because it has to be some kind of sign to see her of all people here tonight—but then I remember our encounter in the Eastwoods bathroom and the fact that she still hates my guts.

"Sorry. I've just— I've had a long day. Please don't leave. I'll go," I say quickly when Kristen glances at her coat.

Kristen sighs. She has a Pepsi and a glass of ice in front of her, and I watch as she dumps the rest of the soda into the glass, stirring it vigorously like she's approximating the experience of a cocktail. I can tell she's annoyed and considering whether she should stay, but at least we're not stuck in a megachurch bathroom staring at each other. With both of us at the bar, the horizontal look we're giving each other is far less confrontational.

"It really threw me to see you out of the blue like that," Kristen says finally. "Back at Eastwoods."

"Yeah. I know." I gingerly slide one seat closer to her, as a test to see if she recoils, but Kristen takes a long sip from her soda and peers at my engagement ring without a word.

"I didn't think you'd still be in town after Christmas," she adds.

"Trust me, I wasn't planning on it." I use the pause that follows this wary consensus as an excuse to study my old best friend in full. The Kristen I remember was long and lean with a tangle of strawberry-blond hair she militantly straightened every morning before school. Now her hair has been cut into a soft pixie and is tucked partially in the hood of her sweatshirt, which she wears zipped to her chest to let the lace edge of a turquoise cami peek out. The obvious roundness of her body seems to exact its own gravitational pull between us.

"Well." I clear my throat. "Congratulations?" I can't tell if Kristen actually seems open to talking or if she's just barely tolerating me here. To test the waters further, I ask when she's due.

"End of May."

"Wow. Soon."

"Yeah." She drums her fingers on the bar, then hesitates for an excruciating minute before saying, "My mom wanted to invite you to the shower."

"Sure. When is it?"

"Well, it *was* last fall."

Christ. I should have let Kristen leave. What did I honestly think I had to say to her?

"I figured, what was the point?" Kristen adds. "Since you didn't come to my wedding. Or Alex's funeral. Or the reunion."

I'm frowning now. "There was a reunion?"

"It was just a five-year thing. Everyone was in town for the funeral anyway." She takes a long exhale. "It helped make things not totally depressing."

"I didn't know about that." I want to add that I didn't even know about Alex's death until a few nights ago.

"Kyle and Nicole planned the whole thing," Kristen says of the reunion. I don't want to admit how much I hate picturing the two of them conspiring together, likely over beers at Sullivan's, too, for any reason. "Kyle didn't tell you?"

"No."

Kristen looks like she wants to say something else about him, but then she shakes her head.

"I wish *you* would have told me," I say in what I hope is a peaceable voice. "I probably would have come."

She gives me a hard glance. "Yeah. Probably."

"I've just been . . ." I trail off and know there isn't a kind way to finish this sentence. I can't say I've been busy, even though that's technically true. "Out of the loop," I finish stiffly. "I'm in New York now."

At this, Kristen rolls her eyes. "I know," she says. "Trust me, we all know."

"What's that supposed to mean?"

"You say it like it's some planet I've never heard of." Kristen's mouth turns up as she says this. "And it's not exactly news, either. We literally all know the great Audrey Zhou made it to New York. My mom brings it up every time we watch *Friends*."

"Well, New York is great," I manage to say while disguising my annoyance. Why did Kristen have to make this so confrontational? If she knew what this day—or even the entire past week—had been like for me, she wouldn't be acting like this. "You should visit," I add.

At this, Kristen snorts and orders another Pepsi, and then turns to face me. "Visit New York, or visit you?" she asks as she cracks into her soda.

"Both?"

"We haven't spoken since college, Audrey."

"Yeah, but . . ." I falter. "You'd like the city."

She scrunches up her face a little and says she doesn't think so. The hostility is tangible now, and I shift in my seat, glancing around the bar to see if people can tell what a terrible reunion is unfolding.

"Look," I say finally, "I'm sorry we didn't keep in touch." I know it's half-assed, but I hope that it clears the air without having to dredge up the memory of when she drove up to Chicago to surprise me for my birthday and I'd laughed at her in front of my new friends, though now, of course, all I can think of is Kristen stuffing her wizard costume back in her trunk, somehow managing to cry and yell at me at the same time. "And I'm sorry I couldn't come to your wedding," I add, thinking of the Vitamix I'd ordered online to send in my stead. "I had a work thing."

Kristen is rubbing her forehead with one hand. "Right. And you've had a work thing for everything else that happened in the last eight years, too, I guess." When I don't answer, she laughs darkly. "God," she says. "I wish you could hear yourself."

"Come on," I say, even though I can feel myself getting heated. "I'm trying here, Kris. I know I've been a shitty friend." When she says nothing back, I tell her I'm sorry about the wedding again. "But you can't blame me for, like, missing a reunion no one told me about," I add. "Or not coming home to visit. You of all people know how much I hated it here."

Kristen makes a face, like she doesn't believe me.

"You don't get it," I snap. "You had a normal family. And boyfriends. And you didn't look like"—I point at my face—"this."

For a minute, Kristen doesn't answer. It's a heavy enough pause to make me realize how wildly off course this entire night has gone. What happened to quietly nursing a beer for an hour before heading back home? Why couldn't I have simply said a polite hi to Kristen when I saw her, then turned around and left, knowing we'd only get into it if I stayed? What exactly is it that I think I'm accomplishing by sitting here and blaming Kristen for not despising high school as much as I did?

"I know it was hard for you," Kristen finally says. For a second, I think she's backing off, but then her brow furrows into a skeptical line. "But come on, Audrey. Growing up here was kind of terrible in general. You weren't so special."

I blink at this. "Excuse me?"

"There are a lot of fucked up things about this place," she says. "Like, last fall, *three* kids overdosed. A bunch of people's parents lost jobs when Caterpillar moved that big plant after the strike. Jesus, remember when everyone called that spot in the cafeteria where Ashley Davis and her friends sat 'the black hole'?" She sucks air through her teeth. "You weren't even here during the election. You haven't seen what it's like. You've been in New York, where, like, nothing actually changed."

The bartender has ducked into some back room to get more ice. I drill my eyes at the doorway, willing him to come back so I can pay for this stupid Blue Moon and leave. I'd been so relieved that Kristen seemed open to talking, but now all I want to do is get out of here.

"I know you hated it here," Kristen clarifies, her voice slightly softening. "I remember how badly we both wanted to get out."

"Yeah," I say. "And you left first, actually."

"Well, I didn't get very far, did I?"

I say nothing and tap the counter impatiently, waiting for the AWOL bartender.

"You know, Aud, when you moved to Chicago for school, I was happy for you. Even when you kept blowing me off," Kristen goes on. "And then you moved to New York. And I knew that's all you wanted, to be as far away as possible. You really did it." I don't know how I'm supposed to feel as she says all this. Being mad because she was mad was easier. Now Kristen appears lost in thought. "But then you didn't come back," she says. "And it made everyone, or, at least, it made *me* feel like you didn't want to have anything to do with us anymore. Like we were only ever a bunch of embarrassing hicks to you."

"That's not true."

She looks at me. "Are you close with *anyone* we grew up with?"

I've started peeling the label off the beer bottle with the edge of my thumbnail, and I pretend to focus on how chipped my nails are. I should tell Kristen about reconnecting with Kyle. But wouldn't that prove her point? I think about the bonfire at Kyle's and that first night at Sullivan's with everyone, how I'd assumed Nicole and Cameron and Luke and that whole gang had nothing to say to me because they never did back in high school, so why should I try to talk to *them* a decade later? Was it like what Kyle said in the car, when we were driving home in the snowstorm? Had I actually unknowingly headed off everything from Joe's crush to countless other potential connections out of a kind of preemptive dismissal, scared to leave myself unguarded from anyone who wasn't Kristen or Kyle? Had everyone I'd grown up with thought of me more as a snob than an outsider, and assumed I completed my bitchy character arc once I left Hickory Grove? Was it possible that they were right?

"You just cut everyone off, didn't you?" Kristen tilts her head. "I guess I'm relieved. I thought it was personal, you know." She exhales like she's taking a drag from an unseen cigarette. "Like, Jesus, Audrey. You were my *best* friend. I didn't think we would always live in the same place or do the same stuff, but like, when I tried to surprise you at college for that dumb convention, you *laughed* at me. And then you weren't even at my wedding. You sent me a blender, but you couldn't be bothered to come?"

"That was a long time ago," I say, thinking about the fight I had with Kyle at the sledding hill, how I'd said the same thing to him in order to minimize my feelings for him, and now I was repurposing it for this fight, or whatever this was, with Kristen.

"It still matters." She looks down now. "I knew you moved on from Hickory Grove, but I never thought you would move on from *me*."

"I had to, okay?" My chest tightens, and I dig my fingernails into my hands, willing myself not to take Kristen by the shoulders and shake her. "It wasn't you, Kris. It was this entire place, and my parents, and that whole fucked up thing with Kyle. I couldn't deal with all of that again." I can feel my voice wobbling, and I know I'm barely minutes away from turning into a total blubbering mess in front of Kristen. "I was finally getting happy," I say. "I got *engaged*. I came back only because Ben wanted to meet my parents, but then I run into you, and I run into Kyle, and of course *that* blew up in my face again."

The bartender emerges at last from the back room, and I dig

through my wallet, praying I have enough cash to leave for my beer so I don't have to finish this conversation with Kristen. But of course, I don't have a single bill on me. Kristen frowns and asks what I'm talking about. I can feel my face burning.

"What happened with Kyle?" she asks again, her voice like an extended palm. For a moment, I could have closed my eyes and easily imagined us in her minivan before school, mainlining gossip and gas station Frappuccinos until the last possible minute before we had to sling our backpacks on and get out. I tell her about Ben and the visit here and how it was supposed to be a quick week, until everything fell apart. When I tell her about running into Kyle at Walmart, and coming here to Sullivan's with him, and confiding in him at the bonfire, I realize this is who I've been wanting to talk to this entire time: not my dad, not my mother, not Zadie, but the one person in the world who could ever understand. I try to slow down as I describe how Kyle and I drove to his house during the snowstorm on Christmas Eve, and everything that came after, and I wait for Kristen's face to change, to see the proof that she, at least, gets it.

"Wow," Kristen says. She's finished her soda, and the tight line of her mouth isn't unkind. But then I realize she's barely holding back laughter. The only thing keeping me from fleeing out the door is the fact that I haven't paid for this stupid beer. Kristen begins shaking her head. "Tell me one thing," she says, smirking now. "Are you actually still in love with Kyle, or did you do it to, like, avoid something else?"

"It wasn't a big deal," I snap. "It just happened."

"Wow," she says again, exhaling in that long, resigned hiss. Somehow, she looks satisfied by this entire story, like it's finally solved a longtime mystery for her. "It's amazing. You really do sound exactly the same."

"Excuse me?"

"You're always so, like, 'things happen to me.'" Kristen shrugs. She shoves her hand in her purse and puts a twenty-dollar bill on the bar. It's enough to cover both our drinks two times over. "Poor me, living in New York. Poor me, I don't get along with my mom.

Poor me, I *kinda* slept with Kyle. This is classic you, and you know it. Kyle deserves better than that. He's the only person who thought you might show up to Alex's funeral. Like, he kept driving by your house to see if you were home. The rest of us knew better."

"Fuck you," I say, watching her slip her coat on and surprising even myself with the force of vitriol in my voice.

Kristen laughs. "There was a point when it would have gutted me to hear you say that. But you know what? We're all grown up now, Audrey. And if that's what you want to say to someone who knows you better than anyone else and will give it to you straight, then okay. Fuck you, too. I don't give a shit anymore."

"Obviously you do," I snap again, "or you wouldn't be running away from me again, like you did at Eastwoods."

"I'm not running away," Kristen says, zipping her coat up with a neat jerk. "I just know when it's time to go. There's a difference, Audrey."

She yanks a knit cap onto her head, and for a second, I can see flashes of the old Kristen, who used to wear that same cap in PE whenever we were forced outside to play flag football—something that I'd hated with this primal aversion that rose from deep within my brain stem, while Kristen loved nothing more. She'd never been afraid of a good brawl even then. She exits the bar and leaves me alone with the sticky scraps of the beer label left on the counter, which I brush into my pocket because I can't stand the thought of leaving evidence behind.

CHAPTER 17

Despite my suspicions that time itself might not escape Hickory Grove's deadening clutches, New Year's Eve finally rolls around. Since my dad's been home from the hospital, he's stayed in his room to catch up on sleep and, I assume, to consider the newly urgent fact of his mortality. But when I knock on his door, I find him sitting with his work laptop open clicking through articles about Fort Lauderdale real estate and cancer treatments. Apparently things are looking up in the grand scheme of both the American economy and medical innovation, he says. I don't know how to respond to this except by returning downstairs and bringing him a pot of tea. I ask if he's feeling okay, and he says he always feels tired this time of the year, that it's not a big deal. Then I leave to put in a few plodding miles on the treadmill at Gold's.

The torturous repetition feels good while I reconsider the four paragraphs I typed out on my phone instead of sleeping last night, part of what I imagined would be an apology note to send Kyle. Compared with my fallout with Kristen two days ago, the task of making up with him feels relatively straightforward—I just needed to get the phrasing right, really. But the more typos I catch now, as I walk off the last mile, the more pathetic this potential email sounds, so I delete the draft entirely and decide I'll start over later. Nicole was the easy one, a matter of spending yesterday morning down at the mall, waiting for the florist to open and consulting the Bentley address listed in the phone book I'd unearthed in the basement. I sent three bouquets: white roses for the long-ago funeral, yellow for friendship, pink because I remember Kyle telling me at prom that those were her favorite. *Sorry I wasn't there,* I scribbled on the card. It's cowardly to try making amends with both her and Kyle from a distance, but if I only have it in me to face one person before I leave Hickory Grove in a week, I know it has to be Kristen, who absolutely won't let an email or bunch of flowers stand in.

When I get home from the gym, someone's Chevy Impala is sitting in the driveway. I figure it's one of my mother's friends from church, dropping by for Bible study in order to get a head start on God's forgiveness for the year ahead. My mother pokes her head out into the garage as I park the car and waves me in.

"Where have you been?" she asks.

As I step around her into the house, I hear the snap of his camera shutter before I see Ben standing at the kitchen island. He puts his camera down and grins. Even though it looks like he hasn't slept or shaved in days, Ben manages to beam that perfect geometric smile when he sees me. "Happy New Year, Audrey," he says.

I'm too stunned to think about anything except how grimy I must look in the picture he just took. He always did like a surprise shot. I squint at my mother. She couldn't have sent a warning text?

"I thought you were still in LA," I blurt out.

Ben's face pinches for a second, but then he smooths it over as he explains how the fires were pretty much done now that the rainy season has begun, and besides, his editors said people were tired of hearing about the fire on the news.

"I flew in this morning," he explains. "Well, to Chicago. And then I got a car and drove down."

"Why?"

He sets his bag down, and now I know he's working to keep the smile on his face. "Because I wanted to spend New Year's Eve with you. Is that so insane?"

I can feel my gym clothes sticking to my back, and I want nothing more than to march upstairs and shower and possibly climb out my bedroom window. It's been two days since we talked on the phone at the hospital and a week since Ben left, but I thought I'd have more time to sort through my feelings before we spoke again.

"Um." I swallow and tell him I have to change, motioning to my clothes.

He holds up his hands in mock surrender and tells me to take my time. I dash up to my room, peeling everything off and replacing it with another sweatshirt and sweatpants from the laundry pile, neither of which smells all that inviting. I know I should be happy to see Ben, and I wait for my brain to knit together basic talking points for our conversation ahead. When I get downstairs, Ben's still standing at the kitchen island and holding his duffel bag. I glance at my mother in the living room. She has CCTV on, but the volume isn't turned up nearly loud enough to provide cover. I guess real-life drama bested any Beijing soap. I motion toward the front door, shrugging on my dad's parka that's hanging on the banister as we step outside. Sweat slides down my back. I begin walking down the Newcastle cul-de-sac briskly, and Ben follows.

"It must have been expensive to get a flight so last minute," I say.

"Points," he explains, like I knew he would.

Ben takes my hand, and I decide to let him hold it. It's obvious he's proud of himself for pulling off this grand gesture. I look at his face again and think about how exhausted he must be, and how much it means that he flew halfway across the country, and drove through all those cornfields and dead little towns after chasing fires around Los Angeles, just to be here. The physicality of Ben's presence is comforting and terrifying all at once, as if now he'll be able to read my thoughts as clearly as a Nasdaq ticker on my forehead. I used to like that about him, I remind myself. I tell Ben that he shouldn't have come all this way. "Again," I add.

"Well," he says, "I kind of have a present for you."

Ben stops and fishes his phone out of his pocket. There's a Band-Aid on the back of his hand—a burn, he says—and noticing it elicits a twinge of affection as I picture the week he must have had in LA, bushwhacking his way through apocalyptic fire and coming home to the station or wherever he'd been bunking to slap the bandage on and then still write those emails to me. So when Ben shows me an image of a familiar brownstone on his phone, I'm caught off guard.

"What's this?" I ask.

"It's our new home."

I blink. "What?" I yank the phone out of his hand and scroll through the listing. It's the Bed-Stuy apartment on Hancock, of course. The one we'd toured in August that Ben loved so much.

"I thought this was just a rental." I think back to when we'd toured the top floor, then remember Ben leaning in conspiratorially when the owners had mentioned they were thinking of selling. "Oh, Ben. You didn't."

"I saw they put the whole place up for sale when I was in LA, and I thought, you know, it was a sign." Ben beams now. "So I put in an offer. I wanted to keep it a surprise for when we got back to New York, but I felt like after everything that's happened, we needed a win." He says this like we're a sports team he's committed to rooting for.

"You bought the whole place," I say slowly, unsure if the cold is making me mis-hear things.

"Yeah." Ben grins and squeezes my hand. I have to work to untangle our fingers. "My parents wired the money and everything. So it's pretty much set. We'll go back to New York to close."

I'm trying to concentrate on breathing through my nose. "You didn't tell me you were doing this," I say.

"Well, yeah. I wanted it to be a surprise."

"You bought a fucking brownstone, and you didn't tell me."

Ben holds his hand up, and I stare at the pitiful Band-Aid dangling off his knuckles. "Okay," he says. "I guess it does sound a little intense when you put it like that. But like, we looked at this one, remember? And we liked it?"

"*You* liked it."

Ben knits his eyebrows together. "Wait. But you didn't say anything. I thought—"

I can barely remember to breathe. "You're unbelievable."

"Hold on," Ben says. He's angry now. "How am I the bad guy here?"

"You really don't get it, do you?" I'm walking so quickly that Ben has to do a little jog to catch up. He puts a hand on my shoulder, and I jerk away. "You always do this," I hiss, not even trying to keep my voice down. "Everything is about you. *You* decide where we live and what we're going to do. You decide when you feel like leaving and then when you feel like showing up again." I'm so worked up that I'm waving my hands around as I say this, as if I'm trying to snatch something intangible from the air.

"You can't still be mad about LA."

I start laughing. "Are you hearing yourself? You're even deciding what I get to be mad at. Jesus, Ben. You're always like, 'Tell me what you think.' I *am* telling you. You're never interested in hearing it."

"It's not like you give me a lot to work with." Ben shakes his head in disgust. "I have to pull this insane grand gesture and fly here just to get you to even face me."

"I didn't ask you to do that."

"Yeah, that's kind of the point, Audrey. I had to be the one to come back and get you to talk."

"And who said I even want to go back to New York?"

Ben asks if I'm joking. We evaluate each other for a minute, and then I look back the way we came down Newcastle. Without taking my eyes off my parents' house, I tell Ben about the diagnosis and the hospital and the doctor who barely spent two minutes giving us the news. He touches my arm.

"Someone has to take care of my dad," I say finally. Ben stares at me like I've suddenly switched languages. He frowns and asks me how bad it is, and I shrug. "They said they caught it early."

"So it's not too bad."

I look at him. "It's not *good*."

Ben exhales through his nose. "Audrey, he's going to be fine," Ben says.

"And what if he's not?"

He shakes his head incredulously. "It could be years before he gets to that point."

"So what, I'm just supposed to live my life and then pencil in a weekend to fly back for the funeral?"

"I mean, kinda? That's what normal people do? What else are you going to do, give up everything and move back to the place you've been telling me you've hated your entire life?" Ben looks at me like he doesn't recognize me anymore. "Think about it," he says. "There are other options. You could visit more. Or your parents could move to New York. Mount Sinai's supposed to be the best, and you could take care of them better if they're nearby. Then they could have time with, like, grandkids, too."

"Are you serious right now?" I say.

"Why not, Audrey? It's not that crazy of an idea. It's definitely better than yours."

For a second, I let myself picture it: finding my parents a place in maybe Sunset Park or Flushing, where Mandarin was simply something else mixed into the air, maybe a nice apartment within walking distance of those little shops that served fresh jiaozi and hand-pulled noodles boiled just long enough to still stay chewy, the way my dad really likes. Surely it would be easier on them both just to have more people like them to talk to. Pros: My mother wouldn't have to make a game out of finding other Asians in the city; they'd be everywhere. They wouldn't have to worry about driving in the snow, or getting looked at funny at Applebee's, or being condescended to by white doctors in suburban hospital systems. I would take the 7 train to visit; on summer weekends, we could be one of those big, happy multigenerational families in Prospect Park, our future children running around Ben and me on a blanket while my mother unloaded congealed tubs of pork buns onto everyone. When Ben traveled out of town for the catastrophe du jour, I could take the kids to stay with their grandparents. When my dad's cancer got worse, I'd take a cab with him into the city, and we'd spend the day getting examined closely by world-class doctors, and maybe we'd even stop at the massage place in Chinatown and have Frank work on his shoulders, then swing by one of the trendy hot pot places on Mott Street for lunch afterward, if he can even still eat that kind of stuff anymore. If there was ever a place where the family I came from and the family I made myself could coexist, wouldn't it be New York City? Everything would be fine, and all I had to do was stay with Ben and let it happen. I could continue to have everything I ever wanted by staying with Ben and letting it all happen to me.

Then I think about how small this imaginary Flushing apartment would be, how my mother would miss her Eastwoods Bible study, how much my dad would miss golfing every weekend. Cons: They would have to give up their house and Whirlpool appliances to live in an apartment a fraction of the size. And what would they *do* in New York? They would hate the noise and the subways, the endless ambulances barreling down the street, the delivery boys whizzing by on their bikes, the daily negotiation with the elements and the landlords and the whims of strangers that it would all require. My parents uprooted their lives for me once, and I could not ask them to do it again. When I try to call back the image of the four of us together with these faceless children in Prospect Park, I can already feel the daydream slipping through my fingers, like a movie at the Angelika that I think I like while I'm watching but promptly forget the moment I step out of the theater. It's possible that together, bound by the partnership of practicality that they cemented into stone over the decades, my parents could pull it off. But if something happened to either one, how alienating it would be to be alone in a terrifying new place. A brief, adjacent thought of being left by myself with my mother for good brings me to tears.

"Audrey?"

Ben stops and wraps his arms around me in what he must imagine is a protective hug. I can feel my wet face getting chapped in the cold, but I don't bother to wipe it off. It'll make my bare hands colder anyway. He tries to kiss me on the side of my head, and I shrug him off almost upon reflex. In that moment I can feel the entire weight of my envy, knowing Ben could crisscross the globe a million times over and take all these exciting photos and live these infinite lives, and then return home via the same JFK terminal each time with the knowledge that everyone he loved lived concentrated on a single cluster of islands and always would. Ben would never know life any other way. I think I hate him for it.

"Audrey," Ben repeats. He looks at me with those huge blue eyes, and I can tell he's on the verge of tears, too. "What's going on? What aren't you telling me?"

I shake my head.

"If you really hate the place, we can figure it out. We can get the deposit back and everything." Ben rakes his hand through his hair. "Maybe I don't totally understand what's been going on, but I'm trying here. Can't you see that?"

I try to picture the Hancock place, filled with the trappings of our life. But I can only imagine where Ben's fixed speed will go, how his photography equipment will take up at least half the guest room, how I'd have to spend all my time pretending to appreciate all the extra space I never asked for. Ben was always going to do exactly what he wanted, wasn't he? He's always going to be the one lying on the massage table, making his contented little noises, while everyone else darts around making him comfortable. No wonder he's had to make a profession out of tracking down other people's discomfort to observe up close. I'm walking fast now as I wait for my heart to stop racing, for my mind to veer back to logic, for something to tell me that I'm hallucinating and making reckless, sleep-deprived decisions, but I think back to that park picnic fantasy and find that Ben's features feel fuzzy in my mind's eye, too, even though he's standing right here.

"Do you really think we can get our money back?"

"Well," he said quietly, "technically, it's my parents' money."

He says this to differentiate it from ours, I know, but the way he lingers on *my*—like he has to specify whose parents have their shit together and whose parents potentially never will—it makes me yank that stupid engagement ring off my finger at last. It comes off so smoothly that I imagine completing its trajectory and flinging the ring into the air, and how satisfying it would be to watch Ben's face as the great Stear family diamond sailed through the gray sky before disappearing forever on some nondescript bank of snow, in the most forgettable part of a state that barely anyone remembered to count in the first place. *This* fantasy I can see in such clarity that I have to check that the ring is actually in my fingers before I grab Ben's wrist and plant it in his palm. Ben looks at it uncomprehendingly, and then he turns to me.

"Audrey," Ben says now in a small voice. "You know we're good together."

"I'm sorry," I say now, barely whispering even though we're alone. There's no one else outside in the whole subdivision. "I don't think this is going to work."

Ben stares ahead at the street where it unfurls into another cul-de-sac. "Is this because of Kyle?" His voice is tight.

I sigh and watch my breath puff out and drift away from my face. Does it make a difference now, whether he knows the truth about Kyle? Ben's still standing within arm's reach, and I can see the tendons of his neck, the soft curls at the edges of his ears, the way his eyelashes slick together as he wipes at his face with his hand, pink from the cold. But all I can think about is the idea of Kyle sitting in his car at the foot of my driveway years ago, patiently waiting to drive me to youth group, or Sullivan's, or Alex Bentley's funeral.

"I wish it were that simple," I say.

We walk silently back to my parents' driveway, where Ben opens the door to the Impala and sits inside for a few minutes with his head in his hands. Afterward, he goes into the house to use the downstairs bathroom and then, without bothering to say goodbye to my parents, he backs his rental out of the driveway.

●

For almost an hour, I stay planted there on the porch, as if I'm waiting on—or maybe guarding against—Ben's return. But the street remains empty, and the only sound carried over by the wind from across the subdivision and the surrounding fields comes from the occasional engine sputtering along the highway in the distance, past a row of tidy silos. When the light starts to fade, I go inside and find my parents in front of my dad's laptop upstairs in the home office, like they've just finished a deep discussion. This surprises me so much that I wipe my face quickly, hoping they can't see that I've been crying. My dad gets up to go make tea in the kitchen, leaving my mother and me to observe each other carefully. I tell her that Ben has left. She shuts the laptop and sighs. I wait for my mother to demand an explanation, or at least for whatever cutting remark she's probably been preparing inside this whole time, but instead she tells me that I look cold and then gestures in the direction of her room. Her voice is softer than it's been since we got home from the hospital, possibly the entire time I've been home. "You should take a bath," she simply says.

The first-floor bedroom used to be my domain, too, back when I was a kid and my mother and I were close. I'd loved climbing onto her bed with my Barbies so I could pretend her floral comforter was the ornate carpet of their doll home. As I got older, though, my mother's room became more of a retreat for her from the rest of the house, and more like the Hague for me, a place I entered only to present myself for judgment. Over the past weeks at home, I haven't set foot in my mother's room aside from the morning I went in to borrow her Pond's. I'm too drained from my breakup with Ben now to protest her suggestion—or even to question this rare invitation back into her side of the house.

It's weird, padding across the plush white carpet of her room and shutting the door to the master bathroom behind me. I'd forgotten about the striped tile and the his-and-hers sinks, installed during that renovation my parents had undertaken when I was in middle school, maybe back when they still talked about their empty-nester years in terms of resale value and European cruises. But the Jacuzzi tub, which came with the house originally, is just as I remembered it: unused and completely occupied by a ninety-six-pack of toilet paper and my mother's drying rack. The dye running off her hand-washed Kohl's sweaters has left violent streaks of red and pink swirling into the drain, and she's draped used towels over the edge of the tub. It's possibly the most immigrant thing I've ever seen, the way this totem of leisure has been converted into something purely functional.

I move the toilet paper and the drying rack and locate Clorox under a sink to clean off the sweater dye and the mildew. The cold marble tile that my mother must have picked out herself from Menards during that renovation is covered in thick, fluffy rugs, so that I can walk between the sinks and the tub without ever actually having to touch the icy floor itself. What was the point of that? Above the toilet my mother has hung a small, framed picture of a lily, probably a stock image she liked so much that she'd never taken it out of the frame. I wait until the water is warm enough to submerge myself, and then I twist the hot water knob all the way to the right. As I lean my head back against the lip of the tub, I survey the rest of the bathroom. Someone has recently painted the walls a soft lilac; judging from the stray brush marks near the ceiling, I wonder if my mother did it herself. Stacked by the sinks are jars of extra Pond's cold cream and Bath & Body Works lotions in varying sizes, half from the gift basket I bought her for Christmas. I never ended up wrapping it after coming home from the mall that day; I'd pushed it toward her the night after my dad's procedure as listlessly as if I were bringing her Lactaid from the grocery store. From the tub, I study the way the various pastel containers have been carefully arranged on the sink counter, with all the labels facing out so that she can read them every time she washes her hands. The effect is neat and a little crushing, this order that my mother has imposed on her life even here. How precious, too, the undiluted *her*ness of my mother that embodied this sliver of space she claimed for herself, down to the bizarre arrangement of the rugs and mismatched pink hand towels and framed stock photos.

I steam myself in the bath until my entire body is red and splotchy. Sleepy from the heat, I manage to drain the tub and go upstairs for a cold shower. In my room, I put on the last clean T-shirt

I have left and then sort the dirty clothes piled onto the carpet into whites and darks. As I tug my hamper out from the back corner of my closet, I have to move the pile of notebooks and books I'd been digging through last week, and my hand closes around the corner of Kristen's copy of *The Prisoner of Azkaban.* This time, I flip through it more carefully. The purple ink she always used to write in the margins smears slightly toward the end, as if one of us had spilled water and left the book sitting in it too long, but I can make out the scrawled note on a page near the end, where Sirius Black flies off on the back of a hippogriff, escaping the school grounds for good. *Can't wait until this is us!!!* Kristen wrote.

After checking on my dad, who has gone to bed early, I go back downstairs to where my mother is in front of the TV, patiently shelling walnuts on the coffee table and watching a broadcast of the New Year's Eve celebration in Times Square. I get on the couch next to her and make sure my hair is wrapped tightly in its towel. As Ryan Seacrest's voice blares on the screen, I watch my mother out of the corner of my eye to gauge her oddly neutral mood. She could still be angry with me, but she hasn't said anything about Ben's surprise visit or the fact that I'm not wearing my ring anymore.

"Well," I say, "I broke up with Ben." It's jarring to hear my words aloud, and part of it makes me want to get in the car and drive after him. Now it's real.

My mother picks up the remote and turns down the volume. "I thought so."

"What do you mean?"

"I called him two days ago. I told him he should come back and try to work things out with you."

Of course she had. The nerve of Ben to not mention the real reason he flew back—somehow it doesn't surprise me at all. I ask my mother how she even got Ben's number, and she shrugs and says he'd given it to her at the Eastwoods show.

I frown. "I thought you hated him," I say.

"I never said that."

"You said you 'expected better.' What does that even mean?"

She sighs warily. "He cares a lot, doesn't he?"

"Yeah, he does."

"Mostly about himself."

I have to hold back a laugh. "Mom!"

"It's true!" she says indignantly. "I know he's a very exciting man. But I don't like all this last-minute travel. And a man builds a home. He doesn't ask his parents to buy it for him. Or for his girlfriend to pay for things while he *chases his dreams.*" This last part she says in English with derision.

"So why'd you even call him?"

"Well . . ." My mother shrugs, like it should be obvious. "I wasn't fair to you the other day. I know I said a lot of things." She's quiet now. "If I can't fix what happened between you and me, I thought I could at least try to fix you and Ben. Because now I don't know what's going to happen to your father. Neither of us will be around forever." Here, her voice breaks.

I reach over and rub her hand. "Mom, come on. Don't say that."

"I know you don't think much of my life, or what I wanted for you," she says now in a small voice. "But I don't want you to end up by yourself, either."

"I'll be fine, okay? I'm sorry for being mad."

My mother swallows and nods without looking at me.

"I shouldn't have said those awful things to you," I say finally. "You're just so hard on me sometimes. You always have been."

"It's because I didn't have a lot of choices like you, Audrey." She sighs now, almost as if she's impatient again. "And you have almost all of them. Is it so bad of me to want you to choose correctly?"

My mother glances over at me as the ball drops on the TV, the excitement of Ryan Seacrest and everyone packed sardine-style in Times Square muted by the remote control. A new year already in New York, but here in Hickory Grove, it's technically only eleven. There's still time.

CHAPTER 18

Because the Andersons' garage door is closed when I drive up, I remind myself not to be optimistic as I ring the doorbell. It's only a few days after New Year's, so it's possible no one's home, or that Kristen has already gone back to Iowa. But then the curtains behind the glass pane of the front door rustle, and I'm not sure if I'm relieved or disappointed to see her mom at the door, frowning in confusion. When I ask if Kristen's home, I wonder if Mrs. Anderson thinks it's funny, too, for us to be reenacting this once-routine scene like this.

"Oh, honey," she says. "I'm sorry, but she's not here."

I try not to look upset as I grip Kristen's paperback tighter in my hand.

"You should try the school," she suggests.

"The high school?"

"She's helping with that winter clinic they're doing for the varsity team. It usually goes for another hour or so."

I think back to when Ben and I sat in the high school parking lot on our first day in Hickory Grove, and we'd watched the girl with the bat bag running into the school. After thanking Mrs. Anderson, I return to my car and drive out to Hickory Grove High again, which only takes ten minutes. Still, I'm nervous that I'll somehow be late—or worse, that I'll have no idea what to do once I'm there. The school's front doors are unlocked, and I try not to think about how

Ben and I could have easily run into Kristen at the start of this entire trip, if only we'd stuck around in the parking lot a little longer that afternoon. But then we wouldn't have crossed paths with Kyle later at Walmart, which maybe meant my whole life would have stayed the same.

Inside, next to the principal's office, I have to stop for a minute as the smell of disinfectant, pencil eraser tips, and the warm insides of countless pairs of shoes overwhelms me. The office lights are off, and the only sound is the vague squeak of sneakers coming from the gym. I move down the main hall, past the trophy cases, past an eighty-inch TV screen cycling through a PowerPoint of semester announcements—a new addition—past the posters of green butcher paper whose corners are curling away from the wall, revealing the useless loops of masking tape underneath. The lights in the cafeteria are half dimmed, the tables folded like sandwiches and pushed against the wall. The double doors to the gym are on the other side, where I can hear someone shouting instructions. To the left is the hallway leading to the upperclassmen wing, where I know I could probably find my senior locker—and Kyle's—if I tried.

A whistle from behind the double doors jerks my attention back, and I cross the cafeteria and push my way into the gym instead. There's that warm shoe smell again, then the pounding of feet as a handful of teenage girls race from one end of the gym to the half-court line in a drill I vaguely remembered being called a "suicide." The short, gray-haired coach stands near the door, watching with approval, and then I spot Kristen at the other end of the court, lightly batting softballs from a bucket toward a line of a dozen other girls crouched down with their gloves. The door closes heavily behind me and causes everyone to turn their heads, but only for a second, though I notice Kristen's glance lingers longer than everyone else's before she turns her attention back to the line. I gingerly seat myself on a row of bleachers in the corner, pulling my knees up to my chest as I pretend to scan the state championship pennants and the beams of the ceiling before I look back at Kristen, who's demonstrating how to field a short hop. For the next half hour, I wait for someone to walk over and tell me to leave, but whether it was due to Kristen's unheard instruction or simply the force of their athletic concentration, no one pays me any attention until the very end, when the girls retreat to their respective Powerade bottles and Kristen starts picking up loose softballs and throwing them back into the bucket. I climb down the bleachers toward her.

"Here," I say. "Let me help."

Kristen eyes me skeptically, but I've already grabbed an empty bucket and head toward the other end of the gym, filling it steadily with satisfying thunks. The girls seem to gauge Kristen's silence as acceptance, and a few run over to help. When it's full, one of the taller ones, who's got strawberry-blond hair just like Kristen's, takes it off my hands and runs off to stash it in the utility closet. I help another girl wheel the pitching machine back behind the bleachers. Kristen stops to chat with the coach, but we're left alone in the gym before long, and she turns to me as she shakes her coat on, frowning slightly.

"So what, you're stalking me now?" she asks.

"Your mom said you'd be here." I hold up the copy of her old Harry Potter book. "Plus, I've been meaning to give this back for a while now."

Despite herself, Kristen's eyes widen and she holds her hand out for it. Like me, she flips through the pages and is clearly amused by the sight of her old handwriting. "Jesus," she murmurs, and then hugs the book to her chest in a motion that makes her seem fourteen again. "This was my favorite one."

"I know," I say. "I'm sorry it took me this long."

We both look at each other, and I dig my hands into my coat pockets in guilt.

"Everything you said at Sullivan's, it's all true," I say finally.

"Yeah?"

"Yeah."

"Well, that's a relief." Kristen raises an eyebrow. "I was thinking maybe I went a little overboard."

"Never." Then I jerk my thumb toward the door, hiking my bag up farther on my shoulder. I tell her I should go, and I'm hoping she'll stop me or that at least we can walk out to our cars together. But Kristen just nods and says that she has to finish up a few things even though, as we stand in the empty gym, it's clear that she's stalling. I decide that's okay.

"See you around," she says, and I say I sure hope so.

●

My parents are making dinner for my last night at home, a proper New Year dinner, they say, even though it's January 5. I can smell the broth for the hot pot all the way from my room: strong and beefy, with the faint prick of chili peppers. My mother told me this morning that I could invite friends. She's clearly feeling sorry for me about the whole breakup with Ben—I left my phone on the kitchen table once when we were having breakfast, and she'd seen the notifications for all ten voicemails I got from Ben after he landed back in New York, which I guess was the moment when he'd felt the need to exorcise an entire relationship's worth of anger and resentment in the space of a cab ride between JFK and our apartment. In his last message, he told me he was going to stay with his parents for a bit, as if warning me that he had better things to do than to wait around for me to come home.

The thought of returning to that apartment we'd so enthusiastically filled together with photogenic houseplants and self-consciously organized bookshelves fills me with dread. If the whole point of New York was being able to pay people to do everything you didn't want to do, then there had to be a service where someone else could move my things out and put them away in a storage unit and possibly light the storage unit on fire, no questions asked. I simply had to ask one of the interns at work for a referral, or Zadie, probably.

Yesterday, she and I spent a few hours on the phone, something we hadn't done properly in years. I kept waiting for Zadie to cut me off as I explained what happened with Ben, what happened with Kyle, and what might happen with my dad. It was usually like her to jump into problem-solving mode, but she stayed quiet on the line as I bumbled my way through the list of events. "*You* broke up with *him*?" she kept saying. I expected her to tell me it was a mistake, that no psychologically sound person would throw away a gift-wrapped brownstone, but instead she tells me we'll figure it out when I'm back. I feel comforted by her use of *we,* like Zadie and I are going through this terrible breakup together, and part of me wonders if she might even secretly be relieved. At least now she won't be the last one married.

But I can't think about that right now. In lieu of the apology note I never sent, I've invited Kyle to dinner tonight, and I keep glancing out my bedroom window in anticipation of when—or if—his car will appear. If he was surprised to hear from me on the phone last night, he didn't let on. "I didn't know you were still in town," Kyle had simply said. In a brighter voice, he pointed out that he'd never had dinner with my parents before and asked what he could bring. The Kyle call shouldn't have been that easy. Even I knew that. I'll have to say something to him tonight that can encompass everything I typed out and deleted over the past days. I want to think that our decades-long familiarity with each other means it doesn't really matter if we get mad or hold on to long-simmering resentments from high school, because at the end of the day, Kyle had been kind of right about what he said at the sledding hill the other day: We never actually owed each other all that much. But maybe it was also simply Kyle being Kyle, calm and measured and midwestern. He said he'd be here at six.

Calling up Kristen was much harder. While confronting her at the high school gym didn't go entirely as I planned, I felt emboldened by the fact that it hadn't totally failed, either. At least she'd spoken to me, right? Even so, I put it off until this morning, when, after an hour of staring pointedly at my phone, I punched in the seven digits I've had memorized since we were thirteen. It was possible Kristen's number had changed since the days when we'd text each other on our Motorola Razrs between class, and I held my breath during the three long rings it took before she picked up. "It's Audrey," I said immediately. I could hear her snorting.

"I know," she says. "I just saw you, like, two days ago."

"I didn't know if this was still your number."

"Well, it's me." There's a pause. "Thanks for coming by the clinic, by the way. And for giving my book back. I reread the whole thing last night." I could hear Kristen pacing over the phone. I remember how she used to do that when cell service was spotty in her room, forcing her to walk in circles around the same mythical patch of carpet that seemed to carry the best clarity.

"So listen," I finally said. "My parents are having this dinner. Sort of a belated New Year's thing. Do you, um, have any plans tonight?"

"You want me to have dinner with you and your family?"

"Yeah. And Kyle's coming."

She snickers. "Of course he is."

"It would mean a lot to me," I said, exhaling slowly like I'm trying not to scare her off. "I know I'm never going to make the last, like, decade up to you. But it was nice to see you the other day at the clinic. And I'm only in town for one more night. It feels right to have you over for dinner, after everything. My parents would really love to see you, too."

There's a pause, then a sigh. "You're lucky I'm too hormonal to hold a grudge right now."

A little before six, the doorbell chimes and I come downstairs to find Kristen standing on the porch, holding up a casserole dish in greeting and grimacing as I open the door.

"Think of this as eight years' worth of Christmas presents," she says dryly, though her mouth is turned into the beginnings of a smile. I sniff the dish, but I already know it's her mom's potatoes au gratin. She steers herself to the kitchen and says hi to my parents, who are soaking ribbons of kelp in bowls on the counter. Even though I'd briefed her on Kristen's pregnancy, my mother nearly drops to the floor in undisguised joy when she sees the baby bump. After sternly instructing Kristen to take a seat on the living room sofa, she scuttles around making a special tea that she says will help improve circulation and soften the cervix for labor. Kristen and I share a look.

Kyle arrives half an hour later, holding a bottle of wine and a bouquet of Gerbera daisies, both of which I know he must have picked up from the Walmart Supercenter. He's wearing his church clothes, and his face and neck have been carefully scraped smooth. I feel my stomach flip over out of habit. "Hey," he says, making no indication to step inside.

"Hi." I close my eyes a bit and take a deep breath. "Thanks for coming."

"I'm glad you called me." He extends the bouquet.

Besides the chat we'd had on the phone, Kyle and I haven't spoken since the afternoon we went to Detweiller Park, and after spending the past week distracting myself with watching my dad's action movie collection with him, driving around Hickory Grove trying to make sense of the new subdivisions, and going to the one theater in town and watching a terrible rom-com at three in the afternoon, and even a few times taking silent but not uncomfortable walks around the subdivision with my mother, the two of us bundled up in our goose-down parkas and swinging our arms in the same determined angles, I can admit now that it was ridiculous to not face him sooner. In the doorway, Kyle rocks on his feet, another habit I recognize from all the nights I spent watching him on the sidelines, waiting to be put in the game.

"Are we cool?" he asks finally. The fact that he's shaved makes him look almost eighteen again if I squint.

I exhale and say that we needed to talk at some point, but that I'm glad to see him. He bows his head knowledgeably.

"Also, I think Ben and I broke up," I say.

"Oh." Kyle blinks. "You *think,* or you *did*?"

"Sorry. I mean, we did." Bizarrely, I laugh. "It's funny to say it out loud."

"Are you okay?"

I nod. He kicks his sneakers off and gives me a careful smile as he comes inside and sets them against the doorway. Everyone else is already in the dining room: My mother and Kristen are sitting on one side of the extendable mahogany table, and Kyle slides in next to my dad on the other, which leaves the chairs at the front and end of the table open. I hesitate.

"You sit at the head," my mom prompts. "Guest of honor."

I pour generous glasses of wine for both Kyle and my dad, plus a splash in the mug that my mother holds out. For Kristen, I pour a Pepsi. My parents, to their credit, have managed an impressive spread. The hot pot has already started bubbling in the middle of the table, and my dad reaches over to turn the temperature dial down as he instructs Kyle and Kristen on the basics. We all take turns dropping our favorites in with little wire strainers: wood ear mushrooms, pale yellow soybean sticks, puffs of gluten, enormous handfuls of glass noodles and bok choy, and blocks of white tofu. I watch Kyle carefully dangle one of the slices of lamb my dad sliced up earlier this afternoon while the meat was still defrosting—the secret to getting the slivers paper thin—with the tine of his fork. There's no prayer, no symbolic "Let's eat." My mother simply plunges a ladle into the pot and asks Kyle to hand his plate over so she can spoon up fish balls for him.

My dad peers at Kristen's casserole. "What's this?" he asks, adding a massive spoonful to his bowl of rice and then turning to offer the dish back to her.

"Just some cheesy potatoes," Kristen says. She points to the glass noodles and asks my dad what they're called, gamely trying to repeat the Mandarin name when he says it patiently for her. A good sport to the end. I feel a surge of affection for her.

As we start eating, I can't keep myself from monitoring Kristen's and Kyle's reactions. It isn't like I know for sure that they've never had hot pot, though judging by Kyle's eagerness with the strainer, that seems likely. I'd forgotten this unease that I guess I must have always carried when it came to anyone eating my parents' cooking, a fear I'd forgotten about until Ben and I were here. This was different from taking my college friends to the nearby Szechuan place or going to a dim sum parlor on Mott Street with Ben. This was presenting a meal, and my home, and my parents by extension, for judgment: Here's what I've had all my life. Here's what it was like for me. I gird myself as I take my first bite, wondering if the broth might be too spicy, the lamb too tough, or the glass noodles too slippery because they aren't fully cooked through. But everything tastes hot and perfect, and I find myself eating carefully, like I want to remember how each bite feels on my tongue. Kyle's face is thoughtful as he tries to ladle a piece of mushroom onto his plate. It splatters everywhere, and we all laugh. For a second I think he's hamming it up a little too much, but then I realize that Kyle probably hasn't had a lot of meals like this since his parents' divorce.

My dad sighs and looks at the empty seat at the table. "I thought Ben would be here," he says.

Everyone else goes still. My mother glances at me in a way that she thinks is subtle.

"He had to leave for LA," I say casually. "Remember, Dad?"

He glances at my mother in a way that makes me realize she must have told him Ben would be back for New Year's, their little surprise. But of course, that was before I kicked him right back out. With a sinking feeling, I realize that despite all the extra good daughter behavior that I'd been putting on in the past few days, as if I could appeal to the moral conscience of the mass of unwelcome cells lining his stomach, I've forgotten to tell my dad about this one important development.

"Actually," I say, tossing a handful of gluten balls into the pot with feigned casualness. "Ben and I had a fight."

"Another one?" My dad is so disappointed that I wonder if marrying Ben wouldn't be so bad if it means I never have to see that look on my dad's face again.

"I don't think it's going to work out," I say.

"Sucks," Kyle chimes in, unhelpfully.

My dad asks me what I mean. I pause to chew through a particularly large piece of tofu as I decide just how much my dad needs to know about how my relationship dissolved from the pressure of a trip that technically had been his idea in the first place. "Ben and I have some things to figure out," I lie. It feels better to pretend there's still a semblance of hope, like it's only a matter of having the right conversation after everything. "I don't know if either of us could do long distance if I were to, like, move home."

My parents both raise their eyebrows now, the bubbling hot pot forgotten. A lone piece of lamb floats to the surface, quickly turning gray. "And why would you do that?" my dad asks.

I look around at them and then back at Kristen, whose brow has furrowed almost imperceptibly. Kyle, on the other hand, raises his eyebrows as if a game he's been watching on TV suddenly got interesting.

"I thought it might be good for you and Mom to have more help around the house," I say.

My dad switches to Mandarin. "Why would we need that? Why now?"

My mother pats his hand and gives him a steady look. She's surprised by this announcement, too, but she's quicker on the uptake. "Because of the cancer, Feng," she murmurs.

"Someone needs to help take care of you. Both of you." I nervously glance over at Kristen and Kyle, who I know aren't able to follow anything now that both my parents have stopped speaking in English.

"So that's what it takes," my dad says, a hard clip in his tone. "For you to come home, I just need to have cancer."

I can feel myself turning red. I can't decide if it's out of horror that Kyle and Kristen are witnessing this quasi-bilingual conversation, or if it's that this grand gesture I had been planning to reveal to my parents over the past few days is going over so badly.

"You should not move home, Audrey," my mother says. "We will be fine." She and my dad share a look.

"You're going to need my help," I insist. "Either I have to move home, or you guys have to move to New York. Which could be good, too. Then I could take care of you from there."

"We don't want to move to New York," my dad says dismissively in English, as if to underline the seriousness of the matter. For a second, I wonder if I've offended him, and I almost miss what he says next. "And you can't move back," he says impatiently. "Because we won't be here. *We're* moving."

I blink. "What?"

Kristen's and Kyle's heads are swiveling between my dad and me like they're watching a tennis match. My dad sits back in his chair.

"We were going to sell the house when I retired in a few years," he explains, less angrily and in English now. "Hearing you and Ben talk about moving got us thinking. And now, there's no reason to wait. I'm not going to live forever, so I'm tired of doing it somewhere so cold." He seems to look off into the middle distance, no doubt thinking about Florida, or Arizona, or one of the other places he's heard about from the elderly snowbirds who used to live in the neighborhood and retirement-track colleagues at work. Then he fishes a chili pepper out of the hot pot and bites into it, as if to illustrate his newly awakened verve.

"We were going to tell you tonight," my mother adds. She's smiling, I realize, and it's so foreign to see that it takes me another second to understand she's actually excited about this.

I feel the urge to laugh. It's unthinkable, the idea of my sick dad and my miserable mom taking off for sandy beaches, like runaway criminals or the leads of a rom-com for old white people. This is what they were plotting together while I was worrying myself into a frenzy this whole past week about how to be the responsible model daughter.

"Where are you going to go?" I say, almost meanly. "Dad, you're *sick*."

He waves his hand at my concern. "There's good hospitals everywhere in America. We'll go somewhere nice. I don't want to deal with shoveling the driveway and things like that anymore."

"You can just pay someone to do that. It's not a big deal. *I'll* pay for it."

My dad makes a face, as if the thought of hiring a stranger to help him take care of his own house is a deep affront.

"This is ridiculous," I say. I look to Kyle and Kristen for backup.

"My great-aunt loves it out in Destin," Kristen says softly.

"See?" my dad announces decisively. "Florida would be good. If I'm going to die in a few years, I want to spend them on a beach."

"Dad." I mean to say it firmly, in the tone of a teacher reprimanding a student for being inappropriate, but instead I force the air through my throat too hard and my voice cracks in front of the four most important people of my life. My mother says something about how they've already been in touch with a real estate agent, and how the property market in Hickory Grove has never been better since everyone wants in on the school district. They'll probably be able to sell the house by summer, my mother adds. A huge item on her list of pros, apparently. They could pay me back for the money I've sent them for the repairs and the renovations over the years, she says, and the thought of my parents wanting to settle up this imaginary account balance with me makes me physically queasy.

"We wanted you to get married at Eastwoods before we moved," my mother adds. "That's why I've been volunteering there so much. You get first pick of the good weekends that way. But I guess a wedding is, um"—she searches for the right English word—"tentative."

I want to ask them how much they've actually thought this through, and if they know how rich it is that they're the ones making an upsetting impulse decision after all this time, but as I watch my parents share a look between themselves, I realize the depth of their uneasy, yet ultimately unwavering, partnership has never been more of a mystery to me. Kyle, who has been quiet this whole time, comes to the realization before I do.

"Now you don't have to come back to Hickory Grove anymore," he chimes in. "For the holidays. Or for anything."

The smell of the food on the table suddenly feels unbearable. I push my chair back from the table as I feel myself sweating through my sweater.

"You're serious about this?" I ask. I'm addressing my mother.

"Why are you so upset?" she asks. "It's not like it's going to make a difference to you. Just fly to a different airport when you feel like visiting every eight years or whatever."

I get up, banging my knee against the table with a thud that makes my eyes water. I suck air in through my teeth furiously. My first instinct is to get the hell out of there, away from my parents, away from the sympathetic gazes of Kristen and Kyle and this fake dining room we never used unless we had someone to impress, and maybe entirely away from this house that I'd shoved into the furthest recesses of my brain but now can't bear the thought of never coming back to, much less the idea of an imaginary happy freckled white family moving in and tearing out the grungy carpet and probably sniggering at how everything smelled vaguely of fish sauce. My car keys are in my coat pocket, which is hanging on the stair banister. I could leave, easily. I could go for a drive and clear my head and be alone, instead of having to manage my reaction to all this in front of Kristen and Kyle, whose presence adds a uniquely humiliating dimension. They probably think I'm insane. Didn't I spend our teenage years telling them how badly I wanted to get out of Hickory Grove and leave it behind? Didn't I go through with it and spend all this time blustering about how happy I've been ever since? They must be so satisfied to know I'd never imagined not having a tether, however flimsy, leading back to this central place. Once my parents realize the final step in their American dream by absconding for some gated community in Fort Lauderdale, the line will be cut, and any trace our family was ever in Hickory Grove—that I was ever here—will be wiped from a town that was already barely a blot on the map. There would be no reason to make anyone fly out to O'Hare and then drive down to this small town in the middle of nowhere again simply so I could march them around empty football fields and parking lots in order to summon the meaning of my childhood here like I'd tried—and failed miserably—to do with Ben.

As I look around the room at the faces of my mother, my father, my best friend, and a guy I thought I would be in love with forever, I feel my panic rising. I was always trying to lose this place; I just hadn't realized what it would mean once I did. For all this to happen right as I self-destruct my life in New York, I think frantically, has to be the cruelest irony of all.

I'm barely able to mutter something about needing a minute before I back out of the dining room, darting straight up to the bathroom so I can yank off my sweater, which is damp with sweat. In the mirror, I can see that my makeup is caking, so I turn on the faucet and let the water run until it is lukewarm, and then I bend over the sink, cupping handfuls of water and splashing them against my face. The little travel-sized bottle of makeup remover that I brought is almost out. I unscrew the top and bang the bottle upside down against my palm until I get a decent gob, which I paw desperately on my face. There's almost a sick satisfaction to be had from how ridiculous I appear in the mirror, standing in a bra and jeans with my hair wet around the edges, eyes red and a rivulet of snot starting to run down my nose.

There's a knock at the door. I turn expecting to see my mother, but it's Kristen.

"Hey," she says. If she also thinks I look awful, she doesn't say anything.

I pretend to be busy rinsing the goop off my face, keeping my face half buried in the sink so I don't have to face her. When I can't stall any longer, I emerge from the sink and try to smile at her, like this is a totally normal night with the two of us together here in my bathroom, as if we're getting ready for a forgettable school function. Kristen hands me a towel to dry my face.

"What am I going to do?" I ask her. I want to think she knows I'm not just talking about my parents moving.

"You'll still have to come back, you know," she says, her voice practical as always. "They always need help with the winter clinic. Plus we have the ten-year reunion coming up. I'm not sending Kyle to spy on your house to see if you're around this time."

Incredibly, I start giggling. A mental image forms of Kristen and Kyle and everyone I've seen this week gathered at Sullivan's and drinking beer and playing flip cup well into our eighties. As if she can tell what I'm thinking about, Kristen now laughs, too, watching me dry my face. "Here," she says. "You missed a spot."

She takes the towel and dabs it at the bottom of my chin. It's incredible how she is pregnant and still manages to tower over me with that pitcher's height. I can smell the perfume she's wearing; it's not quite the same Victoria's Secret body spray she regularly doused both of us in throughout high school, but it feels exactly like Kristen to me. I find myself hugging her. She seems to be surprised for a moment, but then hugs me back.

"I know it's weird," she says. I'm not sure if she is talking about the strange fact of her belly bumping up against me, or the situation with my parents moving out of Hickory Grove, or the fact that we haven't spoken for almost a decade while we became full-grown adults with lives that remain largely question marks to each other, but we're standing here in my dingy bathroom, holding each other up all the same.

CHAPTER 19

By the time I go back downstairs with Kristen, everyone's finished eating, but they're still sitting at the table. Kyle is in deep discussion with my dad over the NFL playoffs, while my mother rubs a Clorox wipe against a soy sauce stain on the dining table. Both parents look up in thinly disguised relief as I reenter the room; Kyle gives me a wink. Wordlessly, my mother dials the hot pot back up so Kristen and I can polish off the remaining tofu and shrimp balls. As we eat, I'm reminded of the long afternoons Kristen and I spent as kids playing in her subdivision, back when there was so much construction that it seemed like a new house materialized on the block every other month. The part when the construction crew installed those rolls of fiberglass insulation, once the rough frame had taken shape, was our favorite. It turned the houses pink and fluffy, like real-life doll mansions. I imagine myself as one of those houses now as I line the beams of my ribs with my parents' soft, starchy cooking and Kristen's reheated potatoes.

Once we finish, my dad asks Kristen and Kyle if they want to stay over and watch a movie. There's a *Mission: Impossible* marathon on USA, he adds hopefully, but Kyle says he has to help Fran take down their Christmas lights. Kristen shakes her head nicely, too. I walk them out to the curb where they've parked, and Kristen gives me a goodbye squeeze as she balances her empty casserole dish in one hand. She doesn't allude to our reconciliation in the bathroom; she just tells me to call her soon and then lightly punches me in the shoulder to show that she means it. Kyle stands with me as we watch Kristen's Honda Civic pull away, then he opens the passenger door of his car in invitation. I hesitate but climb inside. As we both wait for Kyle's car to heat up, I watch him pull off his gloves and unzip his parka. I can feel where my hair is still wet from washing my face.

"So," Kyle says, "that was interesting."

I close my eyes and grimace. "I can't believe I put you through that."

"You know family stuff doesn't scare me."

I ask what his policy is on cancer stuff, and Kyle levels a gaze at me. "Shit," he says. "Tell me everything."

So I fill Kyle in on the parts of the dinner conversation that my parents conducted in Mandarin, and he listens with a grim furrowing of his brow. I thought volunteering to move home to help take care of things was the sacrifice my parents expected of me, I confess. I'd spent so much of the past years dreading a moment like this, when my parents inevitably called in my debt, when they reeled me back at last to where I actually belonged. It felt like a revelation to make the decision myself first. And even though I was only beginning to understand all the reasons why things with Ben would have never worked out, the timing of our breakup at least helped clear a potential return path to Hickory Grove. But it turns out that my parents have no use for my warped sense of duty. After all this time, they didn't actually want me back.

"And now everything is going to change. I might never be back in this house again." I make a face. "I'll be visiting them in, like, *Destin* or something."

Kyle laughs. "Florida's not so bad."

"What if it's a mistake?" I say. "Isn't it reckless for them to pick up and move right now?"

"I don't know. Isn't it cool they're starting a whole new life?"

"Yeah, but," and here I let out a frustrated sigh. "Parents aren't supposed to just leave."

"Trust me, I know."

We fall silent again, and I know Kyle's thinking about his dad.

"Did you mean it, though?" he asks finally. "That you would have moved home?"

I ask if that would have been crazy.

"No. I would have liked having you around."

"Yeah?"

He nods. "You know you can always come back to visit me, if you want. I'll be here."

"Forever?" Neither of us misses the edge of skepticism in my tone.

"For now, I think." Kyle shrugs and looks thoughtfully out to where a neighbor's Christmas lights are still blinking busily. "It's not so bad. Besides, things didn't really work out the one time I tried to leave, with college and everything."

My face reddens for the millionth time tonight, and I apologize now for hassling him at the sledding hill about dropping out of ISU. It was judgmental, I admit, and unfairly so. I'd been upset to think everyone—even my mother—had known about something that happened to Kyle except me, even after I'd been the one to build a firewall to screen out all things Kyle Weber in my life for years.

"If I'm being honest, I didn't want you to find out," Kyle says, and sighs. "Not before I got my life together. And then after a while, I figured you didn't want to hear from me at all."

"I was trying to get over you."

"I know."

"Clearly, it didn't work."

Kyle looks at me, dimples emerging. "Even though I'm not, like, a Ben?"

"Yeah, thank *god,*" I groan, and now we're both doubled over with laughter in spite of ourselves, as if the only way we can convey the full extent of the tangled feelings we still held about each other and the last few weeks and our past lives was through acknowledging the absurdity of sitting here with the engine running, both of us admitting a kind of submission to everything left unexpressed. I pull the sleeve of my sweater down to wipe my nose. Kyle hands me a Kleenex from his cupholder. How much time, I wonder now, did we spend like this as teenagers, staring out a windshield with nowhere to be, talking about the things we thought we wanted and the lives we thought we'd try out, and how much more would Kyle and I get to have? How many total hours was anyone allowed to spend like this, perfect and unguarded, insulated within the concaves of a familiar car like a starship escape pod sealed off from the rest of the galaxy? Would it really have made a difference if I was honest with Kyle that night at Detweiller Park when we both knew we were heading out into the world away from each other? Would we still be in his grown-up Camry laughing together, or would we be married with a split-level in one of those subdivisions off Radnor Road, fighting over mortgage payments and willful kids and regret? Or maybe we wouldn't be in each others' lives at all. I watch Kyle shake his head, smiling. Then he leans over, and I think for a second that he's going to kiss me, but then, instead, he tilts his head onto my shoulder. I can feel him exhale. And I lean my head on his in return. I want to tell him about making up with Kristen, about going back to the high school the other day, and how I could very nearly picture all of us walking down those old hallways. I want to tell him how I never thought I'd miss those years so much, and how I wasn't sure what on earth I was going to do once I leave Hickory Grove again and go back to New York. But I decide that I'll get to it another time. On the radio, a voice croons now about some other girl, some other boy, some lonelier small town. We watch a light dusting of snow drift ghostily and aimlessly through the air. Kyle and I stay until the song is over, and then I get out and we say goodbye and I walk back inside the house, listening to the purr of his car engine wane.

In the kitchen, my parents are murmuring to each other quietly in Mandarin. I start clearing the mess of used napkins and bones and dishes on the table. My mother comes into the dining room, drying her hands on a ripped half of a paper towel, then sets a plate down with an enormous grapefruit, which she begins peeling. I watch her work her thumbnail within the fruit segments to pry the pulp apart and leave the filmy white skins in a mound as she coaxes each section out in one piece. She was always good at leaving each section intact. Once she finishes, my mother slides the plate of pink peeled fruit over to me. She dries her hands on the rest of the paper towel and then folds it into a neat little square for use a third time later. I jab a leftover fork on the table into a glistening pink wedge and lift it to my mouth.

"It's not going to be easy taking care of Dad," I say.

"I know that," my mother says. "But you know, I wasn't there to take care of my parents in the end. So this feels fair."

I move my gaze to the lines on her face, the white baby hairs that she missed during her last dye job now curling at her temples. My dad comes into the dining room now with a packet of watermelon seeds; he pours a little pile of them for me on the table.

"Do you regret it?" I ask my mother. "Not being there for them?"

She shrugs. "No. It wasn't practical for me to fly home over and over. And I had you."

"Well, *I* don't have kids. Or a husband," I say.

"Aiya." She sighs. "What are you trying to prove? Your father and I aren't totally helpless, you know. We built this entire life here together." She looks at me. "You may not approve of our marriage or our life, or even the way we raised you. But it worked, didn't it? This was a good home, wasn't it?"

"Of course." I swallow. "I know that."

"Sometimes you don't act like it."

My dad speaks up now, though he's pretending to focus on cracking a particularly tricky seed. "We didn't only come here because we wanted you to have a fancy job in New York and an American husband," he says finally. "We wanted things for ourselves, too."

My mother nods.

"I'm going to be fine," my dad adds. "It's always you we're worried about."

"So what am I supposed to do now?"

My mother sucks at her teeth and makes a *tsk* sound, a sound I always thought she made when she was mad or annoyed, but now I realize it's just the sound she makes when she can't think of the right word to say. "Anything," she says, shaking her head at me like I'm never going to understand.

"That's not what you used to tell me."

"What would I say?"

"That I always had to be the best. Best grades, best job, best life."

She makes a *hmm* sound. "I wanted you to be afraid, I think. I wanted to teach you to hold on to things tightly, because you'll always be prepared that way. But I guess I scared you too much." Briefly, she buries her head in her hands. "When you left for college, and then New York, I thought it meant I got it all wrong," she says. "I still don't think I'll ever get used to you being so far away. I know it makes no sense. It's what *I* did to my family."

I bite into a forkful of grapefruit, the juice sour and sweet all at once running down my chin. We sit in the soft glow of our conversation until my dad notices the time and hustles us into the living room to catch Tom Cruise dangling off the side of a plane on TV. I watch my dad jab expertly at the remote to adjust the volume for me and leave the English subtitles on for my mother and himself. Then I go back to the kitchen to make us tea, and we sit on the couch, watching the American secret agents get themselves in and out of trouble, the stakes feeling pleasurably thrilling in the way things do when you know nothing bad can truly happen. Halfway through the movie, as Ethan Hunt dives into an underwater vault, I get back up to peel a grapefruit for my mother. It's late by the time we finish, so preoccupied are we with the reassuring dramatics of defeating the bad guys and saving your friends and keeping America safe.

●

In the morning, I get up early to meet the Hertz rep dropping off the rental for my drive back to O'Hare. In the kitchen, my mother is making a plate of tomato egg and warmed-over rice from last night, and we eat it quietly at the kitchen table with my dad.

"Are you going to be okay driving to the airport?" my mother wonders aloud, and my dad looks at me.

"I thought I was taking you back, Audrey."

"It's fine," I say. "I've got it."

"But I like driving you," he says stubbornly.

"Plus, Audrey, you know you're not so good at the interstates," my mother says quickly, then backpedals when I glance at her. We planned this together. "But I'm sure you can handle it," she amends.

"I'll go slow."

"Don't have the radio on too loud. It's distracting," my mother adds.

My dad nods along reluctantly. I clear the table and then go upstairs to get my bags, fitting them into the trunk of the hatchback, next to the American Action Classics DVD set he gave me for Christmas. As I scan my room one last time, like it's a hotel room that I know I'll never see again, the way my parents taught me to do whenever we left on a trip, I pull my phone out and take a picture of the room. Then I tuck my senior yearbook under my arm. My parents come out on the driveway as I stack the yearbook on top of my suitcase in the trunk, and the three of us stand there awkwardly in the cold. My mother is the first to shuffle over and give me a hug, which feels foreign and clumsy as she presses my head against her shoulder. When she pulls away, I'm startled to see that her eyes are red.

"I'll call as soon as I land," I say reflexively, afraid that if I acknowledge her emotion with mine, then we'll both be doomed, and then I'd really never leave. "I could come back for Easter, you know. Help pack things up."

"If you're not too busy with work," my mother says, and then pats my shoulder. "I will keep you updated on your father."

"You can tell me your stuff, too, you know."

She says okay, mostly to herself, and then steps back. I lean over to my dad, and we give each other a nervous little side squeeze, and I tell him I'll be back soon. He peeks over at my mother, who is preoccupied by her phone, and folds three twenty-dollar bills in my hand.

"Dad, I don't need this."

"Do something nice for yourself," he says gruffly. "Go see *Whacked*." I blink uncomprehendingly until I realize he's talking about *Wicked*. I squeeze his shoulder and then, at the last minute, give him a peck on the cheek.

"Okay, I'm going now," I say finally. I get in the car and back slowly out of the driveway, waving until I have to turn around in the cul-de-sac and nose my way out. My laundry hadn't dried completely before I packed everything, so I'm wearing an old University of Minnesota sweatshirt that my dad lent me and a pair of old jeans from my mom. Somehow, they actually fit.

The final snow last night has left the same floury dusting on each rooftop in Hickory Grove, but in the fields, stalks from last season's corn still manage to poke through. At my first stoplight, next to the Presbyterian church, I pause to adjust the rearview mirror and my seat. The quirks of the rental car make me suddenly and deeply miss my Acura. And then I'm on the highway, barreling across the Murray Baker Bridge over the gunmetal depths of the Illinois River, moving on through the neighboring towns and their main streets and their modest churches with the little steeples, the speed limit lowering to thirty to give me time to pick out the Civil War memorials and dive bars. What was it like to grow up here now, when at least things like cellphones and YouTube and the internet have gotten better? Maybe it helped to have more of those surfaces for echolocating your way into place even if it meant knowing how far away everything else really was. Sixty miles out, I see the ramp for I-55 and pull onto the six lanes of traffic that already heave with the new year's frenetic energy.

The trundle of the interstate soothes me in a way that reminds me of falling asleep in Zadie's first ground-floor apartment once when I was too drunk to find my way home, back when we were still at the start of our lives. Last night, after finishing the movie with my parents, she and I talked over the logistics of my return to New York. She offered to go over to Williamsburg and get the stuff I needed for a week from the apartment. What else was that spare key for all these years, she reminded me. On Ben, she pressed only once, gently. "You don't even want to try and talk to him?" she murmured over the phone. I said he was staying with Ann and Clement, which made Zadie content to snap that file closed. "Okay then," she said. "Come straight to my place. We'll have the couch set up for you." She had a cousin who was vacating a little studio in Alphabet City in the coming week, she added. I could stay there if I wanted, but—I could practically hear her making a face—it *was* Manhattan. It'd be something different. I told her I'd think about it.

The rental car has a satellite radio, and it takes a little trial and error before I figure out how to turn it off and go back to the regular FM stations. I hope I'm not yet too far out of range for the one that Kyle and I listened to last night, and I nervously move the dial in and out of the fuzzy static until I catch the end of some new song from the Killers. I let the station settle there until I start losing the signal and the static takes over, so I search for the next closest one and then let that, too, die out, as I drive farther north, leaving central Illinois behind at last after two and a half weeks.

An hour from O'Hare, I pull off at a rest stop to pee and get McDonald's. As I study the menu in line, I become aware of a family of five behind me. Even though I haven't fully turned around, before I tune in to the frequency of their dialect, I know they're Chinese, too. I glance at the three children begging for Happy Meals in a mix of English and Mandarin, while the woman at the register pecks in my order. Behind me, one of the kids rouses the other two in a coordinated tantrum. The clipped, harsh tone the mother deploys makes me sigh in recognition. My food comes out to be barely over five dollars. I pull out the twenties that my dad gave me from my pocket and then look back at the family again. To the cashier, I tilt my head in their direction with an unspoken request. The woman at the register shrugs, and I lay all three bills flat on the counter. She asks if I want change, and I shake my head and go to find a bathroom so I can wash my hands before the food is ready.

CHAPTER 20

The first time my mother and I talk after I've moved into my new place is also the first time we've ever video-chatted with each other. Apparently, one of my mother's Eastwoods friends showed her how to use FaceTime the week before, and she wants the practice. I resist the urge to assume it's because my mother wants to evaluate the apartment, along with the state of my eyebrows and post-move complexion, for herself. She just wants proof of life, I tell myself. Still, I give her plenty of advance warning about the size of Zadie's cousin's studio in Alphabet City and how it's pretty much one long rectangle where the only direct sunlight comes in from the two windows at the end looking out onto Avenue B. I don't mention the third pane in the bathroom, which faces a blank brick wall and may as well not even count; that was the only objectively depressing detail I didn't think I could explain away about the place.

"Well, I guess it's open concept," my mother says, squinting as I slowly pan my phone around the studio, and I'm so surprised by her joke that I startle a pigeon outside the good windows with my laugh. I tilt the screen up to show her what I thought was the apartment's most redeeming detail: a stamped tin ceiling held over from the building's original tenement days, according to the neighbor with the goldendoodle down the hall. I tell my mother that's the thing I love most about New York, the layers of history piled on top of one another and calcifying into a single creaky building. I can almost hear my mother shrugging on the phone. "What's a few hundred years," she sniffs. "You want history, you go to China. We have *dynasties.*" She asks for my new address and says she's going to mail me things for the apartment, as if she suspects I'm actually stranded somewhere in the wilderness instead of living within walking distance of Manhattan's newest Target. The signal is spotty enough that we eventually give up on video-chatting, but a new habit of calling my mother up on Sundays seems to stick.

A few weeks later, after a large box from Illinois appears in the building entryway, I'm on the phone with her as she fills me in on the church's latest Easter pageant preparations and this Fort Lauderdale community college program she'd been researching. The apartment is small enough that I can leave my phone on the kitchen counter and listen through my earbuds as I hunt for a pair of scissors. Even if the call quality isn't better than FaceTime, it makes our conversations easier, without the pressure of facing each other through an intermediating screen. I don't have to check the way I look when we speak, and it's kind of nice as I move around the studio, nudging picture frames and coasters into place, as if my mother is in the room with me. I ask her what she and my dad did for Lunar New Year earlier this week, and she says the variety show on CCTV was pretty good and that one of the presenters had been this white American guy who spoke Mandarin suspiciously well. I tell her Mandarin's so hot now, that everyone's learning it to become more employable. "So if you stuck with it, you'd be CEO of some place right now?" she quips. It's tempting to read into the potential judgment embedded in this comment, but I just snort and say that yeah, I'd *probably* be able to afford to have a separate bedroom then, at least.

Thanks to the overly zealous radiator hissing away in the corner, the apartment has gotten too warm, so I tug open a window at the end of the apartment to let the wet February air inside. If I was being honest, the place was growing on me, despite the jokes I made about it to my mom and the initial misgivings I had when Zadie first handed me the keys. Her cousin had signed the lease weeks ago, only to abandon it to move in with a new girlfriend. "Twenty-two-year-olds," Zadie explained with an eye roll, though we both later agreed aloud that maybe there was something enviable about such bald confidence. I hoped, at least, that taking over her cousin's studio would allow a little of it to rub off and imbue me with the bright-eyed energy of someone still game to let herself be cajoled into buying cat-sized bongs and spending countless hours wandering St. Mark's and waiting in line at windowless basement speakeasies that no one actually knew for sure existed. But I refused to go full bore back to my early twenties: the IKEA set that Zadie's cousin abandoned in the rush of love, for example, had to go. Selling that off piece by piece on Craigslist kept me occupied during the week, and then I'd spent weekends poking around antique shops for replacements, which felt exciting and foreign, since Ben was always the one with the taste and the luck for finding a wayward Eames chair on the curb or, more often, being the receptacle for his parents' castoffs.

When I finally got back to New York, Ben had left on another shoot already. I'd gone to the apartment to get the rest of my belongings, once with Zadie in tow and once by myself when I remembered the potted lily that I kept in the kitchen. I told myself Ben would have wanted me to have it; he always overwatered things anyway. A week later, his mother, Ann, called. She and I had never talked on the phone before, and I'd almost let her go to voicemail before picking up, wondering if I'd left something at their house from Thanksgiving. But she just launched into a convoluted allusion to the private battles she and Clement had waged over the decades, and then said gently that it wasn't too late. She was the one who told me Ben went through with closing on the Hancock brownstone. It did surprise me to hear he still wanted to buy the place—I wasn't even sure if he was making enough money to pay the maintenance fee, until I heard that one of his LA wildfire photos was a favorite for a Pulitzer this year, until I remembered that his parents were probably falling out of their overstuffed sectional to help him out. I told Ann it was nice of her to call and then hung up to go look for a reading chair.

"How's Dad?" I ask my mother now over the phone as I give up on my hunt for scissors and settle for a kitchen knife to open the box she's sent. I hear her call to my dad with a few rapid Mandarin syllables, and I hear the faint sound of my dad shouting hello from what sounded like across the living room.

My mother returns to the phone. "Did you hear that?"

"I did. He sounds good."

"He's doing well. We made an appointment for his gastrectomy for next month. The doctor says maybe that's all we need. He needs to rest for a while. And no more red meat."

"Better for the planet, you know."

"But *you* should keep eating red meat. For strength."

"Sure, Mom."

As I angle the knife under the packing tape, I can't help but chuckle at the dilapidated state of the package my mother has mailed me, which has been shipped in the same cardboard box that our family microwave came in back when we first moved to the house on Newcastle. After more than two decades languishing in my parents' basement, the container had evidently fulfilled its long-awaited usefulness my mother must have envisioned when she first saved it. The box is so unexpectedly heavy, though, that I have to brace the bottom with my knee when I pick it up, and when I peer inside, I see the edges of a stack of plates.

"You really didn't have to send me *dishes,*" I say. "I can get some myself, you know."

"But now you don't have to," she says, as if it were the most obvious thing in the world.

I open the top of the box carefully and lift out the plates, and I realize that they are my parents' nice plates, the ones that we ate on first when Ben and I had been there, then when we had that last dinner with Kyle and Kristen. "You sent me the good ones?" I ask.

She sounds proud of herself. "Of course. We're not really using them here."

I run my finger over the curved edges of a plate. There are eight in all, thick and laughably formal for someone surviving on takeout lo mein and samosas every night. But I remember how I've always liked the weight of them and the earnest blue swirls painted on from several lifetimes ago, before some rich white family bought them and used them and later set them out at a garage sale in Hickory Grove, before my mother snatched them up to mostly showcase in the dining room cabinet. And now they were here with me. I lift the plates out and glance at the bottom of the box, where I see the other reason for its weight: there's a sack of ruby-red grapefruits, slightly squashed from the plates.

"Mom," I groan. "They have grapefruit in New York, you know."

"For ninety-nine cents a pound? I don't think so."

"You're insane. You know that, right?"

"Plus, you said you didn't want me to send you a hong bao for Lunar New Year," she says. "So this seemed like the next best thing."

"I told you I'm too old for that anyway. That stuff's for kids."

"Kids *and* unmarried women."

We both fall silent. I haven't told my mother much about the official coda to the breakup, only that Ben and I tried to work things out one more time after he showed up at Zadie's door one night. We talked for half an hour over coffee at our go-to café, which had been rendered unrecognizable to us from a recent renovation, and that probably doomed the entire conversation to begin with. I'd agreed to talk mostly so I could offer to help pay the rent on our Bedford apartment for another month, but Ben said he had it covered and then gave me a manila envelope as some kind of goodbye present. It was stuffed with the photographs he'd taken in Hickory Grove: shots of my high school and the bristly gray cornfields and all the churches we'd driven past. There was a handful of portraits, too: of the girl from Panera, the drunken girls at Sullivan's who'd hit on him, and my parents. I didn't realize he had taken photos of them, too. There's one of my mother standing in the kitchen; he must have persuaded her to take it that morning when I slept in. She's staring directly at the camera with her arms crossed protectively, a dirty dish towel visible on her right. But the way Ben has her angled in the thin light of the December morning makes her look beautiful. And there's one of my dad, on the golf range, midswing; Ben has got the curve of my dad's form exactly right. There's the one family portrait Ben took, before we went to the Christmas show at Eastwoods, of the three of us standing tensely in the foyer. And there are ones of me, staring ahead in the driver's seat of my car, waiting impatiently at the Eastwoods Christmas extravaganza, sitting on a lawn chair deep in conversation with Kyle, both of our faces aglow from the bonfire. I didn't say anything when I saw that one, because I knew Ben saved it for last on purpose. The whole time, we talked like we were sorting out the details of a business arrangement. Ben spoke only into the foam of his latte. And then it was over, and we parted ways at the G train entrance. I was going to say something like *See you around,* out of habit, but then I heard the train coming and I dashed down the stairs instead, unwilling to wait the extra nine minutes for the next one.

"I know you wanted me to fix things with Ben," I say to my mother on the phone, lifting the sack of grapefruit out and giving one a squeeze. "I bet a wedding at Eastwoods would have been really nice."

"Well, the church isn't going anywhere. You have time," she snorts. "Like, what about Kyle?"

"*Now* you like him? I thought you said he was 'low quality.'"

"He was very polite at dinner. I've changed my mind."

Of course the grapefruit is perfectly ripe. I set the bag on the counter and decide I'll spend the afternoon learning how to peel one properly. "Well, I don't think it's like that with him."

"Still. Kyle's pretty nice-looking, at least."

"Mom!" I think briefly back to the text Kyle sent me a few days ago, about how he was going to try to come up to New York for the summer to visit, that maybe we could go to the Rockaways together. *Like in the Ramones song,* he added, and I felt two things from the pit of my chest all at once: first, the searing strength of my affection for Kyle, and then the absolute truth of the fact that he would never actually visit, that this would just be something we said to each other while our lives unspooled separately until we intersected again either by cosmic chance or my going back to Hickory Grove to help my parents pack up.

My mother is quiet for a moment. Then she says, "Well, your apartment is so small. No room for a man anyway."

I make a sound in agreement.

"Why is it called a 'studio' anyway?" my mother asks. "In China, we would call it a 'dorm.'"

I tell her I'll look it up later, because the actual reason is likely easier to explain than the more romantic one I've started assigning to the term myself, and how I thought it was almost profound that there was a single English word to describe a space for sleeping and working and everything in between, like the fact of life unfolding within three hundred square feet was something like creating a work of art itself. *That* I definitely didn't have the words for in Mandarin, though I wish I did.

Outside on the street, a car idles at a stoplight. Salsa music wafts up. A dog barks; I think it's the one down the hall, and I make a mental note to buy treats for it the next time I'm at the corner store. Someone above me shifts something heavy across the floor, and the radiator hisses villainously even as the brisk February air filters in through the window, rustling the crumpled pages of the *Peoria Journal Star* that my mother packed so carefully between each plate. I ball the paper up and throw it in the empty box I've designated as the recycling bin, reminding myself to swing by Target and get a proper one. A real twenty-eight-year-old should have one of those, I figure, turning over the fact of my birthday in a few days in my hands like a new find from furniture hunting that I don't quite know where to place. In another universe, I'd be celebrating my birthday in Brooklyn and preparing to move into that brownstone with Ben and worrying over sourdough crumb structure and gut health and the correct books *The Current* said everyone should be reading. This theoretical Audrey would be flipping through *Brides* and texting Zadie about centerpieces and wondering whether Ben's parents would think it was too lowbrow to have a karaoke machine at the wedding.

Instead, the real Audrey was here considering the molding grout of the bathroom and thinking back to the visit I made to the hardware store around the corner, where I saw a whole display of grout saws in the back, a scene that struck me as almost luxurious, to sell a knife with only one use. Now, it's reassuring to think someone else stood and stared at the same shower tile grime I had and decided to make this particular tool available for me to buy one February afternoon. Wasn't this country beautiful? I glance at my phone and finish setting the last plate in the cupboard, letting the lip of it nestle against the other seven comfortably and shutting the door. Things were coming along. On the counter are the photographs of Hickory Grove that Ben gave me, which will be the last things I need to hang up. The ones of my father and my mother will go by the door, I think, so I can see them every time I come home.

In anticipation of my lunch date with Zadie, I go to the bathroom to check that none of the poppyseeds from my morning bagel has gotten stuck in my teeth. "I have to go soon," I say to my mother on the phone. "I don't want to keep Zadie waiting."

"Okay, I'll call you next week, after your father's appointment," she says.

"Can you call me before, actually?"

She says it'll be early in the morning, and I say that's fine.

"Won't you have work?" she asks.

"I'll say it's a family emergency."

"*Emergency* makes it sound like it's going to be bad news." I can practically see her leaning against the kitchen counter with the phone against her face, forehead creasing.

"Okay. Not a family emergency. A family *matter*."

"That's good."

"Tell Dad I said hi," I say. "And that I miss you both."

And then my mother says, "I miss you, too, my xin gan," using that old Mandarin phrase for *darling,* which means "my heart and my liver," "my everything."

It's nearly noon. I'm probably still going to be late because Zadie and I are supposed to meet all the way on Houston and Bowery so we can check out that new dim sum parlor with the good reviews. I think Zadie's more excited than I am about my move. She said she was jealous because she never got to live in the city, that she skipped right over from the point where we were young and grateful for a dark corner in a railroad apartment to the part where she got the doorman and the crown molding and the tiny patch of yard in Brooklyn. "You're so lucky," Zadie said. "You're going to be in the middle of everything." I set the empty box by the door. There'll be plenty of time to break it down and take it out later. After putting my coat and boots on, I shut the door carefully behind me, holding my keys tight to my chest.

ACKNOWLEDGMENTS

Thank you, Anne Speyer, Jesse Shuman, and the divine team at Ballantine Books for nurturing and guiding this novel out into the world. To Caroline Eisenmann and Jade Wong-Baxter for believing in this story from the beginning: What a dream it is to be on the Frances Goldin squad (and in such a delightful group chat). To Ryan Wilson and the wonderful folks at Anonymous, for rooting this book on to the great medium beyond. How empowered and sublimely understood you've all made me feel throughout this journey.

I'm grateful to my colleagues at *Vanity Fair* and *BuzzFeed* for giving me generous support (and time!) to become an author. To Matt Ortile, for ushering my fiction debut in *Catapult.* To Alexander Chee for your sage counsel. And to Ari Curtis, for casually telling me once during our time at 60 Madison that you'd be interested in reading anything I had to write about growing up in the Midwest.

To my dearest friends—including Carleigh Cavender, Julia Bush, Madison Feller, Jennifer Chuzhoy, Irene Jiang, and Elian Peltier—thank you for tirelessly cheering me on throughout this wild ride and life in general. To Brandon Choi, and my gorgeous A*Family, for welcoming me home to my place within the community. Kyle Chayka, thank you for all of your words of advice throughout the last years—writerly misery loves company! Kara Cutruzzula, you're the very best mentor. Celia Ampel and Michelle Delgado, I'm forever grateful for your friendship, encouragement, and generosity as the very first readers of this story.

Thank you to everyone who read *Deez Links* over the years, but also everyone who, between 2005 and 2011, happened to come across any works of fiction written by a certain Quizilla user named delilah121c. All I've ever wanted was to chase the high that was writing for you.

To Dunlap and Peoria, Illinois: my hometowns forever. And especially to Mrs. Stubbs, Mrs. Strom, Mr. Friedman, and Mrs. Nelson, for introducing me to a lifelong obsession for writing and literature.

To my family in the Midwest and Jiaxing, especially the family artists: my great-grandpa, Zheng Chuangpu, and my lao lao, Luo Xiheng.

To my brother, Connor, for standing by me and forever surprising me with wisdom beyond your years.

And of course, to my ba ba and ma ma. I love you. You've given me such a beautiful life, and I'll search forever for the right words to thank you.

ABOUT THE AUTHOR

Delia Cai was born in Madison, Wisconsin, and grew up in central Illinois. She is a graduate of the Missouri School of Journalism, and her writing has appeared in *BuzzFeed, GQ, The Cut,* and *Catapult.* Her media newsletter, *Deez Links,* has been highlighted in *The New York Times, New York* magazine, and *Fortune.* She is currently a senior correspondent at *Vanity Fair* and lives in Brooklyn. *Central Places* is her first novel.

Twitter: @delia_cai
Instagram: @deeeliacai

ABOUT THE TYPE

This book was set in Celeste, a typeface that its designer, Chris Burke (b. 1967), classifies as a modern humanistic typeface. Celeste was influenced by Bodoni and Waldman, but the strokeweight contrast is less pronounced. The serifs tend toward the triangular, and the italics harmonize well with the roman in tone and width. It is a robust and readable text face that is less stark and modular than many of the modern fonts, and has many of the friendlier old-face features.